9/21/04

DATE DUE

SEP 3 0 2004			
OCT 0 6 2004			

Mad Dog Summer
and Other Stories

Mad Dog Summer
and Other Stories

Joe R. Lansdale

SUBTERRANEAN PRESS · 2004

FIRST EDITION

ISBN
1-931081-29-8

Subterranean Press
P.O. Box 190106
Burton, MI 48519

email:
subpress@earthlink.net

website:
www.subterraneanpress.com

Contents

· Introduction ·

A HAPPY WRITER SENDS HIS REGARDS
AND HOPES YOU WILL SPEND MONEY ON HIS BOOKS.

This is my latest collection, and I'm proud of it. It covers a lot of ground. From stories of steam and vampires, to stories of the Great Depression, an article about my mother, a story about my popular characters Hap Collins and Leonard Pine, a long novella about a team of superheroes rescuing the devil, a collaboration with my wife. There's also a mule-napping.

Your usual Lansdale collection.

There was to be a story titled "The Senior Girls Bayonette Team," and I really liked it. Through an amazing act of stupidity, when it was near completion, I deleted it and its backup from my computer. I use DOS, so I couldn't recover it.

I have a fragment of it, and will someday, I hope, go back and start over. Right now, too tough to think about. But I will tell you this, it was kind of nifty.

Writing short stories is one of life's great joys. I have learned to love writing novels just about as much, but, for me, the short story always holds sway. I wish there were more markets. I've been fortunate in that there has always been a market for the stories I've written, but if I were writing only short stories, well, that might be a problem. Especially if I wrote a lot of them.

Once upon a time I could write a story in a day to a week. Depending.

Now, it takes me longer. I think the stories are better for the time, though I'm still pretty quick. I think when you've got something to say, you should say it, and that you should maintain as much energy in the creation of it as possible.

Sometimes, I defy that logic and still turn out a good story. Sometimes I start one, put it aside and come back to it years later. But mostly, they come to me in a flash, and I'm off.

An exception to this is "Way Down There." I've thought about this one off and on for years. I wrote a piece of it, put it aside, revised it, wrote some more, and finally, sat down to finish it. It's the strangest piece in the collection, and maybe the one that will have the widest split in opinion. But, I got to tell you, I'm proud of the goofy thing.

The piece on my mother is shorter than I would have liked. It was written to order for an anthology, and to the length restrictions of that anthology. Someday, I hope to write more about my parents. Both were pretty fascinating people.

The collaboration with Andrew, "Veil's Visit," was fun. He and I are extremely close, and it's always a joy to have a chance to visit, or collaborate. We're talking about doing it again.

"Mule Rustlers" was one written in the old way. Quickly.

"Mad Dog Summer." In many ways, a life-changing story. A lot of good things have come my way because of that story.

But enough of all this. I'm not really telling you anything the intros won't tell you, that the stories won't tell you.

I will say this.

Thank you for reading my work. I always appreciate it. It makes me a happy man for you to pick up a book of mine, buy it (the buy part is essential to this equation), and hopefully, like it.

Bless you.

For those of you who steal the books from the library, a problem with many of my books, may you grow like an onion with your head in the ground.

▪ The Mule Rustlers ▪

INTRODUCTION

This one was written specifically for a Mysterious Press anthology. It struck me immediately.

When I was in my twenties, I plowed with a mule. It was the way my wife and I worked our garden, plus some land I used to grow extra food to sell.

I worked a lot of farm jobs then. Picking peas. Digging potatoes. Working in the rose fields, plus doing my own work.

The idea was to grow our own food, work part time, and have time for me to write.

Didn't work out quite that way.

We worked from sunup to sundown, and by the time I was ready to write, I was beat.

I got a job in town.

In time, we used the mule less.

We bought some land with a pond, about twelve acres. Our intention was to build a house. We kept the mule there, going by daily to give it grain, check on it, file down its hooves, as it didn't wear shoes. (I'm talking metal shoes here, nothing from Paris.)

One day I came by to feed my mule, Mattie, and she was gone.

I never found her.

She had been mule-napped.

Somehow, that true life incident led to this.

· The Mule Rustlers ·

On a blustery San Jacinto day, when leggy black clouds appeared against the pearl-gray sky like tromped-on spiders, Elliot and James set about rustling the mule.

A week back, James had spotted the critter while out casing the area for a house to burglarize. The burglary idea went down the tubes because there were too many large dogs in the yards, and too many older people sitting in lawn chairs flexing their false teeth amongst concrete lawn ornaments and sprinklers. Most likely they owned guns.

But on the way out of the neighborhood James observed, on a patch of about ten acres with a small pond and lots of trees, the mule. It was average-sized, brown in color, with a touch of white around the nostrils, and it had ears that tracked the countryside like radar instruments.

All of the property was fenced in barbed wire, but the gate to the property wasn't any great problem. It was made of hog wire stapled to posts, and there was another wire fastened to it and looped over a creosote corner post. There was a chain and padlock, but that was of no consequence. Wire cutters, and you were in.

The road in front of the property was reasonably traveled, and even as he slowed to check out the hog wire, three cars passed him going in the opposite direction.

James discovered if he drove off the gravel road and turned right on a narrow dirt road and parked to the side, he could walk through another piece of unfenced wooded property and climb over the barbed wire fence at the back of the mule's acreage. Better yet, the fence wasn't too good there, was kinda low, two strands only, and was primarily a line that marked ownership, not a boundary. The mule was in there mostly by her own goodwill.

James put a foot on the low, weak fence and pushed it almost to the ground. It was easy to step over then and he wanted to take the mule immediately, for he could see it browsing through a split in the

11

trees, chomping up grass. It was an old mule, and its ears swung forward and back, but if it was aware of his presence, only the ears seemed to know and failed to send the signal to the critter's brain, or maybe the brain got the signal and didn't care.

James studied the situation. There were plenty of little crop farmers who liked a mule to plow their garden, or wanted one just because mules were cool. So there was a market. As for the job, well, the work would be holding the fence down so the mule could step over, then leading it to the truck. Easy money.

Problem was, James didn't have a truck. He had a Volvo that needed front-end work. It had once been crushed up like an accordion, then straightened somewhat, if not enough. It rattled and occasionally threatened to head off to the right without benefit of having the steering wheel turned.

And the damn thing embarrassed him. His hat touched the roof, and if he went out to the Cattleman's Cafe at the auction barn, he felt like a dork climbing out of it amidst mud-splattered pickups, some of them the size of military assault vehicles.

He had owned a huge Dodge Ram, but had lost it in a card game, and the winner, feeling generous, had swapped titles. The card shark got the Dodge, and James got the goddamn Volvo, worn out with the ceiling cloth dripping, the floor rotted away in spots, and the steering wheel slightly bent where an accident, most likely the one that accordioned the front end, must have thrown some un-seat-belted fella against it. At the top of the steering wheel, in the little rubber tubing wrapped around it, were a couple of teeth marks, souvenirs of that same unfortunate episode. Worse yet, the damn Volvo had been painted yellow, and it wasn't a job to be proud of. Baby-shit-hardened-and-aged-on-a-bedpost yellow.

Bottom line was, the mule couldn't ride in the front seat with him. But his friend Elliot owned both a pickup and a horse trailer.

Elliot had once seen himself as a horseman, but the problem was he never owned but one horse, a pinto, and it died from neglect, and had been on its last legs when Elliot purchased it for too much money. It was the only horse James had seen in Elliot's possession outside of stolen ones passing through his hands, and the only one outside of the one in the movie *Cat Ballou* that could lean against a wall at a forty-five-degree angle.

One morning it kept leaning, stiff as a sixteen-year-old's woody, but without the pulse. Having been there, probably dead, for several days, part of its hide had stuck to the wall and gone liquid and gluish. It took him and Elliot both with a two-by-four and a lot of energy to pry it off the stucco and push it down. They'd hooked it up to a chain by the back legs and dragged it to the center of Elliot's property.

Elliot had inherited his land from his grandfather Clemmons, who hated him. Old Man Clemmons had left him the land, but it was rumored he first salted the twenty-five acres and shit in the well. Sure enough, not much grew there except weeds, but as far as Elliot could tell the well water tasted fine.

According to Elliot, besides the salt and maybe the shit, he was given his grandfather's curse that wished him all life's burdens, none of its joys, and an early death. "He didn't like me much," Elliot was fond of saying when deep in his sauce.

They had coated the deceased pinto with gasoline and set it on fire. It had stunk something awful, and since they were involved with a bottle of Wild Turkey while it burned, it had flamed up and caught the back of Elliot's truck on fire, burning out the rubber truck bed lining. James figured they had just managed to beat it out with their coats moments before the gas tank ignited and blew them over and through the trees, along with the burning pinto's hide and bones.

■ ■ ■

James drove over to Elliot's place after his discovery of the mule. Elliot had grown him a few garden vegetables, mostly chocked with bugs, that he had been pushing from his fruit and vegetable stand next to the road.

James found him trying to sell a half bushel of tomatoes to a tall, moderately attractive blonde woman wearing shorts and showing lots of hair on her legs. Short bristly hair like a hog's. James had visions of dropping her in a vat of hot water and scraping that hair off with a knife. Course, he didn't want it hot as hog-scalding water, or she wouldn't be worth much when he got through. He wanted her shaved, not hurt.

Elliot had his brown sweat-stained Stetson pushed up on his head and he was talking the lady up good as he could, considering she was digging through a basket and coming up with some bug-bit tomatoes.

"These are all bit up," she said.

"Bugs attack the good'ns," Elliot said. "Them's the ones you want. These ain't like that crap you get in the store."

"They don't have bugs in them."

"Yeah, but they don't got the flavor these do. You just cut around the spots, and those tomatoes'll taste better than any you ever had."

"That's a crock of shit," the lady said.

"Well now," Elliot said, "that's a matter of opinion."

"It's my opinion you put a few good tomatoes on top of the bug-bit ones," she said. "That's my opinion, and you can keep your tomatoes."

She got in a new red Chevrolet and drove off.

"Good to see you ain't lost your touch," James said.

"Now, these here tomatoes have been goin' pretty fast this morning. Since it's mostly women buyin', I do all right. Fact is that's my first loss. Charm didn't work on her. She's probably a lesbian."

James wanted to call bullshit on that, but right now he wanted Elliot on his side.

"Unless you're doin' so good here you don't need money, I got us a little job."

"You case some spots?" Elliot asked.

"I didn't find nothin' worth doin'. Besides, there's lots of old folks where I was lookin'."

"I don't want no part of them. Always home. Always got dogs and guns."

"Yeah, and lawn gnomes and sprinklers made of wooden animals."

"With the tails that spin and throw water?"

"Yep."

"Kinda like them myself. You know, you picked up some of them things, you could sell them right smart."

"Yeah, well, I got somethin' better."

"Name it."

"Rustlin'."

Elliot worked his mouth a bit. James could see the idea appealed to him. Elliot liked to think of himself as a modern cowboy. "How many head?"

"One."

"One? Hell, that ain't much rustlin'."

"It's a mule. You can get maybe a thousand dollars for one. They're getting rarer, and they're kind of popular now. We rustle it. We could split the money."

Elliot studied on this momentarily. He also liked to think of himself as a respected and experienced thief.

"You know, I know a fella would buy a mule. Let me go up to the house and give him a call."

"It's the same fella I know, ain't it?"

"Yeah," Elliot said.

■ ■ ■

Elliot made the call and came out of the bedroom into the living room with good news.

"George wants it right away. He's offerin' us eight hundred."

"I wanted a thousand."

"He's offering eight hundred, he'll sell it for a thousand or better himself. He said he can't go a thousand. Already got a couple other buys goin' today. It's a deal and it's now."

James considered on that.

"I guess that'll do. We'll need your truck and trailer."

"I figured as much."

"You got any brown shoe polish?"

"Brown shoe polish?"

"That's right," James said.

■ ■ ■

The truck was a big four-seater Dodge with a bed big enough to fill, attach a diving board, and call a pool. The Dodge hummed like a sewing machine as it whizzed along on its huge tires. The trailer clattered behind and wove precariously left and right, as if it might pass the truck at any moment. James and Elliot had their windows down, and the cool April wind snapped at the brims of their hats and made the creases in their crowns deeper.

By the time they drove over to the place where the mule was, the smashed spider clouds had begun to twist their legs together and blend into one messy critter that peed sprinkles of rain all over the truck windshield.

They slowed as they passed the gate, then turned right. No cars or people were visible, so Elliot pulled over to the side of the road, got out quick with James carrying a rope. They went through the woods, stepped over the barbed wire fence, and found the mule grazing. They walked right up to it, and Elliot bribed it with an ear of corn from his garden. The mule sniffed at the corn and bit it. As he did, James slipped the rope over its neck, twisted it so that he put a loop over the mule's nose. Doing this, he brushed the mule's ears, and it kicked at the air, spun and kicked again. It took James several minutes to calm it down.

"It's one of them that's touchy about the ears," Elliot said. "Don't touch the ears again."

"I hear that," James said.

They led the mule to the fence. Elliot pushed it almost to the ground with his boot, and James and the mule stepped over. After that, nothing more was required than to lead the mule to the trailer and load it. It did what was expected without a moment's hesitation.

There was some consternation when it came to turning truck and trailer around, but Elliot managed it and they were soon on the road to a rendezvous with eight hundred dollars.

■ ■ ■

The place they had to go to meet their buyer, George Taylor, was almost to Tyler, and about sixty miles from where they had nabbed the mule. They often sold stolen material there, and George specialized in livestock and just about anything he could buy quick and sell quicker.

The trailer was not enclosed, and it occurred to James that the mule's owner might pass them, but he doubted the mule would be recognized. They were really hauling ass, and the trailer, with the weight of the old mule to aid it, had slowed in its wobbling but still sounded like a train wreck.

When they were about twenty-five miles away from Taylor's place, James had Elliot pull over. He took the brown shoe polish back to the trailer and, reaching between the bars while Elliot fed the mule corn on the cob, painted the white around the mule's nose brown. It was raining lightly, but he managed the touch-up without having it washed away.

He figured this way Taylor might not notice how old the critter was and not try to talk them down. He had given them a price, but they had dealt with Taylor before and what he offered wasn't always what he wanted to give, and it was rare you talked it up. The trick was to keep him from going down. George knew once they had the mule stolen they'd want to get rid of it, and it would be his plan to start finding problems with the animal and to start lowering his price.

When the mule was painted, they got back in the truck and headed out.

Elliot said, "You are one thinker, James."

"Yes sir," James agreed, "you got to get up pretty goddamned early in the morning to get one over on me. It starts raining hard, it won't wash off. That stuff'll hold."

■ ■ ■

When they arrived at Taylor's place, James looked back through the rear truck window and saw the mule with its head lowered, looking at him through sheets of rain. James felt less smart immediately. The brown he had painted on the mule had dried and was darker than the rest of its hide and made it look as if it had dipped its muzzle in a bucket of paint, searching for a carrot on the bottom.

James decided to say nothing to Elliot about this, lest Elliot decide it really wasn't all that necessary to get up early to outsmart him.

Taylor's place was a kind of ranch and junkyard. There were all manner of cars damaged or made thin by the car smasher that Taylor rode with great enthusiasm, wearing a gimme cap with the brim pushed up and his mouth hanging open as if to receive something spoon-fed by a caretaker.

Today, however, the car smasher remained silent near the double-wide where Taylor lived with his bulldog Bullet and his wife, Kay, who was about one ton of woman in a muumuu that might have been made from a circus tent and decorated by children with finger paints. If she owned more than one of these outfits, James was unaware of it. It was possible she had a chest full of them, all the same, folded and ready, with a hole in the center to pull over her head at a moment's notice.

At the back of the place a few cows that looked as if they were ready to be sold for hide and hooves stumbled about. Taylor's station wagon, used to haul a variety of stolen goods, was parked next to the trailer, and next to it was a large red Cadillac with someone at the back of it closing the trunk.

As they drove over the cattle guard and onto the property, the man at the trunk of the Cadillac looked up. He was wearing a blue baseball cap and a blue T-shirt that showed belly at the bottom. He and his belly bounced away from the Caddy, up the steps of the trailer, and inside.

Elliot said, "Who's that?"

"Can't say," James said. "Don't recognize him."

They parked beside the Cadillac, got out, went to the trailer door, and knocked. There was a long pause, then the man with the baseball cap answered the door.

"Yeah," he said.

"We come to see Taylor," Elliot said.

"He ain't here right now," said the man.

"He's expectin' us," James said.

"Say he is?"

"We got a mule to sell him," James said.

"That right?"

"Mrs. Taylor here?" James asked.

"Naw. She ain't. Ain't neither one of them here."

"Where's Bullet?" Elliot asked.

"He don't buy mules, does he?"

"Bullet?" Elliot said.

"Didn't you ask for him?"

"Well, yeah, but not to buy nothin'."

"You boys come on in," came a voice from inside the trailer. "It's all right there, Butch, stand aside. These here boys are wantin' to do some business with George. That's what we're doin'."

Butch stood aside. James and Elliot went inside.

"So is he here?" James asked.

"No. Not just now. But we're expectin' him shortly."

Butch stepped back and leaned against the trailer's kitchen counter, which was stacked with dirty dishes. The place smelled funny. The man who had asked them to come inside was seated on the couch. He was portly, wearing black pants and black shoes with the toes turned up. He had on a big black Hawaiian-style shirt with hula girls in red, blue, and yellow along the bottom. He had greasy black hair combed straight back and tied in a little ponytail. A white short-brimmed hat with a near flat crown was on a coffee table in front of him, along with a can of beer and a white substance in four lines next to a rolled dollar bill. He had his legs crossed and he was playing with the tip of one of his shoes. He had a light growth of beard and he was smiling at them.

"What you boys sellin'?" he asked.

"A mule," James said.

"No shit?"

"That's right," Elliot said. "When's George coming back?"

"Sometime shortly after the Second Coming. But I doubt he'll go with God."

Elliot looked at James. James shrugged, and at that moment he saw past Elliot, and what he saw was Bullet lying on the floor near a doorway to the bedroom, a pool of blood under him. He tried not to let his eyes stay on Bullet long. He said, "Tell you what, boys. I think me and Elliot will come back later, when George is here."

The big man lifted up his Hawaiian shirt and showed him his hairy belly and against it a little flat black automatic pistol. He took the pistol out slowly and put it on his knee and looked at them.

"Naw. He ain't comin' back, and you boys ain't goin' nowhere."

"Aw shit," Elliot said, suddenly getting it. "He ain't no friend of ours. We just come to do business, and if he ain't here to do business, you boys got our blessing. And we'll just leave and not say a word."

Another man came out of the back room. He was naked, and carrying a bowie knife. He was muscular, bug-nosed, with close-cut hair. There was blood on him from thighs to neck. From the back room they heard a moan.

The naked man looked at them, then at the man on the couch.

"Friends of Taylor's," the man on the couch said.

"We ain't," James said. "We hardly know him. We just come to sell a mule."

"A mule, huh," said the naked man. He didn't seem bashful at all. His penis was bloody and stuck to his right leg like some kind of sucker fish. The naked man nodded his head at the open doorway behind him, spoke to the man on the couch. "I've had all of that I want and can take, Viceroy. It's like cutting blubber off a whale."

"You go on and shower," Viceroy said, then smiled, added: "And be sure and wash the parts you don't normally touch."

"Ain't no parts Tim don't touch," Butch said.

"I tell you what," Tim said. "You get in there and go to work, then show me how funny you are. That old woman is hardheaded."

Tim went past Butch, driving the bowie knife into the counter, rattling the dishes.

Viceroy stared at Butch. "Your turn."

"What about you?" Butch said.

"I don't take a turn. Get with it."

Butch put his cap on the counter next to a greasy plate, took off his shirt, pants, underwear, socks, and shoes. He pulled the knife out of the counter and started for the bedroom. He said, "What about these two?"

"Oh, me and them are gonna talk. Any friend of Taylor's is a friend of mine."

"We don't really know him," James said. "We just come to sell a mule."

"Sit down on the floor there, next to the wall, away from the door," Viceroy said, and scratched the side of his cheek with the barrel of the automatic.

A moment later they heard screams from the back room and Butch yelling something, then there was silence, followed shortly by more screams.

"Butch ain't got Tim's touch," Viceroy said. "Tim can skin you and you can walk off before you notice the hide on your back, ass, and legs is missin'. Butch, he's a hacker."

Viceroy leaned forward, took up the dollar bill, and sucked up a couple lines of the white powder. "Goddamn, that'll do it," he said.

Elliot said, "What is that?"

Viceroy laughed. "Boy, you are a rube, ain't you? Would you believe bakin' soda?"

"Really?" Elliot said.

Viceroy hooted. "No. Not really."

From the bedroom you could hear Butch let out a laugh. "Crackers," he said.

"It's cocaine," James said to Elliot. "I seen it in a movie."

"Good God," Elliot said.

"My, you boys are delicate for a couple of thieves," Viceroy said.

Tim came out of the bathroom, still naked, bouncing his balls with a towel.

"Put some clothes on," Viceroy said. "We don't want to see that."

Tim looked hurt, put on his clothes and adjusted his cap. Viceroy snorted the last two lines of coke. "Damn, that's some good stuff: You can step on that multiple."

"Let me have a snort," Tim said.

"Not right now," Viceroy said.

"How come you get to?" Tim said.

"'Cause I'm the biggest bull in the woods, boy. And you can test that anytime you got the urge."

Tim didn't say anything. He went to the refrigerator, found a beer, popped it, and began to sip.

"I don't think she knows nothing," Tim said. "She wouldn't hold back havin' that done to her for a few thousand dollars. Not for a million."

"I reckon you're right," said Viceroy. "I just don't like quittin' half-way. You finish a thing, even if it ain't gonna turn out. Ain't that right, boys?"

James and Elliot didn't reply. Viceroy laughed and picked up the beer on the coffee table and took a jolt of it. He said to himself, "Yeah, that's right. You don't do a thing half-ass. You do it all the way. What time is it?"

Tim reached in his pocket and took out a pocket watch. James recognized it as belonging to George Taylor. "It's four."

"All right," Viceroy said, satisfied, and sipped his beer.

■ ■ ■

After a time Butch came out of the bedroom bloody and looking tired. "She ain't gonna tell nobody nothin'. She's gone. She couldn't take no more. She'd have known somethin', she'd have told it."

"Guess Taylor didn't tell her," Tim said. "Guess she didn't know nothin'."

"George had more in him than I thought, goin' like that, takin' all that pain and not talkin'," Viceroy said. "I wouldn't have expected it of him."

Tim nodded his head. "When you shot his bulldog, I think he was through. Took the heart right out of him. Wasn't a thing we could do to him then that mattered."

"Money's around here somewhere," Viceroy said.

"He might not have had nothin'," Butch said, walking to the bath-room.

"I think he did," Viceroy said. "I don't think he was brave enough to try and cross me. I think he had the money for the blow, but we double-crossed him too soon. We should have had him put the money on the table, then done what we needed to do. Would have been easier on everybody all the way around, them especially."

"They'd have still been dead," Tim said, drinking the last of his beer, crushing the can.

"But they'd have just been dead. Not hurt a lot, then dead. Old fat gal, that wasn't no easy way to go, and in the end she didn't know nothin'. And Taylor, takin' the knife, then out there in that car in the crusher and us telling him we were gonna run him through, and him still not talkin'."

"Like I said, we killed the bulldog I think he was through. Fat woman wasn't nothin' to him, but he seemed to have a hard-on for that dog. He'd just as soon be crushed. But I still think there might not have been any money. I think maybe they was gonna do what we were gonna do. Double cross."

"Yeah, but we brought the blow," Viceroy said.

Tim grinned. "Yeah, but was you gonna give it to 'em?"

Viceroy laughed, then his gaze settled lead-heavy on the mule rustlers. "Well, boys, what do you suggest I do with you pickle heads?"

"Just let us go," James said. "Hell, this ain't our business, and we don't want it to be our business. It ain't like Taylor was a relative of ours."

"That's right," Elliot said. "He's cheated us plenty on little deals."

Viceroy was quiet. He looked at Tim. "What do you say?"

Tim pursed his lips and developed the expression of a man looking in the distance for answers. "I sympathize with these boys. I guess we could let 'em go. Give us their word, show us some ID, so they spill any beans we can find them. You know the littlest bit these days and you can find anybody."

"Damn Internet," Viceroy said.

Butch came out of the bathroom, naked, toweling his hair.

"You think we should 'em go?" Viceroy asked.

Butch looked first at Viceroy and Tim, then at James and Elliot. "Absolutely."

"Get dressed," Viceroy said to Butch, "and we'll let 'em go."

"We won't say a word," Elliot said.

"Sure," Viceroy said. "You look like boys who can be quiet. Don't they?"

"Yeah," Tim said.

"Absolutely," Butch said, tying his shoe.

"Then we'll just go," James said, standing up from his position on the floor, Elliot following suit.

"Not real quick," Viceroy said. "You got a mule, huh?"

James nodded.

"What's he worth?"

"Couple thousand dollars to the right people."

"What about people ain't maybe quite as right?"

"A thousand. Twelve hundred."

"What were you supposed to get?"

"Eight hundred."

"We could do some business, you know."

James didn't say anything. He glanced toward the door where the men had been at work on Mrs. Taylor. He saw the bulldog lying there on the linoleum in its pool of hardened blood, and flowing from the bedroom was fresh blood. The fresh pool flowed around the crusty old pool and bled into the living room of the trailer and died where the patch of carpet near the couch began; the carpet began to slowly absorb it.

James knew these folks weren't going to let them go anywhere.

"I think we'll take the mule," Viceroy said. "Though I ain't sure I'm gonna give you any eight hundred dollars."

"We give it to you as a gift," Elliot said. "Just take it, and the trailer it's in, and let us go."

"That's a mighty nice offer," Viceroy said. "Nice, huh, boys?"

"Damn nice," Tim said.

"Absolutely," Butch said. "They could have held out and tried to deal. You don't get much nicer than that."

"And throwing in the trailer too," Tim said. "Now, that's white of 'em."

James took hold of the doorknob, turned it, said, "We'll show him to you."

"Wait a minute," Viceroy said.

"Come on out," James said.

Butch darted across the room, took hold of James's shoulder. "Hold up."

The door was open now. Rain was really hammering. The mule, its head hung, was visible in the trailer.

"Ain't no need to get wet," Viceroy said.

James had one foot on the steps outside. "You ought to see what you're gettin'."

"It'll do," Viceroy said. "It ain't like we're payin' for it."

Butch tightened his grip on James, and Elliot, seeing how this was going to end up and somehow feeling better about dying out in the open, not eight feet from a deceased bulldog, a room away from a skinned fat woman, pushed against Butch and stepped out behind James and into the yard.

"Damn," Viceroy said.

"Should I?" Butch said, glancing at Viceroy, touching the gun in his pants.

"Hell, let's look at the mule," Viceroy said.

Viceroy put on his odd hat and they all went out in the rain for a look. Viceroy looked as if he were some sort of escapee from a mental institution, wearing a hubcap. The rain ran off of it and made a curtain of water around his head.

They stood by the trailer staring at the mule. Tim said, "Someone's painted its nose, or it's been dippin' it in shit."

James and Elliot said nothing.

James glanced at the trailer, saw there was no underpinning. He glanced at Elliot, nodded his head slightly. Elliot looked carefully. He had an idea what James meant. They might roll under the trailer and get to the other side and start running. It wasn't worth much. Tim and Butch looked as if they could run fast, and all they had to do was run fast enough to get a clear shot.

"This is a goddamn stupid thing," Butch said, the rain hammering his head. "Us all standing out here in the rain lookin' at a goddamn mule. We could be dry and these two could be — "

A horn honked. Coming up the drive was a black Ford pickup with a camper fastened to the bed.

The truck stopped and a man the shape of a pear with the complexion of a marshmallow, dressed in khakis the color of walnut bark, got out smiling teeth all over the place. He had a rooster under his arm.

He said, "Hey, boys. Where's George?"

"He ain't feelin' so good," Viceroy said.

The man with the rooster saw the gun Viceroy was holding. He said, "You boys plinking cans?"

"Somethin' like that," Viceroy said.

"Would you tell George to come out?" the man said.

"He won't come out," Butch said.

The man's smile fell away. "Why not? He knows I'm comin'."

"He's under the weather," Viceroy said.

"Can't we all go inside, it's like being at the bottom of a lake out here."

"Naw. He don't want us in there. Contagious."

"What's he got?"

"You might say a kind of lead poisonin'."

"Well, he wants these here chickens. I got the camper back there full of 'em. They're fightin' chickens. Best damn bunch there is. This'n here, he's special. He's a stud rooster. He ain't fightin' no more. Won his last one. Got a bad shot that put blood in his lungs, but I put his head in my mouth and sucked it out, and he went on to win. Just come back from it and won. I decided to stud him out."

"He's gettin' all wet," Butch said.

"Yeah he is," said the chicken man.

"Let's end this shit," Tim said.

James reached over and pulled the bar on the trailer and the gate came open. He said, "Let's show him to you close-up."

"Not now," Viceroy said, but James was in the trailer now. He took the rope off the trailer rail and tied it around the mule's neck and put a loop over its head, started backing him out.

"That's all right," Viceroy said. "We don't need to see no damn mule."

"He's a good'n," James said when the mule was completely out of the trailer. "A little touchy about the ears."

He turned the mule slightly then, reached up, and grabbed the mule's ears, and it kicked.

The kick was a good one. Both legs shot out and the mule seemed to stand on its front legs like a gymnast that couldn't quite flip over. The shod hooves caught Viceroy in the face and there was a sound like a pound of wet cow shit dropping on a flat rock, and Viceroy's neck turned at a too-far angle and he flew up and fell down.

James bolted, and so did Elliot, slamming into Tim as he went, knocking him down. James hit the ground, rolled under the trailer, scuttled to the other side, Elliot went after him. Butch aimed at the back of Elliot's head and the chicken man said, "Hey, what the hell."

Butch turned and shot the chicken man through the center of the forehead. Chicken man fell and the rooster leaped and squawked, and just for the hell of it, Butch shot the rooster too.

Tim got up cussing. "I'm all muddy."

"Fuck that," Butch said. "They're gettin' away."

Even the mule had bolted, darting across the yard, weaving through the car crusher and a pile of mangled cars. Their last view of it was the tips of its ears over the top of the metallic heap.

Tim ran around the trailer and saw James and Elliot making for a patch of woods in the distance. It was just a little patch that ran along both sides of the creek down there. The land sloped just enough and the rain and wind were hard enough that the shot Tim got off didn't hit James or Elliot. It went past them and smacked a tree.

Tim came back around the trailer and looked at Butch bending over Viceroy, taking his gun, sticking it in his belt.

"He bad?" Tim asked.

"He's dead. Fuckin' neck's broke. If that's bad, he's bad."

"We gonna get them hillbillies?"

"There ain't no hills around here for a billy to live in. They're just the same ole white trash they got everywhere, you idiot."

"Well, this ain't Dallas…We gonna chase 'em?"

"What for? Let's get the TV set and go."

"Got a stereo too. I seen it in there. It's a good'n."

"Get that too. I don't think there is no money. I think he was gonna try and sweet-talk Viceroy out of some of that blow. A pay-later deal."

"He damn sure didn't know Viceroy, did he?"

"No, he didn't. But you know what, I ain't gonna miss him."

A moment later the TV and the stereo were loaded in the Cadillac. Then, just for fun, they put the chicken man and Viceroy in the chicken man's truck and used the car crusher on it. As the truck began to crush, chickens squawked momentarily and the tires blew with a sound like mortar fire.

With Viceroy, the chicken man, and the chickens flattened, they slid the truck onto a pile of rusted metal, got in the Cadillac, and drove out of there, Butch at the wheel.

On the way over the cattle guard, Tim said, "You know, we could have sold them chickens."

"My old man always said don't steal or deal in anything you got to feed. I've stuck by that. Fuck them chickens. Fuck that mule."

Tim considered that, decided it was sage advice, the part about not dealing in livestock. He said, "All right."

■ ■ ■

Along the creek James and Elliot crept. The creek was rising and the sound of the rain through the trees was like someone beating tin with a chain.

The land was low and it was holding water. They kept going and pretty soon they heard a rushing sound. Looking back, they saw a wall of water surging toward them. The lake a mile up had overflowed and the creek and all that rain were causing it to flood.

"Shit," said James.

The water hit them hard and knocked them down, took their hats. When they managed to stand, the water was knee-deep and powerful. It kept bowling them over. Soon they were just flowing with it and logs and limbs were clobbering them at every turn.

They finally got hold of a small tree that had been uprooted and hung to that. The water carried them away from the trees around the creek and out into what had once been a lowland pasture.

They had gone a fair distance like this when they saw the mule swimming. Its neck and back were well out of the water and it held its head as if it were regal and merely about some sort of entertainment.

Their tree homed in on the mule, and as they passed, James grabbed the mule's neck and pulled himself onto it. Elliot got hold of the mule's tail, pulled himself up on its back where James had settled.

The mule was more frantic now, swimming violently. The flood stopped suddenly, and James realized this was in fact where the highway had been cut through what had once been a fairly large hill. The highway was covered and not visible, but this was it, and there was a drop-off as the water flowed over it.

Down they went, and the churning deluge went over them, and they spun that way for a long time, like they were in a washing machine cycle. When they came up, the mule was upside down, feet pointing in the air. Its painted nose sometimes bobbed up and out of the water, but it didn't breathe and it didn't roll over.

James and Elliot clung to its legs and fat belly and washed along like that for about a mile. James said, "I'm through with livestock."

"I hear that," Elliot said.

Then a bolt of lightning, attracted by the mule's upturned, iron-shod hooves, struck them a sizzling, barbecuing strike, so that there was nothing left now but three piles of cooked meat, one with a still visible brown nose and smoking, wilting legs, the other two wearing clothes, hissing smoke, blasting along with the charge of the flood.

The Steam Man of the Prairie
• and the Dark Rider Get Down •

INTRODUCTION

I've always loved Jules Verne. He was the first sf writer I became aware of. First through films based on his work, then the books.

Yeah, I know, it can be argued that he wrote adventure travelogue, not sf, and he certainly did that, but he is undoubtedly one of the greatest sf writers of all time as well, even if no one knew what sf was then.

I should hasten to add, I had read some sf (Tom Swift, Jr.) before Verne, but his was the first name I had ever encountered that made an impact, and therefore, he was the first sf writer I knew of. He was also someone my mother knew of, and she told me about him long before I really understood who he was or what he wrote. I don't think she, herself, ever read a Verne story in her life, but she knew who he was. She was always dropping tidbits like that on me. Anyway, later, Verne became someone whose books I looked for.

Later, I came across H.G. Wells. He was even better. Like Verne, he had a sense of wonder. This is something that seems to have mostly died out in sf, and I don't think it's just being older and jaded that has led me to that belief.

Sometimes I come across older sf books I haven't read, and in the best of them, I can find just this element. For that matter, sometimes in the worst of them I can find it.

Anyway, these writers influenced me greatly when I was growing up. They made me want to be a writer. When I discovered Edgar Rice Burroughs, I went a little crazy. I knew I HAD TO BE A WRITER.

This story is a kind of tribute to the old stuff, with a touch of the new. There is also another influence. Philip José Farmer. If Burroughs is my sentimental favorite of all time, Philip José Farmer is my outright favorite.

He's a mixed bag.

I don't love it all. His prose ranges from sloppy to genius. But, good God, when he's on, he can't be touched. He has that sense of wonder, and he never lost it. He has the magic.

Bless him. He has kept the inner reaches of my heart alive with that sense of wonder and joy. He reminds me that sf, in the broader sense of its term, is in many ways the most wonderful form of fiction in creation.

There are other influences at work here as well. Bram Stoker. Old dime novels, which are in fact the catalyst for this story.

Dime novels were a product of the Old West. They grew out of hero worship.

Wild Bill Hickok and Buffalo Bill had novels written about them, as did others. In fact, a large number of them were reprinted in the 1970s. At least I think it was the 1970s. Sometime in there. The books do not bear copyright information.

I read a number of them. The reprints usually contained a complete dime novel and a story in the back. One I'm looking at right now is titled BUFFALO BILL'S SPY SHADOWER, and it contains a Jesse James story titled "The Boys at Cracker Neck." They're the heroes of the story, despite the fact that in real life they were murdering looters.

The one that was the catalyst for the following story was "Frank Reade, the Inventor, Chasing the James Boys with his Steam Team."

In this, Jesse James was not a hero, and the steam team was a team of metallic stream driven horses.

Cool, huh?

I read this, thought, wow, this isn't that well written, but what a cool idea. (Verne wrote a story about a Steam Elephant called "The Demon of Cawnpore," and it just now occurred to me that it too is an influence.) For some reason, the way James was represented in the dime novel story, I thought of him as a vampire. Can't explain it, but that led to me thinking, always dangerous for me, and pretty soon this came out.

It has only been printed in one place, a collection of novellas called THE LONG ONES. This was the only new piece in that collection, and it's unlikely that many readers have seen it.

The Steam Man of the Prairie
• and the Dark Rider Get Down •

A DIME NOVEL

for Philip José Farmer

FOREWORD

Somewhere out in space the damaged shuttle circled, unable to come down. Its occupants were confused and frightened.

Forever to the left of the ship was a rip in the sky. And through the rip they saw all sorts of things. Daylight and dark. Odd events.

And dat ole shuttle jes go'n roun' and roun' and roun'.

■ ■ ■

(1)
IN SEARCH OF

The shiny steam man, forty feet tall and twenty feet wide, not counting his ten-foot-high conical hat, hissed across the prairie, farted up hills, waded and puffed through streams and rivers. He clanked and clattered. He made good time. His silver metal skin was bright with the sun. The steam from his hat was white as frost. Inside of him, where the four men rode in swaying leather chairs, it was very hot, even with the steam fan blowing.

But they pushed on, working the gears, valves and faucets, forever closing on the Dark Rider. Or so they hoped.

Bill Beadle, captain of the expedition, took off his wool cap and wiped the sweat from his face with an already damp forearm. He tried to do this casually. He did not want the other three to know how near heat exhaustion he was. He took deep breaths, ran a hand through his sweat-soaked hair, and put his cap back on. The cap was hot, and though there was really nothing official about his uniform or his title of captain, he tried to live by a code that maintained the importance of both.

Hamner and Blake looked at him casually. They were red-faced and sweat-popped. They shifted uncomfortably in their blue woolen uniforms. Through the stained glass eyes of the steam man they could see the hills they had entered, see they were burned brown from the sun.

It was midday, and this gave them several hours to reach the land of the Dark Rider, but by then it would be night, and the Dark Rider and his minions, the apes in trousers, would be out and powerful.

Only James Feather, their Indian guide, looked cool in his breech-cloth and headband holding back his long, beaded black hair. He had removed his moccasins and was therefore barefoot. Unlike the others, he was not interested in a uniform, or to be more precise, he was not interested in being hot when he didn't have to be. He could never figure out the ways of white men, though he often considered on them. But mostly he considered the steam man, and thought: neat. This cocksucker can go. A little bouncy on the ass, even in these spring-loaded seats, but the ole boy can go. The white men do come up with a good thing now and then.

They clanked through the hills some more, and through the right ear canal of the steam man, also stained glass, they could see the wrecks.

Beadle was always mystified by the wrecks.

Most people called them saucers. They lay in heaps and shatters all over the place. Strange skeletons that weren't quite bone had been found in some of them, and there were even mummified remains of others. Green squid with multiple eyes and fragments of clothing.

There was no longer anyone alive who really knew what had happened, but what had been handed down was there had been a war, and though damn near everybody came, nobody really won. Not the world, not the saucer people. But the weapons they used, they had brought about strange things.

Like rips in the sky, and the Dark Rider.

Or so it was rumored. No one really knew. Story was the saucers had ripped open the sky and come to this world through a path along-side the sky. And that after the war, when the saucer men gave it up and went home, the earth changed and the rips stayed. What was odd about the rips was you could toss things into them, people could enter them, and things could come out. And there were things to see. Great batlike creatures with monstrous wingspans. Snake-headed critters with flippers and rows of teeth, paddling across the blue-green ether inside the rip. Strange craft jetting across odd landscapes. All manner of things. If you stood near the dark openings, which reached from sky to ground, you could feel them pulling at you, like a vacuum, and if you stepped too close, well then you were gone. Sucked into the beyond. Sometimes the people who were pulled, or went by choice into the rips, came back. Sometime they didn't. But even those that came back bore no real information. It was even reported by a few that the moment they stepped through the rip, they merely exited where they had entered.

Curious.

As for the Dark Rider, no one knew his origin. A disease caused by something from one of the saucers was the usual guess, but that's all it was. A guess. The Dark Rider sucked blood like a vampire, had prodigious strength and odd powers, but had no aversion to crosses, garlic, or any of the classical defenses. Except one. Sunlight. He could not tolerate it. That much had been established.

He also had an army of apelike critters who traveled with him and did most of the shit work. When the Dark Rider was not able to do it, he sent the apes in britches to do his work. Rape. Murder. Torture. Usually by impalement. His method was to have the victim stripped naked and placed on an upright stake with the point in the anus. The pressure of the victim's weight would push him or her down the length of the shaft until the point came out the upper part of the torso. Usually the neck or mouth, or even at times through the top of the head.

Beadle had seen enough of this to give him nightmares for the rest of his life, and he had determined that if it ever appeared he was about to be captured alive by the Dark Rider or his minions, he would kill himself. He kept a double-barreled derringer in his boot for just such a circumstance.

The steam man clanked on.

■ ■ ■

It was near nightfall when they stomped out of the foothills and into the vast forest that grew tall and dark before them and was bordered by a river. It was a good thing, this forest and river. They were out of wood and water, and therefore out of steam.

Though the night brought bad possibilities, it was also preferable to the long hot days. They grabbed their water bags, pulled their Webb rifles over their shoulders on straps, and disembarked from the steam man via a ladder that they poked out of its ass. Like automated turds, they dropped out of the steam man's butt and into the coolness of the night.

The white men left John Feather to guard the steam man with an automatic pistol and a knife on his hip, a Webb rifle slung over his shoulder on a strap, a bow and a quiver of arrows, and went down to the river for water.

John Feather knew he would be better off inside the steam man, in case the Dark Rider and his bunch showed up, but the night air felt great and sucked at a man's common sense. Behind him the steam man popped and crackled as the nocturnal air cooled it.

John Feather tapped the ammo belt strapped across his chest and back, just to make sure it was there. He took one of the heavy clips from his bandolier and squeezed it with his fingers, a habit he had developed when nervous. After a time, he put the oiled clip back on the bandolier and wiped his greasy fingers on his thigh. He looked for a time in every direction, listened intently. Normally, though he liked them, he didn't miss the white men much, but tonight, he would be glad to have them back. Safety in numbers.

■ ■ ■

Beadle, Hamner, and Blake inched down the slick riverbank, stopped at the water and listened to it roar and churn dirt from the bank. There had been a big rain as of late, and the river was wild from it. The reflection of the moon was on the river and it wavered in the water as if it were something bright lying beneath the ripples.

Beadle felt good outside of the metal man. It was wonderful to not have his ass bouncing and his insides shook, to be away from all that hissing and metal clanking.

The roar of the river, the wind through the pines, the moon on the water, the real moon in the sky, bright and gold and nearly full, was soothing.

He eased one of his water bags into the river, listened to it gurgle as it filled.

"We ought to bring Steam down here, Captain," Hamner said. He had removed his cap, which was pretty much the understanding when nightfall came, and fixed it through his belt. The moonlight shone on his red hair and made it appear to be a copper bowl. "We could camp closer to the water."

"I'm afraid Steam's furnaces may be too cold and too low of fuel to walk another inch," Beadle said. "There's just enough left for us to get settled for the night. It would take an hour to heat him up. At least. I'm not sure it's worth it just to have him walk a few hundred feet."

"It is pleasant here, though," Hamner said.

"Not so pleasant we don't need to get this over with and get inside," Beadle said.

This indirect reference to the Dark Rider settled down on them suddenly, and the need for fresh air, wood and water, was eclipsed by a wave of fear. Just a wave. It passed over them and was tucked away. They had grown used to fear. When you hunted the Dark Rider and his boys, you had to learn to put fear on the back burner. You thought about it too much, you'd never breathe night air again. With the Dark Rider, fear and horror were a constant.

Beadle looked at the nearly full moon and wondered if the Dark Rider was looking up at it too. Beadle had sworn to get the Dark Rider. It's what he was being paid for, he and his team. He had formed Steam Man and Company a year back, and during that time he had killed many of the Dark Rider's ape boys, his minions as Beadle liked to call them, and his employers had been very happy, even giving him the honorary title of Captain. But he hadn't gotten the Dark Rider. There was the real deal. And the big money. The reward for the Dark Rider was phenomenal. And Beadle wanted the bastard, reward or not. He thought of him all the time. He wrote dime novels based on his team's exploits, stretching the truth only slightly. He had made a silent vow to pursue the Dark Rider to the ends of the earth.

As Beadle looked at the moon, he saw the last of the white steam that was issuing from the steam man's tall conical hat float across the sky, blurring it, and then the steam dissipated.

"Let's finish," Beadle said.

■　■　■

They made numerous trips with their bags of water, but soon they were famished. Then, leaving John Feather once again to guard Steam, they gathered wood. That accomplished, they took tools from inside the steam man, chopped and sawed the wood and hauled it inside with the water.

As Beadle had expected, the furnaces had cooled. They were lucky they had been able to find water. They might have had to spend a long night in Steam with little to drink until the morning, when it was safe. This way, they could be more comfortable. Even baths could be taken.

"Do you think the Dark Rider is near?" Beadle asked John Feather as they stacked the wood inside the Steam Man.

"He is always near, and always far away," John Feather said.

This was one of the Indian's odd answers that disturbed Beadle. He knew if he asked John Feather to decipher it, he would merely give him another hard to understand remark. It was best to consider the answer given, or just discard it. When John Feather was in this kind of mood, there was no reasoning with him.

Beadle decided to answer his own question, which actually had been foolish, sprung out of fear and the need for something to say. The truth was obvious: they couldn't be too far away from the Dark Rider. Just the day before, they had passed through the burnt and reeking remains of a village with a hundred inhabitants or so with stakes rammed up their asses. Even cats and dogs and three parakeets had been crucified. It was the Dark Rider's calling card. Therefore, he could not be far away. And he always fled to this part of the world, amongst the thick dark woods with its bad things, near the place where the sky was most ripped and you could see into it and view all manner of strange and terrifying things not seen elsewhere.

Beadle pulled up steam's ass flap and locked it for the night with bolt and key. While the wood burned and the water heated, they ate a cold supper of beef jerky and hardtack and washed it down with water, then each retired to his own devices. Beadle had wanted to read, but the kerosene lamps made the place smoky and uncomfortable, even with the Steam man's vents. After first usage of the lamps and a miserable night of smoke and kerosene stink, they had decided to withhold from using them. He could, of course, read by candle light, but he found this uncomfortable and only resorted to this when he was absolutely bored out of his mind.

He did, however, light a candle and put it in a candle hat and used the ladder to descend into one of the steam man's legs, past the machinery that made it walk, and into the foot where he found a can of oil.

Steam had been well-oiled the night before, but it never hurt to do it again. There was always a fear of rusty devices, gritty gears, a metal rod gone bad. And considering who they were hunting, it wouldn't do to have Steam play out.

When he finished there, he went throughout the steam man with his candle hat and his can of oil, dripping the liquid into all of its parts. He paid special attention to the backup controls in the trunk of the steam man. If the head controls failed, these, though simpler, cruder, could manage the machine's basic movements.

After a time the water was heated, and they drew straws for who bathed first, as the others would have the same water. Beadle lucked out. He got naked and climbed in the tub at the top of Steam's head. He set the timer. He had fifteen minutes before the next bather had a shot at the suds, and he greatly enjoyed every minute of his time.

■ ■ ■

Deep in the woods, outside his compound, hanging about for lack of anything else to do, the Dark Rider, alias the Time Traveler, alias many other names, turned his face to the moon as he jerked his dick and thought of blood. At his climax he gave up blood and sperm in thick waddy ropes that splattered on the leaf mold and the body of the dog. He imagined the dog a woman, but it had been days since he had had a woman, tasted a soft throat and sweet blood. He would have settled for a man or child, an old person, but none had been available. Just the dog, and it had been a gamey wild dog at that. Still, feeding on anything made him horny, which was both a blessing and a curse.

Finished, he made the mistake of haste, caught a hunk of dick in his zipper and cursed. The others, who had been patiently waiting for the Dark Rider to finish, said nothing. You didn't laugh at the Dark Rider, not even if he caught his dick in a zipper. Laugh at him, you might find your face on the other side of your head.

The Dark Rider worked for a while, managed his whang free, put it in his pants and zipped up, looked around for anyone with a smile on their face. Most of his minions, as the dime novels written by his nemesis, Beadle, called them, were looking about, as if expecting someone.

In a way they were. Beadle and his regulators, and that infernal tin man.

When the Dark Rider was certain he was fixed, he nodded to his flunkies, and they waddled forward to take the dog and to lick the blood and sperm on the ground. The toadies began to fight amongst themselves, tearing at the dog, rolling and thrashing about in a hungry fury, ripping at the meat, scattering fur, spewing what blood was left in the critter.

After waiting for a while, the Dark Rider became bored. He took hold of one of the apes and threw him on the ground and pulled his britches down. He took out his dong again and ass fucked the beast. It wasn't very pleasant, and he grew angry at himself for resorting to such entertainment, but he went ahead and did it anyway. Consummated, he snapped the animal's neck and gave him to the others as a gift. Some of the ape men fucked the corpse, but pretty soon they were eating it. The dog just hadn't been enough.

The Dark Rider thought about what he had done. If he kept popping the necks of these little beasts, pretty soon he might have to gather wood for the impalement stakes himself. He'd have to go easier on them. They were not limitless. It was too big a pain to get others.

■ ■ ■

When they had all bathed and the water was run out of the tub and down the pipes and out what served as Steam's penis — a tube with a flap over it — they settled in for the night, secure in the giant man.

Beadle, in his hammock at the top of Steam's head, dreamed pleasantly at first of a lost love, but then the dream changed, and the Dark Rider came into it. He was dressed, as always, in dark pants and shirt, high black boots, wide black hat and long black cape. His eyes were flaming sockets, his teeth white as snow, sharp as sin. In the dream, the Dark Rider took Beadle's love, Matilda of the long blonde hair and sleek rich body, and carried her away.

Beadle awoke in a sweat. It was a dream too real.

Matilda. Sucked dry of blood, and then, for the sport of it, impaled through the vagina, left for the heat, bugs and birds. That had been the beginning for Beadle. The beginning of Steam and Company, his hunt for the Dark Rider. His vow to pursue him to the ends of the earth.

(2)
IN THE BAD COUNTRY

The next morning, early, just as light was tearing back the black curtain, they worked the bellows inside the steam man and made the furnace hotter. The steam man began to chug, cough, sput and rock with indigestion. They cranked him up and worked the gears and twisted the faucets and checked the valves. When the steam man's belly was volcanic, they climbed into their chairs, at their controls, Beadle in the command seat.

"Let's do it," Beadle said, and he pulled a gear, twisted a faucet, and took hold of the throttle. The steam man began to walk. He went down the riverbank with a clank and into the river with a splash. The water rose up to his waist, and though there was resistance, and Beadle had to give him nearly full throttle, Steam waded the river and stepped up on the bank. The step would have been a climb for a man.

Now the woods were before the steam man. These woods were the known domain of the Dark Rider, and only a few had ever been this far and returned alive. The survivors told of not only the dark woods, but of the wild creatures there, and of the Dark Rider and his white apes, and beyond the forest, a great rip in the sky. Perhaps the biggest rip there was. A rip so big and wide you could see not only creatures inside it, but stars, and at times, a strange sun, blurred and running like a busted egg yolk. Beadle wondered if the Dark Rider would run again. That was his strategy. Hit and run and hide. But would he run from here, his own stronghold? Would he be prepared to stand and fight? Or would he go to ground, hide and wait them out?

The good thing was they had the day on their side, but even during the day, the Dark Rider had his protection.

It was best not to think about it, Beadle decided. It was best to push on, take it as it came, play it as it laid.

■ ■ ■

Deep down in the cool damp ground, the Dark Rider lay wrapped in clear plastic hauled from one of many possible futures, plastic used to keep dirt off his clothes.

The grave was deep. Twenty feet. It had been dug by the ape men, or as they were more properly known, the Moorlocks. A sheet of lumber had been placed over the top of the grave to keep out stray strands of daylight.

Nearby, in underground catacombs, the Moorlocks rested. Unlike him they were not destroyed by light, just made uncomfortable. It was their eyes; they were like moles, only not really blind, just light sensitive. He had tried building sunglasses for them from pieces of stained glass and wire framing, but the daylight still affected them. Beneath their white fur, their pink skin was highly sensitive. He had taught them to sew shirts and pants, make shoes from skins, but the sun burned right through their clothes. They had abandoned shoes, shirts and glasses, but they still wore the pants. Something about the pants appealed to the Moorlocks. Maybe they liked the confinement of trousers better than letting their hammers swing, their snatches grab dust.

As the Dark Rider lay there, hiding from the light, he began to cry. How in God's name…No, fuck God. God had put him here. Surely it was God. Fate. Whatever. But the bottom line was still…Why?

Once upon a time, though which time he was uncertain, he had been an inventor and had traveled the ages via machine. A time machine.

Then there had been the dimensional juncture.

If he could but do that moment over he would not be what he had become. Sometimes, it was almost as if his old self had never been, and there had always been what he was now, The Dark Rider.

And Weena. How he missed her. She had been the most wonderful moment of his life.

Once upon a time, he had lived as an Englishman in the year 1895, wherever that now existed, if it existed. He had been an inventor, and the result of this invention was a machine that traveled through time.

Oh, but he had been noble. Saw himself as a hero. He traveled to the far future where he discovered a world of soft, simple people who lived above ground, were supplied goods by the machinery of the Moorlocks below ground. And they, without wishing to, supplied the Moorlocks with a food source. Themselves.

These simple people were called the Eloi.

While in this future, he met a beautiful and simple Eloi maiden named Weena. He made love to her, and came to love her. She was stolen by the Moorlocks, and after a desperate but futile battle to find and rescue her, he was forced to escape in the time machine. But he had pushed the gear forward, went farther into the future, to a world with a near burned-out sun, populated by crablike creatures and a dull dead ocean.

He returned then to his own time to tell his tale. But he was not believed when he explained that there were four dimensions, not three. Length, width, depth…and time.

Returning to the era of the Eloi, he discovered Weena had escaped from the Moorlocks, and he decided then and there to become the champion of the Eloi, and within a short time he had taught the mild mannered people how to do for themselves. He traveled through time and brought to the Eloi animals that no longer existed in their future. He taught them to raise meat and vegetables. He taught them how to fight the Moorlocks.

It was a great time, ten years he judged it.

But then he discovered on one of his exploratory journeys through time that there was a fifth dimension. It existed alongside the others; a place where time took different routes, numerous routes.

Somehow, by his travel he had opened some kind of wormhole in time, and now it had all run together and its very fabric had begun to rip. It was believed in this time that the rips had been caused by squid-like invaders in saucers, but in fact, they were the result of his blunders through the Swiss cheese holes of time.

Returning to the Eloi and Weena, he discovered, through his dimensional traveling, he had not only screwed up time and cross-hatched it and connected it in spots and disconnected it in others, but he had also contracted some strange malady.

He craved blood. He was like a vampire. He had to have blood to survive.

Weena stood by him, and he made the Moorlocks his prey. He discovered other side effects of the dimensional plague. He had tremendous strength, speed and agility and a constant erection.

But there was a great sourness in him, and soon he began to change. Even when he did not want to change, he changed. Day became repellant, and he found that he enjoyed being amongst the bodies of the dead Moorlocks that he fed on. He liked the smell of death, of rotting meat.

Weena tried to help him, make him whole again. But there was nothing she could do. And in a moment of anger, he struck her and killed her. It was the final straw. Gloom and doom and the desire to hold destruction in his hand overwhelmed him. He fell in love with the horrors.

Only the memory of Weena remained clean. He had her body mummified in the deep sands beyond the garden world of the Eloi, and he had her placed in a coffin made of oak and maple. Then he buried it in one of the great gardens and a tree was planted to mark it.

Time took the tree and the garden, and now there was just the dirt and her mummified remains, and even that, eventually, his former joy, and now his nemesis, time, would take.

He had made an old museum his home. It housed the wares of many centuries. It was unique. It was a ruined palace of green porcelain, fronted by a giant sphinx that had been some sort of monument. Below the museum, beneath the sphinx, and other sites, were the Moorlocks' tunnels and their machines. Machines that had ground out simple goods for the Eloi.

He became their king, and in time, the Eloi became their food again. And his.

The machines roared below ground once more.

The Eloi quivered again.

And then came the rip.

■ ■ ■

Time lies tight between, within, and behind dimensional curtains, and these curtains are strong and not easy to tear, but somehow, presumed the Dark Rider, his machine had violated the structures of time, and by its presence, its traveling through, it had torn this fabric and other times had slipped into the world of the Eloi and the Moorlocks, slipped in so subtly that a new time was created with a past and a present and a possible future. There was not only a shift in time, but in space, and the Wild West of America collided with a Steam Age where inventors from his own time, who had never made such inventions, were suddenly now building steam ships and flying ships and submarines. Time and space were all a jumble.

The disease in him would not kill him. It just made him live on and on with a burning need to kill, maim and destroy. Perhaps his disease was merely one that all mankind bore in its genes. A disease buried deep in the minds of every human being, dormant in some, active in others, but in him, not buried at all.

Was he not merely a natural device, a plague, helping to monitor a corner(s) of the universe? Was he not nature's way of saying: I'd like to destroy all this and start over. Just take this petri dish and wash it off and disinfect it?

The Dark Rider liked to believe he was the ultimate in Darwinism, and that he was merely doing what needed to be done with a world of losers. Instead of combating evil, did it not make more sense to merely be evil so that mankind could go back to what it had originally been?

Nothing.

■ ■ ■

The sun was scorching again, and inside the steam man it was hotter than the day before. Beadle and his companions sweated profusely, worked the steam man forward with their levers and valves. Steam tore at trees with his great metal hands, uprooting them, tossing them aside, making a path through the forest as they went in search of the Dark Rider's lair, which though not entirely known, was suspected to lie somewhere within, or on the other side of, the great forest.

As the hot day wore on, and more trees were ripped and tossed, a road began to appear through the great forest. Inside the steam man it was hotter yet as Hamner and John Feather tossed logs into the furnace and worked the bellows and stoked the flames that chewed at the wood and boiled the vast tank of water and produced the steam that gave power to the steam man's working parts.

The steam man clanked and hissed on, and finally they broke from the trees, and in the distance they could see a great white sphinx, and near it another building of green stone. Though run down and vine-climbed, both had a majestic air about them.

Beadle said, "If I were the Dark Rider, that would be my den."

John Feather made a grunting noise. The others nodded. The steam man pushed on.

. . .

Then the ground opened up, and the steam man staggered and fell in. His knee struck the rim of the trench and he was knocked backwards, then sideways, came to rest in that position, one leg deep in the hole, the other pushed up and behind him and on the surface. His left shoulder and head leaned against one side of the trench.

The fall caused logs and flames to leap from the furnace, and Blake's pants leg caught on fire. He came out of his chair with a scream, lost control of his levers and valves, and the steam man faltered even more, its hands clutching madly at the edge of the trench, tearing out great clods of soil. Wads of steam spurted from Steam's hat and his metal body heaved and screeched at the grinding of machinery.

John Feather leaped forward, shut the furnace, threw the guard latch in place. Beadle, thrown from his chair, standing on the side of the steam man, since the floor was now askance, wobbled to the controls, turned off the steam.

"We seem to have stepped into a trap," Beadle said, slapping cinders off his pants.

"Goddamn it," Blake said, from his position on the floor. "It's my fault. I let go of my controls."

"No," Beadle said. "You had no choice, and beside, Steam was already falling. It's the Dark Rider's fault. Let's not brood. Let's assess the damage."

They went up the winding staircase to the steam man's hat and used the emergency opening over his ear. They threw open the door and lowered the flexible ramp.

Outside, in the midday sun, what they saw upset them. But it was not as bad as they had feared. Steam's left leg lay on the back side of the trench, while his other leg and lower torso were in it. His head and chest poked out of the deep ditch, and he was leaning to port. The leg that was bent behind him looked to be solidly connected, stretched a bit, but serviceable.

"Maybe he can climb out," Blake said.

Beadle shook his head. "Not with his leg like that. He may pull himself out, but I think there's a chance he'll twist his leg off, then where will we be?"

"Where are we now?" Blake said.

"In a hole," Hamner said. "That's where we are."

"The tripod and winch," John Feather said.

"Yes," Beadle said. "The tripod and winch."

Inside the steam man, stored in a number of connecting parts, was a tripod and winch device. It was there for moving large trees when heating materials were needed and small wood was not available. So far, it had never been used, but it was just the ticket.

They unloaded and fastened the device together, set the tripod up over the trench, fastened the cables to the steam man, then set about lifting him.

The sun was past noon and starting to dip.

* * *

By late day, they had lifted the steam man three times, and each time his great weight had sagged the crane, and he had fallen back into the pit, straining the leg even more.

Finally, in desperation, they cut some of the smaller trees from the forest behind them, and used them to reinforce their apparatus. This was hard business, and the four of them, even with the smaller trees trimmed and topped, had a hard time moving them, pushing them upright and into place, lodging them tight against the ground.

When they had a tripod of trees to reinforce their tripod and winch, John Feather climbed to the top with Hamner, and they bound the trees tightly to their metal tripod with cable.

All set, they checked and tightened the cables, made sure the steam man was solidly fastened, and set about lifting him once more. Shadows spread across the ground as they worked, filled the trench and cooled the air.

Beadle, dirty and sweaty, an itch in his ass, looked up from the winch lever they were working and saw that the sun was falling down behind the sphinx and the building of green stone. "Gentleman," he said. "I suggest we hasten."

(3)
The Dark Rider Awake

Beneath the green rock museum, in the darkness of his grave, the Dark Rider stirred, removed the plastic and sat up. Almost at the same moment, the Moorlocks removed the wooden cover.

Effortlessly, the Dark Rider leaped from the pit, landed at its edge, straightened and looked out at the mass of red eyes around him. When he looked, the red eyes blinked.

In a corner of the dark room sat the Time Machine, draped in spiderwebs. All except the saddle, which the Dark Rider used as his throne.

The Dark Rider took his place on the saddle and a Moorlock brought him his black hat. He sat there, and for a moment, astride his old machine, he felt as if were about to venture again into time and space. A wave of his old self swelled up inside of him and washed him from head to foot. There were warm visions of Weena. But as always, it passed as immediately as it swelled.

His old self was gone, and venturing forth in his machine was impossible. The machine had worn out long ago, and he had never been able to repair it. Certain elements were no longer available. For a while, he searched, but eventually came to the conclusion that what he needed would never be found.

And besides. What was the point? Time and space were collapsing. Not more than a month ago he had come upon men and women from the stone age killing and eating a family in a Winnebago.

He and his Moorlocks fought and impaled the prehistorics, and he only lost ten Moorlocks in the process. Once upon a time the loss of the Moorlocks would not have bothered him at all, but with the death of most of the Moorlock women through sheer chance and his own meanness, there were only a few females left. He kept them in special breeding centers in caverns beneath the ground. But though the Moorlocks loved to fight, they did not dearly love to fuck. Oh, now and then they'd rape some of the women they came across, before they impaled them, but it just wasn't the way it used to be. When they got home they weren't excited like they had been once upon a time; so excited they'd mate with the Moorlock women, impregnating them. Nature was trying desperately to play them out.

Thinking on this, the Dark Rider frowned. It wasn't that he cared all that much for the Moorlocks, it was simply that he liked servants. He supposed he could enslave others, but the Moorlocks were really perfect. Strong, obedient, and not overly bright. Other races had a tendency to revolt, but the Moorlocks actually thrived on stupidity and control, as long as they were allowed their little delights now and then.

But he had more immediate worries tonight. The steam man and the fools inside it. But the whole operation might cost him a kit and caboodle of the Moorlocks.

Sighing, the Dark Rider concluded that their loss was one of the necessities of business. Which was, simply defined, fear and destruction and a good solid meal.

One of the Moorlocks waddled up to the Dark Rider with his head held down.

"What it is it, Asshole?"

Asshole was the Dark Rider's favorite of the Moorlocks.

Asshole leaped about, slapped his chest, made some noise.

"They are near?" asked the Dark Rider.

"Uh, you betcha," Asshole said.

"Then, I suppose, we should go greet them. Get Sticks."

■ ■ ■

Just about everything that could go wrong, had gone wrong. The tripod had turned over. Blake had fallen and sprained an ankle, but was otherwise all right. They cut him a crutch from an oak tree, and he hobbled about, tugging on ropes and struggling to free Steam.

Eventually everything was in place again, and Steam was lifted just enough to free his leg. Beadle climbed back inside and stoked up the dying embers. John Feather climbed in after him and handed him new wood from the stockpile. Beadle put it in on top of the meager flames, then they worked the bellows. The flame flared up and the logs got hot, and still they worked the bellows.

When the fire was going good, Beadle went out on the ramp under Steam's ear and called down to Blake and Hamner. "Crank the winch up tight, then stand back."

When Beadle disappeared back inside Steam, Hamner and Blake took hold of the winch crank together and set to work. They managed to lift Steam even more, allowing his trapped leg to slip into the pit with the other. It was hard work, and when they were finished, it was all they could do to keep standing.

Inside, Beadle and John Feather worked the controls, and Steam climbed easily out of the pit. When he stood on solid ground again, Hamner and Blake cheered, and inside Steam, Beadle and John Feather did the same.

But it was a short-lived celebration. John Feather pointed at one of Steam's eyes, said, "Bad shit coming."

"My God," Beadle said. "Lower the ladder, let them in."

(4)
STICKS A'STEPPIN'

The Dark Rider's contraption was a man made of sticks and it stood at least twenty feet higher than Steam. The sticks had been interlaced with strips of rawhide, woven and strapped, tied to form the shape of a man. There were gaps in the shape, and through the gaps you could see the apes in trousers, as well as flashes of metal. It made cranking and clanking sounds. And the damn thing walked.

John Feather lowered the ladder in Steam's butt, and Hamner scrambled up, followed by the not so scrambling Blake and his crude crutch.

Once inside they took their seats and ran their hands over their controls.

"Steam is bound to be stronger than a man of sticks," Hamner said.

"Don't underestimate the Dark Rider," Beadle said. "We have before, and each time we've regretted it."

Hamner nodded. He remembered when their team had consisted of several others. Mistakes and miscalculations had whittled them down to this.

"What's the game plan then?" Blake asked.

"We approach him cautiously, feel him out."

"I don't think we'll have to worry about approaching him," Hamner said. "He seems to be coming at a right smart clip."

And indeed, he was.

■ ■ ■

Sticks and Steam approached one another. From the rooftop of the museum, the Dark Rider watched. He hoped a kill could be made soon. He was very hungry. And he dearly wanted Beadle. The bastard had been chasing him forever. He would impale the others, but Beadle he would have some fun with first. To humiliate him, he would fuck him. Maybe fuck a wound he would tear in his body with his hands, then he'd torture him some, and drink his blood of course, and call him bad names and pull out his hair, and maybe fuck another wound, then he'd have him impaled after boiling his feet raw, coating them with salt and having a goat lick the soles until the skin stripped off.

Well, he might have to lose that part with the goat. He'd already killed and sucked dry every damn goat in these parts, not to mention sheep, a lot of dogs, a good mess of cats, deer, and of course there wasn't a human outside of Beadle and his bunch within a hundred miles. Not a living one anyway. That was the problem with having his kind of urges. You soon ran out of victims. Rats were plentiful, of course, but even for him they were hard to catch.

Then a thought occurred to him. He could get Asshole to do the foot-licking part. He could be the goat. Asshole, like all the Moorlocks, had a rough tongue, and dearly loved salt any way he could get it. With this in mind, the Dark Rider began to feel content and confident again.

■ ■ ■

Up close, Beadle and his boys could hear machinery inside of Sticks, and they could see into the huge open eyes, and there they saw the apes in trousers, howling, barking, running about, the moonlight illuminating their little red peepers.

Inside Sticks, the Moorlocks worked furiously. Most of their equipment ran on sprockets and cables and bicycle gears, and in the center of the stick man, and at the back of his head, were bicycle seats and pedals, and on the seats, peddling wildly, were the Moorlocks. The pedaling engaged gears and sprockets, and allowed the head Moorlock, Asshole, who sat in a swinging wicker basket, to work levers and guide gears.

As the steam man and the stick man came in range of one another, Asshole pulled levers and yelled and barked at his humanoid engines, and Sticks reached out and grabbed Steam by the head, brought a stick and wicker knee up into his tight tin stomach.

The clang of the knee attack inside of Steam resounded so loudly, Beadle, without thinking, jerked both hands over his ears, and for a moment, Steam wobbled slightly.

Embarrassed, Beadle grabbed at his gears and went to work. He made Steam throw a left, and Sticks took it in the eye, scattering a handful of Moorlocks, but others rushed to take their place.

Blake, who worked the right arm tried to follow with a right cross, but he was late. Sticks brought up his left arm and wrapped it around Steam's right, and they were into a tussle.

Beadle realized quickly that from a striking standpoint Steam was more powerful, but in close, Sticks, with his basket woven parts, was more flexible.

Blake tried to work Steam's right arm free, but it was no go. Sticks brought his right leg around and put it behind Steam's right, kicked back, and threw Steam to the ground, climbed on top of him and tried to pummel him with both tightly woven fists.

Great dents jumped into Steam's metal and poked out in humps on the inside. Sticks used a three-finger poke (he only had four fingers on each hand) to knock out one of Steam's stained glass eyes. The fingers probed inside the gap as if trying to find an eyeball, touched Beadle slightly, and disappeared.

Lying on his back as he was, Steam rocked right and left, and inside of him his parasites worked their gears and valves and cussed. Finally it came to Beadle to have Steam's right leg lift up and latch around Sticks' left leg. Then he did the same with the other side, brought both knees together so Steam could crush Sticks' ribwork and the Moorlocks inside.

But the rib work proved stronger and more flexible than Beadle had imagined. It moved but did not give. He decided it was Steam's turn to grab Sticks' eye sockets. He called out orders, and soon Steam's hands rose and he grabbed at the corners of Sticks' eye sockets with metal thumbs, shook Sticks' head so savagely Moorlocks flew out of the eyeholes.

Moorlocks began to bail through the eyeholes onto Steam's chest, poured in through the busted left eye of Steam.

John Feather leaped out of his harness seat, drew his knife and went at them. Blood flew amidst screams of pain. John Feather slashed and stabbed, killed while he sang his death song. The Moorlocks leaped on top of him. Hamner started to free himself to help John Feather, but Beadle called, "Work the controls."

Sticks' head began to tear and twist off, came loose in a burst of basket work and sticks that flipped and scattered Moorlocks like water drops shaken from a wet dog's back.

Bicycle parts went hither and yon, crashed to the ground. One Moorlock lay with a bicycle chain wrapped around his head, another had a fragment of a pedal in his ass.

Inside Steam, John Feather still fought while Beadle and his crew worked the gears and made Steam roll on his right side. In the process, John Feather crashed about, along with the Moorlocks.

Then Steam stood up. John Feather and the Moorlocks fell back, past the seats and the controls and down the long drop of the left leg to the bottom of Steam's left foot. Beadle heard the horrid crash and winced. It was unlikely there were any survivors, Moorlocks or John Feather.

Beadle steeled himself to his present task, began to walk Steam, stomping fleeing Moorlocks with the machine, spurting them in all directions like overstuffed jelly rolls.

■ ■ ■

From his position atop the museum, the Dark Rider watched and grew angry. Damn dumb Moorlocks. Never give an ape a vampire's job.

The Dark Rider rushed downstairs with a swirl of his cape. He went so fast, the front of his hat blew back.

Near the anterior of the museum stood the Dark Rider's clockwork horse. It stood ten hands high and was made of woven wooden struts and thin metal straps, and at its center, like a heart, was a clockwork mechanism that made it run.

The Dark Rider took a key from his belt, reached inside the horse, inserted the key, turned it, wound the clock. As he wound, the horse lifted its head and made a metal noise. Lights came on behind its wide red eyes.

The Dark Rider pulled himself on top of his horse, whom he had named Clockwork, sat in the bicycle seat there, put his feet on the pedals, and began to pump. Effortless, the bicycle horse moved forward at a rapid gait, its steel hooves pounding the worn floor of the museum, knocking up tile chips.

Two Moorlocks who stood guard at the front of the museum jumped to it and opened the door. With a burst of wind that knocked the Moorlocks down, the Dark Rider blew past them and out into the night.

(5)
THINGS GET PISSY

"The Dark Rider," said Hamner.

Beadle and Blake looked. Sure enough, there he was, bright in the moonlight, astride his well-known mechanical horse. Its hooves threw up chunks of dirt and its head bobbed up and down as the Dark Rider pedaled so furiously his legs were nothing more than the blurs of his black pants.

"He looks pissed off," said Blake.

"He's always pissed off," said Beadle.

Beadle set the course for Steam, and just as the old metal boy made strides in the Dark Rider's direction, a Moorlock, bloodied and angry, came hissing out of the stairway in the left leg of Steam and leaped at Beadle.

Beadle lost control of his business, and Steam suddenly stopped, his left arm dropping to his side and his head lilting. This nearly caused Steam to tip over, and it was all Blake could do to shut down his side of the machine.

The Moorlock opened its mouth wide and bit into Beadle's shoulder. Beadle grabbed it by the scruff of the neck and pulled, but the Moorlock wouldn't come loose. Hamner came out of his seat and jumped at the Moorlock, sticking his thumbs in its eyes, but even though Hamner pushed at the beast's head, causing its eyes to burst into bleeding lumps, still it clung to Beadle.

Beadle beat dramatically at the Moorlock's side, but still it held. Both men hammered at the beast, but still, no go. The old boy was latched in and meant business.

Then John Feather, bloodied and as crazed as the Moorlock, appeared. He had a knife in his teeth. He put it in his hand and said, "Step back, Hamner."

Hamner did, and John Feather cut the Moorlock's throat. With a spew of blood and a gurgle, the Moorlock died, but still its dead head bit tight into Beadle's shoulder.

John Feather sheathed the knife. He and Hamner tried to free the head, but it wouldn't let go. Its teeth were latched deep.

"Cut the head off," Beadle said.

John Feather went to work. As he cut, Beadle said, "I thought you were dead."

"Not hardly," John Feather said. "I got some bumps and my ass hurts, but the Moorlocks cushioned my fall, and I cushioned this guy's."

"Shit," said Blake, who, with his injured leg had not left his chair, "he's on us."

• • •

The Dark Rider, moving at an amazing clip, was riding lickety split around Steam, and he was whirling above his head a hook on a long-ass rope. He let go of the rope with one hand and the hook went out and buried itself in the right tin leg of Steam and held.

The Dark Rider continued to ride furiously around Steam, binding its legs with the rope, pulling them tighter and tighter with the power of the mechanical horse.

Beadle, the head of the Moorlock hanging from his shoulder, struggled at the controls, tried to work the legs to break the rope. But it was too late.

Steam began to topple.

(6)
STEAM ALL MESSED UP

Steam fell with a terrific crash, fell so hard his head, containing Beadle and his crew, came off and rolled over the Dark Rider and his horse, knocking Clockwork for more than a few flips, causing it to shit horse turds of clockwork innards. Steam's head rolled right over the Dark Rider, driving him partially into the ground, but it had no effect.

Inside Steam's torso Beadle unfastened his seat belt, fell out of his seat, got up and wobbled, trying to adjust to the Moorlock's head affixed to his shoulder.

One glance revealed that Hamner was dead. His seat had come unfastened from the floor and had thrown him into Steam's right eye, shattering it, poking glass through him. Blake was loose from his seat and on his crutch. He reached and took a Webb rifle off the wall.

John Feather reached his bow and arrows from the wall, unfastened the top of his quiver and threw it back, slipped the quiver over his shoulder and took his bow and drew an arrow.

Beadle took a Webb rifle off the wall. Beadle looked at John Feather, said: "Today is a good day to die."

"It's night," John Feather said, "and I don't intend to die. I'm gonna kill me some assholes."

Actually, it was Asshole himself who was approaching the be-headed Steam, and with him were a pack of Moorlocks previously scattered from the remains of Stick.

Beadle and his crew went out the hole under Steam's ear. "I'm gonna die," Beadle said, "I'd rather do it out in the open."

Nearby lay Steam's body, leaking from its neck the remains of the exploded furnace: embers, fiery logs, lots of smoke and steam.

The Moorlocks came in a bounding, yelling, growling rush. Strat-egy was not their strong point. All they really knew was what the Dark Rider told them, and good old-fashioned direct ass whipping. The Webb rifles cracked. Arrows flew. Moorlocks went down. But still they closed, and soon the fighting was hand to hand. The Moorlocks were strong and would have won, had not their leader, Asshole, leap-ing up and down and shouting orders, not received one of John Feather's arrows in the mouth.

Asshole, still talking in his barking manner, bit down on the shaft, shattering teeth, then, appearing more than a bit startled, turned him-self completely around and fell on his face, driving the shaft deeper, poking it out of the back of his neck.

In this instant, the Moorlocks lost courage and bolted.

The Dark Rider came then, called: "Get the fuck back here, or I'll impale you all myself."

These seemed like words of wisdom to the Moorlocks. They turned and began to stalk forward. Beadle picked out the Dark Rider and shot at him, hit him full in the chest. The bullet went through him with a jerk of flesh, an explosion of cloth and dust.

The Dark Rider, though knocked down and dazed, was unharmed. Slowly, the Dark Rider stood up.

"That's not good," said Beadle.

"No," John Feather said. "It's not. I guess tonight is a good night to die. And while we're at it, if we're gonna go, I must tell you some-thing, Beadle."

"What?"

"I've always wanted to fuck you."

"Huh," said Beadle, and John Feather let out with a laugh and loosed an arrow that took a Moorlock full in the chest, added: "Not!"

Amidst laughter, Beadle began to fire, and the Moorlocks began to drop.

But the ole Dark Rider, he just keep comin' on.

■ ■ ■

The Dark Rider was on them in a rush. He tossed John Feather hard against Steam's head, grabbed at Beadle, missed, grabbed at Blake who was hitting him with his crutch.

When Beadle regained his feet, the Dark Rider had Blake down and was poking at his ass so hard with the crutch, he had ripped a hole in his pants.

Before the Dark Rider could impale him, Beadle shot the Dark Rider in the back of the head. It was a good shot. No blood came out, just some skull tissue, and the Dark Rider flipped forward and over and came up on his feet, hatless.

He reached down and picked up his hat, dusted it on his knee, and put it on. He looked mad as hell.

■ ■ ■

John Feather had recovered. He let loose an arrow and it struck the Dark Rider in the chest with a thump, stayed there. The Dark Rider sighed, snapped the arrow off close to his chest.

The Moorlocks surrounded them

The Dark Rider said, "And now it ends."

Then the Moorlocks swarmed them. Shots were fired, an arrow flew. But there were too many Moorlocks. In a matter of seconds, it was all over.

(7)
GETTING THE SHAFT

They were carried away to a place outside of the museum, stripped nude, tied with their hands behind their backs, then surrounded by Moorlocks.

Though Hamner was dead, he was the first to be impaled. His body was partially feasted on by the Dark Rider and the Moorlocks, then he was raised into the moonlight with a freshly cut wooden shaft in his ass. The end of it was dropped into a prearranged hole. His dead weight traveled down the length of the stake and the point of it gouged out of his right eye. He continued to slide down it until his bloody buttocks touched the ground.

Second, the Dark Rider, out of some perverse desire for revenge, had Steam impaled. A large sharpened tree was run through the trap door in the steam man's ass, poked through his neck, then the battered, steeple-topped head was placed on top of the stake.

With arms tied behind their backs, Beadle and his Moorlock head, John Feather, and Blake, who could not stand because of his leg, awaited their turn. The Moorlocks were salivating at the thought of their blood and flesh, and Beadle was reminded of a pack of hunting hounds at feeding time. He regretted that he had not gotten to his derringer in time, but the derringer was no longer an issue; like his clothes, it had been taken from him.

The Dark Rider, his hat removed, his face red with Hamner's blood, strands of Hamner's flesh hanging from his teeth, said, "I'm going to save you, Mr. Beadle, until last, and just before you the Indian. And you, what is your name?"

"Blake. Mr. James Blake to you."

"Ah, Blakey. Defiance to the last.

"Moorlocks…" the Dark Rider said.

The Moorlocks all leaned forward, as if listening at a keyhole.

"Gnaw his balls off."

They rushed Blake, and there was an awful commotion. Beadle and John Feather struggled valiantly to loose themselves from their bonds and help their friend, but the best they could manage were some lame, ignored kicks.

Blake was lifted up screaming, and while his legs were held apart by Moorlocks, the others, their heads popping forward like snapping turtles, tore at Blake's testicles, and when they were nothing more than ragged flesh (they got the penis too), a stake was rammed in his ass and he was dropped down on it. He screamed so loud Beadle felt as if the noise was rocking his very bones.

The Moorlocks carried Blake to a prearranged hole, dropped him in, pushed in dirt, and left him there. Courageously, Blake yelled, threw his legs up as high as he could. The movement dropped his weight, and the sharpened stick went through him and out of his throat, killing him quickly.

"That will be the way to do it," John Feather said. "It's how we should do it."

Beadle nodded.

The Dark Rider, who sat in a large wooden chair that had been brought outside from the museum, said, "My, but he was brave. Quite brave."

"Unlike you," Beadle said.

"Ah," the Dark Rider said, "I suppose this is where you are going to challenge me, and with my ego at stake, and your ass at stake, so to speak, I'm going to take you on, one on one, and the winner survives. If I win, you die. If I lose, well, you all go to the house."

"Are you too much of a coward to do that?" Beadle said.

The Dark Rider removed a handkerchief from inside his vest and wiped Hamner's blood from his face and put on his hat. He tossed the handkerchief aside. A Moorlock grabbed it and began to suck at the blood on the cloth. A fight broke out over the handkerchief, and in the struggle one of the Moorlocks was killed.

When this moment had passed, the Dark Rider turned his attention back to Beadle.

"I don't much care how I'm thought of, Mr. Beadle. Since very little causes me damage, and I have the strength of ten men, it's sort of hard to be concerned about such a threat. And besides, in the rare case you did win, my Moorlocks would eat you anyway. In fact, if I should die, they would eat me. Right, boys?"

A murmur of agreement went up from the Moorlocks. Except for those eating the corpse of the loser of the handkerchief battle. They were preoccupied.

"No, I'm not going to do that," the Dark Rider said. "That would be too quick for you. And it would give you some sense of dignity. I'm against that. In fact, I actually have other plans for you. You will get the stake, but not before we've had a bit of torture. As for the red man, well, I can see now that the stake, if you're courageous like your friend, can be beat. I could tie your legs, Indian man, of course, stop that nonsense. But no. I'm going to crucify you. Upside down. And keep the boys off of you for awhile so you'll suffer. As I remember, a saint was crucified upside down. Perhaps, Mr. Red Man, you will be made a saint. But I doubt it."

■ ■ ■

A cross was made and John Feather was put on it and his hands were nailed and his feet, after being overlapped, were also nailed. John Feather made not a sound while the Moorlocks worked, driving the nails into his flesh. The cross was put in the ground upside down, John Feather's head three feet from the dirt, his long hair dangling.

Beadle was taken away to the museum. The Moorlocks were given Blake's body to eat, all except the left arm which was wrapped in cloth and given directly to the Dark Rider for later.

Beadle was placed on a long table and tied to it. The Dark Rider disappeared for a time, about some other mission, and while Beadle waited for the horrors to come, the lone Moorlock left to watch him played with Beadle's dick.

"Lif id ub, pud id down," he said as he played. "Lif id ub, pud id down."

"Would you stop that, for heaven's sake?" Beadle said.

The Moorlock frowned, popped Beadle's balls with the back of his hand, and went back to his game. "Lif id ub, pud id down..."

(8)
A VIEW FROM DOOM

John Feather, in pain so intense he could no longer really feel it, could see the horizon, upside down, and he could see the ground and a bunch of ants. He had been taught that the ants, like all things in nature, were one, his kin. But he didn't like them. He knew what they wanted. Pretty soon they'd be on the cross, then the blood on his hands and feet. Then would come the flies. With kinfolks like ants and flies, who needed enemies? He could kind of get into accepting rocks and trees as his kinfolk, though he was, in fact, crucified on one of his kin, but ants and flies. Uh-uh.

He heard a squawk, lifted his head and looked up. At the top of the cross, waiting patiently, a buzzard had alighted.

John Feather remembered he had never had any use for buzzards, either. Come to think of it, he didn't like coyotes that much, and the way his luck was running, pretty soon they'd show up.

They didn't, but he did hear flies buzzing, and soon felt them alight on his bloody hands and feet.

■ ■ ■

When the Dark Rider showed, the first thing he did was light a kerosene lamp, and the first thing he said was, "I suppose we shall remove the Moorlock head. This will give us a wound to work with."

The Dark Rider took hold of the Moorlock's jaws, pried them apart, tossed the head, sent it bouncing across the floor. The assisting Moorlock watched it bounce. He looked longingly at the Dark Rider.

"Do your job here," the Dark Rider said, "and you can have it all to yourself."

The Moorlock looked pleased.

The Dark Rider, who had brought a roll of leather, placed it just above Beadle's head and uncoiled it. It was full of shiny instruments. The first one he pulled out was a long metal probe, sharpened on one end.

He held it up so Beadle could see it. It caught the lamplight and sparkled.

Beadle told himself he would not scream.

The Dark Rider poked the probe into the bite wound on his shoulder, and Beadle, in spite of himself, screamed. In fact, to his embarrassment, he thought he screamed like a girl, but with less restraint.

. . .

Inside the great time and space cosmic rip, the metal ship hurtled by again, and inside the ship, or as they called it, the shuttle, peering out one of its portholes, was an astronaut named McCormic. He was frightened. He was confused. And he was hungry. He and his partners, a Russian cosmonaut and a French astronaut, had recently finished their last tube of food and the water didn't look good. Another forty-eight hours they'd be out of it, another three or four days they'd be crazy and drinking their urine, maybe starting to think of each other as hot lunches.

Through a series of misfortunes they had lost most of their fuel and could not return to Earth. They were the Flying Dutchman, circling the globe. They had lost contact with home base. The radio waves were silent. It was as if the world beneath them had died. To add tension to all this, their air supply was draining. It would in fact play out at about the same time as the water supply, so maybe they would never get to drink their urine or dine on one another.

To top it off, McCormic was having trouble with his hemorrhoids, which was their way, to appear only at the least opportune time.

And then, there was the rip.

No matter where they were while circling the earth, the rip was always to their left. They watched it constantly, saw inside it strange things. The rip made no sense. It fit nothing they knew or thought they knew. McCormic felt certain it was widening, even as they watched.

McCormic turned to his partners. The Russian was sitting on the floor. His name was Kruschev. Like his companions, he had removed his helmet some time ago. He was reading from the Frenchman's copy of *Huckleberry Finn,* in French. He didn't understand the jokes.

The Frenchman, Gisbone, said, "I know what you are thinking, my friend McCormic. I am thinking of the same."

McCormic glanced at the Russian. The Russian nodded. "It is closer than our earth, comrade."

McCormic said, "It would be easy to use the thrusters. Turn into it. I say we do it."

■ ■ ■

John Feather thought perhaps the best thing he could do was pull with all his might and tear his hands free. The flesh there was not that strong, and if he could pull them through the nails, and was able to free his hands, then...Well, then he could hang upside down by his feet and die slowly of what he was already dying of, only with his hands free. Loss of blood.

But hell, it was something. He balled his hands into fists around the nails and pulled with everything he had.

Boy did it hurt.

Boy did it hurt a lot.

He pulled the flesh of his palms forward until the nails touched his clenched fingers. He jerked forward, and with a scream and burst of blood, John Feather's hands were free.

■ ■ ■

At about that time the shuttle, blasting on the last of its fuel, came hurtling through the crack in the sky, whizzed right by him so hard it caused the impaled steam man to rattle and the cross on which John Feather was crucified to lean dramatically.

The shuttle's wheels came down, but it hit at such an angle they crumpled and the great craft slid along on its belly.

John Feather, from his unique vantage point, watched as the ship tore up dirt, smashed through what was left of the smoldering stick man, turned sideways, spun in several circles and stopped. There was a popping sound from the craft, as if metal were cooling.

After a long moment, the door of the craft opened. John Feather waited for a squid in harness and overalls to appear. But something else came out. Something white and puffy, shaped like a man, but with a bright face that made it look like some kind of insect.

At this moment, John Feather's cross finally came loose in the ground and toppled to the earth with him on top of it. He let out a howl of pain.

Fuck that stoic red man shit.

McCormic was first. He wore his helmet, had his oxygen tank turned on. After a moment, he turned off the oxygen and removed the helmet. He came down the flexible staircase breathing deeply of the air.

"Very fresh," he said.

The Frenchman and the Russian came after him, removing their helmets.

"I believe it ees our earth," said the Frenchman. "Only fugged up."

■ ■ ■

From where he lay, John Feather tried to yell, but found that he had lost his voice. That scream had taken it out of him. He was hoarse and weak. But if he could get their attention, whoever, whatever they were, they might help him. They might eat him too, but considering his condition, he was willing to take the chance.

He tried to yell, but the voice just wasn't there. He tried several times.

The men with parts of their heads in their hands, turned away from the ship, walked around it, and headed away from him, in the direction from which he and his friends and the steam man had come.

When they were dots in the distance, John Feather's voice returned to him in a squeak. But it didn't matter now. They were out of earshot.

All he could manage was a weak, "Shit."

■ ■ ■

The Dark Rider had a lot of fun poking Beadle's wound, but he eventually became bored of that, left, came back with a salt shaker. He shook salt in the wound. Beadle groaned. The Moorlock hopped up and down. He hadn't had this much fun since he'd helped eat his first born young. The Dark Rider smiled, tried not to think of Weena.

■ ■ ■

After lying there for awhile, John Feather sat up and looked at his crucified feet. They hurt like a bitch. It took balls, but he reached down and grabbed both feet with his hands, and jerked with all his might.

The nail groaned, came loose, but not completely. The pain that shot through John Feather was so intense he lay back down. He prayed to the Great Spirit, then to the white man's god Jesus. He threw in a couple words for Buddha as well, even though he couldn't remember if Buddha actually did anything or not. Wasn't he just kind of an inspiration or something? He tried to remember the name of the Arabic god he had heard mentioned, but it wouldn't come to him.

Great Spirit, Jesus, Buddha, all seemed on vacation. The men carrying their heads didn't show up either.

John Feather sat up, took hold of his feet again, wrenched with all his might.

This time the nail came free, and John Feather passed out.

■ ■ ■

With pliers, one by one, the Dark Rider removed, with a slow wrench, Beadle's toenails.

■ ■ ■

John Feather found he could stand, but it was painful. He preferred to go forward on knuckles and knees, but that wasn't doing his hands any good.

Finally, using a combination of stand and crawl, he made it to the steam man, looked up at the spike in its ass, saw there was room to enter inside between shaft and passageway. Painfully, he took hold of the shaft and attempted to climb it. It was very difficult. His hands and feet hurt beyond anything he could imagine and the wounds from them slicked the stake with blood.

He fell twice and hit the ground hard before finally rubbing dirt in his wounds and trying a third time. It was slow and deliberate. But this time he made it.

■ ■ ■

"And this little piggy cried wee-wee-wee, all the way…HOME!"

With that, the Dark Rider jerked out the last toenail on Beadle's left foot.

Beadle groaned so loud, for a moment, even the Moorlock was startled.

"Now," the Dark Rider said, "let's go for the other one. What do you say?"

Beadle was too much in pain to say anything. And besides, what would it matter? He was going to save his breath for groaning and screaming.

■ ■ ■

Inside Steam, John Feather found water and washed the dirt from his wounds and used herbs and roots from his medicine and utility bag, applied them in a quick poultice, then bound them with ripped sheets from one of the locked cabinets. He made a breech cloth from some of the sheet, found his extra pair of soft moccasins and slid inside of them. His feet had swollen, but the leather was soft and stretched. He was able to put them on without too much trouble, and he found the cleansing and dressing had relieved the pain in his feet enough so that he could stand. It wasn't by any means comfortable to do so, but he felt he had to.

He tied his medicine bag around his waist, got a Webb rifle from its rack, his extra bow and quiver of forty-five thin arrows with long steel points.

Then he paused.

He put the rifle, the bow and quiver of arrows aside. He looked out of Steam's ass at the shaft that ran through it and out the neck, looked at the head balanced on top.

John Feather climbed down inside the right leg and took a canister off the wall. He carried it to the gap in Steam's ass and opened it, even though the action caused his hands to bleed. Inside was kerosene. He poured the kerosene down the shaft. He took flint and steel from his medicine pouch and struck up a spark that hit the soaked shaft and caused it to burst into flame. Fire ran down the length of the shaft and it began to burn.

John Feather took wood from the sealed hoppers, built a fire in Steam's belly.

■ ■ ■

"Just two more to go on this foot," the Dark Rider said, "then we start on the fingernails. Then we're going to see if you've been circumcised. And if not, we're going to do that. And if so, we're going to do it really close, if you know what I mean."

"Can I have 'em? Can I have 'em?" the Moorlock asked.

"You can have them, but as it looks to me, you should start on and finish your head."

The Moorlock grabbed the head of his brethren and began chewing on it.

Between bites he said, "Thank you, Master. Thank you."

"Let's do the right thumb first," the Dark Rider said. "What do you say?"

It was a rhetorical question. Beadle knew it was useless to ask for mercy from his enemy. He kept wishing he'd just pass out, but so far, no such luck. This hurt like hell, but was survivable, and therefore stretched out the possibilities. None of them good. It was made all the worse by the fact that the Dark Rider took his time. A little tug here, a little tug there, almost a tug, then a tug, easing the nails out one slow nail at a time.

Not to mention that the Dark Rider liked to pause with his pliers to squeeze the joints themselves, or to pause and poke at the wound in his shoulder.

The Dark Rider seemed to be having the time of his life.

Beadle wished he could say the same.

■ ■ ■

John Feather worked the bellows. The fire was going nicely. It wasn't normally a wise thing to do, but John Feather doused the interior of the furnace with kerosene, and as a result, a rush of fire burst out of it and singed his eyebrows, but the wood blazed.

John Feather checked the shaft in Steam's ass.

Burning nicely.

He went back to the bellows, worked there vigorously, stoking up the flame. The water in the chambers began to heat, and John Feather continued to work the bellows. Smoke came up through Steam's ass as the shaft blazed and caught solid.

■ ■ ■

"Now we have the pinky on the right hand...And, there, isn't that better just having it done with?"

Beadle couldn't understand what the Dark Rider was saying. He couldn't understand because he couldn't quit screaming.

The Dark Rider said, "And now let's do that lefty."

■ ■ ■

Vapor from the pipes pumped up and out of Steam's headless neck. Steam toppled forward and struck the ground hard, throwing John Feather against the side of the furnace, and in that instant, John Feather realized the shaft had burned through. Slightly burned from the furnace, John Feather recovered his feet, closed the furnace door, crawled along the side of Steam and began to work the emergency controls in the mid-body of the machine. They were serviceable at best.

Working these controls, he was able to make Steam put his hands beneath him and right himself.

John Feather clung to a cabinet until Steam was standing straight, then he took his stance on the platform in front of the seats and moved from one position to the other, working levers, observing dials.

It was erratic, but John Feather managed to have Steam lurch forward, find his head, and set it in place. Or almost in place. It set slightly tilted to the left.

John Feather climbed into the head and refastened the steam cables that had come unsnapped when the head came loose. He had to replace one from the backup stock. He tried the main controls. The fall Steam had taken had affected them; they were a little rough, but they worked.

John Feather started Steam toward the museum.

Condensation not only came out of the hole in the steam man's hat, but it hissed out of his eye holes and neck as well. He walked as if drunk.

(9)

RUCKUS

The wall came apart and Steam tore off part of the roof too. He grabbed a rip in the roof and shook it. A big block of granite fell from the ceiling, just missed Beadle on the table, passed to the left elbow of the Dark Rider, and got his Moorlock companion square, just as he was sucking an eyeball from the head he had been eating.

Steam ducked his head and entered the remains of the museum.

"I swore what I'd do to you Beadle," the Dark Rider said. "And I'll do it."

With that, the Dark Rider ducked under the table Beadle was strapped to, lifted it on his back, his arms outstretched, his hands turned backwards to clasp the table's sides, and with little visible effort, darted for the staircase.

Steam, head ducked, tried to pursue him, but as he went up the stairs the ceiling was too low. John Feather made Steam push at the ceiling with his head and shoulders like Atlas bearing the weight of the world, and Steam lifted.

The ceiling began to fall all around and on Steam.

The Dark Rider was up the stairs now, heading for the opening to the roof. When he came to the opening, he flung the table backwards so that Beadle landed on his face, breaking his nose, bamming his knee caps, and in the process, not doing his already maligned toes any good.

The Dark Rider grabbed the table and tore it apart, causing the straps that bound Beadle to be released. He grabbed Beadle by the head, like a kid not knowing how to carry a puppy, and started up a ladder to the roof.

When the Dark Rider reached the summit of the ladder, he used his free hand to throw open the trap, then, still holding the struggling Beadle by the head, pulled him onto the moonlit roof.

To the Dark Rider's right, he saw that the rip in the sky had grown, and that a rip within the rip had opened up a gap of darkness in which strange unidentifiable shapes moved.

Below his feet the roof shook, then exploded. Steam's crooked head poked through. And then rose. It was obvious the steam man was coming up the stairs, and he was tearing the roof apart.

The Dark Rider picked Beadle up by shoulder and thigh, raised him over his head. The Dark Rider thought the easy thing would be to toss Beadle from the roof.

Game over.

But that was the easy thing. He wanted this bastard to suffer.

And then he knew. He'd take his chances inside the rip. If he and Beadle survived it, he'd continue to make Beadle suffer slowly. Nothing else beyond that mattered. He realized suddenly that Beadle had been all that mattered for some time now, and when Beadle was dead, he would have only the memory of Weena again. Nothing else to preoccupy his thoughts. No more Beadle, no more Steam Man or regulators.

With Beadle raised over his head, the Dark Rider growled and started to run toward the rip.

. . .

John Feather saw through the shattered eye of Steam what the Dark Rider planned. Painfully, he grabbed at the quiver he had discarded, picked up his bow, took a coil of thin rope from the wall, tied it to the arrow with one quick loop, and watched as the Dark Rider completed the edge of the museum's roof, which was where the rip in the sky joined it.

The Dark Rider leaped.

John Feather let the arrow fly, dropped the bow, grabbed at the loose end of the rope and listened to the rest of it feed out.

The shot was a good one. It was right on the money. It went through Beadle's left thigh, right on through, and into his inner right thigh.

John Feather heard Beadle yell just as he jerked the rope with all his might. Beadle came loose from the Dark Rider's grasp in midair and was pulled back and slammed onto the museum roof, but the Dark Rider leapt into the dark rip with a curse that reverberated back into this world, then was nothing more than a fading echo.

■ ■ ■

The Dark Rider's leap had carried him into a place of complete cold darkness. His element. Or so it seemed.

He passed between shapes. Giant bats. They snapped smelly teeth at him and missed.

In time, he thought it would have been better had they not missed. Because he was falling.

Falling…falling.

His leap had carried him into an abyss. Seemingly bottomless, because he fell and fell and fell, and if he had been able to keep time, he would have realized that days passed, and still he fell. And had he needed oxygen like normal men he would have long been dead, but he did not need it, and therefore he did not die.

He just continued to fall.

He thought of Weena. He wondered if there really was a plane on which her soul survived, wondered if he could join her there, if she would want him now that he was what he was.

And he fell and he fell…and he is falling still…

■ ■ ■

But, back to John Feather and Beadle.

John Feather found a knife, dropped the ladder out from under Steam's ear, hobbled down it and out to Beadle. John Feather, while Beadle protested, cut the arrowhead out of Beadle's thigh, hacked the arrow off at the shaft, and using one injured, bleeding foot against the outside of Beadle's leg, jerked it free.

"We're going to have to help one another," John Feather said. "I'm not feeling too strong. My hands are seizing up."

"Did you have to shoot me with an arrow?"

"It was that, or follow him. And if he had gone into that rip, I would not have followed. I'm not that much of a friend."

The two of them, supporting one another, hobbled back to Steam.

Inside, Beadle found spare pants and shirt and boots and put them on. John Feather doctored his wounds again. Then, in their control chairs, they worked Steam and brought him out of the remains of the museum. They saw a few Moorlocks through Steam's eyes, but they were scattering. The sun was coming up.

"We should try and kill them all," Beadle said.

"I'm not up to killing much of anything," John Feather said.

"Yeah," Beadle said. "Me either."

"Without their leader, they aren't much."

"I think we're making a mistake."

John Feather sighed. "You may be right. But…"

"Yeah. Let's take Steam home."

John Feather, in considerable pain, looked through one of Steam's eyes at the landscape bathed in the orange-red light of the rising sun. There were more rips out there than before, and he saw things spilling out of some of them.

"If we still have a home," said John Feather.

EPILOGUE

The astronauts, who had shed their heavy pressure suits and were wearing orange jumps, stopped walking as a green Dodge Caravan driven by a blonde woman with two kids in it, a boy and a girl, stopped beside them.

She lowered an electric window.

"You look lost," she said.

"Very," said McCormic.

"I suggest you get in." She nodded to the rear.

The astronauts glanced in that direction. A herd of small but very aggressive looking dinosaurs were thundering in their direction.

"We'll take you up on that suggestion," McCormic said.

They hustled inside. The boy and girl looked terrified. The astronauts smiled at them.

The blonde woman put her foot to the gas and they tore off.

Behind them the dinosaurs continued to pursue. The woman soon had the Caravan up to eighty and the dinosaurs were no longer visible.

"How much gas do you have?" asked McCormic.

"Over half a tank," she said. "Where are we?"

McCormic looked at the others. They shrugged. He said, "We haven't a clue. But I think we're home, and yet, we aren't."

"I guess," said the blonde woman, "that's as good an answer as I'm going to find."

The Caravan drove on.

All about, earth and sky resounded with the sounds of time and space coming apart.

▪ Screwup ▪

(WITH KAREN LANSDALE)
INTRODUCTION

This one is Jill Morgan's fault. She asked my wife and me to do a story for a book of stories written by husbands and wives. Karen had a couple of ideas, and one of them sparked something. I changed it a bit, told her what I had in mind, she suggested changes, I wrote a draft, she worked it over a bit, and I revised, and this came out.

This is the second time Karen and I have done a story together. The first was "Change of Lifestyle" which first appeared in TWILIGHT ZONE MAGAZINE.

We also co-edited an anthology together.

No one got hurt.

· Screwup ·

(WITH KAREN LANSDALE)

As he drove, Miller could hear his wife's voice in the back of his head telling him what a screwup he was. The thought of her, the memory of her voice, were normally things he did not like to think about, but now, with her tucked nice and dead in the car trunk, thinking about her wasn't so bad.

It had been a simple thing, really. He had considered it for years, almost immediately after the wedding. Nothing he did or had done suited Caroline.

She didn't like his job and wanted better for him, she said, so he left it, and when his new job turned sour she scolded him for leaving the old job, never remembered, or admitted she remembered, that she was the one who had asked him to leave.

It was always that way. One thing after another. If he took the garbage out, he took it out wrong. He should have double-bagged it. If he double-bagged it, she felt he was wasting bags. He was supposed to know the difference in trash that needed double-bagging and trash that needed a single bag. Now and then Caroline suggested triple-bagging for something especially nasty.

Miller smiled.

She was tripled-bagged. Very bloody, so three bags were necessary. He was sure she would approve since the axe blows to her head had made a terrible mess, and would have made an even worse mess in her car.

Her car. He owned the Cadillac before they met, but now it was her car. As everything they owned was hers. Including him.

But not now. Not anymore.

Miller was smiling to himself when he noticed the flashing lights in the rearview mirror. His stomach turned sour immediately. He pulled over and rolled down the window and waited, watched the cop in the rearview mirror. The cop parked his car, got out, came around to the window.

"I'm sorry, Officer," Miller said. "Was I speeding?"

The cop was a tall lean fellow with sunglasses on. Miller could see himself in the glasses. Somehow, those glasses made him feel as if he were looking into the cold calculating eyes of an insect.

"License please," the officer asked.

"I must have been driving faster than I thought," Miller said, pulling his wallet out and opening it to his license.

The cop took the wallet, looked at the license. "Nothing like that, sir." The officer gave him his wallet back. "Could you get out of the car please? And bring your car keys."

Miller got out and the officer walked him around to the rear of the automobile. He pointed at the left taillight.

"When you put on the brakes, going around the curve there, I noticed your light wasn't working."

"Oh," Miller said, and he tried not to look overly relieved.

"Cars like this," the officer said, "sometimes something in the trunk falls against the wire inside, disconnects it. It's easy to connect."

"Good. I'll take care of it as soon as I get home."

"No sir," the officer said. "We'll take care of it right now. You need to have your taillight working. If it isn't a loose wire, I'll follow you to a filling station where you can have it fixed."

"I'm going straight home. I can fix it myself."

"Your license says you live on Timberridge, that's in the other direction, so you're not going straight home."

"Well, I meant after I run some errands."

· "Open the trunk, sir."

Miller found the correct key on his ring and opened the trunk. The big plastic bag, like a cocoon, filled most of the space.

"You don't have a spare back here?" the cop said.

"No sir. I took it out. I had some things I wanted to donate to Goodwill. I bagged them up, and the bag was so large I had to take the tire out."

"That's certainly a nice new shoe you're donating there," the officer said. "My wife has some just like it."

"What?"

"The shoe."

Miller looked. The bottom of the bag had broken open, and Caroline's shoe was poking through the break. You couldn't see her ankle, just the shoe, the heel of which was resting against a tire iron.

"Oh, yeah," Miller said. "My wife, she's like that. Buys shoes by the dozens. Soon as she thinks something is out of style, out it goes. Good tax write off, though. Goodwill, I mean."

"Let's look at that light," the officer said. The cop leaned forward, looked inside the trunk. "Here's your problem," he said. "This bag of clothes has rolled up against the wiring here."

The cop struggled to move the bag, hesitated, turned and looked at Miller with those bug-eye glasses. Miller could see himself in their mirrored reflection. He looked red and sweaty in the glasses.

"You say that bag is full of clothes?" the officer asked.

Miller nodded.

"Awful heavy," the officer said.

"Stuffed tight," Miller said.

The officer reached out and touched the bag and shifted it. Caroline's leg, which had been bent, suddenly extended through the bag, showing not only the shoe, but half a sleek leg in hose.

As the officer reached for his gun, Miller reached for the tire tool. Miller was faster. The tool came down on the cop's cowboy hat and creased it, then creased the head beneath it. The cop fell straight into Miller's arms. Miller dropped the cop and hit him three times in the head with the tire tool, making sure.

When Miller was finished, he boosted the cop into the trunk. He was about to close the lid when he heard a sound. He looked to his left, and there, across the highway, standing on a trail on the side of a wooded hill, was a young man with a pack on his back, holding a hiking stick.

The hiker turned quickly, started scuttling up the hill, back into the undergrowth.

"Darn," Miller said. He pulled the cop's gun free, closed the trunk, and ran after the hiker.

Miller was in decent shape, and the man was wearing a pack, so it wasn't long before he had him in sight. The hiker had abandoned his walking stick, and was trying to work out of his pack as he ran. He was making strange sounds, like a trapped animal. He worked out of the pack and veered off the trail into the woods.

Miller followed.

As the man scrambled up a vine covered hill, Miller pointed the gun and pulled the trigger. The bullet slammed into the side of the hill, but missed the hiker. The hiker made it to the summit of the hill, and was just about to start down the other side when Miller fired again.

This time, Miller was on the money. The hiker took it in the back, rolled down the hill, bounced against a few thin trees, tumbled to the ground right in front of Miller.

The hiker looked up at Miller with pleading eyes.

"Nothing personal," Miller said. "Really."

He shot the hiker in the head. Twice.

Miller considered leaving the hiker, but thought it might be best to rid himself of the body, along with the cop and his wife. He had plans to sink Caroline in an old well he knew about on some abandoned property. He was sure the cop and the hiker would also fit in.

Miller jammed the pistol into his pants waistband and pulled his shirt over it. He gathered up the hiker's pack and walking stick, tied the walking stick to the pack and put the pack on. He hoisted the hiker's body onto his back in a fireman's cradle, headed toward the highway and his car.

■ ■ ■

By the time Miller made the highway, he was exhausted. The man was not a big man, but carrying pack, man, stick, and doing it on rough terrain, was no easy chore.

When Miller got to the edge of the highway, he looked to see if cars were coming. None were. Finally, luck was with him.

He carried the body across the highway, dropped it on the ground, hustled the car keys out of his pocket, and opened the trunk. He picked up the body and tried to shove it in with the cop and Caroline. It wouldn't fit.

He pulled the body out, and in the process, the man's hand caught on the bag containing Caroline, and tore it, all three layers.

Caroline's face was revealed. Miller dropped the dead hiker on the ground and looked at the pretty but mocking face. It seemed to say: "You're a screwup. Always a screwup."

Miller slammed the lid, dragged the hiker to the side of the Cadillac, opened the back door and hoisted the hiker's body inside. He put the pack and the stick in there with him.

Covered in sweat, Miller climbed behind the wheel.

He hadn't gone far when the car began to handle roughly, and in a moment of anger, Miller realized it was his right rear tire. The one

Caroline told him needed air. She had bitched about it for an hour, about how he should get air in the tire, about how he should keep the car up, so on and so on, and then he got the axe and made her quiet.

But she was right. The tire needed air. He couldn't just stop at a station and get air. Someone might see the hiker's body in the back seat.

Miller pulled off the highway onto a dirt road, got out and opened the trunk. Caroline's body had rolled to the side and now her lips were against the dead cop's lips.

Unfaithful even in death, thought Miller. She had started messing around a month after the wedding, and now, dead, she was still doing it.

Suddenly, Miller remembered he had no spare.

"Damn," he said.

And then he heard a car pull over and stop. Two teenagers, a boy and a girl were parked just behind him. They got out, smiling. "Hey, you need some help, mister?" said the boy.

"No," Miller said, but already they were near him. He saw the girl's eyes go wide as she looked in the trunk.

"Johnny!" she said, but Johnny had also seen the bodies. Johnny took off running for his car. Miller pulled out the pistol and shot him in the back and dropped him. The girl took off running down the road in the opposite direction. Miller stepped into the road, leveled the gun, and fired. The girl went face down on the dirt road, slid, then rolled on her back.

Miller, exhausted, pushed the gun into his waistband, gathered up the girl's body, then the boy's, and placed them in the back seat with the hiker.

He checked the teenager's tires. Too small. They wouldn't work on the Caddy.

Exhausted, angry, Miller took bullets from the cop's gunbelt and reloaded the pistol. He might as well be ready for anything. He closed up the trunk, drove out of there on the dying tire.

∎ ∎ ∎

Eventually, Miller located a serve yourself filling station, pulled in there. He feared the tire would be so worn that airing it up would be useless. But he found he was wrong. The tire swelled up to normal size.

But it wasn't all good news. There was a slow leak. He could hear it hissing. He filled the tire as best he could, then drove off, heading for the well. He hoped it was deep enough to hold everybody.

■ ■ ■

When Miller reached the well it was almost dark. The well was near the remains of an old house and the house was in the middle of a weed-grown pasture. The house had been scourged and raped and left for dead by the elements. The brick curbing around the well was mostly crumbled away, and the mouth of it was covered with an old piece of rotting plyboard.

Miller parked the Caddy near the old gate, got out and opened it, drove through and on up to the old house and well.

As he pulled up, pigeons took flight from the rotting ruins of the house, spotted the gray sky for a moment, then they were gone and the world was silent.

Miller pulled the plyboard off the well and took a look. It was too dark to see the bottom, but he could tell a lot of the well had crumbled. He used to play here as a kid, and just last year, out of nostalgia, he had stopped here to look at the old house and the old well.

When he was eleven, he and Trudy Jo Terrence had played here. He had kissed her inside the old house. The roof had been on the place then, and the walls were standing.

He wondered what ever happened to Trudy Jo. He should have married her. Marrying Caroline had been a huge mistake. She drove him crazy, and now, just to get rid of her, he had been forced to kill four innocent people.

Miller started with the occupants of the back seat. He dropped the teenage girl into the well head first. Her body gave off a sound like someone dropping a tea service. Miller flinched. She had been a pretty girl.

He dropped the teenage boy next. The coward had taken off running. Hadn't even tried to help the girl. Miller dropped him down the shaft. The sound he gave off was a thud. Next came the hiker's pack and walking stick and the hiker himself.

From the trunk, he dragged the cop to the well curbing and dropped him down. Miller was amazed when he dropped the cop. The man's feet stuck up and out of the well. The damned thing was full. Miller worked on pushing the cop deeper, but no go. The well was tucked tight.

Miller got the tire iron he had used on the cop out of the trunk and beat the cop's legs with it until he broke enough bones to make the legs bend. He forced them down with a crunch. Now there was room to pull the plyboard over the well. The only problem was, he still had Caroline to take care of.

She was always a problem.

Miller pulled the plyboard over the well, went back to the Caddy and drove toward town.

■ ■ ■

As Miller neared town, he began to feel the car rock. The tire was going flat again. He stopped at a station and aired it. He wasn't as tense this time, though he was somewhat worried about the bloodstains on the back seat. He assumed they would wipe off easily, since the seats were vinyl. He'd clean the trunk too, from top to bottom. No telltale blood stains or hair samples. He'd do the best job ever done in the history of cleaning up after a murder. Well, murders. And he would do the same for the house.

There was a loud wham, and the air hose popped free of the tire with an ear splitting hiss. A car had rammed the back of the Caddy, knocking it forward a good three feet!

"Hey," Miller said.

A young man, obviously drunk, climbed out of an ancient Ford. "Ah, man, I'm sorry. I didn't see you there."

"You didn't see a blue Cadillac parked in front of you at a service station air hose!"

"Nope."

"You idiot!"

"Hey, it's no reason to get testy, fella. I'll poke you in the nose."

"I doubt it," Miller said. Then thought: Great, I'm making a scene. I don't want to draw attention to myself. What's wrong with me?

"Forget it," Miller said, and drove away.

■ ■ ■

Miller drove around town for an hour on his leaking tire, trying to think of a good place to ditch Caroline's body. Nothing came to mind.

He finally decided to air up the tire one more time, take the body home, leave it in the trunk overnight. That would give him a chance to clean up the living room. No one would even know she was missing. Tomorrow, he'd find a place to ditch her.

He found a station and put air in the tire and started home.

As he pulled into his driveway, a sense of defeat came over Miller. Maybe Caroline was right. He was a screwup. None of this was working out. He should have planned her murder instead of doing it spontaneously, and maybe he could have handled the cop better.

No, he assured himself. He had to kill her when he had the chance and the urge.

And the cop. The others. He had no choice.

As Miller closed the Caddy door, a voice said, "Hey, Miller, how about some gin rummy?"

It was Terrence, his next door neighbor. Ever since the guy's wife had died this fellow had been trying to be his good buddy. He suspicioned it was Caroline that Terrence was after. He always had eyes for her, and Miller had half hoped they'd run off together, but Caroline never showed any interest in Terrence. She liked screwing around with the guys at her work, or at Christmas parties. She didn't want to run off with any of them. She liked it the way she had it. Screw around with the guys, come home and nag him.

Terrence was standing at the back of Miller's Cadillac, outlined by the streetlights, waving a deck of cards.

"I don't think so, Terrence," Miller said. "Not tonight. I'm tired."

"Oh, okay," Terrence said. "What about Caroline?"

"Oh no, she's simply dead, Terrence. Wouldn't be able to."

"Oh," Terrence said. "Hey, look at the back of your car."

Miller walked around slowly to the back of the Caddy. He hadn't really looked at it before. The bumper was bent and the trunk was creased.

"You know this happened?"

"Yeah. Guy ran into me at the filling station."

"Hope you got his name and insurance."

"Yeah. Sure."

"Hey, look at this," Terrence said, grasping the bent edge of the trunk. "This is loose."

The trunk flew up. Caroline, the bag completely torn away from her head was in a bizarre squatting position, that nagging look on her face, a dried blood crevasse in the top of her head.

"Oh, my goodness," said Terrence.

"Yep," said Miller, pulling the cop's revolver from under his shirt. He pushed the gun straight into Terrence's gut and pulled the trigger. There was a muffled bark, and Terrence and his cards were sprawled on the driveway.

Terrence was heavy and Miller was tired, but he got the body boosted into the trunk and pushed Caroline down on her side and closed the lid. He gathered up Terrence's cards, put them in his back pocket, went to the garage for wire to tie the trunk down. All he could find was some thin copper wire, but it would have to do.

When he finished fastening down the trunk, he decided now that he had two bodies, he better get rid of them tonight. Terrence had a nosy sister, and by tomorrow she'd be hunting for Terrence. Miller knew, as a next door neighbor, he'd be questioned, and it wouldn't do to have Terrence in his car trunk. He also had to come up with a reason Caroline was gone. Maybe he could make it look as if she ran off with Terrence.

Now there was an idea.

Man, he thought, I got a lot to wrap up tonight. Get rid of the bodies, clean up the blood in the living room, clean up the car trunk. It was all too much to think about.

He drove across town again. The car begin to list. Oh, dammit, Miller thought, I didn't change the tire! What a screwup.

But, now that no one was in the back seat, Miller decided to have the tire plugged. He pulled into a service station and drank a Coke and had some peanuts while he waited for the tire to be plugged.

The station was manned by one man, and he stayed busy running up front to take money for serve yourself gas, then back to Miller's tire.

When he had the tire fixed and ready to go on the car, he said, "Hey, Mister, come here."

Miller and the station man, who wore a shirt with Alex written above his pocket said, "You know, you're leaking something out of the trunk here."

Miller looked. It was a dark stream of blood.

"Oil," Miller said.

"No, I don't think so," said Alex squatting down for a look, touching the wet run with his fingers. "This looks like blood."

"All right," Miller said. "I shot a dog. It was digging up my wife's flower beds. I hate myself for doing it, but it's been going on for a while, so I shot it. I was carrying it off."

"Oh," said Alex. "I like dogs myself."

"Me too," Miller said, "but not in my wife's flower beds."

Alex pulled a shop rag from his pocket, wiped the blood off his fingers.

"I'm about wrapped up here," Alex said.

"Sure," Miller said, and walked back toward the station. He stopped and turned for a look. Alex was bending down next to the trunk. He had a pair of wire cutters and was cutting the copper wire. The trunk lid sprang open. Alex looked inside and let out his breath.

When Alex turned Miller was standing behind him with a jack handle. It took three blows to drop Alex.

Miller put Alex in the back seat with his shop rag and wire cutters. He wired the trunk shut again.

All that was needed to finish up the tire job was to put the tire on the wheel and fasten the lug bolts. Miller did this himself, and let the jack down. Before he could get all of this finished, however, he took in thirty-five dollars for gas from customers, sold a can of oil and turned down a job to fix a flat.

Miller finally settled on the lake outside of town. It wasn't his first choice, but it would have to do. He took some heavy jacks from the station and piled them in the back seat on top of Alex. When he drove off, the car was weighed down considerably.

Just outside of town a highway patrolman pulled him over about his taillight. Damn that Caroline, or maybe that nosy Terrence. One of them had fallen against the wire again.

The cop didn't get to say much, however. Miller shot him right away with the first cop's gun.

Sighing, Miller pulled the policeman into the front seat beside him, sat him up neatly, pulled the officer's hat down over the bullet hole in his forehead.

"Screwup," he could hear Caroline say.

Miller sighed. "You're right, darling. You're right."

Miller drove out to the lake.

■ ■ ■

When Miller arrived, he was surprised to find the place deserted. No cops. No hikers. No drunks to run into the back of his car. No nosy neighbors. No helpful teenagers. Just the woods and the lake, wide and wet with moonlight on it.

Miller was about to tie the cop and Alex the station man to the heavy jacks when he had another idea. What he'd do was just push the car off in the water. He could say Caroline went away with the car. Went away with Terrence. That would work. He could make up a story about how he had found them in bed together once. Something along that line. When he got home, he'd give it some serious thought.

Home. He'd have to walk home, and that would take some time, but it would be best to be rid of the clue filled car. With it missing, he could strengthen the scenario he was trying to create. The poor husband whose wife ran off with the next door neighbor in their car.

By the time anyone thought to look in the lake, he would have already figured a way to change his identity and move. Yeah, that's what he'd do. He'd start over completely. It had been done before. The information was out there on how to accomplish it, all you had to do was research. There were even books on the subject. He could do it. Caroline was wrong. He wasn't a screwup. He was a clear thinker, that's what he was.

Miller drove the car to a perfect drop off place. He put the gear in neutral, got out and walked to the rear of the Caddy and gave it a push.

Just before it went over the side of the sloping bank, the wire on the trunk snapped. The trunk flew up, hit Miller under the chin and sent him sliding after the car.

Next thing he knew he was under the water. The car was going down before him, and he was being pulled after it. He couldn't figure how, but he was being pulled down, and fast.

He finally realized the wire that had held the trunk shut was twisted in his shirt and one end was still attached to the bumper, and he was being dragged down with it. Miller snatched at the wire, ripped his shirt, freed himself.

As he bobbed to the surface, Caroline bobbed up too, completely free of her plastic bags. She splashed down on top of him. Miller tried to swim away from her, but his legs wouldn't work.

Miller kicked and struggled, but his legs became more confined. He bent under the water to free them. The three plastic bags that had held Caroline were twisted around his ankles, it was impossible to tear them loose, and he was going down, down, down.

Miller fought the plastic until he was exhausted. He was sinking toward bottom, his breath all gone, one thought left in his head.

Caroline was right. He was a screwup.

Passing him in the wet darkness, sinking down with him was Caroline, spinning around and around like a happy ballerina.

• The Big Blow •

INTRODUCTION

This is one of my all-time favorite pieces. I wrote it very quickly for an anthology Doug Winter was editing called MILLENNIUM, or REVELATIONS. I forget which was the British, which was the American. The idea was, beginning with nineteen hundred, until two thousand, a writer would have a ten year period in which to write a story about those times. Any kind of story, but something that touched on the era. Some real event that anchored it. All of this was bookended by a piece by Clive Barker. It was an interesting book, to say the least.

I chose the great Galveston storm of nineteen hundred.

And what a bitch that was.

This was before hurricanes were named, and before warnings were as quick as they are now, but even so, Galveston knew it was coming. But they weren't concerned. Not really.

Thing was, they had ridden out some awful hurricanes. But this one.

Oh my.

This was the mother of all hurricanes. Maybe the greatest hurricane to ever touch ground.

It blew Galveston away.

Literally.

Galveston was a bright and shining city then, a real rival to New York as the most sophisticated city in the U.S.

That storm came along and took it away, like the story of Atlantis. It never fully recovered.

The historical figures mentioned in the story, well, most of them were there. Many of the events are real or are based on real events.

I don't actually know what happened to Jack Johnson's family. My contribution is poetic license.

At the end of it all, there were so many bodies, not only of the recent dead, but those that were washed up from the cemetery, they hauled them out to sea and dumped them.

They washed back. They piled them up and burned them.

85

No one knows how many people died, because they didn't count the black deaths. Some estimates put the death toll at six thousand or higher.

It was an almost supernatural storm.

Jack Johnson, my main character, went on to be the first black heavyweight champion of the world.

This is the story I wrote about the storm and about Johnson. It won a Bram Stoker, was later expanded into a novel, and has been under option for film for years. David Lynch at one point, now with Neal Edelstein and Ridley Scott of Scott Free productions.

So now, into my time machine, and back to 1900 Galveston, Texas. Bring a life preserver.

· The Big Blow ·

TUESDAY, SEPTEMBER 4, 1900, 4:00 P.M.

Telegraphed Message from Washington, D.C., Weather Bureau, Central Office, to Issac Cline, Galveston, Texas, Weather Bureau:

Tropical storm disturbance moving northward over Cuba.

6:38 P.M.

On an afternoon hotter than two rats fucking in a wool sock, John McBride, six-foot one-and-a-half inches, 220 pounds, ham-handed, built like a wild boar and of similar disposition, arrived by ferry from mainland Texas to Galveston Island, a six-gun under his coat and a razor in his shoe.

As the ferry docked, McBride set his suitcase down, removed his bowler, took a crisp white handkerchief from inside his coat, wiped the bowler's sweatband with it, used it to mop his forehead, ran it over his thinning black hair, and put the hat back on.

An old Chinese guy in San Francisco told him he was losing his hair because he always wore hats, and McBride decided maybe he was right, but now he wore the hats to hide his baldness. At thirty he felt he was too young to lose his hair. The Chinaman had given him a tonic for his problem at a considerable sum. McBride used it religiously, rubbed it into his scalp. So far, all he could see it had done was shine his bald spot. He ever got back to Frisco, he was gonna look that Chinaman up, maybe knock a few knots in his head.

As McBride picked up his suitcase and stepped off the ferry with the others, he observed the sky. It appeared green as a pooltable cloth. As the sun dipped down to drink from the Gulf, McBride almost expected to see steam rise up from beyond the island. He took in a deep

87

breath of sea air and thought it tasted all right. It made him hungry. That was why he was here. He was hungry. First on the menu was a woman, then a steak, then some rest before the final meal — the thing he had come for. To whip a nigger.

He hired a buggy to take him to a poke house he had been told about by his employers, the fellows who had paid his way from Chicago. According to what they said, there was a redhead there so good and tight she'd make you sing soprano. Way he felt, if she was redheaded, female, and ready, he'd be all right, and to hell with the song. It was on another's tab anyway.

As the coach trotted along, McBride took in Galveston. It was a Southerner's version of New York, with a touch of the tropics. Houses were upraised on stilts — thick support posts actually — against the washing of storm waters, and in the city proper the houses looked to be fresh off Deep South plantations.

City Hall had apparently been designed by an architect with a Moorish background. It was ripe with domes and spirals. The style collided with a magnificent clock housed in the building's highest point, a peaked tower. The clock was like a miniature Big Ben. England meets the Middle East.

Electric streetcars hissed along the streets, and there were a large number of bicycles, carriages, buggies, and pedestrians. McBride even saw one automobile.

The streets themselves were made of buried wooden blocks that McBride identified as ships' ballast. Some of the sidestreets were made of white shell, and some were hardened sand. He liked what he saw, thought: Maybe, after I do in the nigger, I'll stick around a while. Take in the sun at the beach. Find a way to get my fingers in a little solid graft of some sort.

When McBride finally got to the whorehouse, it was full dark. He gave the black driver a big tip, cocked his bowler, grabbed his suitcase, went through the ornate iron gate, up the steps, and inside to get his tumblers clicked right.

After giving his name to the plump madam, who looked as if she could still grind out a customer or two herself, he was given the royalty treatment. The madam herself took him upstairs, undressed him, bathed him, fondled him a bit.

When he was clean, she dried him off, nestled him in bed, kissed him on the forehead as if he were her little boy, then toddled off. The moment she left, he climbed out of bed, got in front of the mirror on the dresser and combed his hair, trying to push as much as possible over the bald spot. He had just gotten it arranged and gone back to bed when the redhead entered.

She was green-eyed and a little thick-waisted, but not bad to look at. She had fire-red hair on her head and a darker fire between her legs, which were white as sheets and smooth as a newborn pig.

He started off by hurting her a little, tweaking her nipples, just to show her who was boss. She pretended to like it. Kind of money his employers were paying, he figured she'd dip a turd in gravel and push it around the floor with her nose and pretend to like it.

McBride roughed her bottom some, then got in the saddle and bucked a few. Later on, when she got a little slow about doing what he wanted, he blacked one of her eyes.

When the representatives of the Galveston Sporting Club showed up, he was lying in bed with the redhead, uncovered, letting a hot wind blow through the open windows and dry his and the redhead's juices.

The madam let the club members in and went away. There were four of them, all dressed in evening wear with top hats in their hands. Two were gray-haired and gray-whiskered. The other two were younger men. One was large, had a face that looked as if it regularly stopped cannonballs. Both eyes were black from a recent encounter. His nose was flat and strayed to the left of his face. He did his breathing through his mouth. He didn't have any top front teeth.

The other young man was slight and a dandy. This, McBride assumed, would be Ronald Beems, the man who had written him on behalf of the Sporting Club.

Everything about Beems annoyed McBride. His suit, unlike the wrinkled and drooping suits of the others, looked fresh-pressed, unresponsive to the afternoon's humidity. He smelled faintly of mothballs and naphtha, and some sort of hair tonic that had ginger as a base. He wore a thin little moustache and the sort of hair McBride wished he had. Black, full, and longish, with muttonchop sideburns. He had perfect features. No fist had ever touched him. He stood stiff, as if he had a hoe handle up his ass.

Beems, like the others, looked at McBride and the redhead with more than a little astonishment. McBride lay with his legs spread and his back propped against a pillow. He looked very big there. His legs and shoulders and arms were thick and twisted with muscle and glazed in sweat. His stomach protruded a bit, but it was hard-looking.

The whore, sweaty, eye blacked, legs spread, breasts slouching from the heat, looked more embarrassed than McBride. She wanted to cover, but she didn't move. Fresh in her memory was that punch to the eye.

"For heaven's sake, man," Beems said. "Cover yourself."

"What the hell you think we've been doin' here?" McBride said. "Playin' checkers?"

"There's no need to be open about it. A man's pleasure is taken in private."

"Certainly you've seen balls before," McBride said, reaching for a cigar that lay on the table next to his revolver and a box of matches. Then he smiled and studied Beems. "Then maybe you ain't...And then again, maybe, well, you've seen plenty and close up. You look to me the sort that would rather hear a fat boy fart than a pretty girl sing."

"You disgusting brute," Beems said.

"That's telling me," McBride said. "Now I'm hurt. Cut to the goddamn core." McBride patted the redhead's inner thigh. "You recognize this business, don't you? You don't, I got to tell you about it. We men call it a woman, and that thing between her legs is the ole red snapper."

"We'll not conduct our affairs in this fashion," Beems said.

McBride smiled, took a match from the box, and lit the cigar. He puffed, said, "You dressed up pieces of dirt brought me all the way down here from Chicago. I didn't ask to come. You offered me a job, and I took it, and I can untake it, it suits me. I got round-trip money from you already. You sent for me, and I came, and you set me up with a paid hair hole, and you're here for a meeting at a whorehouse, and now you're gonna tell me you're too special to look at my balls. Too prudish to look at pussy. Go on out, let me finish what I really want to finish. I'll be out of here come tomorrow, and you can whip your own nigger."

There was a moment of foot shuffling, and one of the elderly men leaned over and whispered to Beems. Beems breathed once, like a fish out of water, said, "Very well. There's not that much needs to be said. We want this nigger whipped, and we want him whipped bad. We understand in your last bout, the man died."

"Yeah," McBride said. "I killed him and dipped my wick in his old lady. Same night."

This was a lie, but McBride liked the sound of it. He liked the way their faces looked when he told it. The woman had actually been the man's half sister, and the man had died three days later from the beating.

"And this was a white man?" Beems said.

"White as snow. Dead as a stone. Talk money."

"We've explained our financial offer."

"Talk it again. I like the sound of money."

"Hundred dollars before you get in the ring with the nigger. Two hundred more if you beat him. A bonus of five hundred if you kill him. This is a short fight. Not forty-five rounds. No prizefighter makes money like that for so little work. Not even John L. Sullivan."

"This must be one hated nigger. Why? He mountin' your dog?"

"That's our business."

"All right. But I'll take half of that money now."

"That wasn't our deal."

"Now it is. And I'll be runnin' me a tab while I'm here, too. Pick it up."

More foot shuffling. Finally, the two elderly men got their heads together, pulled out their wallets. They pooled their money, gave it to Beems. "These gentlemen are our backers," Beems said. "This is Mr. —"

"I don't care who they are," McBride said. "Give me the money."

Beems tossed it on the foot of the bed.

"Pick it up and bring it here," McBride said to Beems.

"I will not."

"Yes, you will, 'cause you want me to beat this nigger. You want me to do it bad. And another reason is this: You don't, I'll get up and whip your dainty little ass all over this room."

Beems shook a little. "But why?"

"Because I can."

Beems, his face red as infection, gathered the bills from the bed, carried them around to McBride. He thrust them at McBride. McBride, fast as a duck on a June bug, grabbed Beems's wrist and pulled him forward, causing him to let go of the money and drop it onto McBride's chest. McBride pulled the cigar from his mouth with his free hand, stuck it against the back of Beems's thumb. Beems let out a squeal, said, "Forrest!"

The big man with no teeth and black eyes started around the bed toward McBride. McBride said, "Step back, Charlie, or you'll have to hire someone to yank this fella out of your ass."

Forrest hesitated, looked as if he might keep coming, then stepped back and hung his head.

McBride pulled Beems's captured hand between his legs and rubbed it over his sweaty balls a few times, then pushed him away. Beems stood with his mouth open, stared at his hand.

"I'm bull of the woods here," McBride said, "and it stays that way from here on out. You treat me with respect. I say, hold my rope while I pee, you hold it, I say, hold my sacks off the sheet while I get a piece, you hold 'em."

Beems said, "You bastard. I could have you killed."

"Then do it. I hate your type. I hate someone I think's your type. I hate someone who likes your type or wants to be your type. I'd kill a dog liked to be with you. I hate all of you expensive bastards with money and no guts. I hate you 'cause you can't whip your own nigger, and I'm glad you can't, 'cause I can. And you'll pay me. So go ahead, send your killers around. See where it gets them. Where it gets you. And I hate your goddamn hair, Beems."

"When this is over," Beems said, "you leave immediately!"

"I will, but not because of you. Because I can't stand you or your little pack of turds."

The big man with missing teeth raised his head, glared at McBride. McBride said, "Nigger whipped your ass, didn't he, Forrest?"

Forrest didn't say anything, but his face said a lot. McBride said, "You can't whip the nigger, so your boss sent for me. I can whip the nigger. So don't think for a moment you can whip me."

"Come on," Beems said. "Let's leave. The man makes me sick."

Beems joined the others, his hand held out to his side. The elderly gentlemen looked as if they had just realized they were lost in the forest. They organized themselves enough to start out the door. Beems followed, turned before exiting, glared at McBride.

McBride said, "Don't wash that hand, Beems. You can say, 'Shake the hand of the man who shook the balls of John McBride.'"

"You go to hell," Beems said.

"Keep me posted," McBride said. Beems left. McBride yelled after him and his crowd, "And gentlemen, enjoyed doing business with you."

9:12 P.M.

Later in the night the redhead displeased him and McBride popped her other eye, stretched her out, lay across her, and slept. While he slept, he dreamed he had a head of hair like Mr. Ronald Beems.

Outside, the wind picked up slightly, blew hot, brine-scented air down Galveston's streets and through the whorehouse window.

9:34 P.M.

Bill Cooper was working outside on the second-floor deck he was building. He had it completed except for a bit of trim work. It had gone dark on him sometime back, and he was trying to finish by lantern light. He was hammering a sidewall board into place when he felt a drop of rain. He stopped hammering and looked up. The night sky had a peculiar appearance, and for a moment it gave him pause. He studied the heavens a moment longer, decided it didn't look all that bad. It was just the starlight that gave it that look. No more drops fell on him.

Bill tossed the hammer on the deck, leaving the nail only partially driven, picked up the lantern, and went inside the house to be with his wife and baby son. He'd had enough for one day.

11:01 P.M.

The waves came in loud against the beach and the air was surprisingly heavy for so late at night. It lay hot and sweaty on "Lil" Arthur John Johnson's bare chest. He breathed in the air and blew it out, pounded the railroad tie with all his might for the hundredth time. His right fist struck it, and the tie moved in the sand. He hooked it with a left, jammed it with a straight right, putting his entire six-foot, two-hundred-pound frame into it. The tie went backwards, came out of the sand, and hit the beach.

Arthur stepped back and held out his broad, black hands and examined them in the moonlight. They were scuffed, but essentially sound. He walked down to the water and squatted and stuck his hands in, let the surf roll over them. The salt didn't even burn. His hands were like leather. He rubbed them together, being sure to coat them completely with seawater. He cupped water in his palms, rubbed it on his face, over his shaved, bullet head.

Along with a number of other pounding exercises, he had been doing this for months, conditioning his hands and face with work and brine. Rumor was, this man he was to fight, this McBride, had fists like razors, fists that cut right through the gloves and tore the flesh.

"Lil" Arthur took another breath, and this one was filled not only with the smell of saltwater and dead fish, but of raw sewage, which was regularly dumped offshore in the Gulf.

He took his shovel and redug the hole in the sand and dropped the tie back in, patted it down, went back to work. This time, two socks and it came up. He repeated the washing of his hands and face, then picked up the tie, placed it on a broad shoulder and began to run down the beach. When he had gone a good distance, he switched shoulders and ran back. He didn't even feel winded.

He collected his shovel, and with the tie on one shoulder, headed toward his family's shack in the Flats, also known as Nigger Town.

"Lil" Arthur left the tie in front of the shack and put the shovel on the sagging porch. He was about to go inside when he saw a man start across the little excuse of a yard. The man was white. He was wearing dress clothes and a top hat.

When he was near the front porch, he stopped, took off his hat. It was Forrest Thomas, the man "Lil" Arthur had beaten unconscious three weeks back. It had taken only till the middle of the third round.

Even in the cloud-hazy moonlight, "Lil" Arthur could see Forrest looked rough. For a moment, a fleeting moment, he almost felt bad about inflicting so much damage. But then he began to wonder if the man had a gun.

"Arthur," Forrest said. "I come to talk a minute, if'n it's all right."

This was certainly different from the night "Lil" Arthur had climbed into the ring with him. Then, Forrest Thomas had been conceited and full of piss and vinegar and wore the word nigger on his lips as firmly as a mole. He was angry he had been reduced by his employer to fighting a black man. To hear him tell it, he deserved no less than John L. Sullivan, who refused to fight a Negro, considering it a debasement to the heavyweight title.

"Yeah," "Lil" Arthur said. "What you want?"

"I ain't got nothing against you," Forrest said.

"Don't matter you do," "Lil" Arthur said.

"You whupped me fair and square."

"I know, and I can do it again."

"I didn't think so before, but I know you can now."

"That's what you come to say? You got all dressed up, just to come talk to a nigger that whupped you?"

"I come to say more."

"Say it. I'm tired."

"McBride's come in."

"That ain't tellin' me nothin'. I reckoned he'd come in sometime. How'm I gonna fight him, he don't come in?"

"You don't know anything about McBride. Not really. He killed a man in the ring, his last fight in Chicago. That's why Beems brought him in, to kill you. Beems and his bunch want you dead 'cause you whipped a white man. They don't care you whipped me. They care you whipped a white man. Beems figures it's an insult to the white race, a white man being beat by a colored. This McBride, he's got a shot at the Championship of the World. He's that good."

"You tellin' me you concerned for me?"

"I'm tellin' you Beems and the members of the Sportin' Club can't take it. They lost a lot of money on bets, too. They got to set it right, see. I ain't no friend of yours, but I figure I owe you that. I come to warn you this McBride is a killer."

"Lil" Arthur listened to the crickets saw their legs a moment, then said, "If that worried me, this man being a killer, and I didn't fight him, that would look pretty good for your boss, wouldn't it? Beems could say the bad nigger didn't show up. That he was scared of a white man."

"You fight this McBride, there's a good chance he'll kill you or cripple you. Boxing bein' against the law, there won't be nobody there legal to keep check on things. Not really. Audience gonna be there ain't gonna say nothin'. They ain't supposed to be there anyway. You died, got hurt bad, you'd end up out there in the Gulf with a block of granite tied to your dick, and that'd be that."

"Sayin' I should run?"

"You run, it gives Beems face, and you don't take a beatin', maybe get killed. You figure it."

"You ain't doin' nothin' for me. You're just pimpin' for Beems. You tryin' to beat me with your mouth. Well, I ain't gonna take no beatin'. White. Colored. Striped. It don't matter. McBride gets in the ring, I'll knock him down. You go on back to Beems. Tell him I ain't scared, and I ain't gonna run. And ain't none of this workin'."

Forrest put his hat on. "Have it your way, nigger." He turned and walked away.

"Lil" Arthur started inside the house, but before he could open the door, his father, Henry, came out. He dragged his left leg behind him as he came, leaned on his cane. He wore a ragged undershirt and work pants. He was sweaty. Tired. Gray. Grayer yet in the muted moonlight.

"You ought not talk to a white man that way," Henry said. "Them Ku Kluxers'll come 'round."

"I ain't afraid of no Ku Kluxers."

"Yeah, well I am, and we be seein' what you say when you swingin' from a rope, a peckerwood cuttin' off yo balls. You ain't lived none yet. You ain't nothin' but twenty-two years. Sit down, boy."

"Papa, you ain't me. I ain't got no bad leg. I ain't scared of nobody."

"I ain't always had no bad leg. Sit down."

"Lil" Arthur sat down beside his father. Henry said, "A colored man, he got to play the game, to win the game. You hear me?"

"I ain't seen you winnin' much."

Henry slapped "Lil" Arthur quickly. It was fast, and "Lil" Arthur realized where he had inherited his hand speed. "You shut yo face," Henry said. "Don't talk to your papa like that."

"Lil" Arthur reached up and touched his cheek, not because it hurt, but because he was still a little amazed. Henry said, "For a colored man, winnin' is stayin' alive to live out the time God give you."

"But how you spend what time you got, Papa, that ain't up to God. I'm gonna be the Heavyweight Champion of the World someday. You'll see."

"There ain't never gonna be no colored Champion of the World, 'Lil' Arthur. And there ain't no talkin' to you. You a fool. I'm gonna be cuttin' you down from a tree some morning, yo neck all stretched out. Help me up. I'm goin' to bed."

"Lil" Arthur helped his father up, and the old man, balanced on his cane, dragged himself inside the shack.

A moment later, "Lil" Arthur's mother, Tina, came out. She was a broad-faced woman, short and stocky, nearly twenty years younger than her husband.

"You don't need talk yo papa that way," she said.

"He don't do nothin', and he don't want me to do nothin'," "Lil" Arthur said.

"He know what he been through, Arthur. He born a slave. He made to fight for white mens like he was some kinda fightin' rooster, and he got his leg paralyzed cause he had to fight for them Rebels in the war. You think on that. He in one hell of a fix. Him a colored man out there shootin' at Yankees, 'cause if he don't, they gonna shoot him, and them Rebels gonna shoot him he don't fight the Yankees."

"I ain't all that fond of Yankees myself. They ain't likin' niggers any more than anyone else."

"That's true. But, yo papa, he right about one thing. You ain't lived enough to know nothin' about nothin'. You want to be a white man so bad it hurt you. You is African, boy. You is born of slaves come from slaves come from Africa."

"You sayin what he's sayin'?"

"Naw, I ain't. I'm sayin', you whup this fella, and you whup him good. Remember when them bullies used to chase you home, and I tell you, you come back without fightin', I'm gonna whup you harder than them?"

"Yes ma'am."

"And you got so you whupped 'em good, just so I wouldn't whup yo ass?"

"Yes ma'am."

"Well, these here white men hire out this man against you, threaten you, they're bullies. You go in there, and you whup this fella, and you use what God give you in them hands, and you make your way. But you remember, you ain't gonna have nothin' easy. Only way a white man gonna get respect for you is you knock him down, you hear? And you can knock him down in that ring better than out here, 'cause then you just a bad nigger they gonna hang. But you don't talk to yo papa that way. He better than most. He got him a steady job, and he hold this family together."

"He's a janitor."

"That's more than you is."

"And you hold this family together."

"It a two-person job, son."

"Yes, ma'am."

"Good night, son."

"Lil" Arthur hugged her, kissed her cheek, and she went inside. He followed, but the smallness of the two-room house, all those bodies on pallets — his parents, three sisters, two brothers, and a brother-in-law — made him feel crowded. And the pigeons sickened him. Always the pigeons. They had found a hole in the roof — the one that had been covered with tar paper — and now they were roosting inside on the rafters. Tomorrow, half the house would be covered in bird shit. He needed to get up there and put some fresh tar paper on the roof. He kept meaning to. Papa couldn't do it, and he spent his own time training. He had to do more for the family besides bring in a few dollars from fighting.

"Lil" Arthur got the stick they kept by the door for just such an occasion, used it to roust the pigeons by poking at them. In the long run, it wouldn't matter. They would fly as high as the roof, then gradually creep back down to roost. But the explosion of bird wings, their rise to the sky through the hole in the roof, lifted his spirits.

His brother-in-law, Clement, rose up on an elbow from his pallet, and his wife, "Lil" Arthur's sister Lucy, stirred and rolled over, stretched her arm across Clement's chest, but didn't wake up.

"What you doin', Arthur?" Clement whispered. "You don't know a man's got to sleep? I got work to do 'morrow. Ain't all of us sleep all day."

"Sleep then. And stay out of my sister. Lucy don't need no kids now. We got a house full a folks."

"She my wife. We supposed to do that. And multiply."

"Then get your own place and multiply. We packed tight as turds here."

"You crazy, Arthur."

Arthur cocked the pigeon stick. "Lay down and shut up."

Clement lay down, and Arthur put the stick back and gathered up his pallet and went outside. He inspected the pallet for bird shit, found none, stretched out on the porch, and tried to sleep. He thought about getting his guitar, going back to the beach to strum it, but he was too tired for that. Too tired to do anything, too awake to sleep.

His mother had told him time and again that when he was a baby, an old Negro lady with the second sight had picked up his little hand and said, "This child gonna eat his bread in many countries."

It was something that had always sustained him. But now, he began to wonder. Except for trying to leave Galveston by train once, falling asleep in the boxcar, only to discover it had been making circles in the train yard all night as supplies were unloaded, he'd had no adventures, and was still eating his bread in Galveston.

All night he fought mosquitoes, the heat, and his own ambition. By morning he was exhausted.

WEDNESDAY, SEPTEMBER 5, 10:20 A.M.

Telegraphed Message from Washington, D.C., Weather Bureau, Central Office, to Issac Cline, Galveston, Texas, Weather Bureau:

> *Disturbance center near Key West moving northwest. Vessels bound for Florida and Cuban ports should exercise caution. Storm likely to become dangerous.*

10:23 A.M.

McBride awoke, fucked the redhead, sat up in bed, and cracked his knuckles, said, "I'm going to eat and train, Red. You have your ass here when I get back, and put it on the Sportin' Club's bill. And wash yourself, for heaven's sake."

"Yes sir, Mr. McBride," she said.

McBride got up, poured water into a washbasin, washed his dick, under his arms, splashed water on his face. Then he sat at the dresser in front of the mirror and spent twenty minutes putting on the Chinaman's remedy and combing his hair. As soon as he had it just right, he put on a cap.

He got dressed in loose pants, a short-sleeved shirt, soft shoes, wrapped his knuckles with gauze, put a little notebook and pencil in his back pocket, then pulled on soft leather gloves. When the redhead wasn't looking, he wrapped his revolver and razor in a washrag, stuffed them between his shirt and his stomach.

Downstairs, making sure no one was about, he removed the rag containing his revolver and razor, stuck them into the drooping greenness of a potted plant, then went away.

He strolled down the street to a café and ordered steak and eggs and lots of coffee. He ate with his gloves and hat on. He paid for the meal, but got a receipt.

Comfortably full, he went out to train.

He began at the docks. There were a number of men hard at work. They were loading bags of cottonseed onto a ship. He stood with his hands behind his back and watched. The scent of the sea was strong. The water lapped at the pilings enthusiastically, and the air was as heavy as a cotton sack.

After a while, he strolled over to a large bald man with arms and legs like plantation columns. The man wore faded overalls without a shirt, and his chest was as hairy as a bear's ass. He had on heavy work boots with the sides burst out. McBride could see his bare feet through the openings. McBride hated a man that didn't keep up his appearance, even when he was working. Pride was like a dog. You didn't feed it regularly, it died.

McBride said, "What's your name?"

The man, a bag of cottonseed under each arm, stopped and looked at him, taken aback. "Ketchum," he said. "Warner Ketchum."

"Yeah," McBride said. "Thought so. So, you're the one."

The man glared at him. "One what?"

The other men stopped working, turned to look.

"I just wanted to see you," McBride said. "Yeah, you fit the description. I just never thought there was a white man would stoop to such a thing. Fact is, hard to imagine any man stooping to such a thing."

"What are you talkin' about, fella?"

"Well, word is, Warner Ketchum that works at the dock has been known to suck a little nigger dick in his time."

Ketchum dropped the cottonseed bags. "Who the hell are you? Where you hear that?"

McBride put his gloved hands behind his back and held them. "They say, on a good night, you can do more with a nigger's dick than a cat can with a ball of twine."

The man was fuming. "You got me mixed up with somebody else, you Yankee-talkin' sonofabitch."

"Naw, I ain't got you mixed up. Your name's Warner Ketchum. You look how you was described to me by the nigger whose stick you slicked."

Warner stepped forward with his right foot and swung a right punch so looped it looked like a sickle blade. McBride ducked it without removing his hands from behind his back, slipped inside and twisted his hips as he brought a right uppercut into Warner's midsection.

Warner's air exploded and he wobbled back, and McBride was in again, a left hook to the ribs, a straight right to the solar plexus. Warner doubled and went to his knees.

McBride leaned over and kissed him on the ear, said, "Tell me. Them nigger dicks taste like licorice?"

Warner came up then, and he was wild. He threw a right, then a left. McBride bobbed beneath them. Warner kicked at him. McBride turned sideways, let the kick go by, unloaded a left hand that caught Warner on the jaw, followed it with a right that struck with a sound like the impact of an artillery shell.

Warner dropped to one knee. McBride grabbed him by the head and swung his knee into Warner's face, busting his nose all over the dock. Warner fell face forward, caught himself on his hands, almost got up. Then, very slowly, he collapsed, lay down, and didn't move.

McBride looked at the men who were watching him. He said, "He didn't suck no nigger dicks. I made that up." He got out his pad and pencil and wrote: Owed me. Price of one sparring partner, FIVE DOL-LARS.

He put the pad and pencil away. Got five dollars out of his wallet, folded it, put it in the man's back pocket. He turned to the other men who stood staring at him as if he were one of Jesus' miracles.

"Frankly, I think you're all a bunch of sorry assholes, and I think, one at a time, I can lick every goddamn one of you Southern white trash pieces of shit. Any takers?"

"Not likely," said a stocky man at the front of the crowd. "You're a ringer." He picked up a sack of cottonseed he had put down, started toward the ship. The other men did the same.

McBride said, "Okay," and walked away.

He thought, maybe, on down the docks he might find another sparring partner.

5:23 P.M.

By the end of the day, near dark, McBride checked his notepad for expenses, saw the Sporting Club owed him forty-five dollars in spar-ring partners, and a new pair of gloves, as well as breakfast and din-ner to come. He added money for a shoeshine. A clumsy sonofabitch had scuffed one of his shoes.

He got the shoeshine and ate a steak, flexed his muscles as he arrived at the whorehouse. He felt loose still, like he could take on another two or three yokels.

He went inside, got his goods out of the potted plant, and climbed the stairs.

THURSDAY, SEPTEMBER 6, 6:00 P.M.

Telegraphed Message from Washington, D.C., Weather Bureau, Central Office, to Issac Cline, Galveston, Texas, Weather Bureau:

Storm center just northwest of Key West.

7:30 P.M.

"Lil" Arthur ran down to the Sporting Club that night and stood in front of it, his hands in his pants pockets. The wind was brisk, and the air was just plain sour.

Saturday, he was going to fight a heavyweight crown contender, and though it would not be listed as an official bout, and McBride was just in it to pick up some money, "Lil" Arthur was glad to have the chance to fight a man who might fight for the championship someday. And if he could beat him, even if it didn't affect McBride's record, "Lil" Arthur knew he'd have that; he would have beaten a contender for the Heavyweight Championship of the World.

It was a far cry from the Battle Royales he had first participated in. There was a time when he looked upon those degrading events with favor.

He remembered his first Battle Royale. His friend Ernest had talked him into it. Once a month, sometimes more often, white "sporting men" liked to get a bunch of colored boys and men to come down to the club for a free-for-all. They'd put nine or ten of them in a ring, sometimes make them strip naked and wear Sambo masks. He'd done that once himself.

While the coloreds fought, the whites would toss money and yell for them to kill one another. Sometimes they'd tie two coloreds together by the ankles, let them go at it. Blood flowed thick as molasses on flapjacks. Bones were broken. Muscles torn. For the whites, it was great fun, watching a couple of coons knock each other about.

"Lil" Arthur found he was good at all that fighting, and even knocked Ernest out, effectively ending their friendship. He couldn't help himself. He got in there, got the battling blood up, he would hit whoever came near him.

He started boxing regularly, gained some skill. No more Battle Royales. He got a reputation with the colored boxers, and in time that spread to the whites.

The Sporting Club, plumb out of new white contenders for their champion, Forrest Thomas, gave "Lil" Arthur twenty-five dollars to mix it up with their man, thinking a colored and a white would be a novelty, and the superiority of the white race would be proved in a match of skill and timing.

Right before the fight, "Lil" Arthur said his prayers, and then considering he was going to be fighting in front of a bunch of angry, mean-spirited whites, and for the first time, white women—sporting women, but women—who wanted to see a black man knocked to jelly, he took gauze and wrapped his dick. He wrapped it so that it was as thick as a blackjack. He figured he'd give them white folks something to look at. The thing they feared the most. A black as coal stud nigger.

He whipped Forrest Thomas like he was a redheaded stepchild; whipped him so badly, they stopped the fight so no one would see a colored man knock a white man out.

Against their wishes, the Sporting Club was forced to hand the championship over to "Lil" Arthur John Johnson, and the fact that a colored now held the club's precious boxing crown was like a chicken bone in the club's throat. Primarily Beems's throat. As the current president of the Sporting Club, the match had been Beems's idea, and Forrest Thomas had been Beems's man.

Enter McBride. Beems, on the side, talked a couple of the Sporting Club's more wealthy members into financing a fight. One where a true contender to the heavyweight crown would whip "Lil" Arthur and return the local championship to a white man, even if that white man relinquished the crown when he returned to Chicago, leaving it vacant. In that case, "Lil" Arthur was certain he'd never get another shot at the Sporting Club championship. They wanted him out, by hook or crook.

"Lil" Arthur had never seen McBride. Didn't know how he fought. He'd just heard he was as tough as stone and had balls like a brass monkey. He liked to think he was the same way. He didn't intend to give the championship up. Saturday, he'd find out if he had to.

9:00 P.M.

The redhead, nursing a fat lip, two black eyes, and a bruise on her belly, rolled over gingerly and put her arm across McBride's hairy chest. "You had enough?"

"I'll say when I've had enough."

"I was just thinking, I might go downstairs and get something to eat. Come back in a few minutes."

"You had time to eat before I got back. You didn't eat, you just messed up. I'm paying for this. Or rather the Sporting Club is."

"An engine's got to have coal, if you want that engine to go."

"Yeah?"

"Yeah." The redhead reached up and ran her fingers through McBride's hair.

McBride reached across his chest and slapped the redhead. "Don't touch my hair. Stay out of my hair. And shut up. I don't care you want to fuck or not. I want to fuck, we fuck. Got it?"

"Yes, sir."

"Listen here, I'm gonna take a shit. I get back, I want you to wash that goddamn nasty hole of yours. You think I like stickin' my wick in that, it not being clean? You got to get clean."

"It's so hot. I sweat. And you're just gonna mess me up again."

"I don't care. You wash that thing. I went around with my johnson like that, it'd fall off. I get a disease, girl, I'll come back here, kick your ass so hard your butthole will swap places with your cunt."

"I ain't got no disease, Mr. McBride."

"Good."

"Why you got to be so mean?" the redhead asked suddenly, then couldn't believe it had come out of her mouth. She realized, not only would a remark like that anger McBride, but the question was stupid. It was like asking a chicken why it pecked shit. It just did. McBride was mean because he was, and that was that.

But even as the redhead flinched, McBride turned philosophical. "It isn't a matter of mean. It's because I can do what I want, and others can't. You got that, sister?"

"Sure. I didn't mean nothing by it."

"Someone can do to me what I do to them, then all right, that's how it is. Isn't a man, woman, or animal on earth that's worth a damn. You know that?"

"Sure. You're right."

"You bet I am. Only thing pure in this world is a baby. Human or animal, a baby is born hungry and innocent. It can't do a thing for itself. Then it grows up and gets just like everyone else. A baby is all right until it's about two. Then, it ought to just be smothered and save the world the room. My sister, she was all right till she was about two, then it wasn't nothing but her wanting stuff and my mother giving it to her. Later on, Mama didn't have nothing to do with her either, same as me. She got over two years old, she was just trouble. Like I was. Like everybody else is."

"Sure," the redhead said.

"Oh, shut up, you don't know your ass from a pig track."

McBride got up and went to the john. He took his revolver and his wallet and his razor with him. He didn't trust a whore—any woman for that matter—far as he could hurl one.

While he was in the can trying out the new flush toilet, the red-head eased out of bed wearing only a sheet. She slipped out the door, went downstairs and outside, into the streets. She flagged down a man in a buggy, talked him into a ride, for a ride, then she was out of there, destination unimportant.

9:49 P.M.

Later, pissed at the redhead, McBride used the madam herself, blacked both her eyes when she suggested that a lot of sex before a fight might not be a good idea for an athlete.

The madam, lying in bed with McBride's muscular arm across her ample breasts, sighed and watched the glow of the gas streetlights play on the ceiling.

Well, she thought, *it's a living.*

FRIDAY, SEPTEMBER 7, 10:35 A.M.

Telegraphed Message from Washington, D.C., Weather Bureau, Central Office, to Issac Cline, Galveston, Texas, Weather Bureau:

Storm warning. Galveston, Texas. Take precautions.

Issac Cline, head of the Galveston Weather Bureau, sat at his desk on the third floor of the Levy Building and read the telegram. He went downstairs and outside for a look-see.

The weather was certainly in a stormy mood, but it didn't look like serious hurricane weather. He had been with the Weather Bureau for eight years, and he thought he ought to know a hurricane by now, and this wasn't it. The sky wasn't the right color.

He walked until he got to the beach. By then the wind was picking up, and the sea was swelling. The clouds were like wads of duck down ripped from a pillow. He walked a little farther down the beach, found a turtle wrapped in seaweed, poked it with a stick. It was dead as a stone.

Issac returned to the Levy Building, and by the time he made his way back, the wind had picked up considerably. He climbed the stairs to the roof. The roof barometer was dropping quickly, and the wind was serious. He revised his opinion on how much he knew about storms. He estimated the wind to be blowing at twenty miles an hour, and growing. He pushed against it, made his way to the weather pole, hoisted two flags. The top flag was actually a white pennant. It whipped in the wind like a gossip's tongue. Anyone who saw it knew it meant the wind was coming from the northwest. Beneath it was a red flag with a black center; this flag meant the wind was coming ass over teakettle, and that a seriously violent storm was expected within hours.

The air smelled dank and fishy. For a moment, Cline thought perhaps he had actually touched the dead turtle and brought its stink back with him. But no, it was the wind.

At about this same time, the steamship *Pensacola*, commanded by Captain James Slater, left the port of Galveston from Pier 34, destination Pensacola, Florida.

Slater had read the hurricane reports of the day before, and though the wind was picking up and was oddly steamy, the sky failed to show what he was watching for. A dusty, brick red color a sure sign of a hurricane. He felt the whole Weather Bureau business was about as much guess and luck as it was anything else. He figured he could do that and be as accurate.

He gave orders to ease the *Pensacola* into the Gulf.

1:06 P.M.

The pigeons fluttered through the opening in the Johnsons' roof. Tar paper lifted, tore, blew away, tumbled through the sky as if they were little black pieces of the structure's soul.

"It's them birds again," his mother said.

"Lil" Arthur stopped doing push-ups, looked to the ceiling. Pigeons were thick on the rafters. So was pigeon shit. The sky was very visible through the roof. And very black. It looked venomous.

"Shit," "Lil" Arthur said.

"It's okay," she said. "Leave 'em be. They scared. So am I."

"Lil" Arthur stood up, said, "Ain't nothin' be scared of. We been through all kinda storms. We're on a rise here. Water don't never get this high."

"I ain't never liked no storm. I be glad when yo daddy and the young'uns gets home."

"Papa's got an old tarp I might can put over that hole. Keep out the rain."

"You think you can, go on."

"I already shoulda," "Lil" Arthur said.

"Lil" Arthur went outside, crawled under the upraised porch, and got hold of the old tarp. It was pretty rotten, but it might serve his purpose, at least temporarily. He dragged it into the yard, crawled back under, tugged out the creaking ladder and a rusty hammer. He was about to go inside and get the nails when he heard a kind of odd roaring. He stopped, listened, recognized it.

It was the surf. He had certainly heard it before, but not this loud and this far from the beach. He got the nails and put the ladder against the side of the house and carried the tarp onto the roof. The tarp nearly took to the air when he spread it, almost carried him with it. With considerable effort he got it nailed over the hole, trapping what pigeons didn't flee inside the house.

2:30 P.M.

Inside the whorehouse, the madam, a fat lip added to her black eyes, watched from the bed as McBride, naked, seated in a chair before the dresser mirror, carefully oiled and combed his hair over his bald spot. The windows were closed, and the wind rattled them like dice in a gambler's fist. The air inside the whorehouse was as stuffy as a minister's wife.

"What's that smell?" she asked.

It was the tonic the Chinaman had given him. He said, "You don't want your tits pinched, shut the fuck up."

"All right," she said.

The windows rattled again. Pops of rain flecked the glass.

McBride went to the window, his limp dick resting on the windowsill, almost touching the glass, like a large, wrinkled grub looking for a way out.

"Storm coming," he said.

The madam thought: *No shit.*

McBride opened the window. The wind blew a comb and hairbrush off the dresser. A man, walking along the sandy street, one hand on his hat to save it from the wind, glanced up at McBride. McBride took hold of his dick and wagged it at him. The man turned his head and picked up his pace.

McBride said, "Spread those fat legs, honey-ass, 'cause I'm sailing into port, and I'm ready to drop anchor."

Sighing, the madam rolled onto her back, and McBride mounted her. "Don't mess up my hair this time," he said.

4:30 P.M.

The study smelled of stale cigar smoke and sweat, and faintly of baby oil. The grandfather clock chimed four-thirty. The air was humid and sticky as it shoved through the open windows and fluttered the dark curtains. The sunlight, which was tinted with a green cloud haze, flashed in and out, giving brightness to the false eyes and the yellowed teeth of a dozen mounted animal heads on the walls. Bears. Boar. Deer. Even a wolf.

Beems, the source of much of the sweat smell, thought: It's at least another hour before my wife gets home. Good.

Forrest drove him so hard Beems's forehead slammed into the wall, rocking the head of the wild boar that was mounted there, causing the boar to look as if it had turned its head in response to a distant sound, a peculiar sight.

"It's not because I'm one of them kind I do this," Beems said. "It's just, oh yeah, honey...The wife, you know, she don't do nothing for me. I mean, you got to get a little pleasure where you can. A man's got to get his pleasure, don't you think...Oh, yes. That's it...A man, he's got to get his pleasure, right? Even if there's nothing funny about him?"

Forrest rested his hands on Beems's naked shoulders, pushing him down until his head rested on top of the couch cushion. Forrest cocked his hips, drove forward with teeth clenched, penetrating deep into Beems's ass. He said, "Yeah. Sure."

"You mean that? This don't make me queer?"

"No," Forrest panted. "Never has. Never will. Don't mean nothin'. Not a damn thing. It's all right. You're a man's man. Let me concentrate."

Forrest had to concentrate. He hated this business, but it was part of the job. And, of course, unknown to Beems, he was putting the meat to Beems's wife. So, if he wanted to keep doing that, he had to stay in with the boss. And Mrs. Beems, of course, had no idea he was reaming her husband's dirty ditch, or that her husband had about as much interest in women as a pig does a silver tea service.

What a joke. He was fucking Beems's old lady, doing the dog work for Beems, for a good price, and was reaming Beems's asshole and assuring Beems he wasn't what he was, a fairy. And as an added benefit, he didn't have to fight the nigger tomorrow night. That was a big plus. That sonofabitch hit like a mule kicked. He hoped this McBride would tap him good. The nigger died, he'd make a point of shitting on his grave. Right at the head of it.

Well, maybe, Forrest decided, as he drove his hips forward hard enough to make Beems scream a little, he didn't hate this business after all. Not completely. He took so much crap from Beems, this was kinda nice, having the bastard bent over a couch, dicking him so hard his head slammed the wall. Goddamn, nutless queer, insulting him in public, trying to act tough.

Forrest took the bottle of baby oil off the end table and poured it onto Beems's ass. He put the bottle back and realized he was going soft. He tried to imagine he was plunging into Mrs. Beems, who had the smoothest ass and the brightest blonde pubic hair he had ever seen. "I'm almost there," Forrest said.

"Stroke, Forrest! Stroke, man. Stroke!"

In the moment of orgasm, Beems imagined that the dick plunging into his hairy ass belonged to the big nigger, "Lil" Arthur. He thought about "Lil" Arthur all the time. Ever since he had seen him fight naked in a Battle Royale while wearing a Sambo mask for the enjoyment of the crowd.

And the way "Lil" Arthur had whipped Forrest. Oh, God. So thoroughly. So expertly. Forrest had been the man until then, and that made him want Forrest, but now, he wanted the nigger.

Oh God, Beems thought, to have him in me, wearing that mask, that would do it for all time. Just once. Or twice. Jesus, I want it so bad I got to be sure the nigger gets killed. I got to be sure I don't try to pay the nigger money to do this, because he lives after the fight with McBride, I know I'll break down and try. And I break down and he doesn't do it, and word gets around, or he does it, and word gets around, or I get caught...I couldn't bear that. This is bad enough. But a nigger...?

Then there was McBride. He thought about him. He had touched McBride's balls and feigned disgust, but he hadn't washed that hand yet, just as McBride suggested.

McBride won the fight with the nigger, better yet, killed him, maybe McBride would do it with him. McBride was a gent that liked money, and he liked to hurt whoever he was fucking. Beems could tell that from the way the redhead was battered. That would be good. That would be all right. McBride was the type who'd fuck anyone or anything, Beems could tell.

He imagined it was McBride at work instead of Forrest. McBride, naked, except for the bowler.

Forrest, in his moment of orgasm, grunted, said, "Oh yeah," and almost called Mrs. Beems's name. He lifted his head as he finished, saw the hard glass eyes of the stuffed wild boar. The eyes were full of sunlight. Then the curtains fluttered and the eyes were full of darkness.

4:45 P.M.

The steamship *Pensacola,* outbound from Galveston, reached the Gulf, and a wind reached the *Pensacola.* Captain Slater felt his heart clinch. The sea came high and savage from the east, and the ship rose up and dived back down, and the waves, dark green and shadowed by the thick clouds overhead, reared up on either side of the steamship, hissed, plunged back down, and the *Pensacola* rode up.

Jake Bernard, the pilot commissioner, came onto the bridge looking green as the waves. He was Slater's guest on this voyage, and now he wished he were back home. He couldn't believe how ill he felt. Never, in all his years, had he encountered seas like this, and he had thought himself immune to seasickness.

"I don't know about you, Slater," Bernard said, "but I ain't had this much fun since a bulldog gutted my daddy."

Slater tried to smile, but couldn't make it. He saw that Bernard, in spite of his joshing, didn't look particularly jovial. Slater said, "Look at the glass."

Bernard checked the barometer. It was falling fast.

"Never seen it that low," Bernard said.

"Me either," Slater said. He ordered his crew then. Told them to take in the awning, to batten the hatches, and to prepare for water.

Bernard, who had not left the barometer, said, "God. Look at this, man!"

Slater looked. The barometer read 28.55.

Bernard said, "Way I heard it, ever gets that low, you're supposed to bend forward, kiss your root, and tell it good-bye."

6:30 P.M.

The Coopers, Bill and Angelique and their eighteen-month-old baby, Teddy, were on their way to dinner at a restaurant by buggy, when their horse, Bess, a beautiful chocolate-colored mare, made a run at the crashing sea.

It was the sea that frightened the horse, but in its moment of fear, it had tried to plunge headlong toward the source of its fright, assuring Bill that horses were, in fact, the most stupid animals in God's creation.

Bill jerked the reins and cussed the horse. Bess wheeled, lurched the buggy so hard Bill thought they might tip, but the buggy bounced on line, and he maneuvered Bess back on track.

Angelique, dark-haired and pretty, said, "I think I soiled my bloomers...I smell it...No, that's Teddy. Thank goodness."

Bill stopped the buggy outside the restaurant, which was situated on high posts near the beach, and Angelique changed the baby's diaper, put the soiled cloth in the back of the buggy.

When she was finished, they tied up the reins and went in for a steak dinner. They sat by a window where they could see the buggy. The horse bucked and reared and tugged so much, Bill feared she might break the reins and bolt. Above them, they could hear the rocks that covered the flat roof rolling and tumbling about like mice battling over morsels. Teddy sat in a high chair provided by the restaurant; whammed a spoon in a plate of applesauce.

"Had I known the weather was this bad," Angelique said, "we'd have stayed home. I'm sorry, Bill."

"We stay home too much," Bill said, realizing the crash of the surf was causing him to raise his voice. "Building that upper deck on the house isn't doing much for my nerves either. I'm beginning to realize I'm not much of a carpenter."

Angelique widened her dark brown eyes. "No? You, not a carpenter?"

Bill smiled at her.

"I could have told you that, just by listening to all the cussing you were doing. How many times did you hit your thumb, dear?"

"Too many to count."

Angelique grew serious. "Bill. Look."

Many of the restaurant's patrons had abandoned their meals and were standing at the large windows, watching the sea. The tide was high and it was washing up to the restaurant's pilings, splashing against them hard, throwing spray against the glass.

"Goodness," Bill said. "It wasn't this bad just minutes ago."

"Hurricane?" Angelique asked.

"Yeah. It's a hurricane all right. The flags are up. I saw them."

"Why so nervous? We've had hurricanes before."

"I don't know. This feels different, I guess...It's all right. I'm just jittery is all."

They ate quickly and drove the buggy home, Bess pulling briskly all the way. The sea crashed behind them and the clouds raced above them like apparitions.

8:00 P.M.

Captain Slater figured the wind was easily eighty knots. A hurricane. The *Pensacola* was jumping like a frog. Crockery was crashing below. A medicine chest so heavy two men couldn't move it leaped up and struck the window of the bridge, went through onto the deck, slid across it, hit the railing, bounced high, and dropped into the boiling sea.

Slater and Bernard bumped heads so hard they nearly knocked each other out. When Slater got off the floor, he got a thick rope out from under a shelf and tossed it around a support post, made a couple of wraps, then used the loose ends to tie bowlines around his and Bernard's waists. That way, he and Bernard could move about the bridge if they had to, but they wouldn't end up following the path of the medicine chest.

Slater tried to think of something to do, but all he knew to do he had done. He'd had the crew drop anchor in the open Gulf; down to a hundred fathoms, and he'd instructed them to find the best shelter possible close to their posts, and to pray.

The *Pensacola* swung to the anchor, struggled like a bull on a leash. Slater could hear the bolts and plates that held the ship together screaming in agony. Those bolts broke, the plates cracked, he didn't need Captain Ahab to tell him they'd go down to Davy Jones's locker so fast they wouldn't have time to take in a lungful of air.

Using the wall for support, Slater edged along to where the bridge glass had been broken by the flying chest. Sea spray slammed against him like needles shot from a cannon. He was concentrating on the foredeck, watching it dip, when he heard Bernard make a noise that was not quite a word, yet more expressive than a grunt.

Slater turned, saw Bernard clutching the latch on one of the bridge windows so tightly he thought he would surely twist it off. Then he saw what Bernard saw.

The sea had turned black as a Dutch oven, the sky the color of gangrene, and between sea and sky there appeared to be something rising out of the water, something huge and oddly shaped, and then

Slater realized what it was. It was a great wall of water, many times taller than the ship, and it was moving directly toward and over them.

SATURDAY, SEPTEMBER 8, 3:30 A.M.

Bill Cooper opened his eyes. He had been overwhelmed by a feeling of dread. He rose carefully, so as not to wake Angelique, went into the bedroom across the hall and checked on Teddy. The boy slept soundly, his thumb in his mouth.

Bill smiled at the child, reached down, and gently touched him. The boy was sweaty, and Bill noted that the air in the room smelled foul. He opened a window, stuck his head out, and looked up. The sky had cleared and the moon was bright. Suddenly, he felt silly. Perhaps this storm business, the deck he was building on the upper floor of the house, had made him restless and worried. Certainly, it looked as if the storm had passed them by.

Then his feeling of satisfaction passed. For when he examined the yard, he saw it had turned to molten silver. And then he realized it was moonlight on water. The Gulf had crept all the way up to the house. A small rowboat, loose from its moorings, floated by.

8:06 A.M.

Issac Cline had driven his buggy down the beach, warning residents near the water to evacuate. Some had. Some had not. Most had weathered many storms and felt they could weather another.

Still, many residents and tourists made for the long wooden trestle bridge to mainland Texas. Already, the water was leaping to the bottom of the bridge, slapping at it, testing its strength.

Wagons, buggies, horses, pedestrians were as thick on the bridge as ants on gingerbread. The sky, which had been oddly clear and bright and full of moon early that morning, had now grown gray and it was raining. Of the three railway bridges that led to the mainland, one was already underwater.

3:45 P.M.

Henry Johnson, aided by "Lil" Arthur, climbed up on the wagon beside his wife. Tina held an umbrella over their heads. In the back of the wagon was the rest of the family, protected by upright posts planted in the corners, covered with the tarp that had formerly been on the roof of the house.

All day Henry had debated whether they should leave. But by 2:00, he realized this wasn't going to be just another storm. This was going to be a goddamn, wet-assed humdinger. He had organized his family, and now, by hook or crook, he was leaving. He glanced at his shack, the water pouring through the roof like the falls of Niagara. It wasn't much, but it was all he had. He doubted it could stand much of this storm, but he tried not to think about that. He had greater concerns. He said to "Lil" Arthur, "You come on with us."

"I got to fight," "Lil" Arthur said.

"You got to do nothin'. This storm'll wash your ass to sea."

"I got to, Papa."

Tina said, "Maybe yo papa's right, baby. You ought to come."

"You know I can't. Soon as the fight's over, I'll head on out. I promise. In fact, weather's so bad, I'll knock this McBride out early."

"You do that," Tina said.

"Lil" Arthur climbed on the wagon and hugged his mama and shook his father's hand. Henry spoke quickly without looking at "Lil" Arthur, said, "Good luck, son. Knock him out."

"Lil" Arthur nodded. "Thanks, Papa." He climbed down and went around to the back of the wagon and threw up the tarp and hugged his sisters one at a time and shook hands with his brother-in-law, Clement. He pulled Clement close to him, said, "You stay out of my sister, hear?"

"Yeah, Arthur. Sure. But I think maybe we done got a problem. She's already swole up."

"Ah, shit," "Lil" Arthur said.

4:03 P.M.

As Henry Johnson drove the horses onto the wooden bridge that connected Galveston to the mainland, he felt ill. The water was washing over the sides, against the wagon wheels. The horses were nervous, and the line of would-be escapees on the bridge was tremendous. It would take them a long time to cross, maybe hours, and from the look of things, the way the water was rising, wouldn't be long before the bridge was underwater.

He said a private prayer: "Lord, take care of my family. And especially that fool son of mine, 'Lil' Arthur."

It didn't occur to him to include himself in the prayer.

4:37 P.M.

Bill and Angelique Cooper moved everything of value they could carry to the second floor of the house. Already the water was sloshing in the doorway. Rain splattered against the windows violently enough to shake them, and shingles flapped boisterously on the roof.

Bill paused in his work and shuffled through ankle-deep water to a window and looked out. He said, "Angelique, I think we can stop carrying."

"But I haven't carried up the—"

"We're leaving."

"Leaving? It's that bad?"

"Not yet."

Bess was difficult to hook to the buggy. She was wild-eyed and skittish. The barn was leaking badly. Angelique held an umbrella over her head, waiting for the buggy to be fastened. She could feel water rising above her high button shoes.

Bill paused for a moment to calm the horse, glanced at Angelique, thought she looked oddly beautiful, the water running off the umbrella in streams. She held Teddy close to her. Teddy was asleep, totally unaware of what was going on around him. Any other time, the baby would be squalling, annoyed. The rain and the wind were actually helping him to sleep. At least, thought Bill, I am grateful for that.

By the time the buggy was hooked, they were standing in calf-deep water. Bill opened the barn door with great difficulty, saw that the yard was gone, and so was the street. He would have to guess at directions. Worse yet, it wasn't rain water running through the street. It was definitely seawater; the water of the Gulf had risen up as if to swallow Galveston the way the ocean was said to have swallowed Atlantis.

Bill helped Angelique and Teddy into the buggy, took hold of the reins, clucked to Bess. Bess jerked and reared, and finally, by reins and voice, Bill calmed her. She began to plod forward through the dark, powerful water.

5:00 P.M.

McBride awoke. The wind was howling. The window glass was rattling violently, even though the windows were raised. The air was cool for a change, but damp. It was dark in the room.

The madam, wrapped in a blanket, sat in a chair pulled up against the far wall. She turned and looked at McBride. She said, "All hell's broken loose."

"Say it has?" McBride got up, walked naked to the windows. The wind was so furious it pushed him. "Damn," he said. "It's dark as midnight. This looks bad."

"Bad?" The madam laughed. "Worst hurricane I've ever seen, and I don't even think it's cranked up good yet."

"You don't think they'll call off the fight do you?"

"Can you fight in a boat?"

"Hell, honey, I can fight and fuck at the same time on a boat. Come to think of it, I can fight and fuck on a rolling log, I have to. I used to be a lumberjack up north."

"I was you, I'd find a log, and get to crackin'."

A bolt of lightning, white as eternity, split the sky, and when it did, the darkness outside subsided, and in that instant, McBride saw the street was covered in waist-deep water.

"Reckon I better start on over there," he said. "It may take me a while."

The madam thought: Well, honey, go right ahead, and I hope you drown.

5:20 P.M.

"Lil" Arthur was standing on the porch, trying to decide if he should brave the water, which was now up to the lip of the porch, when he saw a loose rowboat drift by.

Suddenly he was in the water, swimming, and the force of the water carried him after the boat, and soon he had hold of it. When he climbed inside, he found the boat was a third filled with water.

He found a paddle and a pail half-filled with dirt. The dirt had turned to mud and was beginning to flow over the top of the bucket. A few dead worms swirled in the mess. The world was atumble with wind, water, and darkness.

"Lil" Arthur took the bucket and poured out the mud and the worms and started to bail. Now and then he put the bucket aside and used the boat paddle. Not that he needed it much. The water was carrying him where he wanted to go. Uptown.

5:46 P.M.

Uptown the water was not so deep, but it took McBride almost an hour to get to the Sporting Club. He waded through waist-deep water for a block, then knee-deep, and finally ankle-deep. His bowler hat had lost all its shape when he arrived, and his clothes were ruined. The water hadn't done his revolver or his razor any good either.

When he arrived at the building, he was surprised to find a crowd of men had gathered on the steps. Most stood under umbrellas, but many were bareheaded. There were a few women among them. Whores mostly. Decent women didn't go to prizefights.

McBride went up the steps, and the crowd blocked him. He said, "Look here. I'm McBride. I'm to fight the nigger."

The crowd parted, and McBride, with words of encouragement and pats on the back, was allowed indoors. Inside, the wind could still be heard, but it sounded distant. The rain was just a hum.

Beems, Forrest, and the two oldsters were standing in the foyer, looking tense as fat hens at noontime. As soon as they saw McBride, their faces relaxed, and the elderly gentlemen went away. Beems said, "We were afraid you wouldn't make it."

"Worried about your investment?"

"I suppose."

"I'd have come if I had to swim."

"The nigger doesn't show, the title and the money's yours."

"I don't want it like that," McBride said. "I want to hit him. Course, he don't show, I'll take the money. You seen it this bad before?"

"No," Beems said.

"I didn't expect nobody to be here."

"Gamblers always show," Forrest said. "They gamble their money, they gamble their lives."

"Go find something to do, Forrest," Beems said. "I'll show Mr. McBride the dressing room."

Forrest looked at Beems, grinned a little, showed Beems he knew what he had in mind. Beems fumed. Forrest went away. Beems took hold of McBride's elbow and began to guide him.

"I ain't no dog got to be led," McBride said.

"Very well," Beems said, and McBride followed him through a side door and down into a locker room. The room had two inches of water in it.

"My God," Beems said. "We've sprung a leak somewhere."

"Water like this," McBride said. "The force...it's washing out the mortar in the bricks, seeping through the chinks in the wall...Hell, it's all right for what I got to do."

"There's shorts and boots in the locker there," Beems said. "You could go ahead and change."

McBride sloshed water, sat on a bench and pulled off his shoes and socks with his feet resting on the bench. Beems stood where he was, watching the water rise.

McBride took the razor out of the side of one of the shoes, held it up for Beems to see, said, "Mexican boxing glove."

Beems grinned. He watched as McBride removed his bowler, coat and shirt. He watched carefully as he removed his pants and shorts. McBride reached into the locker Beems had recommended, paused, turned, stared at Beems.

"You're liking what you're seein', ain't you, buddy?"

Beems didn't say anything. His heart was in his throat.

McBride grinned at him. "I knew first time I seen you, you was an Alice."

"No," Beems said. "Nothing like that. It's not like that at all."

McBride smiled. He looked very gentle in that moment. He said, "It's all right. Come here. I don't mind that."

"Well..."

"Naw. Really. It's just, you know, you got to be careful. Not let everyone know. Not everyone understands, see."

Beems, almost licking his lips, went over to McBride. When he was close, McBride's smile widened, and he unloaded a right upper-cut into Beems's stomach. He hit him so hard Beems dropped to his knees in the water, nodded forward, and banged his head on the bench. His top hat came off, hit the water, sailed along the row of lockers, made a right turn near the wall, flowed out of sight behind a bench.

McBride picked Beems up by the hair and pulled his head close to his dick, said, "Look at it a minute, 'cause that's all you're gonna do."

Then McBride pulled Beems to his feet by his pretty hair and went to work on him. Lefts and rights. Nothing too hard. But more than Beems had ever gotten. When he finished, he left Beems lying in the water next to the bench, coughing.

McBride said, "Next time you piss, you'll piss blood, Alice." McBride got a towel out of the locker and sat on the bench and put his feet up and dried them. He put on the boxing shorts. There was a mirror on the inside of the locker, and McBride was upset to see his hair. It was a mess. He spent several minutes putting it in place. When he finished, he glanced down at Beems, who was pretending to be dead.

McBride said, "Get up, fairy-ass. Show me where I'm gonna fight."

"Don't tell anybody," Beems said. "I got a wife. A reputation. Don't tell anybody."

"I'll make you a promise," McBride said, closing the locker door. "That goddamn nigger beats me, I'll fuck you. Shit, I'll let you fuck me. But don't get your butthole all apucker. I ain't losin' nothin'. Tonight, way I feel, I could knock John L. Sullivan on his ass."

McBride started out of the locker room, carrying his socks and the boxing shoes with him. Beems lay in the water, giving him plenty of head start.

6:00 P.M.

Henry couldn't believe how slow the line was moving. Hundreds of people, crawling for hours. When the Johnsons were near the end of the bridge, almost to the mainland, the water rushed in a dark brown wave and washed the buggy in front of them off the bridge. The Johnsons' wagon felt the wave, too, but only slid to the railing. But the buggy hit the railing, bounced, went over, pulling the horse into the railing after it. For a moment the horse hung there, its back legs slipping through, pulling with its front legs, then the railing cracked and the whole kit and kaboodle went over.

"Oh Jesus," Tina said.

"Hang on," Henry said. He knew he had to hurry, before another wave washed in, because if it was bigger, or caught them near the gap the buggy had made, they, too, were gone.

Behind them the Johnsons could hear screams of people fleeing the storm. The water was rising rapidly over the bridge, and those to the middle and the rear realized that if they didn't get across quickly, they weren't going to make it. As they fought to move forward, the bridge cracked and moaned as if with a human voice.

The wind ripped at the tarp over the wagon and tore it away. "Shit," said Clement. "Ain't that something?"

A horse bearing a man and a woman, the woman wearing a great straw hat that drooped down on each side of her head, raced by the Johnsons. The bridge was too slick and the horse was moving too fast. Its legs splayed and it went down and started sliding. Slid right through the opening the buggy had made. Disappeared immediately beneath the water. When Henry ventured a look in that direction, he saw the woman's straw hat come up once, then blend with the water.

When Henry's wagon was even with the gap, a fresh brown wave came over the bridge, higher and harder this time. It hit his horses and the wagon broadside. The sound of it, the impact of it, reminded Henry of when he was in the Civil War and a wagon he was riding in was hit by Yankee cannon fire. The impact had knocked him spinning, and when he tried to get up, his leg had been ruined. He thought he would never be that frightened again. But now, he was even more afraid.

The wagon drifted sideways, hit the gap, but was too wide for it. It hung on the ragged railing, the sideboards cracking with the impact. Henry's family screamed and lay down flat in the wagon as the water came down on them like a heavy hand. The pressure of the water snapped the wagon's wheels off the axle, slammed the bottom of the wagon against the bridge, but the sideboards held together.

"Everybody out!" Henry said.

Henry, his weak leg failing to respond, tumbled out of the wagon onto the bridge, which was now under a foot of water. He got hold of a sideboard and pulled himself up, helped Tina down, reached up, and snatched his cane off the seat.

Clement and the others jumped down, started hustling toward the end of the bridge on foot. As they came even with Henry, he said, "Go on, hurry. Don't worry none about me."

Tina clutched his arm. "Go on, woman," he said. "You got young'uns to care about. I got to free these horses." He patted her hand. She moved on with the others.

Henry pulled out his pocketknife and set to cutting the horses free of the harness. As soon as they were loose, both fool animals bolted directly into the railing. One of them bounced off of it, pivoted, made for the end of the bridge at a splashing gallop, but the other horse hit with such impact it flipped over, turning its feet to the sky. It pierced the water and was gone.

Henry turned to look for his family. They were no longer visible. Surely, they had made the mainland by now.

Others had come along to fill their place; people in wagons, and buggies, on horseback and on foot. People who seemed to be scrambling on top of water, since the bridge was now completely below sea level.

Then Henry heard a roar. He turned to the east side of the bridge. There was a heavy sheet of water cocked high above him, and it was coming down, like a monstrous wet flyswatter. And when it struck Henry and the bridge, and all those on it, it smashed them flat and drove them into the churning belly of the sea.

6:14 P.M.

Bill and Angelique Cooper, their buggy half-submerged in water, saw the bridge through the driving rain, then suddenly they saw it no more. The bridge and the people were wadded together and washed down.

The bridge rose up on the waves a moment later, like a writhing spinal column. People still clung to it. It leaped forward into the water, the end of it lashing the air, then it was gone and the people with it.

"God have mercy on their souls," Angelique said.

Bill said, "That's it then."

He turned the buggy around in the water with difficulty, headed home. All around him, shingles and rocks from the roofs of structures flew like shrapnel.

7:39 P.M.

"Lil" Arthur, as he floated toward town, realized it was less deep here. It was just as well, the rain was pounding his boat and filling it with water. He couldn't bail and paddle as fast as it went in. He climbed over the side and let the current carry the boat away.

The water surprised him with its force. He was almost swept away, but it was shallow enough to get a foothold and push against the flow. He waded to the Sporting Club, went around back to the colored entrance. When he got there, an elderly black man known as Uncle Cooter let him in, said, "Man, I'd been you, I'd stayed home."

"What," "Lil" Arthur said. "And missed a boat ride?"

"A boat ride?"

"Lil" Arthur told him how he had gotten this far.

"Damnation," Uncle Cooter said. "God gonna put this island underwater 'cause it's so evil. Like that Sodom and Gomorrah place."

"What have you and me done to God?"

Uncle Cooter smiled. "Why, we is the only good children God's got. He gonna watch after us. Well, me anyway. You done gonna get in with this Mr. McBride, and he's some bad stuff, 'Lil' Arthur. God ain't gonna help you there. And this Mr. McBride, he ain't got no sense neither. He done beat up Mr. Beems, and Mr. Beems the one settin' this up, gonna pay him money."

"Why'd he beat him up?"

"Hell, you can't figure white people. They all fucked up. But Mr. Beems damn sure look like a raccoon now. Both his eyes all black, his lip pouched out."

"Where do I change?"

"Janitor's closet. They done put your shorts and shoes in there. And there's some gauze for your hands."

"Lil" Arthur found the shorts. They were old and faded. The boxing shoes weren't too good either. He found some soiled rags and used those to dry himself. He used the gauze to wrap his hands, then his dick. He figured, once you start a custom, you stick with it.

7:45 P.M.

When Bill and Angelique and Teddy arrived at their house, they saw that the water had pushed against the front door so violently, it had come open. Water was flowing into the hall and onto the bottom step of the stairs. Bill looked up and saw a lamp burning upstairs. They had left so quickly, they had forgotten to extinguish it.

With a snort, Bess bolted. The buggy jerked forward, hit a curb, and the harness snapped so abruptly Bill and his family were not thrown from their seat, but merely whipped forward and back against the seat. The reins popped through Bill's hands so swiftly, the leather cut his palms.

Bess rushed across the yard and through the open doorway of the house, and slowly and carefully, began to climb the stairs.

Angelique said, "My lands."

Bill, a little stunned, climbed down, went around, and helped Angelique and the baby out of the buggy. The baby was wet and crying, and Angelique tried to cover him with the umbrella, but now the wind and rain seemed to come from all directions. The umbrella was little more than a wad of cloth.

They waded inside the house, tried to close the door, but the water was too much for them. They gave it up.

Bess had reached the top landing and disappeared. They followed her up. The bedroom door was open and the horse had gone in there. She stood near the table bearing the kerosene lamp. Shaking.

"Poor thing," Angelique said, gathering some towels from a chifforobe. "She's more terrified than we are."

Bill removed the harness that remained on Bess, stroked her, tried to soothe her. When he went to the window and looked out, the horse went with him. The world had not miraculously dried up. The water was obviously rising.

"Maybe we'll be all right here," Angelique said. She was drying Teddy, who was crying violently because he was cold and wet. "Water can't get this high, can it?"

Bill idly stroked Bess's mane, thought of the bridge. The way it had snapped like a wooden toy. He said, "Of course not."

8:15 P.M.

The fight had started late, right after two one-legged colored boys had gone a couple of rounds, hopping about, trying to club each other senseless with oversized boxing gloves.

The crowd was sparse but vocal. Loud enough that "Lil" Arthur forgot the raging storm outside. The crowd kept yelling, "Kill the nigger," and had struck up a chorus of "All coons look alike to me" — a catchy little number that "Lil" Arthur liked in spite of himself.

The yelling, the song, was meant to drop his spirits, but he found it fired him up. He liked being the underdog. He liked to make ass holes eat their words. Besides, he was the Galveston Champion, not McBride, no matter what the crowd wanted. He was the one who would step through the ropes tonight the victor. And he had made a change. He would no longer allow himself to be introduced as "Lil" Arthur. When his name had been called, and he had been reluctantly named Galveston Sporting Club Champion by the announcer, the announcer had done as he had asked. He had called him by the name he preferred from here on. Not "Lil" Arthur Johnson. Not Arthur John Johnson, but the name he called him, the name he called himself. Jack Johnson.

So far, however, the fight wasn't going either way, and he had to hand it to McBride, the fella could hit. He had a way of throwing short, sharp punches to the ribs, punches that felt like knife stabs.

Before the fight, Jack, as McBride had surely done, had used his thumbs to rearrange as much of the cotton in his gloves as possible. Arrange it so that his knuckles would be against the leather and would make good contact with McBride's flesh. But so far McBride had avoided most of his blows. The man was a master of slipping and sliding the punches. Jack had never seen anything like that before. McBride could also pick off shots with a flick of his forearms. It was very professional and enlightening.

Even so, Jack found he was managing to take the punches pretty well, and he'd discovered something astonishing. The few times he'd hit McBride was when he got excited, leaned forward, went flat-footed, and threw the uppercut. This was not a thing he had trained for much, and when he had, he usually threw the uppercut by coming up on his toes, twisting his body, the prescribed way to throw it. But he found, against all logic, he could throw it flat-footed and leaning forward, and he could throw it hard.

He thought he had seen a bit of surprise on McBride's face when he'd hit him with it. He knew that he'd certainly surprised himself.

It went like that until the beginning of the fourth round, then when McBride came out, he said, "I've carried you enough, nigger. Now you got to fight."

Then Jack saw stuff he'd never seen before. The way this guy moved, it was something. Bounced around like a cat, like the way he'd heard Gentleman Jim fought, and the guy was fast with those hands. Tossed bullets, and the bullets stunned a whole lot worse than before. Jack realized McBride had been holding back, trying to make the fight interesting. And he realized something else. Something important about himself. He didn't know as much about boxing as he thought.

He tried hooking McBride, but McBride turned the hooks away with his arms, and Jack tried his surprise weapon, the uppercut, found he could catch McBride a little with that, in the stomach, but not enough to send McBride to the canvas. When the fifth round came up, Jack was scared. And hurt. And the referee — a skinny bastard with a handlebar moustache — wasn't helping. Anytime he tied McBride up, the referee separated them. McBride tied him up, thumbed him in the eye, butted him, the referee grinned like he was eating jelly.

Jack was thinking maybe of taking a dive. Just going down and lying there, getting himself out of this misery next time McBride threw one of those short ones that connected solid, but then the bell rang and he sat on his bench, and Uncle Cooter, who was the only man in his corner, sprayed water in his mouth and let him spit blood in a bucket.

Uncle Cooter said, "I was you, son, I'd play possum. Just hit that goddamn canvas and lay there like you axed. You don't, this shithead gonna cut you to pieces. This way, you get a little payday and you don't die. Paydays is all right. Dyin' ain't nothin' to rush."

"Jesus, he's good. How can I beat him?"

Uncle Cooter rubbed Jack's shoulders. "You can't. Play dead."

"There's got to be a way."

"Yeah," Uncle Cooter said. "He might die on you. That's the only way you gonna beat him. He got to just die."

"Thanks, Cooter. You're a lot of help."

"You welcome."

Jack feared the sound of the bell. He looked in McBride's corner, and McBride was sitting on his stool as if he were lounging, drinking from a bottle of beer, chatting with a man in the audience. He was asking the man to go get him a sandwich.

Forrest Thomas was in McBride's corner, holding a folded towel over his arm, in case McBride might need it, which, considering he needed to break a good sweat first, wasn't likely.

Forrest looked at Jack, pointed a finger, and lowered his thumb like it was the hammer of a revolver. Jack could see a word on Forrest's lips. The word was: POW!

The referee wandered over to McBride's corner, leaned on the ring post, had a laugh with McBride over something.

The bell rang. McBride gave the bottle of beer to Forrest and came out. Jack rose, saw Beems, eyes blacked, looking rough, sitting in the front row. Rough or not, Beems seemed happy. He looked at Jack and smiled like a gravedigger.

This time out, Jack took a severe pounding. He just couldn't stop those short little hooks of McBride's, and he couldn't seem to hit McBride any kind of blow but the uppercut, and that not hard enough. McBride was getting better as he went along, getting warmed up. If he had another beer and a sandwich, hell, he might go ahead and knock Jack out so he could have coffee and pie.

Jack decided to quit trying to hit the head and the ribs, and just go in and pound McBride on the arms. That way, he could at least hit something. He did, and was amazed at the end of the round to find McBride lowering his guard.

Jack went back to his corner and Uncle Cooter said, "Keep hittin' him on the arms. That's gettin' to him. You wreckin' his tools."

"I figured that much. Thanks a lot."

"You welcome."

Jack examined the crowd in the Sporting Club bleachers. They were not watching the ring. They had turned their heads toward the east wall, and for good reason. It was vibrating. Water was seeping in, and it had filled the floor beneath the ring six inches deep. The people occupying the bottom row of bleachers, all around the ring, had been forced to lift their feet. Above him, Jack heard a noise that sounded like something big and mean peeling skin off an elephant's head.

By the time the bell rang and Jack shuffled out, he noticed that the water had gone up another two inches.

8:46 P.M.

Bill held the lantern in front of him at arm's length as he crouched at the top of the stairs. The water was halfway up the steps. The house was shaking like a fat man's ass on a bucking bronco. He could hear shingles ripping loose, blowing away.

He went back to the bedroom. The wind was screaming. The windows were vibrating; panes had blown out of a couple of them. The baby was crying. Angelique sat in the middle of the bed, trying to nurse the child, but Teddy wouldn't have any of that. Bess was facing a corner of the room, had her head pushed against the wall. The horse lashed her tail back and forth nervously, made nickering noises.

Bill went around and opened all the windows to help take away some of the force of the wind. Something he knew he should have done long ago, but he was trying to spare the baby the howl of the wind, the dampness.

The wind charged through the open windows and the rain charged with it. Bill could hardly stand before them, they were so powerful.

Fifteen minutes later, he heard the furniture below thumping on the ceiling, floating against the floor on which he stood.

9:00 P.M.

My God, thought Jack, how many rounds this thing gonna go? His head ached and his ribs ached worse and his insides felt as if he had swallowed hot tacks and was trying to regurgitate them. His legs, though strong, were beginning to feel the wear. He had thought this was a fifteen-round affair, but realized now it was twenty, and if he wasn't losing by then, he might get word it would go twenty-five.

Jack slammed a glove against McBride's left elbow, saw McBride grimace, drop the arm. Jack followed with the uppercut, and this time he not only hit McBride, he hit him solid. McBride took the shot so hard, he farted. The sandwich he'd eaten between rounds probably didn't seem like such a good idea now.

Next time Jack threw the combination, he connected with the uppercut again. McBride moved back, and Jack followed, hitting him on the arms, slipping in the uppercut now and then, even starting to make contact with hooks and straight rights.

Then every light in the building went out as the walls came apart and the bleachers soared up on a great surge of water and dumped the boxing patrons into the wet darkness. The ring itself began to move, to rise to the ceiling, but before it tilted out from under Jack, McBride hit him a blow so hard Jack thought he felt past lives cease to exist;

ancestors fresh from the slime rocked from that blow, and the reverberations of it rippled back to the present and into the future, and back again. The ceiling went away on a torrent of wind, Jack reached out and got hold of something and clung for dear life.

"You stupid sonofabitch," Uncle Cooter said, "you got me by the goddamn head."

9:05 P.M.

Captain Slater thought they would be at the bottom of the Gulf by now, and was greatly surprised they were not. A great wave of water had hit them so hard the night before it had snapped the anchor chain. The ship was driven down, way down, and then all the water in the world washed over them and there was total darkness and horror, and then, what seemed like hours later but could only have been seconds, the water broke and the *Pensacola* flew high up as if shot from a cannon, came down again, leaned starboard so far it took water, then, miraculously, corrected itself. The sea had been choppy and wild ever since.

Slater shook shit and seawater out of his pants legs and followed the rope around his waist to the support post. He got hold of the post, felt for the rest of the rope. In the darkness, he cried out, "Bernard. You there?"

"I think so," came Bernard's voice from the darkness. And then they heard a couple of bolts pop free, fire off like rifle blasts. Then: "Oh, Jesus," Bernard said. "Feel that swell? Here it comes again."

Slater turned his head and looked out. There was nothing but a great wall of blackness moving toward them. It made the first great wave seem like a mere rise; this one was bigger than the Great Wall of China.

10:00 P.M.

Bill and Angelique lay on the bed with Teddy. The water was washing over the edges of the feather mattress, blowing wet, cold wind over them. They had started the Edison and a gospel record had been playing, but the wind and rain had finally gotten into the mechanism and killed it.

As it went dead, the far wall cracked and leaned in and a ripple of cracking lumber went across the floor and the ceiling sagged and so did the bed. Bess suddenly disappeared through a hole in the floor. One moment she was there, the next she was gone, beneath the water.

Bill grabbed Angelique by the arm, pulled her to her feet in the knee-deep water. She held Teddy close to her. He pulled them across the room as the floor shifted, pulled them through the door that led onto the unfinished deck, stumbled over a hammer that lay beneath the water, but managed to keep his feet.

Bill couldn't help but think of all the work he had put in on this deck. Now it would never be finished. He hated to leave anything unfinished. He hated worse that it was starting to lean.

There was one central post that seemed to stand well enough, and they took position behind that. The post was one of several that the house was built around; a support post to lift the house above the normal rise of water. It connected bedroom to deck.

Bill tried to look through the driving rain. All he could see was water. Galveston was covered by the sea. It had risen up and swallowed the city and the island.

The house began to shake violently. They heard lumber splintering, felt it shimmying. The deck swayed more dynamically.

"We're not going to make it, are we, Bill?" Angelique said.

"No, darling. We aren't."

"I love you."

"I love you."

He held her and kissed her. She said, "It doesn't matter, you and I. But Teddy. He doesn't know. He doesn't understand. God, why Teddy? He's only a baby...How do I drown, darling?"

"One deep breath and it's over. Just one deep pull of the water, and don't fight it."

Angelique started to cry. Bill squatted, ran his hand under the water and over the deck. He found the hammer. It was lodged in its spot because it was caught in a gap in the unfinished deck. Bill brought the hammer out. There was a big nail sticking out of the main support post. He had driven it there the day before, to find it easily enough. It was his last big nail and it was his intent to save it.

He used the claw of the hammer to pull it out. He looked at Angelique. "We can give Teddy a chance."

Angelique couldn't see Bill well in the darkness, but she somehow felt what his face was saying. "Oh, Bill."

"It's a chance."

"But..."

"We can't stand against this, but the support post—"

"Oh Lord, Bill," and Angelique sagged, holding Teddy close to her chest. Bill grabbed her shoulders, said, "Give me my son."

Angelique sobbed, then the house slouched far to the right—except for the support post. All the other supports were washing loose, but so far, this one hadn't budged.

Angelique gave Teddy to Bill. Bill kissed the child, lifted him as high on the post as he could, pushed the child's back against the wood, and lifted its arm. Angelique was suddenly there, supporting the baby. Bill kissed her. He took the hammer and the nail, and placing the nail squarely against Teddy's little wrist, drove it through the child's flesh with one swift blow.

Then the storm blew more furious and the deck turned to gelatin. Bill clutched Angelique, and Angelique almost managed to say, "Teddy," then all the powers of nature took them and the flimsy house away.

High above it all, water lapping around the post, Teddy, wet and cold, squalled with pain.

Bess surfaced among lumber and junk. She began to paddle her legs furiously, snorting water. A nail on a board cut across her muzzle, opening a deep gash. The horse nickered, thrashed its legs violently, lifted its head, trying to stay afloat.

SUNDAY, SEPTEMBER 9, 4:00 A.M.

The mechanism that revolved the Bolivar lighthouse beam had stopped working. The stairs that led up to the lighthouse had gradually filled with people fleeing the storm, and as the water rose, so did the people. One man with a young boy had come in last, and therefore was on the constantly rising bottom rung. He kept saying, "Move up. Move up, lessen' you want to see a man and his boy drown." And everyone would move up. And then the man would soon repeat his refrain as the water rose.

The lighthouse was becoming congested. The lighthouse tower had begun to sway. The lighthouse operator, Jim Marlin, and his wife, Elizabeth, lit the kerosene lamp and placed it in the center of the cir-

cular, magnifying lens, and tried to turn the beam by hand. They
wanted someone to know there was shelter here, even though it was
overcrowded, and might soon cease to exist. The best thing to do was
to douse the light and hope they could save those who were already
there, and save themselves. But Jim and Elizabeth couldn't do that.
Elizabeth said, "Way I see it, Jim. It's all or nothing, and the good
Lord would want it that way. I want it that way."

All night long they had heard screams and cries for help, and
once, when the lighthouse beam was operating, they had seen a young
man clinging to a timber. When the light swung back to where the
young man had been, he had vanished.

Now, as they tried to turn the light by hand, they found it was too
much of a chore. Finally, they let it shine in one direction, and there in
the light they saw a couple of bodies being dragged by a large patch
of canvas from which dangled ropes, like jellyfish tentacles. The ropes
had grouped and twisted around the pair, and the canvas seemed to
operate with design, folded and opened like a pair of great wings, as
if it were an exotic sea creature bearing them off to a secret lair where
they could be eaten in privacy.

Neither Jim nor Elizabeth Marlin knew the bloated men tangled
in the ropes together, had no idea they were named Ronald Beems
and Forrest Thomas.

5:00 A.M.

A crack of light. Dawn. Jim and Elizabeth had fallen asleep leaning against the base of the great light, and at the first ray of sunshine,
they awoke, saw a ship's bow at the lighthouse window, and standing at the bow, looking in at them, was a bedraggled man in uniform,
and he was crying savagely.

Jim went to the window. The ship had been lifted up on piles of
sand and lumber. Across the bow he could see the letters *PENSACOLA*.
The man was leaning against the glass. He wore a captain's hat. He
held out his hand, palm first. Jim put his hand to the glass, trying to
match the span of the crying captain's hand.

Behind the captain a number of wet men appeared. When they
saw the lighthouse they fell to their knees and lifted their heads to the
heavens in prayer, having forgotten that it was in fact the heavens
that had devastated them.

6:00 A.M.

The day broke above the shining water, and the water began to go down, rapidly, and John McBride sat comfortably on the great hour hand of what was left of the City Hall clock. He sat there with his arms wrapped around debris that dangled from the clock. In the night, a huge spring mechanism had jumped from the face of the clock and hit him a glancing blow in the head, and for a moment, McBride had thought he was still battling the nigger. He wasn't sure which was worse to fight. The hurricane or the nigger. But through the night he had become grateful for the spring to hold on to.

Below him he saw much of what was left of the Sporting Club, including the lockers where he had put his belongings. The whole damn place had washed up beneath the clock tower.

McBride used his teeth to work off the binds of his boxing gloves and slip his hands free. All through the night the gloves had been a burden. He feared his lack of grip would cause him to fall. It felt good to have his hands out of the tight, wet leather.

McBride ventured to take hold of the minute hand of the clock, swing on it a little, and cause it to lower him onto a pile of rubble. He climbed over lumber and junk and found a mass of bloated bodies, men, women, and children, most of them sporting shingles that had cut into their heads and bodies. He searched their pockets for money and found none, but one of the women—he could tell it was a woman by her hair and dress only, her features were lost in the fleshy swelling of her face—had a ring. He tried to pull it off her finger, but it wouldn't come off. The water had swollen her flesh all around it.

He sloshed his way to the pile of lockers. He searched through them until he found the one where he had put his clothes. They were so filthy with mud, he left them. But he got the razor and the revolver. The revolver was full of grit. He took out the shells and shook them and put them back. He stuck the gun in his soaked boxing trunks. He opened the razor and shook out the silt and went over to the woman and used the razor to cut off her finger. The blade cut easily through the flesh, and he whacked through the bone. He pushed the ring on his little finger, closed the razor, and slipped it into the waistband of his trunks, next to his revolver.

This was a hell of a thing to happen. He had hidden his money back at the whorehouse, and he figured it and the plump madam were probably far at sea, the madam possibly full of harpoon wounds.

And the shitasses who were to pay him were now all choked, including the main one, the queer Beems. And if they weren't, they were certainly no longer men of means.

This had been one shitty trip. No clothes. No money. No whipped nigger. And no more pussy. He'd come with more than he was leaving with.

What the hell else could go wrong?

He decided to wade toward the whorehouse, see if it was possibly standing, maybe find some bodies along the way to loot—something to make up for his losses.

As he started in that direction, he saw a dog on top of a doghouse float by. The dog was chained to the house and the chain had gotten tangled around some floating rubble and it had pulled the dog flat against the roof. It lifted its eyes and saw McBride, barked wearily for help. McBride determined it was well within pistol shot.

McBride lifted the revolver and pulled the trigger. It clicked, but nothing happened. He tried again, hoping against hope. It fired this time and the dog took a blast in the skull and rolled off the house, and hung by the chain, then sailed out of sight.

McBride said, "Poor thing."

7:03 A.M.

The water was falling away rapidly, returning to the sea, leaving in its wake thousands of bodies and the debris that had once been Galveston. The stench was awful. Jack and Cooter, who had spent the night in a child's tree house, awoke, amazed they were alive.

The huge oak tree they were in was stripped of leaves and limbs, but the tree house was unharmed. It was remarkable. They had washed right up to it, just climbed off the lumber to which they had been clinging, and went inside. It was dry in there, and they found three hard biscuits in a tin and three hot bottles of that good ole Waco, Texas, drink, Dr Pepper. There was a phone on the wall, but it was a fake, made of lumber and tin cans. Jack had the urge to try it, as if it might be a line to God, for surely, it was God who had brought them here.

Cooter had helped Jack remove his gloves, then they ate the biscuits, drank a bottle of Dr Pepper apiece, then split the last bottle and slept.

When it was good and light, they decided to climb down. The ladder, a series of boards nailed to the tree, had washed away, but they made it to the ground by sliding down like firemen on a pole.

When they reached the earth, they started walking, sloshing through the mud and water that had rolled back to ankle-deep. The world they had known was gone. Galveston was a wet mulch of bloated bodies — humans, dogs, mules, and horses — and mashed lumber. In the distance they saw a bedraggled family walking along like ducks in a row. Jack recognized them. He had seen them around town. They were Issac Cline, his brother Joseph, Issac's wife and children. He wondered if they knew where they were going, or were they like him and Cooter, just out there? He decided on the latter.

Jack and Cooter decided to head for higher ground, back uptown. Soon they could see the tower of City Hall, in sad shape but still standing, the clock having sprung a great spring. It poked from the face of the mechanism like a twisted, metal tongue.

They hadn't gone too far toward the tower when they encountered a man coming toward them. He was wearing shorts and shoes like Jack and was riding a chocolate brown mare bareback. He had looped a piece of frayed rope around the horse's muzzle and was using that as a primitive bridle. His hair was combed to perfection. It was McBride.

"Shit," Cooter said. "Ain't this somethin'? Well, Jack, you take care, I gonna be seein' you."

"Asshole," Jack said.

Cooter put his hands in his pockets and turned right, headed over piles of junk and bodies on his way to who knew where.

McBride spotted Jack, yelled, "You somethin', nigger. A hurricane can't even drown you."

"You neither," Jack said. They were within twenty feet of one another now. Jack could see the revolver and the razor in McBride's waistband. The horse, a beautiful animal with a deep cut on its muzzle, suddenly buckled and lay down with its legs folded beneath it, dropped its head into the mud.

McBride stepped off the animal, said, "Can you believe that? Goddamn horse survived all this and it can't carry me no ways at all."

McBride pulled his pistol and shot the horse through the head. It rolled over gently, lay on its side without so much as one last heave of its belly. McBride turned back to Jack. The revolver lay loose in his hand. He said, "Had it misfired, I'd have had to beat that horse to death with a board. I don't believe in animals suffering. Gun's been underwater, and it's worked two out of three. Can you believe that?"

"That horse would have been all right," Jack said.

"Naw, it wouldn't," McBride said. "Why don't you shake it, see if it'll come around?" McBride pushed the revolver into the waistband of his shorts. "How's about you and me? Want to finish where we left off?"

"You got to be jokin'," Jack said.

"You hear me laughin'?"

"I don't know about you, peckerwood, but I feel like I been in a hurricane, then swam a few miles in boxing gloves, then slept all night in a tree house and had biscuits and Dr Pepper for breakfast."

"I ain't even had no breakfast, nigger. Listen here. I can't go home not knowing I can whip you or not. Hell, I might never get home. I want to know I can take you. You want to know."

"Yeah. I do. But I don't want to fight no pistol and razor."

McBride removed the pistol and razor from his trunks, found a dry spot and put them there. He said, "Come on."

"Where?"

"Here's all we got."

Jack turned and looked. He could see a slight rise of dirt beyond the piles of wreckage. A house had stood there. One of its great support poles was still visible.

"Over there," Jack said.

They went over there and found a spot about the size of a boxing ring. Down below them on each side were heaps of bodies and heaps of gulls on the bodies, scrambling for soft flesh and eyeballs. McBride studied the bodies, what was left of Galveston, turned to Jack, said, "Fuck the rules."

They waded into each other, bare knuckle. It was obvious after only moments that they were exhausted. They were throwing hammers, not punches, and the sounds of their strikes mixed with the caws and cries of the gulls. McBride ducked his head beneath Jack's chin, drove it up. Jack locked his hands behind McBride's neck, kneed him in the groin.

They rolled on the ground and in the mud, then came apart. They regained their feet and went at it again. Then the sounds of their blows and the shrieks of the gulls were overwhelmed by a cry so unique and savage, they ceased punching.

"Time," Jack said.

"What in hell is that?" McBride said.

They walked toward the sound of the cry, leaned on the great support post. Once a fine house had stood here, and now, there was only this. McBride said, "I don't know about you, nigger, but I'm one tired sonofabitch."

The cry came again. Above him. He looked up. A baby was nailed near the top of the support. Its upraised, nailed arm was covered in caked blood. Gulls were flapping around its head, making a kind of halo.

"I'll be goddamned," Jack said. "Boost me, McBride."

"What?"

"Boost me."

"You got to be kidding."

Jack lifted his leg. McBride sighed, made a stirrup with his cupped hands, and Jack stood, got hold of the post and worked his way painfully up. At the bottom, McBride picked up garbage and hurled it at the gulls.

"You gonna hit the baby, you jackass," Jack said.

When he got up there, Jack found the nail was sticking out of the baby's wrist by an inch or so. He wrapped his legs tight around the post, held on with one arm while he took hold of the nail and tried to work it free with his fingers. It wouldn't budge.

"Can't get it loose," Jack yelled down. He was about to drop; his legs and arms had turned to butter.

"Hang on," McBride said, and went away.

It seemed like forever before he came back. He had the revolver with him. He looked up at Jack and the baby. He looked at them for a long moment. Jack watched him, didn't move. McBride said, "Listen up, nigger. Catch this, use it to work out the nail."

McBride emptied the remaining cartridges from the revolver and tossed it up. Jack caught it on the third try. He used the trigger guard to snag the nail, but mostly mashed the baby's wrist. The baby had stopped crying. It was making a kind of mewing sound, like a dying goat.

The nail came loose, and Jack nearly didn't grab the baby in time and when he did, he got hold of its nailed arm and he felt and heard its shoulder snap out of place. He was weakening, and he knew he was about to fall.

"McBride," he said, "catch."

The baby dropped and so did the revolver. McBride reached out and grabbed the child. It screamed when he caught it, and McBride raised it over his head and laughed. He laid the baby on top of a pile of wide lumber and looked at it.

Jack was about halfway down the post when he fell, landing on his back, knocking the wind out of him. By the time he got it together enough to get up and find the revolver and wobble over to McBride, McBride had worked the child's shoulder back into place and was cooing to him.

Jack said, "He ain't gonna make it. He's lost lots of blood."

McBride stood up with the baby on his shoulder. He said, "Naw. He's tough as a warthog. Worse this little shit will have is a scar. Elastic as he is, there ain't no real damage. And he didn't bleed out bad neither. He gets some milk in him, fifteen, sixteen years from now, he'll be chasin' pussy. Course, best thing is, come around when he's about two and go on and kill him. He'll just grow up to be men like us."

McBride held the child out and away from him, looked him over. The baby's penis lifted and the child peed all over him. McBride laughed uproariously.

"Well, shit, nigger. I reckon today ain't my day, and it ain't the day you and me gonna find out who's the best. Here. I don't know no one here. Take 'em."

Jack took the child, gave McBride his revolver, said, "I don't know there's anyone I know anymore."

"I tell you, you're one lucky nigger," McBride said. "I'm gonna forgo you a beating, maybe a killing."

"That right?"

"Uh-huh. Someone's got to tote this kid to safety, and if'n I kept him, I might get tired of him in an hour. Put his little head underwater."

"You would, wouldn't you?"

"I might. And you know, you're a fool to give me back my gun."

"Naw. I broke it gettin' that nail loose."

McBride grinned, tossed the gun in the mud, shaded his eyes, and looked at the sky. "Can you beat that? Looks like it's gonna be a nice day."

Jack nodded. The baby sucked on his shoulder. He decided McBride was right. This was one tough kid. It was snuggled against him as if nothing had happened, trying to get milk. Jack wondered about the child's family. Wondered about his own. Where were they? Were they alive?

McBride grinned, said, "Nigger, you got a hell of an uppercut." Then he turned and walked away.

Jack patted the baby's back, watched McBride find his razor, then walk on. Jack watched him until he disappeared behind a swell of lumber and bodies, and he never saw him again.

· Veil's Visit ·

(WITH ANDREW VACHSS)
INTRODUCTION

This was fun. For me, maybe not for Andrew. I can be an odd duck to work with on collaborations.

Andrew, after reading my series about Hap and Leonard, told me he wanted to defend Leonard in a court of law.

It should be noted that Andrew Vachss is one of the world's premier lawyers. His law practice is for children, and children only. But, he's still a lawyer, and he thought it might be fun to defend my character Leonard, who in a couple of the books, takes to burning down a crackhouse.

So, I'm not saying Veil is Andrew, but there is a strong resemblance. He mentioned this idea several times.

I thought it was a nifty idea, but I kept going on about my work. He finally just did a draft of the story. Sent it to me, waited.

Nothing.

I kept meaning to get to it, really.

Then he sent me a disk so I could put it on my machine and do my draft more easily.

I lost the disk.

He sent me another.

I finally revised it, making Hap and Leonard fit my idea of Hap and Leonard. Andrew had suggestions. They were made. The results follow.

I really love the courtroom scenes.

They are so…so Andrew.

· Veil's Visit ·

(WITH ANDREW VACHSS)

(1)

Leonard eyed Veil for a long hard moment, said, "If you're a lawyer, then I can shit a perfectly round turd through a hoop at twenty paces. Blindfolded."

"I am a lawyer," Veil said. "But I'll let your accomplishments speak for themselves."

Veil was average height, dark hair touched with gray, one good eye. The other one roamed a little. He had a beard that could have been used as a Brillo pad, and he was dressed in an expensive suit and shiny shoes, a fancy wristwatch and ring. He was the only guy I'd ever seen with the kind of presence Leonard has. Scary.

"You still don't look like any kind of lawyer to me," Leonard said.

"He means that as a compliment," I said to Veil. "Leonard doesn't think real highly of your brethren at the bar."

"Oh, you're a bigot?" Veil asked pleasantly, looking directly at Leonard with his one good eye. A very icy eye indeed—I remembered it well.

"The fuck you talking about? Lawyers are all right. They got their purpose. You never know when you might want one of them to weigh down a rock at the bottom of a lake." Leonard's tone had shifted from mildly inquisitive to that of a man who might like to perform a live dissection.

"You think all lawyers are alike, right? But if I said all blacks are alike, you'd think you know something about *me*, right?"

"I knew you were coming to that," Leonard said.

"Well," I said. "I think this is really going well. What about you boys?"

Veil and Leonard may not have bonded as well as I had hoped, but they certainly had some things in common. In a way, they were both assholes. I, of course, exist on a higher plane.

"You wearing an Armani suit, must have set you back a thousand dollars—" Leonard said.

"You know a joint where I can get suits like this for a lousy one grand, I'll stop there on my way back and pick up a couple dozen," Veil said.

"Yeah, fine," Leonard said. "Gold Rolex, diamond ring...How much all *that* set you back?"

"It was a gift," Veil said.

"Sure," Leonard said. "You know what you look like?"

"What's that?"

"You look like Central Casting for a mob movie."

"And you look like a candidate for a chain gang. Which is kind of why I'm here."

"You gonna defend me? How you gonna do that? I may not know exactly what you are, but I can bet the farm on this—you ain't no *Texas* lawyer. Hell, you ain't no Texan, period."

"No problem. I can just go *pro hac vice.*"

"I hope that isn't some kind of sexual act," Leonard said. "Especially if it involves me and you."

"It just means I get admitted to the bar for one case. For the specific litigation. I'll need local counsel to handle the pleadings, of course..."

"Do I look like a goddamned pleader to you? And you best not say yes."

"'Pleadings' just means the papers," Veil said, his voice a model of patience. "Motions, applications...stuff like that. You wanted to cop a plea to this, Hap wouldn't need me. I don't do that kind of thing. And by the way, I'm doing this for Hap, not you."

"What is it makes you so special to Hap?" Leonard asked, studying Veil's face carefully. "What is it that you *do* do?"

"Fight," Veil said.

"Yeah," I said. "He *can* do that."

"Yeah, so can you and me, but that and a rubber will get us a jack off without mess." Leonard sighed. He said to Veil, "You know what my problem is?"

"Besides attitude, sure. Says so right on the indictment. You burned down a crackhouse. For at least the...what was it, fourth time? That's first degree arson, malicious destruction of property, attempted murder—"

"I didn't—"

"What? Know anyone was home when you firebombed the dump? Doesn't matter — the charge is still valid."

"Yeah, well they can valid *this*," Leonard said, making a gesture appropriate to his speech.

"You're looking at a flat dime down in Huntsville," Veil told him. "That a good enough summary of your 'problem?'"

"No, it ain't close," Leonard said. "Here's my problem. You come in here wearing a few thousand bucks of fancy stuff, tell me you're a fighter, but your face looks like you lost a lot more fights than you won. You don't know jack about Texas law, but you're gonna work a local jury. And that's still not my big problem. You know what my big problem is?"

"I figure you're going to tell me sometime before visiting hours are over," Veil said.

"My problem is this. Why the hell should I trust you?"

"I trust him," I said.

"I know, brother. And I trust you. What I don't trust, on the other hand, is your judgment. The two ain't necessarily the same thing."

"Try this, then." Veil told him. "Homicide. A murder. And nobody's said a word about it. For almost twenty years."

"You telling me you and Hap — ?"

"I'm telling you there was a homicide. No statute of limitations on that, right? It's still unsolved. And nobody's talking."

"I don't know. Me and Hap been tight a long time. He'd tell me something like that. I mean, he dropped the rock on someone, I'd know." Leonard turned to me. "Wouldn't I?"

I didn't say anything. Veil was doing the talking.

Veil leaned in close, dropping his voice. "It wasn't Hap who did it. But Hap knows all about it. And you if keep your mouth shut long enough, you will too. Then you can decide who to trust. Deal?"

Leonard gave Veil a long, deep look. "Deal," he finally said, leaning back, waiting to hear the story.

Veil turned and looked at me, and I knew that was my cue to tell it.

(2)

"It was back in my semi-hippie days," I said to Leonard. "Remember when I was all about peace and love?"

"The only 'piece' I ever knew you to be about was a piece of ass," Leonard said kindly. "I always thought you had that long hair so's it could help you get into fights."

"Just tell him the fucking story," Veil said. "Okay? I've got work to do, and I can't do it without Leonard. You two keep screwing around and the guard's going to roll on back here and — "

"It was in this house on the coast," I said. "In Oregon. I was living with some folks."

"Some of those folks being women, of course."

"Yeah. I was experimenting with different ways of life. I told you about it. Anyway, I hadn't been there long. This house, it wasn't like it was a commune or nothing, but people just…came and went, understand? So, one day, this guy comes strolling up. Nice-looking guy. Photographer, he said he was. All loaded down with equipment in his van. He was a traveling man, just working his way around the country. Taking pictures for this book he was doing. He fit in pretty good. You know, he looked the part. Long hair, but a little neater than the rest of us. Suave manner. Took pictures a lot. Nobody really cared. He did his share of the work, kicked in a few bucks for grub. No big deal. I was a little suspicious at first. We always got photographers wanting to 'document' us, you know? Mostly wanted pictures of the girls. Especially Sunflower — she had this thing about clothes being 'inhibiting' and all. In other words she was quick to shuck drawers and throw the hair triangle around. But this guy was real peaceful, real calm. I remember one of the guys there said this one had a calm presence. Like the eye of a hurricane."

"This is motherfucking fascinating and all," Leonard said, "but considering my particular situation, I wonder if you couldn't, you know, get to the point?"

Seeing as how Leonard never read that part of the Good Book that talked about patience being a virtue, I sped it up a bit. "I was out in the back yard one night," I said. "Meditating."

"Masturbating, you mean," Leonard said.

"I was just getting to that stage with the martial arts and I didn't want any of the damn marijuana smoke getting in my eyes. I guess I was more conservative about that sort of thing than I realized. It made me nervous just being around it. So I needed some privacy. I wasn't doing the classic meditation thing. Just being alone with my thoughts, trying to find my center."

"Which you never have," Leonard said.

"I'm sitting there, thinking about whatever it was I was thinking about—"

"Pussy," Leonard said.

"And I open my eyes and there he is. Veil."

"That'd be some scary shit," Leonard said.

"Looked about the same he does now."

"Yeah? Was he wearing that Armani suit?"

"Matter a fact, he wasn't," I said. "He looked like everyone else did around there then. Only difference was the pistol."

"I can see how that got your attention," Leonard said.

"It was dark. And I'm no modern firearms expert. But it wasn't the stuff I grew up with, hunting rifles, shotguns and revolvers. This was a seriously big-ass gun, I can tell you that. I couldn't tell if he was pointing it at me or not. Finally I decided he was just kind of...holding it. I asked him, politely, I might add, if there was anything I could do for him, short of volunteering to be shot, and he said, yeah, matter of fact, there was. What he wanted was some information about this photographer guy.

"Now hippie types weren't all that different from cons back then, at least when it came to giving out information to the cops. Cops had a way of thinking you had long hair you had to be something from Mars out to destroy Mom, apple pie and the American way."

"Does that mean Texas too?" Leonard asked.

"I believe it did, yes."

"Well, I can see their point. And the apple pie part."

"I could tell this guy was no cop. And he wasn't asking me for evidence-type stuff anyway. Just when the guy had showed up, stuff like that."

Leonard yawned. Sometimes he can be a very crude individual. Veil looked like he always does. Calm.

"Anyway, I started to say I didn't know the guy, then...I don't know. There was something about his manner that made me trust him."

"Thank you," Veil said. I wasn't sure if he was being sarcastic or not.

I nodded. "I told him the truth. It wasn't any big deal. Like I said, he wasn't asking anything weird, but I was a little worried. I mean, you know, the gun and all. Then I got stupid and—"

"Oh, *that's* when it happened?" Leonard asked. "That's like the moment it set in?"

I maintained patience—which is what Leonard is always complaining he has to do with *me*—and went on like he hadn't said a word: " —asked him how come he wanted to know all about this guy, and maybe I ought not to be saying anything, and how he ought to take his pistol and go on. I didn't want any trouble, and no one at the place did either.

"So Veil asks the big question. Where is the guy right now? I told him he was out somewhere. Or maybe gone, for all I knew. That's the way things were then. People came and went like cats and you didn't tend to get uptight about it. It was the times."

"Groovy," Leonard said.

"We talk for a while, but, truth was, I didn't *know* anything about the guy, so I really got nothing to say of importance. But, you know, I'm thinking it isn't every day you see a guy looks like Veil walking around with a gun almost the size of my dick."

"Jesus," Leonard said. "Can't ever get away from your dick."

"No, it tends to stay with me."

"How about staying with the story," Veil said, still calm but with an edge to his voice now.

"So I ask Veil, it's okay with him, I'm going back in the house and get some sleep, and like maybe could he put the gun up 'cause it's making me nervous. I know I mentioned that gun several times. I'm trying to kind of glide out of there because I figure a guy with a gun has more on this mind than just small talk. I thought he might even be a druggie, though he didn't look like one. Veil here, he says no problem. But I see he's not going anywhere so I don't move. Somehow, the idea of getting my back to that gun doesn't appeal to me, and we're kind of close, and I'm thinking he gets a little closer I got a small chance of taking the gun away from him. Anyway, we both stick. Studying each other, I think. Neither of us going anywhere."

"Neither the fuck am I," Leonard said. "Matter of fact, I think moss is starting to grow on the north side of my ass."

"All right, partner," I told him, "here's the finale. I decide to not go in the house, just sit out there with Veil. We talk a bit about this and that, anything but guns, and we're quiet a bit. Gets to be real late, I don't know, maybe four in the morning, and we both hear a motor. Something pulling into the driveway. Then we hear a car door close. Another minute or so, the front door to the house closes too. Veil, without a word to me, gets up and walks around to the drive. I follow him. Even then I think I'm some kind of mediator. That whatever's going on, maybe I can fix it. I was hell for fixing people's problems then."

"You're still hell for that," Leonard said.

"Sure enough, there's the guy's van. I'm starting to finally snap that Veil hasn't just showed up for an assassination. He's investigating, and, well, I don't know how, but I'm just sort of falling in with him. In spite of his sweet personality, there's something about me and him that clicked."

"I adore a love story," Leonard said.

"So anyway, I wasn't exactly shocked when Veil put the pistol away, stuck a little flashlight in his teeth, worked the locks on the guy's van like he had a key. We both climbed in, being real quiet. In the back, under a pile of equipment, we found the…pictures."

"Guy was a blackmailer?" Leonard asked, a little interested now.

"They were pictures of kids," I told him. Quiet, so's he'd know what kind of pictures I meant.

Leonard's face changed. I knew then he was thinking about what kind of pictures they were and not liking having to think about it.

"I'd never seen anything like that before, and didn't know that sort of thing existed. Oh, I guess, in theory, but not in reality. And the times then, lot of folks were thinking free love and sex was okay for anyone, grown-ups, kids. People who didn't really know anything about life and what this sort of thing was all about, but one look at those pictures and I was educated, and it was an education I didn't want. I've never got over it.

. "So he," I said, nodding my head over at Veil, "asks me, where does the guy with the van sleep? Where inside the house, I mean. I tried to explain to him what a crash pad was. I couldn't be sure where he was, or even who he might be with, you understand? Anyway, Veil just looks at me, says it would be a real mess if they found this guy in the house. A mess for us, you know? So he asks me, how about if I go inside, tell the guy it looks like someone tried to break into his van?

"I won't kid you. I hesitated. Not because I felt any sympathy for that sonofabitch, but because it's not my nature to walk someone off a plank. I was trying to sort of think my way out of it when Veil here told me to take a look at the pictures again. A good look."

"The guy's toast," Leonard said. "Fucker like that, he's toast. I know you, Hap. He's toast."

I nodded at Leonard. "Yeah," I said. "I went inside. Brought the guy out with me. He opens the door to the van, climbs in the front seat. And there's Veil, in the passenger seat. Veil and that pistol. I went back in the house, watched from the window. I heard the van start up, saw it pull out. I never saw the photographer again. And to tell you the truth, I've never lost a minute's sleep over it. I don't know what that says about me, but I haven't felt a moment of regret."

"It says you have good character," Veil said.

"What I want to know," Leonard said looking at Veil, "is what did you do with the body?"

Veil didn't say anything.

Leonard tried again. "You was a hit man? Is that what Hap here's trying to tell me?"

"It was a long time ago," Veil told him. "It doesn't matter, does it? What matters is: You want to talk to me now?"

(3)

The judge looked like nothing so much as a turkey buzzard: tiny head on a long, wrinkled neck and cold little eyes. Everybody stood up when he entered the courtroom. Lester Rommerly — the local lawyer I went and hired like Veil told me — he told the judge that Veil would be representing Leonard. The judge looked down at Veil.

"Where are you admitted to practice, sir?"

"In New York State, your honor. And in the Federal District Courts of New York, New Jersey, Rhode Island, Pennsylvania, Illinois, Michigan, California, and Massachusetts."

"Get around a bit, do you?"

"On occasion," Veil replied.

"Well sir, you can represent this defendant here. Nothing against the law about that, as you apparently know. I can't help wondering, I must say, how you managed to find yourself way down here."

Veil didn't say anything. And it was obvious after a minute that he wasn't going to. He and the judge just kind of watched each other.

Then the trial started.

The first few witnesses were all government. The fire department guy testified about "the presence of an accelerant" being the tip-off that this was arson, not some accidental fire. Veil got up slowly, started to walk over to the witness box, then stopped. His voice was low, but it carried right through the courtroom.

"Officer, you have any experience with alcoholics?"

"Objection!" the DA shouted.

"Sustained," the judge said, not even looking at Veil.

"Officer," Veil went on like nothing had happened, "you have any experience with dope fiends?"

"Objection!" the DA was on his feet, red-faced.

"Counsel, you are to desist from this line of questioning," the judge said. "The witness is a fireman, not a psychologist."

"Oh, excuse me, your honor," Veil said sweetly. "I misphrased my inquiry. Let me try again: Officer," he said, turning his attention back to the witness, "by 'accelerant,' you mean something like gasoline or kerosene, isn't that correct?"

"Yes," the witness said, cautious in spite of Veil's mild tone.

"Hmmm," Veil said. "Be pretty stupid to keep a can of gasoline right in the house, wouldn't it?"

"Your honor…" the DA pleaded.

"Well, I believe he can answer that one," the judge said.

"Yeah, it would," the fire marshall said. "But some folks keep kerosene inside. You know, for heating and all."

"*Thank* you, officer," Veil said, like the witness had just given him this great gift. "And it'd be even stupider to smoke cigarettes in the same house where you kept gasoline…or kerosene, wouldn't it?"

"Well, *sure*. I mean, if—"

"Objection!" the DA yelled. "There is no evidence to show that anyone was smoking cigarettes in the house!"

"Ah, my apologies," Veil said, bowing slightly. "Please consider the question withdrawn. Officer: Be pretty stupid to smoke *crack* in a house with gasoline or kerosene in it, right?"

"Your honor!" the DA cut in. "This is nothing but trickery. This man is trying to tell the jury there was gasoline in the house. And this officer has clearly testified that—"

" — That there *was* either gasoline or kerosene in the house at the time the fire started," Veil interrupted.

"Not in a damn *can,*" the DA said again.

"Your honor," Veil said, his voice the soul of reasonableness, "the witness testified that he found a charred can of gasoline in the house. Now it was his expert *opinion* that someone had poured gasoline all over the floor and the walls and then dropped a match. I am merely inquiring if there couldn't be some *other* way the fire had started."

The judge, obviously irritated, said, "Then why don't you just ask him that?"

"Well, judge, I kind of was doing that. I mean, if one of the crackheads living there had maybe fallen asleep after he got high, you know, nodded out the way they do…and the crack pipe fell to the ground, and there was a can of kerosene lying around and—"

"That is *enough!*" the judge cut in. "You are well aware, sir, that when the fire trucks arrived, the house was empty."

"But the trucks weren't there when the fire *started,* judge. Maybe the dope fiend felt the flames and ran for his life. I don't know. I wasn't there. And I thought the jury—"

"The jury will *disregard* your entire line of questioning, sir. And unless you have *another* line of questioning for this witness, he is excused."

Veil bowed.

(4)

At the lunch break, I asked him, "What the hell are you doing? Leonard already *told* the police it was him who burned down the crackhouse."

"Sure. You just said the magic word: crackhouse. I want to make sure the jury hears that enough times, that's all."

"You think they're gonna let him off just because—?"

"We're just getting started," Veil told me.

(5)

"Now officer, prior to placing the defendant under arrest, did you issue the appropriate Miranda warnings?" the DA asked the sheriff's deputy.

"Yes sir, I did."

"And did the defendant agree to speak with you?"

"Well…he didn't exactly 'agree.' I mean, this ain't the first time for old Leonard there. We knowed it was him, living right across the road and all. So when we went over there to arrest him, he was just sitting on the porch."

"But he *did* tell you that he was responsible for the arson, isn't that correct, Officer?"

"Oh yeah. Leonard said he burned it down. Said he'd do it again if those—well, I don't want to use the language he used here—he'd just burn it down again."

"No further questions," the DA said, turning away in triumph.

"Did the defendant resist arrest?" Veil asked on cross-examination.

"Not at all," the deputy said. "Matter of fact, you could see he was waiting on us."

"But if he *wanted* to resist arrest, he could have, couldn't he?"

"I don't get your meaning," the deputy said.

"The man means I could kick your ass without breaking a sweat," Leonard volunteered from the defendant's table.

The judge pounded his gavel a few times. Leonard shrugged, like he'd just been trying to be helpful.

"Deputy, were you familiar with the location of the fire? You had been there before? In your professional capacity, I mean." Veil asked him.

"Sure enough," the deputy answered.

"Fair to say the place was a crackhouse?" Veil asked.

"No question about that. We probably made a couple of dozen arrests there during the past year alone."

"You made any *since* the house burned down?"

"You mean…at that same address? Of course not."

"Thank you, officer," Veil said.

(6)

"Doctor, you were on duty on the night of the thirteenth, is that correct?"

"That is correct," the doctor said, eyeing Veil like a man waiting for the doctor to grease up and begin his proctology exam.

"And your specialty is Emergency Medicine, is that also correct?"

"It is."

"And when you say 'on duty,' you mean you're in the ER, right?"

"Yes sir."

"In fact, you're in *charge* of the ER, aren't you?"

"I am the physician in charge, if that is what you're asking me, sir. I have nothing to do with administration, so…."

"I understand," Veil said in a voice sweet as a preacher explaining scripture. "Now, Doctor, have you ever treated patients with burns?"

"Of course," the doctor snapped at him.

"And those range, don't they? I mean, from first degree to third degree burns. Which are the worst?"

"Third degree."

"Hmmm...I wonder if that's where they got the term, 'Give him the third degree'...?"

"Your Honor...." the DA protested again.

"Mr. Veil, where are you going with this?" the judge asked.

"To the heart of the truth, your honor. And if you'll permit me...."

The judge waved a disgusted hand in Veil's direction. Veil kind of waved back. The big diamond glinted on his hand, catching the sun's rays through the high courthouse windows. "Doctor, you treat anybody with third degree burns the night of the thirteenth?"

"I did not."

"Second degree burns?"

"No."

"Even *first* degree burns?"

"You know quite well I did not, sir. This isn't the first time you have asked me these questions."

"Sure, *I* know the answers. But you're telling the jury, Doctor, not me. Now you've seen the photographs of the house that was burnt to the ground. Could anyone have been *inside* that house and *not* been burned?"

"I don't see how," the doctor snapped. "But that doesn't mean—"

"Let's let the jury decide what it means," Veil cut him off. "Am I right, judge?"

The judge knew when he was being jerked off, but, having told Veil those exact same words a couple of dozen times during the trial already, he was smart enough to keep his lipless mouth shut.

"All right, Doctor. Now we're coming to the heart of your testimony. See, the reason we have *expert* testimony is that experts, well, they know stuff the average person doesn't. And they get to explain it to us so we can understand things that happen."

"Your honor, he's making a speech!" the DA complained, for maybe the two hundredth time.

But Veil rolled on like he hadn't heard a word. "Doctor, can you explain what causes the plague?"

One of the elderly ladies on the jury gasped when Veil said "the plague," but the doctor went right on: "Well, actually, it is caused by fleas which are the primary carriers."

"Fleas? And here all along I thought it was carried by rats," Veil replied, turning to the jury as if embracing them all in his viewpoint.

"Yes, fleas," the doctor said. "They are, in fact, fleas especially common to rodents, but *wild* rodents — prairie dogs, chipmunks, and the like."

"Not squirrels?"

"Only *ground* squirrels," the doctor answered.

"So, in other words, you mean varmints, right, Doctor?"

"I do."

"The kind of varmints folks go shooting just for sport?"

"Well, some do. But mostly it's farmers who kill them. And that's not for sport — that's to protect their crops," the doctor said, self-righteously, looking to the jury for support.

"Uh, isn't it true, Doctor, that if you kill *enough* varmints, the fleas just jump over to rats?"

"Well, that's true...."

"That's what happened a long time ago, wasn't it, Doctor? The Black Death in Europe — that was bubonic plague, right? Caused by rats with these fleas you talked about? And it killed, what? Twenty-five *million* people?"

"Yes. That's true. But today, we have certain antibiotics that can — "

"Sure. But plague is still a danger, isn't it? I mean, if it got loose, it could still kill a whole bunch of innocent folks, right?"

"Yes, that is true."

"Doctor, just a couple of more questions and we'll be done. Before there were these special antibiotics, how did folks deal with rat infestation? You know, to protect themselves against plague? What would they do if there was a bunch of these rats in a house?"

"Burn it down," the doctor said. "Fire is the only — "

"Objection! Relevancy!" the DA shouted.

"Approach the bench," the judge roared.

Veil didn't move. "Judge, is he saying that crack *isn't* a plague? Because it's my belief — and I know others share it — that the Lord is testing us with this new plague. It's killing our children, your honor. And it's sweeping across the — "

"That is *enough!*" the judge shrieked at Veil. "One more word from you, sir, and you will be joining your client in jail tonight."

"You want me to defend Leonard using sign language?" Veil asked.

A number of folks laughed.

The judge cracked his gavel a few times and, when he was done, they took Veil out in handcuffs.

(7)

When I went to visit that night, I was able to talk to both of them. Someone had brought a chess board and pieces in and they were playing. "You're crazy," I told Veil.

"Like a fuckin' fox," Leonard said. "My man here is right on the money. I mean, he *gets* it. Check."

"You moved a piece off the board," Veil said.

"Did not."

"Yeah, you did."

"Damn," Leonard said pulling the piece out from between his legs and returning it to the board. "For a man with one eye you see a lot. Still check though."

I shook my head. "Sure. Veil gets it. You, you're gonna get life by the time he's done," I said.

"Everything'll be fine," Veil said, studying the chess board. "We can always go to Plan B."

"And what's Plan B?" I asked him.

He and Leonard exchanged looks.

(8)

"The defense of *what?*" the judge yelled at Veil the next morning.

"The defense of necessity, your honor. It's right here, in Texas law. In fact, the case of *Texas v. Whitehouse* is directly on point. A man was charged with stealing water from his neighbor by constructing a si-phon-system. And he did it, all right. But it was during a drought, and if he hadn't done it, his cattle would've starved. So he had to *pay* for the water he took, and that was fair, but he didn't have to go to prison."

"And it is your position that your client *had* to burn down the crack…I mean, the occupied dwelling across the street from his house to prevent the spread of disease?"

"Exactly, your honor. Like the bubonic plague."

"Well, you're not going to argue that nonsense in my court. Go ahead and take your appeal. By the time the court even hears it, your client'll have been locked down for a good seven-eight years. That'll hold him."

(9)

Veil faced the jury, his face grim and set. He walked back and forth in front of them for a few minutes, as if getting the feel of the ground. Then he spun around and looked them in the eyes, one by one.

"You think the police can protect you from the plague? From the invasion? No, I'm not talking about aliens, or UFOs, or AIDS, now — I'm talking crack. And it's here, folks. Right here. You think it can't happen in your town? You think it's only Dallas and Houston where they grow those sort of folks? Take a look around. Even in this little town, you all lock your doors at night now, don't you? And you've had shootings right at the high school, haven't you? You see the churches as full as they used to be? No you don't. Because things are *changing,* people. The plague is coming, just like the Good Book says. Only it's not locusts, it's that crack cocaine. It's a plague, all right. And it's carried by rats, just like always. And, like we learned, there isn't but one way to turn that tide. Fire!

"Now I'm not saying my client set that fire. In fact, I'm asking you to find that he did *not* set that fire. I'm asking you to turn this good citizen, this man who cared about his community, loose. So he can be with you. That's where he belongs. He stood with you…now it's time for you to stand with him."

Veil sat down, exhausted like he'd just gone ten rounds with a rough opponent. But, the way they do trials, it's always the prosecutor who gets to throw the last punch.

And that chubby little bastard of a DA gave it his best shot, going on and on about how two wrongs don't make a right. But you could see him slip a few times. He'd make this snide reference to Leonard being black, or being gay, or just being…Leonard, I guess, and, of course that part is kind of understandable. But, exactly like Veil predicted, every time he did it, there was at least one member of the jury who didn't like it. Sure, it's easy to play on people's prejudices—and we got no shortage of *those* down this way, I know—but if there wasn't more good folks than bad, well, the Klan would've been running the state a long time ago.

The judge told the jury what the law was, and told them to go out there and come back when they were done. Everybody got up to go to lunch, but Veil didn't move. He motioned me over.

"This is going to be over with real quick, Hap," he said. "One way or the other."

"What if it's the other?"

"Plan B," he said, his face flat as a piece of slate.

(10)

The jury was out about an hour. The foreman stood up and said "Not Guilty" about two dozen times—once for every crime they had charged Leonard with.

I was hugging Leonard when Veil tapped me on the shoulder. "Leonard," he said, "you need to go over there and thank those jury people. One at a time. Sin*cere,* you understand?"

"What for?" Leonard asked.

"Because this is going to happen again," Veil said. "And maybe next time, one of the rats'll get burned."

Knowing Leonard, I couldn't argue with that. He walked over to the jury and I turned around to say something to Veil. But he was gone.

· Way Down There ·

Way Down There" is an exercise in weirdness. It's not a brain storm, though I would argue, lightly, that it does contain within it a number of philosophical and theological concepts, as if discussed by Groucho Marx in a thoughtful mood while drinking pure alcohol.

"Way Down There" may not change your life, but for better or worse, there aren't two just like it. I've always found the general view of Hell fascinating. And silly, really. And I thought, what if it was literal? In fact, what if all the hells that existed were literal? Which one applies to who? What if God is an Existentialist?

That can't be good.

My own belief is that he/she/it doesn't exist, unless one wants to call an energy form that is mindless and thoughtless and therefore unconcerned with the lives of humans, because it doesn't even know we exist, and in fact knows nothing because knowledge and intent are not factors, God. Well, go ahead.

But where did it all begin?

Has God always existed?

If there is no God, how could nothing exist and become something?

And if there is a God, how could he/she/it always be?

Seems to me, you're asking the same question, and there is no answer.

But I love the basis of religion. I love the myths. It's curious to me that when one believes in a particular myth, call it Christianity, for example, the believers think of it differently from Islam, or Greek myths, or whatever religion you want to name.

Christianity to the Christian is the real thing. The rest of that stuff, well, it's just made up, even if like Greek myths, it has people ascending to heaven via chariot.

I once had a friend give me his view of the Christian religion, and in it, God was always warring with the dark side. Light and Dark fought this constant battle with swords, the good and the bad. Dressed the way they did in ancient times.

I thought, well, why swords?

Why doesn't God move with the times?

Why would God maintain primitive devices?

Why would he have primitive dress?

Why dress at all?

And if God existed before the times of swords and these particular outfits, what did he wear then?

Skins? The old ass hanging out? The stone knife and stick?

Entwining religion with history doesn't make it any more real.

In the Old Testament only Jews were saved. In the New Testament, a Jew named Jesus forms a new branch of the Jewish faith, and later, others make it into Christianity. Peter and Saul help bring it to Gentiles.

What happened before Gentiles received it?

Did they all go to hell just because the religion didn't exist?

Did they go to hell after it existed but was denied to them?

It's a quandary, and if you want to believe on faith that it's all real, go for it.

But, there's lots of things people believe on faith.

The world is flat.

Yep. Some folks still truly believe that, and no matter what you tell them, they believe it. But, believing it, having faith, doesn't make it so.

We never landed on the moon. It's all a big hoax.

Despite oodles of evidence to the contrary, plenty of solid reasons to know we went to the moon, there are still the faithful who disbelieve.

Faith, like patriotism, being a Democrat or Republican, Liberal or Conservative, is not necessarily a virtue.

I have faith in my wife and my dog, myself and a few friends, but after that...

Still. The whole business fascinates me.

I also like comic books and pulps and cheap sf and horror movies and old style sf of the Jules Verne and H.G. Wells and Edgar Rice Burroughs variety. I also love the idea of a hollow earth, and have read much about it. I'd like to have faith this is true, but alas, we've come back to that faith business again.

Comic books can make silliness seem real. But that doesn't always translate to fiction.

I know. I've tried.

The Batman series of the sixties with Adam West was camp, but in a way, it was just like the comic stories about Batman in the fifties and sixties. But, somehow, on those brightly painted comic pages, the stories and characters didn't seem camp. They worked differently in the head.

So, we come to "Way Down There."

I'll let you be the judge.

Anyway, all of this business, comics, superheroes, religion, philosophy, the hollow earth theories, me being in a fun mood, all came together and became this.

No need to have your pocket mythology book handy.

Or your pocket theology or comparative religion book.

No need to have your pocket book of philosophers at your fingertips. Have fun.

Just don't get paint from the animation on your fingers.

And for heaven sakes, don't think too hard. You sure shouldn't need to.

· Way Down There ·

Dedicated to Warner Brothers cartoons, Chuck Jones, Tex Avery,
the pulps and comic books everywhere.

FROM THE SPECIAL ARCHIVES OF WEIRD BUT TRUE GEOGRAPHIC STORIES:

Report filed by John George Emerson under the heading "The Profundity of Subterranean Life, Demonology, and Its Influence on The Outer Regions of the Planet Earth," read aloud to the meeting of the Special Archives by John George Emerson prior to the playing on CD of the tune, "Up Jumped the Debil and He Tossed Dem Bones," by Jimmy Joe Smith and the Hurricane Hunters, followed by quotes from Professor Edgar Rice Burroughs' treatise on Subterranean Activity at The Earth's Core, and this excerpt from John Cleve Symmes, creator of the Theory of Concentric Spheres and Polar Voids: "I declare that the earth is hollow and habitable within."

The actual reports, however, are boring, so we will cut straight to the story, and it goes like this:

One day the wind picked up and blew cold around the world, causing much of the Northern Atlantic to chill over. In Scotland, sheep became wool-sicles and in barns cows dove nose forward into the dirt and didn't rise, their tails crooks of ice.

In Africa, heavy coats and ear-flap hats became the need of the day, and the Red Cross was on full-time alert delivering them by snowmobile.

It was so cold in North America, trucks with chains on their tires began driving over sheets of ice that covered the Great Lakes, or, as they quickly became known, the Great Ices. In fact, all the lakes up there went solid. Frozen fish were excavated from them with hydraulic drills and chugging back hoes, hauled off by dump truck.

These frozen fish became a standard food, considering they kept without rotting. Few crops could be grown, just a smidgen of vegetables brought up from South America, and even down south it was cold and the vegetables were small and sick and pithy as cork and the growing season was the blink of an eye.

Wind wagons were in, racing along on ski runners. Mutts went from lying about to sledding supplies and fat-ass couch potatoes over stretches of whiteness in search of food.

Air travel didn't work out so well. Had to be given up. Too much wind. There were all kinds of plane pieces in trees, dotted on mountainsides. Balloons, ultra-lights, and zeppelins weren't even considered.

In Texas, short sleeve weather disappeared, and the Miami Keys were soon invaded by icebergs pushing down from the north. People took to living on that floating ice, wrapped up and padded, spitting frost that was as chilly as a meat-lockered side of bacon. These folks became known as Floaters. They drifted on their homes of ice, putting up tent cities, building wooden floors, heating with oil squeezed from the fish they could find.

There were no real vacation spots.

Some animals went extinct. Sloths for instance. They couldn't take it. Lizards took a dive too. But polar bears multiplied. They seemed happy. As did seals and walruses and foxes and arctic wolves. Amongst those groups was much happy mating. The whales adapted. A lot of insects went belly up and it was all over for the flea, the mosquito, and the blue bottle fly. No wakes were held.

Looting was common. Store owners carried guns and used them. There were rumors of cannibalism, and a TV show featuring ways to fix mystery meat became a hit.

Years rolled one into the other, each more icy than the last. The world shivered and shook. And still that uncommon wind blew.

Eventually came the shadows.

Long, lean and wraithlike, wind-whipped and grimy, not quite flesh, not quite spirit, hooded, no coat, no shoes. They blew with the wind. Where they showed, disease popped up. Red pustules, white lesions, rips in the skin, bleeding from nose, mouth and eyes. The shadows came and went, delivering their unnamed misery like angry mailmen without vacations.

John George Emerson, the Brain, thought the answer was beneath the world. He had his reasons. He knew the best way to find out. That the only way to solve things was to drive down to the center of the earth in his '57 Chevy and set things right.

The Chevy was black with super high beams. It had been stretched. Had six doors instead of four, extra seats, and in the back, a long, long trunk with four hammocks, a magazine rack and a series of cup holders. Low ceiling back there. Watch your head.

The '57 was also wide. Much wider than the original. It had fine leather seats and a diamond shaped suicide knob about the size of a lumberjack's fist, fastened down tight with a thick metal clamp on a false cheetah skin steering wheel cover.

There was an eight speed gearshift that would allow it to climb straight up the face of a wall, do the dipsy-do over lumpy topography, float in water, dive beneath, fly short distances, though not too high, and, of course, cruise on highways.

The '57 flexed in the middle if need be. This due to the Brain's special blend of metal and rubber and a goo of his own creation. The car had tires that wouldn't go flat and they molded with the terrain when needed, worked like grippers.

Windshields and side glasses were as thick as Mike Tyson's head and could go dark when the need arose. Watertight when closed, of course. Or with the touch of a button, so clear you could hardly tell glass was there. As an added precaution, they were bulletproof.

Red, fuzzy dice with black dots hung from the rearview mirror, and the outside wing mirrors could fold in or out, controlled by buttons close to the driver, next to the steering wheel.

The lights were good, standard and infra-red. Fluids were up and the windshield wipers worked. There was a slight shimmy when it reached speeds at the max of six hundred and seventy-five.

John named the car after a scientist he had read about. He called the car the Abner Perry. A.P. for short.

Besides the car, John The Brain also had a map.

And a book with silver clasps. Much of the book was written in what his assistant Buck Shaver called deedly-bops. Hieroglyphics of a sort, but with more squiggles and slashes, and what John the Brain told Buck were some very rude passages that would give even Buck pause. And Buck had been the cuss-fight champion of Cut and Shoot, Texas.

Buck, though known for cursing, wasn't known for his math or science abilities, but, due to an accidental exposure to radiation while trying to find a cookie when he was five in his father's lab, he could twist a tire tool into a knot, bench press six hundred pounds for two hundred reps, take a blast from a .38 revolver full in the chest with no more concern than being hit by a speeding beetle. And he could wear cowboy boots for long periods of time without walking funny, even if his feet were like the feet of the ape. The rest of him was apelike as well. In fact, he appeared to be a six foot-four, two thousand pound gorilla with a large penis. Because of this special attribute, he wore a loose pair of designer boxer shorts, hearts for Valentine's Day, Santas for Christmas, multi-colors the rest of the year round. His cowboy boots were special made, quite wide. Green and blue with the shape of Texas on the boot top.

The same radiation that gave him strength and apeness knocked his I.Q. off the shelf, left only two thirds of it standing, and that two thirds wobbled from time to time.

This book John owned had been spat up by a volcano. It was inside a rock. When the rock cooled, it split open. And there it was. The book. Big enough and heavy enough to give a fella a hernia. Drop that on a duck, you could then use him to sail like a Frisbee.

John could read the book, could translate the deedly-bops because he had been Down There — not Way Down There, but down enough — and had found an ancient stone that was a key to the language in the book. A language old as language, but without all the double meanings, puns, and no "exception" rules. It was what it was, and it was more than enough. It was the guide that led to the reading of *The Book of Htrae Wolloh,* which along with *The Necronomicon,* and *The Book of Doches,* was an essential for any evil bastard's shelf. And, of course, anyone interested in evil bastards, as was John.

The book was sandwiched between thick slabs of formica. The pages were thin sheets of leather written on with an ink that appeared sometimes green and sometimes black and had a constant unpleasant aroma. Sometimes the words squirmed.

The book was how John decided he knew what to do. The book contained certain prophecies, explained there were powers beyond cable TV and missile ballistics. The book, in deedly-bops, talked of cold-making wizards, mean-spirited sprites, and disease-dropping shadows. John, using a special scanner he had designed, put the book on disk. This way, he didn't have to deal with the smell or its unwieldy construct. Could pop it in a handheld and read it.

When first the cold came, John remembered the prophecy. He had been working on understanding the book for years, and once he understood it, he believed it. But he had delayed to do anything about it. He was too busy with Andie, Buck's sister. He spent all his free time, which was minimal, dating her. Wining and dining and boinking. Talking about science, all his inventions. And boinking.

The same radiation that had made Buck strong and not too sharp, had affected her as well. She had been in the room when Buck pulled the towel on which sat the experiment.

They had crept in there together. Their father had locked the door, but they had watched and seen where he stuck the key. They got it, went in after their father's personal collection of cookies, and the accident happened.

Buck was the one who pulled it down on them. Because of it, as stated, he went dumb and strong.

Andie got the opposite end of the switch. She went real-damn-smart, grew tall and lean with golden skin. Her blue eyes turned silver with flecks of gold. Her hair was like a shoulder-length head of flame that whipped and turned and waved.

Andie was so good-looking, when supermodels saw her they cried. When men saw her they sat down. If they were sitting, they laid down. If they were lying down...Well, they cried. The really weak ones opened their flies and got it and went to work.

There was another side effect: she could crawl up flat surfaces, across the ceiling like a lizard. She could flex her body and stretch it as if it were made of rubber. John, and everyone else, called her Stretch.

John had had his own intelligence boosted through electromagnetism and some kind of oily liquid the military had invented. You had to watch that liquid, got on your hands and in your eyes it burned, worse than jalapeno juice. And heaven forbid you should scratch yourself, you know, down there. That was some heat that stuff put out.

John was brainy to begin with, and not bad looking. Women didn't cry when they saw him, but they looked twice. He was tall, broad shouldered with a heroic face. How he came about the extra stack of brains was a college experiment.

Usually, in those experiments, you ended up with sugar pills or syphilis or some kind of psychedelic color explosion head trip. But this one had worked out. John didn't know it right away, though. It was the kind of thing where he hired on to be a guinea pig, and when it was over, nothing seemed to change, so the lab technicians destroyed their notes, gave him some dough and a handshake, told him not to let the door hit him in the ass on the way out.

Three years later. Bam! He got up one morning feeling as if his brain were bigger, hotter, and full of juice. He could learn languages quick as night to day. Mathematic problems were nothing, popped them into his head like popping jujubes into his mouth, spat out the answers.

Another side effect was prehensile toes.

Andie liked that.

Being a man of science had its benefits.

Already these three and the special '57 Chevy had a rep. They had taken up crime fighting. Whipped the pure-dee-ole dog shit out of bad guys using their powers, riding the streets in the black '57, ready to rock, ready to roll.

This world freezing business, however, was a little different. That and the wraiths. You didn't whip those wraiths' asses. No, sir. They didn't have asses. You couldn't get hold of them, but they could get hold of you.

The plague part was something else. One day you're you, next day you're a giant pustule. Even the Team, as they called themselves, were scared of that stuff.

It all had to be stopped at the source.

Way Down There at the center of the world.

The secret Team Center is one cool as hell spot in the mountains. You look up, you can't see it. It's hidden from below. For that matter, it's hidden from above. Just looks like mountains and trees. Worm's eye or bird's eye, you don't see dick.

There's a road winds up there, and cars go on it, but there's a stand of trees alongside it, and they're close to the mountainside. They're made of plastic, but they look real. They feel real. They even give off a scent. Pine and oak, and sometimes cinnamon.

A press of a button from inside the mountain, or from the console of the '57, and they sink into the ground, limbs, leaves, false blue jays that squawk and flap, the whole nine yards. They do this faster than a teenage girl can answer a phone.

The '57 can ride right over where the "trees" have been, and with another click of a button, the mountain opens up, slides back like an Ali Baba thing.

Open, sesame, baby.

Once inside, the mountain closes up.

And boy is it neat in there.

Chemistry set heaven. Glowing tubes and boiling beakers, fired by Bunsen burners blowing blue flame and red licks. A throbbing, humming, nuclear powered generator that makes everything run smooth, keeps them warm during all this horrible coolness. If it were actually to turn hot, it could cool them.

Team's got their own pop-eyed dwarf who's their butler/valet, and no slow shakes at science and mathematics himself. All of his brains are natural, of course, as is the hump on his back. The cotton suit and bowler he wears are imported and tailored from London, England.

There's all manner of TV screens and videos, crime files on computer, a library and scientific doodads, and a nice little shop where you can park the '57 and work on it, if it needs it. Can't beat the tools there. Boxes of them. Stack them all together, they'd be twelve feet high.

Inside the mountain there's this jet sleigh ride on a runner. Get in that, you can ride a few miles through the mountain and come to a wall. With a touch of a button on the sleigh, the wall will part, the sleigh will stop, and you can walk inside a house to die for.

When you close up the mountain wall, you're standing in nothing but well furnished glass walls and hardwood flooring overhanging a three hundred foot drop to the river below.

Buck likes to watch down there with high-powered binoculars, sometimes a telescope, because in the summer, on boats, women will occasionally get naked.

Or used to. Now all you see is ice and wraiths and the blowing clouds, low down and gray, like cotton balls that have been used to sop up pus.

Nice place, this room. Lots of talking goes on here. Superhero plans galore. And if you want, the hunchback dwarf will fix you a sandwich and freshen your drink.

He's got a stereotypical role, the dwarf does. Right out of central casting. (Needed: One dwarf. Domestic. Must cook. Must clean. Must be helpful. Respectful. Courteous.)

So, this day we're talking about, they're inside this glass room, the whole team. The heroes. Fact is, they haven't been out in ages. Not since the wraiths and all that cold. It's not safe out there. Not even for heroes.

They're in the glass room, as they call it, and Buck is sitting in a soft chair drinking a tall glass of milk, and John and Andie are sitting on the couch, snuggling, and the dwarf, who is named Montawn, is watching them carefully, as Andie is wearing a loose blouse and no bra and he's hoping a tit will fall out.

"So you're sure about this book," Buck asks. "It knows what it's talking about?"

"Oh, yeah," John says. "Just to make sure, I used a spell in it. I called up Virgil's ghost. You know, Dante's guide?"

"I don't know," Buck said. "You and Andie, you're the brains. Montawn too, he's got more brains than me. What I got is chest hair and a dong about the length of a ball peen hammer. Frankly, maybe because I'm dumb, I don't consider this a drawback."

"Get Virgil, will you, Montawn?" John said.

Montawn went away.

"Isn't a ghost able to walk through walls and shit?" Buck said.

"Not when you summon him with a spell. I called him up last night, put him in the broom closet, told him to stay there. I was too tired to deal with him then. It was an arduous spell."

Andie grinned. "Yeah, it was a kind of anniversary for us."

"What anniversary?" Buck said.

"It's the first time since the first time," Andie said.

"Oh," Buck said. "Well, your brother dear doesn't need to hear about it."

A wraith went by the window, turned its dark, eyeless face toward them.

Andie (Stretch) shot it the finger.

It fluttered, made scootchy sounds against the glass, fluttered off leaving a spot of goo.

"Damn," Stretch said. "I hate those things."

"We're safe in here, Stretch," John said. "An artillery shell couldn't break that glass."

"I know. But I just don't like them."

"What's to like?"

Montawn came back with Virgil. Virgil was about five feet tall, wearing a white robe and sandals. He had too-black hair that smacked of cheap dye. It was cut short and combed down in front across his forehead. He looked a little bit like Moe Howard of the Three Stooges. He was carrying a lyre. He smelled like patchouli oil.

"Hello," Virgil said.

"Virgil," John said. "Please tell Buck here, and the others, about yourself."

"I am the shade of the great poet, Virgil," he said.

Montawn said, "I don't know how great you were. The Iliad and the Odyssey read better."

"Written by committee," Virgil said. "There was no blind poet Homer. Well, there was, but he didn't write it. He just took credit for everyone else's work."

"Done by committee, and still better than the Aeneid," Montawn said.

"That's enough, Montawn," John said. "I'm proud to have an autographed scroll…Thank you, Virgil…Go wash the car, Montawn."

"But, of course, sir," Montawn said, and left.

"Summarize yourself, Virgil," John said.

"I am a guide through hell," Virgil said.

"That's where we'll be going," John said. "But give us a little more."

Virgil nodded, said, "There are several levels of hell. We can sidestep a few of them, not all. But, I assure you, I will make one hell of a guide. That's a joke."

"We get you," John said.

"Lot of sinners down there," Buck said. "Am I right?"

"Of course," Virgil said.

"Then maybe there's someone down there would like the idea of a little monkey business, if you get my drift," Buck said. "Oh, now, don't sour up. I'm just joking."

"You do not joke about hell," Virgil said.

"You just did."

"I suppose I did."

"Sure you did," Buck said. "Besides. It don't matter. I'm a Baptist. After we're baptized, we can do all manner of fucking around. We're already saved, baby…It does work that way, doesn't it, Virgil? Baptists count?"

"Every religion counts."

"Even that Rastafarian business?"

"I suppose there are exceptions. I will say this. Hell is full of Methodists, so it can't be as choosy as some might think."

"Continue," John said. "And this time, Buck, no interruptions."

"Hell is a big place," Virgil said. "I have been summoned, and I should go on the record and say, against my will, to be your guide."

"How do you know English?"

"Buck," John said. "I asked you not to interrupt."

"Just this one question and I'll be quiet."

"I can do this in most any language you want, including signing for the deaf, or the use of American Indian sign language. Would you like it in song?"

"Just talk will do," John said.

Virgil looked disappointed, but he went on with it.

"To explain what's happening, there is a renegade demon who has decided to give the upper earth...Well, hell. That's not the way it's supposed to work. Up here, you get choices. Make the right ones, depending on religion, and you get a reward or a punishment. Some religions, you don't get dick.

"But, we will not get into theological matters, I'm a Jupiter man, myself. Still go by the Roman Gods, you know? But, sometimes the demons want people who do not want to be down there. Satan, believe it or not, evil as he is, is a stand-up guy. He only takes those he can trick or persuade or those who want to go down there. In other words, he leaves it up to you."

"If there are other hells, wouldn't this conflict with them?" Stretch asked.

"Could," Virgil said. "Might. There are so many parallel worlds and hells and heavens. It gets to be quite confusing. But we'll stick to the Christian hell. Actually, there are different versions of that as well, and there are overlaps. But to make it simple, hell is trying to take over the world."

"Shouldn't it be hot instead of cold?" Buck asked.

"That one seems logical, but hell is not that logical," Virgil said. "But, Satan, he abides by certain rules. Good has control unless you give yourself to Evil. Satan is up with that. However, Beelzebub and a couple other guys, they don't like this way of thinking."

"Wait a minute," Buck said. "I don't mean to interrupt — "

"Of course you do," Stretch said.

" — but isn't Beelzebub just another name for the devil?"

"People get that confused. He is actually a demon, and that is a very general way of describing him. Technically it's not accurate, but for your understanding, close enough. Excuse me, you are a gorilla, are you not?"

"Not," Buck said. "How many six foot four gorillas do you see that sit in chairs and wear boxer shots and cowboy boots?"

"Due to an accident, Buck sprouted some apelike DNA," Stretch said."

"You were telling us how Beelzebub is not the devil," John said.

"Beelzebub overthrew Satan some time back. No more Mr. Nice Guy. He wants to take over this world and move up here. Down there it's far too warm, another reason he's making it cold here by means of magic spells. Still, hell is nothing like you would think. You know, fire everywhere, people burning...Well, actually, that does go on, but it isn't like that all over. There are even people who are happy down there...though, I suppose you couldn't exactly call them people now. They are shadows, somewhere between spirit and flesh."

"Stick to the point," John said. "Now I know why the Aeneid is so windy."

"Et tu? To put it in a nutshell, Satan is under arrest and is being tortured and the world will continue to have all manner of bad things going on until he is freed, Beelzebub is disposed of, and the proper balance between good and evil is restored."

"So our mission," Buck said, "is to rescue the devil?"

"That's it on the nosey," John said.

"Guess I better change into my combat shorts," Buck said.

"We should all get on our duds," John said. "This business has gone on long enough. Now that I got the book translated, we can do something. No more time for messing around. It's time for ACTION. He pressed the intercom on the couch. "Montawn. Quit messing around out there in the garage. Come pack us a lunch. We're on our way to hell."

> *Up jump the debil*
> *and go boo-boo-boo*
> *Lawd! screams the bad and the*
> *innocent too.*
> *Look here, debil says to all dem foks*
> *Gonna cast duh bones, see who*
> *gonna get the pokes*

Jimmy Joe Smith and The Hurricane Hunters

The super long, super wide '57's ultra-generator buzzed like a super bee. Something about the sound of it, way it throbbed and vibrated the chassis, way it felt when you put your hand on the automobile, always gave Buck the sensation of needing to pee.

He thought he might spend the entire trip on the toilet with that buzzing going on. But he knew in reality, after one good trip to the crapper he'd be all right. It was just the psychology of it.

And he never got used to John calling their ride a '57 Chevy. It only vaguely resembled the Chevy from which it was formed. He loaded in an ice chest Montawn handed him while Stretch and John loaded up the back and prepared the chemical toilet.

Virgil was lounging near the great television set, strumming his lyre.

"You could help us," Buck said.

"Not my department," Virgil said. "You want a guide through hell, a little song, a poem, I can help you out. I don't do luggage. You got a dwarf, use him."

"Ungrateful," Buck said.

"For what?" Virgil said. "I'm not getting paid. I'm having to respond to a spell. Tell him, John."

"That's right," John said, pushing a suitcase into a spot beneath a seat.

"You know, it's Good Friday. Last time I did work on Good Friday, it was for Dante Alighieri. He wrote a good account of it, though I don't suppose you've read it, have you, Ape Man? I doubt you'd read anything without pictures, and they would have to be of naked women, am I right?"

"I don't like they way you talk," Buck said.

"I don't like your looks," Virgil said.

"I ought to tie you in a knot."

"Hey, I'm a ghost. You can't hurt a ghost."

"You look solid to me."

"Well, I suppose I am. For now. The spell, you know. But you don't want to hurt the guide. That wouldn't be good. Tell him, John."

"That wouldn't be good," John said.

Soon they were loaded and in the car, Buck at the wheel. Buck didn't like the car much, but he could drive it better than any of them. He gave it the gas, and away they went, out of the hideaway, out there in the world.

The car went fast and it went through cold and it went through dark and wraiths flittered by it and smashed against it, went SPLAT, like big black bugs, and still the car rolled on.

It darted into the Rockies, a hidden crevasse its goal. A crevasse that led to the center of the earth.

John knew this because of scientific articles written by Edgar Rice Burroughs and John Uri Lloyd's account of a visit to the underworld. As well as the works of Dante, and Arne Saknussemm.

He had studied them, deduced by all manner of math and geology, and just plain guessing, that there was a crevasse in this spot, and that it was in fact a path that led to the center of the earth, and hell.

So they inched down the sides of the mountain. The car hung to the earth like a spider. They went between the trees and rocks, and the car flexed around them, eased about like a weasel, and went

down,
way
down
there.
Over
all
manner
of
BUMPS
and HUMPS
and realtightsqueezes.
After the initial twistsandturnsand
d
r
o
p
s,

they came to a wide tunnel with polished walls, and their speedpickeduprealgoddamnquick, and soon they were cruising and Virgil was playing his harp, giving them a song of his own.

Jesus was a tough guy.
Though it ain't well known.
When they nailed him to the cross
you know he got a bone?
Jesus was a tough guy.
Though it ain't well known.
Bitch slapped money changers on the temple stones.
Intimidated loaves and fishes till they multiplied.
Fucked Mary Magdalene
It's in the book implied.

Jesus was a tough guy,
though it ain't well known.
When they nailed him to the cross
you know he got a bone.
Gave him wine and vinegar,
stuck him with a spear.
He said, oh hell that hurt,
cut a fart and was out of here.

"Perhaps something a little more melodious and sweet?" Stretch
said. "Less sacrilegious."

"Sacrilegious?" Virgil said, strumming his lyre a few notes. "Only
if that's your religion. How about a song about love? Looking at you,
I think of love."

"Sure, love is good," Stretch said.

"All right, here we go:

Knew a gal named Alice.
Came from some place roun' Dallas.
Wore her hair in a bouffant way
stacked up high as a bale of hay.
I said Alice, suck my phallus,
this pleasure she denied
So I offered her another, though it
hurt my pride.
She said, you ain't so hot, not from what I see.
Not a thing that you done offered, really appeals to me.
Ooooh, baby, ooooh, baby, ain't nothing you got good.
(Brief instrumental interlude on the lyre using a Coke
bottle slide.)
I said now, baby, you know that done a lie.
Way I can love you, will make a kitty cry.
Oh, yeah, pretty baby.
It's true to the bone.
Bend over, Alice, honey,
and I'll drive you home.
Yeah, baby, I'll drive you home."

"That's enough," Stretch said. "That's not love. That's lust. And it
sounds…Well, fucked up. Sing something in Greek. Sing the same songs
if you must, but in Greek. At least I won't know what you're saying."

"I kind of like those tunes," said Buck with a shift of gears. "Makes drivin' more of a pleasure."

"You would like them," Stretch said. "Virgil. In Greek. Got me?"

"Anything for you, fair lady. Actually, I thought that last little ditty was catchy."

"What I think," John said, "is you resent being called up as a guide and are trying to make us uncomfortable so I'll get irritated and send you back to where you came from."

"I thought of that," Virgil said, "but actually, now that Satan is no longer in command, I'm not quite the favorite I once was in that section of hell. Before, I had free rein everywhere. This new guy, this Beelzebub, he's got no sense of humor and doesn't like music."

"Maybe it's your music he doesn't like," Stretch said.

"I suggest we put in a CD," John said. "Give you a rest, Virg."

John flicked one from a CD box, stuck it into the player, hit a button. Jimmy Dale Gilmore began singing "Red Chevrolet."

Virgil was angry at first, but pretty soon, he too was tapping his foot.

Finally, the song came to an end.

John said, "This is as far as I been down."

"That was before the team, I take it?" Virgil said. "The time you went down before, I mean."

John nodded. "I wrote about it.[1] It's also been put on CD with a bad actor reading it. But this is nowhere deep as we have to go."

"You must go beyond deep," Virgil said. "At a certain point, you go cosmic. Inside, way down, the interior shifts and all the worlds overlap one another. Like small hoops inside larger hoops inside larger hoops, and so on. Then there are tunnels."

"What exactly does that mean?" Stretch said.

"The best way to explain it," Virgil said, "is, you'll see."

"I'm putting the pedal to the metal, folks," Buck said, and he geared and geared, and the car screamed and moaned.

"Yee-ha," Virgil said. "Down we go."

Abandon All Hope, Ye Who Enter Here

Dante's INFERNO

---

1. See "The Adventure of the Serpent Man" in STARTLING TALES: Volume 2, Number 17. (One page was misprinted and was corrected in the following issue, Volume 2, 18.)

The tunnel widened and the walls glowed with phosphorescent light and made the inside of the Chevy green as rank cheese. And it grew warm in the car, drip-sweat warm, and John said, "Crank up the air conditioner. It's on nuclear pellets. We need to, we can chill it in here enough to hang meat."

"Well, in the immortal words of someone," Virgil said, "'Hell be a hot muthafucka.' So, you may not be hanging all that much meat."

"Well," Buck said. "Personally, me, I can always hang meat."

"How gauche," Stretch said.

Buck flicked the conditioner on. Pretty soon it was cool and the sweat dried. And—

—DOWN

they

went.

ZIIIIIIIIIIIIIIIIIIIIIIIIIIP

AND

D

R

O

P, and they're all thinking (except Virgil, well, Buck isn't thinking much either): Where's bottom?

Now, swelling up from the floor, jutting out of the walls, there were flames. They licked the Chevy like a treat, but all it did was boil a bit of paint, puff it up in bubbles. That Chevy, it was well-built and well-painted.

The Chevy kept going. Buck flipped some switches. Put the car on auto pilot and feel-along-mode. That way, it could probe its way along the rocks, the tires molding and pulling the machine forward. Any fancy maneuvering, well, that had to be done by hand.

Way it was now, with the flames and all, thick as they were, red as they were, well, Buck couldn't see to do any fancy stuff anyway. Therefore, the autopilot.

As they continued, the flames grew thinner, and they saw along the cavernous walls, on narrow trails, naked men and women. They were sweaty and dirty, but didn't look any worse for wear. Buck liked looking at some of the women. When the hell folks saw the car, they waved.

Dropping another twenty miles, they saw men and women hanging from flaming chains by their eyelids, breasts, and genitals.

"How come they're like this?" Butch asked. "I mean, the ones above, they got it different. Easier, it seems."

"The ones above, on the trails, they're minor sinners," Virgil said. "They may even leave someday, take a ride up to the cool cloud place. Things they did, cheat on tests, lie to friends, that kind of stuff, it doesn't doom them for long. The ones hanging, they were greater sinners. They won't be leaving."

"But what did they do?" Butch asked.

"Wore white after Labor Day."

"What?"

"A joke. I don't know. Various things. Adultery. Rape. Incest."

"Adultery is a hell offense?" Stretch asked.

"Well, Bill Clinton got out of it. It's not entirely fair, way it works. But some people, they can talk their way out of almost anything."

"Richard Nixon?"

"Gets along with the boss. Or did. I don't know now. Boss isn't the boss anymore. But before the overthrow, Dick had it pretty cushy. Had a chair right up there by Satan himself. That Dick, what a cutup. Always with the jokes."

"Dick Nixon?" John said. "The ex-president. The crook. Jokes? I've seen vids of him. I've seen documentaries. Cutup? He didn't look to have a sense of humor."

"Oh yeah. Down here Tricky Dicky can be himself, and he's quite the jokester. One of my favorites of his is: How many Democrats does it take to roof a house?"

"I'll bite," Stretch said. "How many?"

"About twelve, if you slice them real thin."

Virgil began to hoot.

"Hey," Buck said, flipping off the autopilot, taking the wheel, laughing a bit, "That's funny. I like that. That ain't bad."

> *Pitchfork's hot,*
> *pointy too.*
> *When the Debil poke it quick*
> *it stick in you.*
> *Oh, up jump the Debil, and he's*
> *feelin' fine.*
> *Lawd screams the bad*
> *and the innocent kind.*
> *Don't do it, Debil, we beg of you*

But, dat ole Debil, he go
boo, boo, boo —

Jimmy Joe Smith and The Hurricane Hunters

They went down, level after level, through flames and darkness. Sometimes one or two slept. One drove. And way up above, on the surface, the wind blew hard and the air stayed cold. And John, he remembered what he had read in the book. The big heavy book of bad things he had found down here.

Remembering made him toss. Made him moan. Up there, it was bad now, but it was going to get worse, and in time, it would be so bad that bad or good was no longer significant.

The end of the world you could call it.

That's what it was.

No. Worse than that.

What it was, was the end of the universe.

The end of…well…The End.

Down there, even in their air-conditioned car, it was warm. Towels were passed around to wipe sweaty faces. And they drove on.

The team came to places where it was clear of fire and the walls were lit with phosphorescence. And at each level of descent there was some horror or curiosity.

This is some of what they saw:

bodies on fire and mouths open in screams the team could not hear inside the comfort of the '57;

bodies hanging by razor wire and little red imps with little sharp pitchforks, poking at skin that was forever festered with wounds, boiling with pus;

pots containing men and women, boiling in oil;

bodies on racks where demons with sharp knives peeled the skin away from victims in bloody, dripping strips (instantly to grow back again for a replay);

cats being beat and flayed and mashed, which prompted Ape Man Buck to say:

"I don't see any dogs."

"Oh, no," Virgil said. "Dogs don't go to hell. Even the bad ones. That isn't right. Nor children under twelve. No matter what they've done."

"What did the cats do?"

"They're cats."

They came to a place where a man was tied to a stone and a large piano was being cranked up and dropped on him repeatedly.

"What a weird punishment," Stretch said.

"Oh, that's Barry Manilow. Crimes against music."

"All right," Stretch said. "I can see that."

The dark tunnel curved and Buck took them around it fast and furious, causing their seat belts to snap tight. As they went, John said, "Question. Hitler?"

"Beelzebub's butt-hole buddy," Virgil said. "Adolph's asshole is as big as a dinner platter, and he's in good with the man."

"You mean…?" Buck asked.

"That's right," Virgil said. "He's Beezel's bitch."

"My guess is, 'cause of that," Buck said, "Hitler got to keep the mustache."

"Oh, yeah," Virgil said.

The tunnel leveled and widened and there were many forks.

"Which one do we take?" John asked.

"They lead to all the different hells of the different religions, different beliefs. That little tunnel over there. That's a hell one man believes in. He believes in it so strong, it has come to exist. He's pretty unique, that man. He's the only one that's got his own tunnel."

"Who is he?"

"You wouldn't know him. Just a guy. But he has a great imagination. You want the tunnel in the middle."

"Is it in the middle because it's the most important?" Stretch asked.

"No. The middle leads to several major religions. Once, way back, Hades was in the middle."

"Isn't hell Hades?" Stretch asked. "I'm still confused on all this."

"Yes, and no. Hades is my version of hell. It's the one I believe in. I'm an ancient Roman guy, you know."

"But don't you believe in them all?"

"I do. Because I am a guide. I don't live in hell. I just tour the dead about. Some to stay permanently, some in an astral state, just taking the tour. But for me, the one that is most real is the one most ingrained in my earthly consciousness. That's the same for you. The one in the middle comes closer to that. It's not exactly what you suspect, but there are connections."

"What about Muslim hell?" John asked.

"Mormons?" Stretch said.

"They all overlap," Virgil said. "Oscar Ziegler said: 'There are as many afterlives as there are caverns in the earth, and each one is a unique ecology, godless and strange.' He was right."

"I've got a question," John said. "Atheists? Do they automatically go to hell?"

"They just die. They get their wish. They aren't punished or rewarded."

"I'll be damned," John said. "Agnostics?"

"They have to roll the dice."

"Dice?"

"Yeah, and sometimes the game is crooked. But that's how it works. They go to a waiting room, watch a little TV, nothing on there but game shows and a constant rerun of THE POSTMAN. Death shows up, gives them the dice, and they roll."

"Death?" Stretch said. "In a black robe? All bony? And he gives you dice?"

"Sometimes he wears a hat," Virgil said. "Pork pie. And leisure suits from the seventies. He is bony though. And yes, he has dice."

"That's different than I thought," John said.

"I thought Satan and Death were the same," Stretch said.

"No," Virgil said. "Death is a subcontractor."

"So, hey diddle diddle, right up the middle," Buck said.

The car jetted toward the tunnel and was sucked in. It was sucked in so fast it was no longer touching ground. That was okay. The car could fly. Buck flipped a switch and along they went. They came to a cavern so vast it was a world. A world of fire. There was a black boiling sun above it all, and out of the blackness licked red flames, and in spite of the blackness, the world below was more than well lit. It was overlit. Everything appeared red and orange and yellow and tarnished gold, and shadows, creepier than the wraiths topside, flowed about like malignant oil spills.

There were rocks and ledges and valleys of fire, bodies boiling in lava, screams and wails, razors blades blown on the wind like butterflies, cutting at men and women running like deer.

"Park it here," Virgil said.

They were no longer flying, but were riding along a ledge, easy as a goat, when Virgil pointed at a cavern. There were cars in there. In fact, it was a garage. One car was huge and black and looked somewhat like an old Cadillac, but wasn't. It was longer and wider than a Caddy.

There were other cars there as well. None of them identifiable, except for a De Lorean.

Buck whipped in next to the big black car and jerked the Chevy in park.

"Who do those belong to?" John asked.

"Satan," Virgil said. "Or did. I guess Beelzebub now."

"Should we be sneakier?" Stretch asked.

"They are way under here. They don't like it hot."

"I thought they were devils, demons," Stretch said.

"Oh, they run the place," Virgil said. "But where they are, it's very different. Comfy, in fact. Warm by earthly standards, I suppose. But quite bearable. No worse than Texas. And in the offices, private quarters, cool, almost arctic cool."

"Course," John said, "you know what General Sherman said. He said if he owned Hell and Texas, he'd live in Hell and rent out Texas."

"Well, he'd be wrong," Virgil said. "We park the car here, in the garage, no one will probably notice. We can go on foot from this point."

"But why?" Buck asked. "We got the car."

"Well, the car has done well," Virgil said. "But it can't go where we need to go. Didn't John tell you?"

"No, I didn't," John said. "But now I am. That's why we brought the gear, team. Let's break it out and go. And, of course, I've got the Book. On disk."

Now, unknown and fearful dangers we were about to encounter.

JOURNEY TO THE CENTRE OF THE EARTH by Jules Verne

Got air-conditioned body suits, miner hats with straps and lights, grappling hooks and ropes and pulleys, pegs and mountain picks, a six-day supply of food for four, a handheld computer with disks of information, including a copy of the Book, toilet paper, combs, a mirror, bottles of water, a canteen, all in fifty-pound packs strapped to their backs. And in Buck's pack, four to five girlie magazines. BOOBS AND BUTTS, BUTTS AND BOOBS, TITS AND ASS, ASS AND TITS, PENTHOUSE.

And when the packs were on their backs, Virgil led them to a hole in the floor of the garage. Not a wide hole, just enough for folks with packs, but it was a deep hole, dropped way the hell down, so to speak, and there was a hot strong wind blowing up through the hole, and down there, you could hear screams and sounds that were beyond the human voice. And it stank a little.

Virgil said, "When the wind dies. Just leap in. There's a downdraft that will carry us."

Stretch removed her pack, and stretched. Her elasto-plastic suit stretched with her. She stretched and stuck her elongated neck and head and upper body down the hole.

Stretch popped back out of the hole, compressed back to normal, slipped on her pack, said, "Man, it stinks down there."

"Even if there's a wind," Buck said, "won't it still drop us fast enough to go splat?"

"No," Virgil said. "It'll float us down. It'll be like cushions under our feet. It blows up for awhile, then it drops down…There. It's dying. Jump!"

And in leaped Virgil, followed by Stretch and John and Buck.

On the way down, Virgil said, "I like this part."

They went for miles and miles. Buck even had time to take a candy bar out of his pocket and eat it. He also scratched his ape head and ate a few fleas. Finally the wind began to die, and just as worry set in, it lowered them on a narrow ledge. Looking over the ledge, all you could see was darkness. Behind them was a narrow cavern. The ledge was littered with dark piles of stinking refuse.

"We'll have to step in quick-like, before the wind reverses and carries us back up. It'll snap us off this ledge like a sheet of paper if we're not careful. Got to watch the backdraft. You don't, up you'll go, through the hole."

"We don't want to ride it down anymore?" Stretch said.

"There's not much ride left. Dies out just below us. Then up it blows again. Come on, we're on foot now. And once we're in the cavern, we have to start climbing down. Just walking at first. Then the gear."

Just as they managed themselves inside the cavern, the wind blew back, burst up, warm and foul-smelling.

"Wow," Stretch said. "That stinks worse than before."

"Sometimes the wind catches more of the sewer smell."

"Sewer smell?" Stretch asked.

"Well, that hole is Satan's shitter," Virgil said.

"He don't have plumbing?" Buck said.

"He's modern in some ways, but there are some throwbacks."

"That's what's on the ledge, I take it," John said. "Satan mess."

"Correct," Virgil said.

"Man, if his ass fits over that hole," Buck said, "he must be some size."

"He's a big boy," Virgil said.

"Then I guess the De Lorean isn't his," Stretch said.

"Nixon's."

From there the going got rough. No car to ride in. No air to ride on. It was assholes and elbows, climbing down into heat and steam.

"I don't understand how all this works," Stretch said as they went. "These people have bodies. How do their bodies get here? Bodies rot."

"They are made flesh again," Virgil said. "Their spirits are made solid. Souls, if you prefer. That way, they can suffer the physical pain, but not die, due to the power of the soul. Sometimes they come here young, sometimes old. As long as they are contained in hell, a physical body will survive, and survive, but it will feel all the pain of damnation. American Indians, at least some, they have a hell where you come here the way you died. That's why they often mutilated bodies after combat. Wanted to send their foes to the other world without parts of themselves. If a person was killed and mutilated and was of another religion, it had no effect."

"But if we go to this hell," Butch said, "this Christian hell, how will that solve the problem upstairs considering there are all these other hells?"

"This is the one we want. This is the one causing all the trouble. Sometimes it's one of the others, but now, it's this one. The Christian branch of hell, in all its divisions."

"How come you know so much about all the hells?" Butch asked.

"I entertain in most of them," Virgil said. "Me and Woody Guthrie and a few others. We're troubadours. We get to leave when we want. The individual hells. But really, there's no place to go. I'm glad you called me up. It's given me a change of pace."

"Why not heaven?" Stretch asked. "Why can't you go there?"

"Well, unlike some," Virgil said, "me and Woody, we got a job. Various Gods got their heads together, decided we should be entertainers. We can occasionally visit heaven or earth, especially if we're under a spell, but it's not our domain. Your God and Satan are mostly about choices. But now and then, they violate their own rules. Everyone likes a little music, so, we're on tap."

"Why would they want to make people in hell happy?" Stretch asked.

"I assume they are making the rulers of hell happy," John said.

"You assume right," Virgil said, "though now and then I play a tune for the masses. Not supposed to. Good deed and all."

"Good for you," Stretch said.

"Remember this, you might see someone you want to help along the way," Virgil said. "But most of the people here belong here. Now and then there's a mistake, but not often. Bookkeeping is not what it used to be throughout the hells. So many souls, you know. But don't help. Got me?"

Everyone agreed.

Climbing down became more difficult and the equipment came out and the talk stopped. They used picks and ropes and mountain climbing stuff and such to lower themselves farther down into the darkness. It grew so dark, without the fire and phosphorescence and all, it became necessary for them to put on their miner caps and flick on the lights.

Along the way, impaled on spikes in the shadows, identified by their moans and screams, they passed a series of politicians, mostly Republicans and political radio show hosts.

The impaled souls asked for help.

The group kept going.

After hours of descent, they stopped to rest in a cavern. It was warm in the cavern and there was lots of steam, but it wasn't too uncomfortable. In fact, it made them drowsy.

They ate and slept. When they awoke, they continued on, using the ropes and the equipment.

But then, there was an accident.

Buck slipped. He put a peg in wrong, it came loose, and he fell, and when he fell, the safety line, which was attached to his companions, caught him. He hung in midair as the others held their spots and supported his weight.

Stretch stretched. She bent over backwards, her whole body went down past John and Virgil to where Buck hung in the air, thrashing his ape arms.

She pushed up under and behind him and tried to lift him. He was a little too heavy. John began to pull on the rope as Stretch pushed. Virgil just remained still, clinging to his place on the rock wall.

Finally they pushed and pulled Buck up. Then they all climbed up a piece, sat on the a ledge above them, and rested.

"Man," Buck said, scratching the fur on his head. "That was close."

"I'll say," Stretch said. "You okay, brother?"

"I am. Hey, you won't believe what I saw. When I fell, I saw something really strange."

"We're in hell," John said. "What do you expect?"

"No. This was strange in a different way. When we go back down, you ought to see it. It's in a cavern, directly below us. That's how I got messed up. I put a foot out and it went into a cave. I sort of, well, panicked, grabbed at my peg, and instead of hanging to it, pulled it out. When I dropped, turned upside down, my light shown in there, and I saw it."

"What?" John asked.

"I don't know. But I think we should take a look. Are you guys having flea trouble? I mean, is hell full of fleas, Virgil?"

"Parts of it are, in fact," Virgil said. "But these fleas, you brought them with you. They belong to you."

"Whatever," Buck said. "But you guys, you got to see what I saw."

"This is not a sightseeing tour," John said. "Upstairs is going through a real mess. We got to find Satan, cut him loose, let him make things right again."

"All right," Buck said. "But I think you ought to look."

The worked their way down on the ropes and swung into the cave and found what Buck had seen.

A large clay shape in the image of a man lying face up.

"My goodness," John said. "It looks like—"

"It is," Virgil said.

"Is what?" Buck said.

"The Golem," John said.

"I thought it was a myth," Stretch said.

"Oh, no," Virgil said. "It is quite real. But I'm surprised to find it here."

The Golem was large, made of dark clay, and its features were cut into it in a crude manner. A line for a mouth, circles for eyes. No nose. No ears. A smudge on the forehead. No penis; it was as smooth down there as a Barbie doll. It had fingers like frankfurters, thick hands, chunky arms, a barrel body and legs like oaks, feet that were wide and flat, stubby toes. There was a pile of mud above its head and the pile went up in a thick dried line, up into the darkness of a tunnel.

Virgil leaned forward, looked up the tunnel. He had been given a lighted helmet, same as the others, and after a moment of looking up there, he said, "My guess is, way above us, is the city of Prague. And our friend here came down on a mud slide."

"And why would you guess that?" Buck asked.

"The Golem was kept there," John said. "In Prague."

"And who is the Golem?" Buck asked. "I still don't get it."

"The word is Hebrew," John said. "It means unformed mass."

"Or fetus," Virgil said. "There may have been more than one Golem, but the one that is for sure is the one created by Rabbi Low, in what you call the sixteenth century."

"And what makes it so famous, other than being ugly?" Buck said.

"To simplify the story, it was made for vengeance," John said.

"Then later hidden away," Virgil said. "In Prague. Until needed again. See the smudge on its forehead. A word in Hebrew was marked there in the clay. That's what brought it to life. When it was no longer needed, the mark was rubbed out."

"No shit," Buck said.

"No shit," Virgil said.

"It might be handy," John said.

"True," Virgil said.

"The word is 'Emet,'" John said. "Meaning truth. Am I right?"

"You are," Virgil said. He leaned forward, and examined the Golem's forehead. "Water," he said.

John provided some from his canteen, pouring it gently on the Golem's head.

"It's still not soft enough," Virgil said. "Loan me a knife."

John did. Virgil cut crudely into the Golem's forehead the Hebrew word "Emet."

Immediately the Golem's circle eyes filled with light and its mouth moved from side to side as if it were tasting a sour persimmon. Its great chest heaved. It made a sound like thick goo gurgling down a drain.

"Commands must be simple," Virgil said. "The Golem is very literal."

"Stand," said Virgil, and the Golem stood. Its clay body made a cracking sound and thin lines ran all through the body like veins.

"Wow," said Buck. "That sonofagun must be…What, eight feet tall?"

"More like nine," Stretch said.

"How do you think it got here?" John asked Virgil.

"My guess is, without anyone knowing it, its hiding place eroded some century or two ago and it began a slow slide down to hell on a trail of sometimes dry, sometimes slick mud. That's my guess. It has been sliding this way for centuries. The mud, perhaps made wet by a water leak in the synagog, must have loosened the ground beneath it. Underneath was a natural tunnel, and in it went. With the Golem's hiding place in the synagog long forgotten — they've been looking for him for centuries, you know — the Golem is lost without being known to be lost. It's down here in hell."

"Cool," Buck said. "But I have a feeling it isn't going to climb down so good."

"I don't think we need to climb down any more," Virgil said. "I haven't been in this tunnel, but I know this vicinity well. This most likely leads to where we need to go. The underground River Styx."

"Isn't that in a different mythology than the one we need?" Stretch asked.

"The River Styx runs through all the mythologies," Virgil. "It's the sewer system. Where do you think Satan's bowel movement goes after he drops it through the hole up there? The stuff that misses the ledge."

"Yuk," Stretch said.

"I still think," Buck said, "if you're Satan, got all those powers, you ought to put in some real plumbing. Something you can flush."

"If all works out," John said, "you might have an opportunity to discuss it with him."

The three of the Earth, Virgil the Guide, and the man made of clay began to walk. They went deeper into the cave, and soon it widened and inclined. After a while, Buck said, "Golem, pick me up and carry me."

The Golem turned, grabbed Buck by the head and lifted him, started walking.

"Put me down!" Buck said, and the Golem dropped him.

Buck, lying on the ground, rubbed his hairy neck. "Damn," he said.

Virgil said: "As I was saying. He takes things literally."

The Dark Design had no pattern.

From THE DARK DESIGN by Philip José Farmer

When they started out again, Buck looked down, and there on the ground, he saw a quarter.

"Look here, a bit of luck," he said, and put it in his pocket.

"Let me see that," Virgil said.

Buck produced it.

"Look close," Virgil said.

Buck looked. "Hey, whose head is that?"

"It's imprinted with Satan's head," Virgil said.

"Wow," Buck said. "He is one ugly dude. But, hey, it'll spend down here, won't it? I mean, surely they got a concession stand."

"Not while Beelzebub is in control," Virgil said. "Right now, it's like Confederate money. Well, maybe not. Not in other sections. It is silver."

"What would you buy here anyway?" Stretch said.

"Ice water," Buck said.

"Well, actually," Virgil said, "sometimes Satan does favors. He does allow a bit of money to be earned, in a fashion. And spent at the General Store. Ice water is popular. Most, however, well, they never get a break."

"Hell is nothing like what I expected," Stretch said.

"It's just like life," Virgil said. "That's what makes it scary."

In time the great tunnel emptied out into a larger cavern, the walls of which were lit up with phosphorescence. A wide dark river ran through the center of the cavern and twisted between great rock walls and out of sight, enveloped by darkness.

Rows and rows of people, and things unidentifiable, stood on the bank of dirt and stone, looking out at the brown churning water.

"Who are they?" Stretch asked.

"Souls and demons waiting to take the trip," Virgil said. "They made the trip here, same as we did, only slower. Some have been traveling for centuries. They're waiting on Charon."

"I thought we were in Christian hell," John said. "There's no Charon."

Virgil shook his head. "Like I said, this river winds through all the hells. Some demons just use it for travel, when they're on vacation, want to visit different sections of hell."

"They get vacations?" Stretch said.

"If they work for one of the hells," Virgil said. "They get paid vacations. Also, a hundred sick days a century, paid. Lot of other health benefits as well. Also, now and then, visitors from Heaven take the tour. Makes them feel superior."

"So, we want Charon and his boat?" John said.

"Exactly," Virgil said.

"We could swim across," Buck said.

"Well, you, John and Stretch might try it," Virgil said. "Stretch could stretch across it, pop on over to the other side. You and John might even swim it, strong as you are. But even with your strength, I don't think so. Rapids. Sharp rocks in spots. And it's deep. And, it's the sewer. That's why it's brown…and lumpy."

"Oh, my," Stretch said.

"And even if you could swim it, I couldn't. I'm not up to that. I don't have those kinds of powers. I'm very limited, even more so when I'm under your sway, your magic. As for Golem, well, it'd sink like…like a lot of clay."

"Look," Buck said.

Out of the dark end of the cavern came a great, black, paddle wheel boat. It was large, and on the deck, at the wheel, was a shape in black.

As the boat paddled forward, mixing turds in the water like a buttermilk churn, they saw that the shape was a hooded robe with a skeletal face in it. Bony hands held the wheel.

"We better hustle on down closer to where it docks," Virgil said.

They went down and got in line behind some very strange looking people. Virgil said, "Oh, shit."

"What?" John said.

"We have to pay Charon to take the ride."

"Hey, I got that devil's quarter."

"It's silver," Virgil said. "Charon doesn't care what kind of silver. He'd take silver spoons, you had them."

"And I'm the one's supposed to be stupid," Buck said. "I knew that quarter would come in handy."

"Will it work for all of us?" John asked.

"Well, maybe you could leave him something else," Virgil said. "Hey, you have a spare flashlight?"

"I do." John said. "A pen light."

"He might like that."

The boat paddled up to a wooden dock and stopped. The dock hadn't been there a moment before.

A plank, unassisted, jammed out of the side of the boat. Charon locked the wheel with a chain, came down the ramp and stood on the dock. He took coins of bronze and silver as the line entered onto the boat. When it came to Buck, he gave Charon the devil's quarter. Charon's face, though skeletal, had features, as if the bones were made of rubber. He bit the coin Buck offered him, jerked a bony thumb over his shoulder, and Buck boarded.

"Charon," Virgil said. "Hey, man, how's the old bone hanging. So to speak. We don't all have silver — "

Charon raised his arm quickly and one bony finger poked out of his robe. Poked in the direction they had come.

"No. No. Now listen. We got something really cool. A light. A little light. A pen light. Wouldn't you like that? Look, I know three of the group here aren't dead. And one is, well, neither dead nor alive. It's clay. But, hey, a pen light. Think about it."

Charon held up three fingers.

"He'll let three of us on," Virgil said.

"Then we leave the Golem," John said.

"We might need him later," Virgil said. "We'll need all of us."

Virgil looked back at Charon.

"What else," Virgil said. "We got packs full of things here."

Charon shook his head, bared his teeth, leaned forward, put his mouth near Virgil's ear.

"Oh," Virgil said.

After a moment, Virgil turned to John and Stretch. "Well, he will let us on, but…Well…"

"What?" Stretch said.

"You got to show him your tits."

"For heaven's sake," Stretch said. "The lecher."

"He does work in hell," Virgil said.

Stretch sighed. "Very well. You two go on board. Don't look back…Not that you haven't seen it all before, John, but it's undignified enough."

"I don't like it," John said.

"No time to get prudish," Stretch said.

Virgil took the pen light from John and gave it to Charon. It disappeared inside Charon's robe. John, grumbling, went on board, Virgil behind him. When the Golem stepped on board, the boat lowered a full foot in the water.

"All right," Stretch said, unfastening her air-conditioned body suit, lowering it over her shoulders. "Does this work for you?"

Charon stuck his bony hand in his mouth and bit it.

After a moment of ogling, he stepped aside and poked his bony finger at the boat.

Stretch readjusted herself, stepped on board.

"I really hate that guy," John said.

A three-headed dog came out of the cabin and went over and stood by Charon as he unchained the wheel. Steam charged out of the pipes, and the paddle wheel began to turn, thrashing the turd-water. The boat rolled forward.

John said, "Isn't that Cerberus?"

"Yep, that's him," Virgil said.

"I thought he guarded the entrance to the underworld."

"Did you see him as we went down?"

"Well, no."

"Then he doesn't. He's actually quite tame. Or, pretty tame. He used to do that some, guard the opening, but he's such a favorite of everyone, he just wanders around down here now. I mean, why guard the opening? People are dying to get in."

"You're such a comedian," Buck said.

"I did do a little stand up. I was all right. Again, why guard the place? Satan always says: 'Everyone's welcome.' He's the only dog down here. Like I said, dogs don't go to hell. He's free to leave at any time. He likes it here. Lately, Cerberus spends a lot of time on board with Charon. He likes the boat ride, I guess."

Paddle like a motherfucker
do what you will.
No matter how you do,
you go there still.

Jimmy Joe Smith and the Hurricane Hunters

The heroes and the souls churned down the great river and as they went, it widened. Soon they were on an inland sea. The brown water stretched beneath the phosphorescent kingdom as far as the eye could see.

"I'm getting seasick," Buck said.

"I have some dramamine," Stretch said, dug around in her pack till she found it.

Buck took it and they churned on.

And on.

And on.

And on.

They came to a place where the river was on fire, and they went right through that. John, Buck, and Stretch had to go inside because they were flesh and not spirit of flesh, and they watched through the glass as the boat went through the flames.

The inferno wrapped around Virgil, Charon, Cerberus, the Golem, and the others. A few jerked back in fear, but after a moment, stood up, bathing in it, realizing they were not to be consumed.

"If the fire doesn't hurt these souls," Stretch said, "what's the punishment?"

"I think it hurts when the powers that be are ready to punish them," John said. "That's when they crank up the juice. Right now, those powers are just scaring them. Showing them Charon, all dark and spooky, the river of shit, the fire on the river. They will be sorted out later, sent to where they need to go."

"It's scaring me," Buck said.

"Yeah, me too," John said. "Thing that surprises me is what Virgil said about vacationers from Heaven. That's hard to believe."

John was tapped on the shoulder. "That would be us."

He turned to see a man, a woman, and a young girl clumped up together. "Car wreck got us. On our way to church. We were very pious. We're from up there, you know. Way Up There. But, we thought we'd see how the other half lives. Well, actually, it's quite a bit more than half down here. But here we are. Super really. Quite the vacation. Just thought I'd let you know. Didn't mean to eavesdrop."

"No problem," John said. "Thanks."

After some time — though time was hard to judge, and in fact non-existent now — the boat paddled toward shore. The fire on the river had long gone out, and when they arrived at the shore, there were naked bodies writhing in the mud, howling in agony. As souls disembarked, they stepped on the bodies, which continued to twist and squirm, but never rose up.

John, Buck and Stretch came out of the viewer's port, looked out at the bank, the bodies in the mud.

"What's their problem?" John said. "A little mud never hurt anybody."

"They aren't allowed to get up," Virgil said. "They can't get up.
They have a spell on them. So, here they lie, day after day, with biting
worms and sores from the bites. They are the mat for everyone who
disembarks. Forever. It gets old. And by the way, that isn't mud. It's
dung. Hence all those flies."

"I thought that was stinky mud," Buck said.

They stepped off the boat plank, onto the bodies, found it hard to
keep their footing.

"Don't fall, or you stay," Virgil said.

"Shit," Buck said. "That one grabbed at me."

"Kick him," Virgil said. "Better yet, Golem, come."

The Golem came down the plank and the boat rose two feet in the
water. The heroes stepped aside. The Golem came and stood by Virgil.
"Golem. You lead the way, and we will follow in your path."

The Golem walked, stepping on the contorting souls, who disappeared beneath its heavy feet, bogged deep in the dung and mud.

"Follow it," Virgil said.

It flickered eternally in a state between flesh and spirit.

"The Mound" by H.P. Lovecraft and Zealia Bishop.

They went along briskly, moving over the mashed down bodies,
and by the time they were through the muck and to the other side on
solid ground, they looked back to see a few souls go down, their clothes
torn from them by the wallowers. Soon, these unfortunate souls had
joined the squirming.

"Man," John said, "that's got to suck."

"In the case of most," Virgil said, "it wouldn't matter. They're
going to be punished anyway. But if you're just here on holiday, that
has to suck."

"Big time," Buck said.

Virgil turned and led them on, commanding the Golem to follow
behind. The moaning masses moved along with them.

"We're getting close to our goal," Virgil said. "There will be fire,
then there will be all manner of ugliness. In other words, you haven't
seen anything yet."

"You're saying we need our helmets?" John asked.

"I am. I, of course, am immune. As is the Golem."

"Are you immune from death?" Stretch asked.

"Death, yes. Pain? No. For helping you, even though it is against my will, I will be punished."

"I didn't realize that," Stretch said.

"He did," Virgil said, nodding at John the Brain.

"I did," John said. "I thought the world was worth the price of one lyre player. And three superheroes."

"I don't feel all that super right now," Stretch said.

"Me either," Buck said. "I feel like an itty-bitty ape man in a hot place."

"I can give you one bit of peace, Stretch," Virgil said. "Hell must function the way it is supposed to. Magic isn't supposed to be a daily part of earthly life. The wraiths, the disease, they are supernatural. The earth is made only for the natural. If the natural order fails, earth is doomed, and so are heaven and hell. The wraiths, the plague, it's nothing. John knows this."

John nodded.

"So, my choice is to maintain my cushy life as tour guide. And to make sure those who are supposed to be punished for eternity, are. And that the world doesn't end."

"The world would actually end?" Buck said.

"The universe will collapse on itself," John said, "and in the end, nothing will remain. Neither heaven nor earth nor hell, Satan nor God, demon or angel. There will be only void."

"You kind of left some of that out," Buck said.

"I know," John said. "It was just to take the edge off worry."

"Well, now I'm worried," Buck said.

"Sorry," Virgil said.

"It doesn't matter," Buck said. "We came here to do a job, and no matter what, we'll do it as well as we can."

"That's the spirit," Virgil said.

"Doesn't Beelzebub know all this?" Stretch said. "That the universe will end?"

"It's what Beelzebub wants," John said.

"And I thought Satan was the bad guy?" Buck said.

"He is," John said. "But he is a bad guy with a job to do, and he knows his limits. Beelzebub doesn't."

"Why can't God stop him?" Stretch asked.

"Because the God you're talking about, all the Gods, have their limits," Virgil said. "The all powerful business…Well, it isn't true, you know. For that matter, God doesn't really mess much in the lives of individuals unless it's for his own amusement. God's job is to keep the universe in order when possible. Satan keeps up with the trivia. Who's fucking who. Who killed who. He's really responsible for knowing who goes to heaven, and who comes here."

"Like Santa Claus," Buck said. "He's making a list and checking it twice."

"You got it," Virgil said.

"Does God know we're here?" Stretch said. "That we're his emissaries?"

"He does," Virgil said. "And he really isn't a he, or a she, or exactly an it. But *he* is as good a term as any."

"Did…it…he, send us?"

"Do you remember him asking you?" Virgil said. "He doesn't make choices for humans. Unless, as I said, it's for his amusement. You know, like giving babies AIDS. He's sort of got it made, you know. Something goes well, he gets credit. Goes wrong, it's God's will. Guy's in a wreck, loses a leg, both arms and his dick, but if he survives, it's a miracle. I don't think so."

"Will God help us?" Stretch asked.

"To do what?" Virgil said.

"Succeed."

"It's up to us. That's the way it works."

"It seems evil has all the power," Buck said.

"If it's not stopped, it does."

"But surely, the end of the world, all that, God would want to intervene," Stretch said.

"It's not up to your God," Virgil said. "He works as part of a multi-faceted heaven. He allows. He rewards. In the meantime, might I suggest a bit of air-conditioning. Those helmets."

The heroes took off their miner helmets, fished from their packs little flat helmets with flexible plastic face plates and headlamps, shook them so they were full, put them on, fastening them to the shoulders of their air-conditioned suits with snaps and flaps. They adjusted near flat knobs on their belts, picked up the level of air-conditioning. When they spoke, their voices came through the little speakers in the face plates loud and clear, if a bit metallic sounding.

"I sound like a throat cancer victim," Buck said.

"You sound like a talking ape," John said.

They moved along with the moaning, trudging masses for awhile, then Virgil said, "I've been on this spot many times. There's a little path. You can't see it from the main tunnel, but it's behind that large boulder shaped like buttocks. We can go that way."

"So could the others, couldn't they?" Buck said. "I don't know what all these people did, but I feel sorry for them. Maybe we could let them use the path with us, as a way out of where they're going."

"Don't feel sorry for them, " Virgil said. "They deserve their punishment. They must travel that way. They can't go any other way. Not once they reach this point. And, even if they could go the path, it doesn't lead to something pleasant."

"Great," Buck said.

"But we can go that way without problems?" Stretch said.

"I am a guide, the Golem is supernatural clay, and you are living, so, we can. But not without problems."

It was a narrow trail and they had to turn on their headlamps to see. As they went down it grew warmer, even inside their suits, so they knew the temperature outside was phenomenal, because the suits were designed to handle heat beyond any known to man. In those suits, you could have walked into the face of the sun and felt nothing.

As they worked their way down, the rocks glowed red with fire, and finally they turned white hot. Beneath their boots they could feel the heat, and their toes sweated.

Virgil and the Golem moved through the heat without problems. Virgil tucked his lyre under his arm, said, "If you were to remove your helmets, you would be eaten by flames in less than an instant. The very air is alive with heat. Even I sweat. It's a kind of sympathy thing, I believe. Careful not to touch the rocks at all. Some of them are sharp and could tear your suits, and the heat has been accumulating in them forever. Literally. Gather yourself. Down here, you can never be certain what's just around the corner."

As they turned the corner they came upon a dancing troupe, singers, and actors.

They were not attractive people, not by any means, though Buck did notice that a couple of the fat women in chain mail had nice legs, in a kind of dirty, over-muscular sort of way. They were dancing from one side of the trail to the other, and they were bad. They danced hard and fast, and as the heroes tried to pass, the dancers moved in a chain in front of them.

"Bad summer stock," Virgil said. "Dance theater. Goddamn Renaissance Festival folk. They go straight to here. Do not pass Go. Straight to here. They don't even get to ride on the boat."

"God," Stretch said, "they're awful. I thought I was dance impaired, but they're actually dreadful. Why won't they let us pass?"

"It's their job," Virgil said.

The troupe, the number of which was impossible to determine, and seemed to change at any given moment, moved faster and faster, and then they began to sing.

They were really bad.

"Jesus," Buck said. "I just thought I hated opera."

"It isn't opera," Virgil said. "It's worse than that. It's contemporary show tunes."

Buck slugged one of the dancers, a woman. She went flying back and out of sight, mixed into the heat waves and was gone. But then, another, perhaps even a worse singer and dancer, took her place.

Stretch said, "I can't do anything. Not in this suit. I can't stretch. It's not made like my body suit."

"Yeah," Virgil said, "you're pretty much fucked there."

The dancers flowed back, and the actors moved forward, began to perform Pal Joey.

"Jesus," John said, "I never thought anyone could be so bad as to make you weak. Oh, my God, look. They've got clowns and mimes with them."

"You have to expect that," Stretch said. "It is, after all, hell."

The crowd of dancers, singers, mimes and juggling clowns closed in on the heroes. The music of John Tesh echoed through the air. The mimes touched nothing with their palms, feigned being trapped by invisible walls, pretended to climb. The clowns honked horns and juggled balls, made with inane skits. Even through their air-conditioned suits, the heroes could feel the wind from their fast dancing, the sourness of their singing voices, the horrible embarrassment of seeing mimes perform, the overwhelming sadness of clowns. The horrible recitations of Hamlet and Macbeth by voices non-sublime.

There were even bad rappers,[2] making stupid gang signs, throwing fingers left and right, sounding one and the same, modern man's commercial Gongorism.

"Growing weak," Stretch said, and she went to one knee.

---

2. bad rappers (redundant)

The other heroes sagged.

John the Brain thought even the Golem looked sour.

"Play," John said to Virgil.

"What?"

"Play, Virgil. Play something. Strike back. Play Barry Manilow. No. Kenny Loggins. Some rap or heavy metal. Do something."

"They love that shit," Virgil said.

"Then play well," John said.

Virgil swung his lyre up and began to play, and soon he began to sing.

The music was divine, and Virgil's voice was...Well, it was the voice of Caruso, Streisand, Patsy Cline and Elvis and every beautiful voice that had ever sung. Nothing like the way he had sung before, and the lyre was sweet. And finally Virgil sang no more, but played the blues, almost as fine and pure as Eric Clapton and B.B. King.

Slowly, the crowd moved back, hands over their ears.

"It's too good for them," Buck said. "They can't stand it."

Virgil played, walked ahead of the others. John helped Stretch up, and they followed.

"Stay close," John said.

As they went, the crowd of rejected summer stock, performance artists, mimes, clowns, and small-town theater actors, Renaissance idiots, closed in around them for a moment. But they couldn't stand it, not when Virgil took on the voice of Roy Orbison and hit a note so high the heat waves trembled. The bad performers leaped aside, were sucked into the heat, and were, except for one red clown nose, gone.

Stretch kicked the clown nose ahead of her, and as they went forward, she kicked it again. And again. Until she managed to knock it behind some rocks and out of sight.

They went along for a ways, then came to a room of flying paper. The papers were pages from books, and the books fluttered about and whipped this way and that. Chained to rocks, dangling, were human shapes, bloody from where the pages had darted against them, administering paper cuts to the bone.

"My God," Stretch said. "Who are they?"

"The parasites of literature, and of the talented. Editors, publishers, agents and critics."

"Surely there are good ones?" Stretch said.

"Yes, and all four have a place in heaven," Virgil said.

"How do we get through?" Buck asked. "Figure we get these suits cut, we can just add barbecue sauce."

"You wouldn't have time," Vigil said. "The paper won't bother us, though. We're not their prey...Uh, none of you work in publishing in any kind of way, do you?"

Everyone shook their heads, including the Golem.

"Good," Virgil said. "Let's proceed."

They howl against Things As They Are, like monkeys in a tree, but they never give constructive criticism. They want to destroy without any thought of what to do after the destruction.

From SEXUAL IMPLICATIONS IN THE CHARGE OF THE LIGHT BRIGADE, by Philip José Farmer.

They saw all manner of horrors. There were rock walls on which continuous reruns of bad television shows were projected by a bright red light. Young men sat in chairs and watched and screamed. There were rooms full of acne-pocked teenage boys playing video games. Their eyes weeped blood.

"How is watching TV and playing video games a punishment, especially to teenagers?" Buck asked.

"Oh, the ones watching TV. They're the ones who created those shitty shows. They were little more than teenagers when they did it, so now, they're always teenagers. And they have to watch their own garbage, over and over. And as for the video games, they may look like teenagers, but they're actually honor society students who crossed the good and bad line somehow."

"That warrants this level of hell?" John said.

"Oh, yeah," Virgil said. "You betcha."

"What happens to video game fans that cross the line?" Stretch asked.

"They work in the library," Virgil said.

There were rooms of endless snacks, full of sweetness and calories. Fat people lay bloated and sugar-stained amongst them, and still they were poking the junk down.

There were so many other terrible things, the heroes had to look straight ahead, lest they be mesmerized by the horrors.

They heard a terrible racket ahead of them, and finally they came to a vast crater. They crept up on the noise and laid down on the edge of the crater and looked below. Except for the Golem. It stood stiff and silent as always. Way it stood, the color of its false flesh, it nearly blended in with the cavern walls.

Down there, fastened to a rock by twisting vines of poison ivy and anklets and bracelets made of hissing snakes, was the face on the coin. Satan.

Satan was huge and dark red and had little knobby black horns and cloven, hairy feet. His black greasy wings were folded against his back and pressed against the rock wall. He was muscular with knees that bent the wrong way. A ropy penis hung long and large between his bowed legs and dragged the ground. The head of it was the size of grapefruit. It oozed infection. It writhed like a snake. Stuck through it was a pitchfork, white-hot and smoking. Satan's testicles were missing, and where they should have been was a bloody wound. You could have dropped a bowling ball into that wound and it wouldn't have touched the sides of the rip.

Satan screamed and moaned and groaned, and the little devils, wearing ear muffs, leaped and laughed and poked. Some stood on his chest and jammed into his eye sockets with white-hot pokers, pinched his wide lips with pliers. Others urinated on his legs, and some just stood in a bored line and called him names.

Still others read aloud from a Rod McKuen poetry book, read it straight.

"Cover your ears," Virgil said.

The heroes did. After a moment, without being asked, the Golem did the same.

Finally they eased back from the ledge, away from the poetry. When they were safely distanced, Buck said, "Where's Beelzebub? I want to hit him."

"My guess, the room beyond," Virgil said. "Notice that it's cooler?"

"Now that you mention it," John said.

"There's cool air blowing up from a cavern nearby," Virgil said. "That's where he will be."

"Should we go down there and kick some ass?" Buck said. "Throw devils this way and that, save Satan."

"No," Virgil said. "We'll go to the source."

"But wouldn't it be nice to have Satan himself for an ally?" Stretch said.

"What holds him is not the vines or what those demons and imps are doing to him," Virgil said. "It's a spell. We wouldn't be able to break that spell. We have to destroy Beelzebub, steal the Orbs of Gandar, say some magic words from the book, which, if done right, should fix things up. Then we head out while our good will is working."

"What are the Orbs of Gandar?" Buck asked.

"Actually, they're Satan's nuts," John said. "I read about the ritual in the book. That's because after he was subdued by Beelzebub and his cohorts, they de-nutted him. His power is in his gonads. Much bad and powerful magic can be brought forth from those. They're the Orbs of Gandar."

"Eeeeeewwwwww," Stretch said. "Unwashed Satan balls."

"Why are they called that?" Buck asked. "The orbs of whatchamacallit."

"Satan's pet names for them," Virgil said. "He calls his penis Leroy."

They took a little tunnel through the rock, and soon the air was cooler yet.

"We can leave the suits here," Virgil said.

"Damn," Buck said, "who would have thought hell had air-conditioning."

The heroes removed the suits, folded them up, found a place to hide them in the rocks. After John removed his handheld computer from his pack, they stowed their packs away as well. John the Brain and Stretch wore only skintight blue and red suits. Buck wore fur and a pair of shorts. The Golem, as always, stood at attention. Virgil said, "I should have asked you for one of those suits. They look good. Especially on Stretch."

"Thank you, Virgil," Stretch said.

"Now," John said. "Pay attention. We can't beat Beelzebub. He's too powerful—"

"Whoa!" Buck said. "Then what's the point? I could have died Up There just as good as Down Here, and without all the effort."

"Point is," John said, "we can't beat him alone. Not the way we've beaten others in the past. We have to have the book. The book's spell is our only chance. But, Beelzebub and his forces have to be held at bay long enough for me to read the spell. Trick is, not only do I need time to read the spell. Beelzebub's got to bleed, and I have to have some of that blood to make the spell work."

"That won't be too fucking hard," Buck said.

"Actually," Virgil said. "It will. The blood's acidic."

"I was worried about that," John said. "I read about the blood. Its qualities. But, we've had a stroke of fortune."

"How so?" Buck said.

"The Golem," John said.

They turned their head and looked at the Golem standing mute and still in the shadows.

"Ah," said the others.

"One other thing," Virgil said. "It just occurred to me. I know you brought candles. We'll need back in a pack so I can have one. And we'll need a match."

They went into a large cavern by means of a wide open archway. It was mucho air-conditioned in there. The walls were white and the floor was covered in beautiful Moroccan tile. There was pleasant music playing. The air was scented with jasmine and strawberry.

Beelzebub, huge and reptilian, a crest of bone on his head, a bowler hat containing one long white feather perched on that, had Hitler bent over a couch and was porking him in the ass while red, horned imps cheered him on, leaped and cavorted, clicked their goat-like hooves on the smooth tile floor.

"You the man," one imp cried.

"Give him the root," said another.

Hitler, wearing his classic mustache, bored-looking, his head toward the heroes, was smoking a large stogie and blowing smoke swastikas from out of his nose.

In a cage, naked, swinging from the ceiling, was Dick Nixon, peeling a banana.

The heroes strolled in. They could have been on their way to church, way they came. Just walked in, upright and eager-looking, humming "Up Jumped the Devil" by the Hurricane Hunters. Doing that, because that's the way they always worked. Looking cool, even if they weren't.[3]

John held the computer book in his hand, Virgil his lyre, the others were empty-handed. The Golem puffed bits of dried clay dust as it walked.

Virgil jerked up the lyre, hit a note so high, Beelzebub jumped back, whipped his forked dick out of Hitler's ass, sprayed black jism. The imps screamed. Hitler hopped back three feet, did a little knee dip

---

3. This shows the team at the height of their abilities. Being cool in Hell, even in the air-conditioned unit, takes special poise.

and put his hands over his ears. Dick Nixon made a hooting sound, shit in his hand, threw it on the floor and passed out.

The heroes were affected not at all. Virgil had melted candle wax and filled the human's ears. He and the Golem hadn't needed any. They were immune.

Hitler bolted, showing them his ass, which hung open like a puffer fish's mouth.

Stretch began to expand after him.

Virgil said, "Let him go. He's of no use. We want the big guy."

Beelzebub slapped his hands over his ears and began bellowing. He snatched up the couch and tossed it.

Virgil tried to leap out of the way, but it was too late. The corner of the couch caught his jaw and knocked him back. His lyre went skittering across the tile floor. Virgil, unconscious, went skittering after it.

Stretch stretched, long and lean, her beautiful head looking large and unwieldy on her flat elastic neck; her body was as thin as a stretched piece of chewed gum. She wrapped herself around Beelzebub's legs, pulled them together tight, brought him down.

Beelzebub's bowler went flying. His head cracked on the floor like a rotten watermelon, and out of the crack a clutch of fat juicy spiders rushed. They went straight for John and Buck. The imps rushed them too.

Beelzebub shivered and twisted. Next instant, Stretch was no longer squeezing his legs, but squeezing the body of a barrel-thick, twenty foot long snake with a cracked open head.

"Hold him, baby," John said, and flicked open the computer book as Buck went to work stomping spiders, slapping at imps. The spiders smashed to black goo. The imps to red goo. The spiders were so thick, they managed to run up Buck's legs and disappear into his fur, their positions identified only by painful bites that made Buck yip like a pup. The imps swarmed his head. Some of them leaped onto John.

John pulled imps from his hair as if they were burrs. He tossed them hard against the wall. They exploded like pouches of strawberry Kool Aid. John punched a key on his handheld. The screen lit up. Black and red symbols rushed across the lighted "page," began to squirm like ants on a hot skillet, skipped and hopped like fleas.

Struggling to concentrate on the racing glyphs, John read the symbols, yelled out the words, the long lost names. Hiddly-diddly, Cthulu-Dooloo. Or so it sounded to Buck's ears. He wasn't all that concentrated on it. He was slapping and stomping at the biting spiders, the clutching imps.

The snake (Beelzebub) twisted and squirmed, wrapped around Stretch's legs, which up until this point had not left their original position. She had merely elongated her upper body, left her legs anchored. But now the snake had them.

Stretch went thin as thread, slid out of the snake's coils, sent one arm out way long, grabbed at the edge of the room's entrance, jerked herself forward, allowing her body to whip back into shape. This resulted in her being popped forward at an incredible rate. She just managed to avoid colliding with the wall. But it was still enough to swing her through the archway, cause her to drop on her back, which, at the last moment she arched and made wide and flat, so it was like dropping a large piece of elastic. She fell to the floor so softly there was no sound.

The snake lifted its head and lifted half of its great body off the floor, slithered forward, its tail thrashing this way and that.

"Golem," John said, but the Golem did not respond. It stood still, as if it were a new piece of furniture in the room.

"GOLEM!" John said. But the Golem didn't move.

Buck leaped forward, spiders biting at him, imps clinging to him, and grabbed the snake. He wrapped his short powerful legs around it and squeezed. The snake let forth with a hissing sound that sounded as if all the tires in the universe had suddenly lost their air. Its great triangular head split open to show fangs dripping with poison. Its yellow eyes squirmed in their sockets.

Buck let go of the snake long enough to sock the head a good one. Knocked it so hard it flew back, then slammed against the ground. With a leap, Buck grabbed the snake's body again, began to squeeze.

Writhing, the snake beat its own body on the ground to do harm to Buck. It worked. Beelzebub knocked Buck lose. It widened its mouth, dropped it over Buck's head, lifted him high in the air. The fangs were so wide, they just missed Buck, coming down on either side of his shoulders.

Stretch grabbed Virgil, was lifting him up by coiling her body around him. She spat in his face. "Wake up!"

Virgil's eyes opened.

"We need the Golem," she said.

"Hey, baby," Virgil said. "I like kisses, but not that wet."

Stretch let loose of him, whipped back into shape. Virgil fell to the floor. "Ouch," he said.

"Now," she said. "We need him now."

Virgil took in the situation, said, "Golem. Fuck up that snake."

The Golem turned its head, looked at the snake waving its head in the air, Buck's body and feet sticking out of its mouth.

The Golem went forward. Its pace was deliberate, but not fast. It grabbed the snake with both hands and squeezed. Squeezed so hard the rock-like muscles in its back clashed together and dust exploded off its back and made a brief clay cloud.

The Golem squeezed so hard Buck's head shot out of the snake's mouth like a cannonball. Buck hit the floor. His head was lathered up and he blinked his eyes as if he were coming out of a darkened theater.

"It stunk in there," he said.

The snake wasn't a snake now.

It split into two snakes, connected at the tail. The tail sprouted a rattler. The rattle rattled, loud as an entire civilization working maracas. Both of its heads whipped forward, snapped their fangs at the Golem. One head hit so hard the fangs snapped off, but the Golem didn't move.

"Stand on its tail, Golem," Virgil said.

The Golem moved between the snakes, stood on the creature where the tail connected to the two elongated bodies. The snakes wrapped around the Golem and squeezed, high and low. Clay dust puffed. The snake strained so hard coal-black snake shit shot out of it ass and slid across the floor. But the Golem didn't move.

Both snake heads hissed around in front of the Golem, and the Golem, moving surprisingly fast, grabbed them and banged them together. The snake dropped to the floor and there was a twist and a turn and whip and a whirl, and there lay Beelzebub, unconscious, forked tongue hanging out on his cheek, forked dick hanging out on his thigh.

Buck was standing now, still picking spiders and imps from his fur. Stretch came over to help him.

John said, "We need its blood."

Virgil pulled a little knife from inside his robe, went over to the snake and cut its throat. "Golem. Catch that blood in your hands."

As dark blood spurted from Beelzebub, the Golem squatted, held its hands together. Blood filled them, began to run over the sides, hit the tile floor, eat right through it, making holes that went on forever.

"Have him bring it here," John said.

"Bring the blood to him, Golem," Virgil said, pointing at John. "But don't get it on him."

"Everyone stand back, please," John said.

"It's about time you did something," Buck said.

"He's doing what we can't do," Stretch said. "He's translating the book."

John had been reciting the words as he was able to read them, but now, even though they jumped and squirmed on the screen, he recognized a pattern, and he could translate them more quickly.

"Indonreluxtaderron. Godollacon, Jorolla Corolla, Coundertapcondientharytimsubell."

The Golem thudded over to John, carrying the blood in its palms.

"Won't it burn through its hands?" Stretch asked.

"I don't think so," Virgil said.

After a moment John read a word. Hesitated. Made a clicking noise with his tongue. Whistled. Then read another word. He made a kind of scratching sound inside his mouth.

"What the fuck?" said Buck.

"Quiet," Virgil said. "It's a language few know, and fewer yet can make the sounds. Don't distract him."

The air hardened. Turned thick and gooey as amber.

"Tell him to pour the blood over my head," John said.

"Are you crazy!" Stretch said.

"He knows what he's doing," Virgil said. "Golem. Carefully, pour the blood over John's head."

"Does he know who John is?" Buck asked.

"He does," Virgil said. "He is literal. But he has insights. He is, after all, supernatural."

The Golem poured the blood over John's head. To do so, it had to move slowly because the air was dense. The blood came out of its hands slow and thick as fresh molasses. It seemed to hang in the air before trickling down in lumps and bumps, and just as it was about to strike John's head, it spread and flowed around him in a kind of gooey, dark barrier.

John read more glyphs, said more chants.

And then an odd thing happened in a series of odd things. Beelzebub's forked tongue expanded, slithered toward its crotch. His forked dick got long and hard and stuck upright. Tongue and dick collided, embraced one another, and began to tug at one another. They pulled until head and crotch were close together, then Beelzebub's asshole flared open and puckered and trembled like a volcano about to erupt, made with a sucking sound. The air turned foul as a chili supper in an old age home. And slowly Beelzebub's ugly head was pulled toward that sucking asshole, and slowly, the asshole expanded and took in the head and pulled and sucked and slurped.

John kept reading the incantation.

He finished with a powerful noise that made everyone in the room but the Golem's bowels loosen (technically, it had no bowels), in spite of the wax in their ears. Even Virgil felt a twinge.

Beelzebub was pulled completely into his own asshole, and there was a popping sound.

The asshole fell to the floor, puckered a couple of times, as if gulping air, then unpuckered and was an empty flesh ring lying on the floor.

John said, "Virgil, tell the Golem to step on that."

Virgil told him.

The Golem did it. The asshole ring crunched under the Golem's foot with a sound like the dried skin of a locust. When the Golem lifted its foot, there was only dust.

"Man," Buck said. "That was some cool shit."

They looked about the room until they found Satan's balls in a large fruit jar. A piece of white tape had been put across the jar, and on it was written, Orbs of Gandar, aka, Satan's Nuts.

They left Nixon in the cage. The imps and spiders had disappeared somewhere during all the chanting, and when they re-suited and got back to the devil, the imps were gone. The Rod McKuen poetry book lay open face down on the ground.

The devil lay weak and ugly against the wall. The vines had died. The snakes were gone. The devil's blind orbs filled up with yellow, black-slitted eyes. He rose slowly, stretched and flapped his wings.

He stood easily twenty feet high on his cloven hooves. The wound between his legs dripped black blood.

Virgil held up the big fruit jar. "Got your balls, big guy."

Satan was happy. The balls were replaced. Virgil burned the poetry book with a match borrowed from John. Satan, powerful now, got on the telephone in his office, recently the office of one Beelzebub, now popped out of existence.

Everyone was on Satan's side now.

Satan ordered up a hot air balloon manned by imps. The same imps who had tortured him. But they were forgiven. A thing that surprised the heroes.

"Damn," Buck said. "We had this guy all wrong."

Virgil leaned over, said, "Don't expect too much. He's feeling friendly right now. Got his balls back. Best thing to do is just move on."

The hot air balloon arrived just outside of Satan's air-conditioned office. The men shook hands with Satan. Even the Golem. Satan patted Stretch on the ass. He was, after all, Satan.

They climbed into the big basket with six little red hopping imps. The imps were all over the place, firing up the burner, filling the balloon with hot air.

Up they went.

"I never heard Satan speak," Buck said. "Not even when he was on the phone."

"You can't hear him unless he speaks directly to you," Virgil said. "And it's best if he doesn't."

"He didn't say thanks, you know."

"Don't push it."

The balloon rose and drifted, sailed high over the great River Styx. It floated down a dark tunnel, and then it rose again, and Buck said, "Hey, we're inside Satan's shitter."

And they were.

They rose up and hung for awhile until the updraft came, and up they shot, through the crapper hole, into the garage.

The imps said nothing. Just made chattering noises. But the heroes understood. They climbed out quickly.

The downdraft came. The balloon was sucked down and away.

"What do we do with the Golem?" Stretch asked.

"It will stay here with me," Virgil said. "I'll find a place for it, erase the name on its forehead, send it back to sleep. Or back to its nonexistence."

"I'll miss him," Stretch said. She leaned forward and kissed Virgil on the cheek. "And I'll miss you too."

Virgil blushed. "Not since I met the daughter of Zeus, Helen of Troy, have I met such a beauty and a charmer as you."

"Oh, that's sweet," Stretch said.

"Let me draw you a map," Virgil said.

The cold went away. Airplanes and flying devices took to the air. Wind wagons went into museums or were recycled or burned. Polar bears headed north and far south, depending on where they were at the time. Along with them went other cold-loving animals. Some people had the nerve to complain about the change. Mostly looters and snowmobile salesmen.

From a history book of a later century

They took a different route out than the way they came. John asked Virgil for that. Wanted to go out the arctic opening he had heard so much about.

They drove the Chevy hard, climbed up from hell into a tunnel that widened so gradually it was hard to realize they were rising up, coming out of the center of the earth and into a great green valley.

Along the sides of the enormous earthen bowl they entered were all manner of mechanical ruins. Crashed zeppelins. Bi-planes. Even a few semi-modern planes. Dog sleds. As they rose up higher and ice began to appear, they even saw a great ship.

"Must have got caught in the ice," John said. "Then, over the years, the ice floe carried it down into this valley."

"My God," Stretch said. "What is that?"

John, who was driving, slowed. They looked. There, frozen in the ice was a huge, scarred man."

"I believe, friends," John said, "that is the Frankenstein Monster."

"Neat," Buck said. "Shall we look?"

"No," John said, gunning the motor. "This is close enough. It's time to get back."

They drove and came to the ice of the polar cap, but the Chevy handled that. They came to the sea, and the super Chevy navigated that as well. It did what it had to do. It rolled on tires, it swam with fins, it flew on wings, and in a short time, the heroes arrived at their mountain sanctuary, slid in through the secret passage, pulled into the garage, took the elevator up to the great room where their hunchback served them cocoa and cookies.

They watched at the great windows all day. Saw that the wraiths still whipped and wisped through the sky.

But early the next morning the day turned clear and the sun shone bright, and down below, they noticed the frozen river was melting.

No wraiths were seen.

They flicked on television. There had been no new cases of the plague. People were wandering about more freely. Green grass had been seen poking through melting ice.

Down below them they could see boats on the river, women wearing bikinis. Buck spent a lot of time with the binoculars checking this phenomenon out. Hell, it had been a long time since the river below had wiggled boats and ass on its mighty stream.

"It's going to be all right, isn't it?" Stretch said.

"I think so," John said.

Montawn cleared his throat. "Well, sir. There is one thing."

"And what is that?" John asked.

"Your friend, Professor Bazza, called."

"And?"

"Seems, sir, that there's a disturbance on Mars."

"What kind of disturbance?"

"An alternate disturbance."

Buck said, "What?"

John said, "You mean the alternate universe Mars, don't you?"

"I do, sir. As you know, the professor has been traveling there from time to time. Well, sir, things have gone haywire, and he's contacted you, using that device similar to the Gridley Wave. You know the one, sir."

"Of course."

"I thought I'd wait until you had your cocoa, but, his messages sounded quite desperate."

John looked at Stretch and Buck.

"Hey, I'm for anything after what we just did. We saved the goddamn world. I could do with saving Mars. Even if it's an alternate Mars."

"A quickie first," Stretch said. "Then Mars."

"Sounds like a plan," John said. "Montawn, check out the car. Make sure she's ready to go. And pack some sandwiches. And ease up on the pickle loaf."

Below is a list, not in alphabetical order, of references that were used in reconstructing the events of this true adventure. In some cases, publications have been so many, and are such well known works, that I haven't bothered to list dates or publishers. This is meant to be nothing more than an informal guide.

ACME PRODUCTS AND THEIR USAGE, A Definitive Examination and Price Guide, by Wilie Coyote, Translated from the Original by Mel Blanc. SUBTERRANEAN PRESS, 1999.

Musical references:

THE COMPLETE WORKS OF JIMMY JOE SMITH AND THE HURRICANE HUNTERS, (On Pellet Drive Connections) from BOOGER-DOODLE PRODUCTIONS, 1956.
VIRGIL'S GREATEST HITS, by Virgil, AENEAS RECORDINGS, (date?)
SONGS TO ACCOMPANY THE READING OF THE AENEID, by Virgil, AENEAS RECORDINGS. (date?)

Nonfiction:

AT THE EARTH'S CORE, (First published as "The Inner World") by Edgar Rice Burroughs, 1913), 1922 as the novel.
TARZAN AT THE EARTH'S CORE, Edgar Rice Burroughs, 1930. (Burroughs' acquaintances David Innes and Abner Perry, like Verne's explorers, only succeeded in exploring the level above hell, and thought it was the core. Several massive pockets, or worlds, as well as natural "suns" exist throughout the earth. But the true core, is hell. Burroughs also wrote other books about the center of the earth, and though certain truths are hidden within, they are generally fiction based on the early adventures of Abner Perry and David Innes best described in the volume below.)
THE TRUTH ABOUT THE CENTER OF THE WORLD, Abner Perry, 1918, SUBTERRANEAN PRESS. (A tedious but informative work said to have been submitted via Gridley Wave from the center of the earth (see above), outlining their adventures in a land called Pellucidar.)
JOURNEY TO THE CENTER OF THE EARTH, by Jules Verne, 1871 (English Version).
FIVE THOUSAND MILES UNDERGROUND, Roy Rockwood, 1908.
PILGRIM'S PROGRESS, John Bunyan, Part One, 1678. Part Two, 1684.
THE ART OF HELL, by Adolph Hitler, BEELZEBUB PRODUCTIONS, 1948. (Very rare.)
THE COMPLETE WORKS OF SUBTERRANEAN EXPLORER CAVE CARSON, by Cave Carson, SUBTERRANEAN PRESS. 1965.
A DESCENT INTO THE MAELSTROM, by Edgar Allan Poe, 1841.
THE NARRATIVE OF A. GORDON PYM OF NANTUCKET, by Edgar Allan Poe, 1850.
BLACK AS THE PIT FROM POLE TO POLE, Howard Waldrop and Steve Utley, from CUSTER'S LAST JUMP, and Other Collaborations, GOLDEN GRYPHON PRESS, 2003.
THE SECRET PEOPLE, by John Benyon Harris, 1964.

THE AENEID, 19 B.C.

THE ARMOR OF VULCAN, A Descriptive Price Guide. Date written is unknown, but only two of this volume are known to exist. The book is transcribed on sheet metal so thin at first glance it looks like paper. The transcription was done by use of a small hammer and an even smaller chisel. THE ARMOR OF VULCAN is bound in bull hide and bronze clasp. Considered priceless. Found in a volcano near Mt. Etna in Sicily. The author is rumored to be Vulcan himself, known to the Greeks as Hephaestus.

· O'Reta, Snapshot Memories ·

INTRODUCTION

This one was commissioned for a book titled MOTHERS AND SONS, edited by Jill Morgan. I jumped at the chance. My mother and I were close, but we also had our differences. We went through the usual teen/parent conflicts, but we weathered them quite well, and stayed friends through it all. But our relationship was not "friends" as many modern folks like to think it should be between parents and offspring. My mother was a parent in the best sense of the word, as was my father. They were truly people for me to admire and look up to. I still do.

We lived in poverty much of the time, but I didn't know it, partly because our poverty was nowhere as bad as that of others around us, and my parents were always able to make me feel special and managed to get whatever it was I needed growing up. We never thought of ourselves as poor. Just broke.

My mother was an amazing woman, made do with little to nothing, was able to stretch five dollars into twenty, and was at the same time one of the most generous and kind souls I've ever known.

She was constantly inspiring me, encouraging me. Without her, I doubt I would have become a writer. From early on, she spotted something in me that had to do with the written word, and she encouraged it. I think, for her, a teacher and/or writer, was the top of life's food chain.

I pretty much agree.

One reviewer of the book this appeared in seemed upset at my piece, because she thought I made a saint of my mother. I think if you read the piece, you'll see she's a human being. But, I feel sorry for the reviewer who must have never known what it was like to have a family in the true sense of the word. In many ways, I feel like the pro-family values folks sometimes, hopefully without the self-righteousness. But these days, you look around, and most families are shattered asunder. Multiple marriages. Kids here and there. Shattered hearts, broken spirits, children raising children, wearing white after Labor Day. What has the world come to?

215

This is not to say that people should not divorce if they are unhappy, or that folks should make a bad situation "work" by staying in it. But it is to say, people quit awfully easy these days. Part of that is a negative hangover from the Baby Boomers, of which I'm one. First off, I'm going to say that in many ways, the Baby Boomers are a great generation. It's an argument I can make and you can pass on if you like. Being tested under fire is not the only measure of greatness. But that is all for another time.

My point is, respect for my generation or not, one of the many negative things we brought into the current generation is selfishness. We came through an idealistic time, and therefore, have tried to transfer that to our children. I think we overdid it. We are a young-minded generation for one, and therefore, it's hard for us to grow old gracefully. This becomes a selfish endeavor, staying young. I don't think it's all negative, but much of it is, and we've passed on, if nothing else, this selfish feeling of entitlement to our children. When everything is about you, it's easy to see every little stress and strife as not something to get through, but something to abandon.

Too many abandon too quickly.

Too many fail to consider our children over ourselves.

Too many of us want what we want right now.

Too many have situational ethics.

We reap what we sow.

I miss those tough-minded people of my parents' generation.

I miss my mother, who could make bad times good, turn the worst situation into a game, and who was willing to sacrifice for the greater good of the family.

Well, I could go on with this, but I'm starting to ramble and repeat myself.

Let me put it like this.

I miss her.

Thanks, Mom.

· O'Reta, Snapshot Memories ·

Her maiden name was O'Reta Wood. Most everyone called her Reta, or Reeter, with the exception of my dad. He called her O'Reeter, which, akin to Reeter, is one of those rural Southern peculiarities I never have figured out. It's like Cinderella becoming Cindereller. Who added the "er," and why was it added? But I loved to hear my daddy call her name, and I think she did too.

My first memory of my mother is her sitting in a chair beside me, before a long row of curtainless windows, looking out at the night.

I guess I was three or four years old. We were in the first house I remember, and below us was a honky-tonk, and beyond that, across the highway, a drive-in theater.

On the huge drive-in screen were cartoon figures (most likely Warner Brothers), and sometimes actors going through their paces, and from that distance cartoons and humans were about the size they would be on a television screen, which we didn't have.

Since we couldn't hear what the characters were saying, my mother translated their silence to words. I had no idea then she was making it up; I thought she was omniscient. What I do know is I enjoyed it. It was my introduction to storytelling.

When I think of my mother, this is most often the first memory that comes to mind. That and her reading me Uncle Remus, and of course, the tornado.

One day, while my father was off at work, which was a lot of the time, the birds went quiet and the sky turned greenish, and my mother suddenly grew agitated. She threw open the windows and the doors, and from those same windows where we had watched the drive-in theater, we saw something else.

In the distance, beyond the drive-in, trees leaped up and swirled in a cone, and the cone danced. It was a tornado, a Texas cyclone, a twister, looking not too unlike the tornado I would see later on television (when we finally got one) while watching The Wizard of Oz.

Mom scooped me up and ran to the next-door neighbor's house. He had a storm shelter. Once inside with the neighbor's family, we found ourselves at least a foot deep in water. There were jars of canned food on shelves, and the man who owned the shelter, a person I barely remember, stood with flashlight and club. As we watched, he killed a water moccasin that had crawled in down there. Above us the storm hollered and stomped and tugged at the latched double wooden doors like a maniac with a knife. My mother stood in the water and held me in a death grip.

I don't remember being afraid of the storm, just excited. But the snake, my first, had scared me. Never have liked them since. Maybe I got that from my mother. She was scared of snakes, water, drinking alcohol, and electricity. So am I.

The storm was over almost as fast as it happened. All I remember is that when we came out into the light, our house was untouched, as were the handful of houses in the immediate area, but the drive-in screen was gone and partly in our yard, and some of the honky-tonk's roof had been taken away. It had all seemed like a dream.

Later, I remember it being said that a house some distance behind us had the tornado drop in, as if for a visit, only to leave the place in shambles. We were lucky. The damn thing had jumped over us and gone on.

Other memories of that time: Wandering bums. They call them homeless now, but they called them bums then. They were sometimes men down on their luck, more often than not lost souls who claimed to be preachers. They'd come to our door and ask for food. My mother nearly always fixed them something. Sometimes they did a little work around the house in return. Sometimes they preached, or gave us a little story of how they had come to where they now stood, or wobbled, as was the case with some.

If my mother smelled alcohol on their breath, they not only didn't get fed, she ran them off by locking the screen door and lecturing at them through it about the depravities of drink. They usually took hat in hand (as everyone seemed to wear hats then) and slunk off apologetically.

None of this sympathetic twelve-step stuff. These guys were drunks. Mom was a fanatic teetotaler and viewed 1920s prohibition exponent and saloon smasher Carrie Nation as a kind of saint. My father viewed her as an annoying busybody who might have served more good if she had been hit by a truck.

Looking back, seeing a number of friends of mine who took to the bottle, fell in and didn't come out, the number of social drunks I've been around, I'm glad mom scolded me at an early age. I don't see the occasional drink as quite the resident evil my mother did, but drunkenness I've never liked and have never been drunk myself. A legacy from my mother: have no respect for the bottle, because it has none for you.

■ ■ ■

My mother was pulled into this century as if by a tornado of technology. Future shock. And she never quite adjusted to it.

My mother's Scotch-Irish mother, my grandmother, Ole, was born in the 1880s in Oklahoma Territory. It didn't become a state until a few years later. She traveled by covered wagon and actually saw Buffalo Bill's Wild West Show. I remember her telling me about it. White horses. Stagecoaches being chased by wild Indians, gunfire, sharpshooters (maybe Annie Oakley), and the old man himself, white-bearded, handsome, magnificent. Wild Bill Hickok had only been dead about ten years when she was born.

She told me of seeing Indian encampments as a child. Of attempting to homestead land (most likely Oklahoma during the land rush), where snakes tried to climb in the wagon all night and were fought off by her family. But the snakes were so thick and persistent, the very next day they abandoned their homesteading adventure and departed.

She told me Irish ghost stories about birds that appeared before the death of loved ones. Family stories, like how her husband's brother, George, an older man, fought in the Civil War in place of his son, George, Jr., who had deserted. George Sr., however, was later shot and killed for stealing horses.

Ole saw a number of her children buried. She lived to be ninety-eight years old, and in pretty good health until the end. She loved the modern world and thought the good old days weren't all that damn good. I think she adjusted to the changing times better than my parents, who were born in this century.

At the beginning of the twentieth century, shortly after the death of the Wild West, my parents were born. My father in 1909, my mother in 1916. Buffalo Bill was still alive, as was Wyatt Earp, Bat Masterson, and Emmett Dalton, the lone survivor of the Dalton gang's last raid.

Frank James died a year before my mother was born. My father was approximately six years old at the time.

My mother's family moved to Texas, where she met and grew up with the man who was to become my father. She and A. B. Lansdale were married in 1933. My father wanted to be a mechanic. Mom bought Dad a Model T with some money she had earned from berry picking. She told him to take it apart and put it back together until he could do it without thinking. He took her advice, and that was how he learned his trade.

My brother was born in 1935. Emmett Dalton was still alive and writing for the movies. Wyatt Earp had only been dead six years. Pretty Boy Floyd was about to meet his end. It was the middle of the Great Depression.

Sixteen years later, in 1951, I was born. World War II was but six years gone. It was the Eisenhower generation. The nuclear age. The baby boom. Hank Williams and Ernest Tubb were on the radio. The birth of rock and roll was on the very near horizon. Prosperity ruled the nation, if not East Texas. Some dumbass was going to invent the hula hoop.

This to me is the most amazing thing about my family. That they had a foot in so many different generations. The Wild West, the Great Depression, the nuclear age. I think this was part of what made them who they were.

My mother and father were very close, and very different. They argued a lot. My father was uneducated. He had begun helping raise his family at eight years old when his mother died. His father was a mean-spirited jackass who was quick with the whip, and my father had scars to prove it. As well as brawling scars, snakebite scars, and smallpox scars. He never so much as spanked me.

My mother had come from a family that wasn't overly educated, but had a respect for education — especially her father. Her father, my grandfather, was her hero. She adored him, told me stories of him, and praised him. He was no saint, however. Besides her four brothers and one sister, her two half brothers from a previous marriage, there was a simultaneous marriage to a woman on the other side of the Ozarks. The result of that second union was a half sister. When we found out about her, met her years later, there was no denying she was kin. She was the spitting image of my mother.

When I was growing up, the Depression was constantly in our house, even if it was supposedly long over. We pinched pennies. We ate what was on our plates. We saved bits of cloth, paper, damn near anything we could get our hands on. My mom ran the coffee grounds through twice, sometimes three times. We saved the grease from frying and made soap out of it with lye.

My mother never could get hold of the idea that times were better. For her the wolf was always at the door. She had a terrible fear of going hungry. She was absolutely paranoid about it. And it wasn't something my father took lightly either. I remember Dad hunting squirrels, and it wasn't just for recreation. My mother made meals from polk salad and wild dandelions, made jelly out of wild grapes and persimmons, tea from sassafras. We raised a garden, hogs, and chickens a lot of the time.

There was never a moment in my mother's life when the future was secure, and because of this, I think it was hard for her to plan too far ahead for herself. For her family, yes, but she and my father constantly denied themselves things to make sure it was there for the family.

In spite of this, my parents probably did better during the early fifties than at any other time in their lives, and it's the only time I remember living in a close neighborhood with a house immediately next door. Then my mother was a full-time housewife, and my father worked at Wanda Petroleum, a butane company. He was a mechanic troubleshooter, on the road a lot of the time fixing broken-down trucks. Sometimes he'd work in horrible weather and be out late and far away, have to lie in puddles of water on freezing nights working on a motor. I've seen him come in the door with freezing chills and icicles in his hair. Next morning, he'd be up and gone before daylight, back to work.

My mother was a great lover of books, especially nonfiction. She was interested in comparative religion, and it's my belief she wrestled with her views on religion all her life. There were times when her views were strictly hard-shell Baptist, and times when she was somewhat agnostic. Most of the time she was what I would call a liberal Baptist. An oxymoron to many, but the truth is they did and do exist. My mother loved reading the Bible, and she hooked me on the habit. I'm not religious, but I still read the Bible. Great stories. Great lessons for life. Lots of sex, murder, and perversion.

She loved William Faulkner, more for what he accomplished than for his books, which to my knowledge, she had never read. Faulkner, for some reason, reminded her of her father, a conclusion I presume she gleaned from reading about his life. I doubt she knew Faulkner was a notorious drunk.

My mother had a natural knack for color. She loved to paint, often did her painting with her fingers, using boards, or squares of plywood for her canvases.

She would just suddenly have the urge, and she would paint. Perhaps for days on end. When she was finished, occasionally these paintings would find their way on our walls, or she would give them away, or sell them, and sometimes, she would just toss them. Usually the paintings were of flowers. My mother loved flowers. Sometimes they were just colorful, and not obviously anything but fine displays of color.

The paintings, no matter what they were of, always had a kind of, well, fuzzy weirdness about them. They were art, and they were unique, but they weren't at all traditional. Later, when I saw Van Gogh's work, I realized that it had much the same appearance. Not on the same level, but the same sort of technique. My mother had never taken an art lesson, and had never even heard of Vincent Van Gogh. Maybe part of the result was due to the weakness of her eyes, but I tend to think she painted what she saw. A world bright and beautiful, but fuzzy around the edges.

She was great at making something out of nothing. From food to throw rugs to coffee tables to flower arrangements, she could take nothing—which is mostly what she had to work with—and turn it into something.

When I was young, she was very optimistic. Always looking for a better day. She instilled that in me. Unfortunately for her, this wasn't her true nature. She was subject to tremendous ups and downs. I think now she would most likely be diagnosed as a manic depressive. In later years, it got worse.

■ ■ ■

Growing up, my mother was always there to read to me, tell me she loved me, impress on me how intelligent and special I was, but how I should keep in mind that others didn't have all the advantages I had, and that I should respect every human being, no matter their race, color, religion, or financial station in life. Do unto others as you would have them do unto you.

It never occurred to me that we were poor. We thought of ourselves as broke. It wasn't until years later that I realized it.

There was no reason I should have felt poor. When I was young my mother made my shirts and even jackets, sewed them on a pedal Singer sewing machine.

She always found money for me to buy comic books and the occasional paperback book. At Christmas I always received a book or two, because I was a fanatic for the stuff. At the time I loved D.C. comics especially, and some offbeat comics like Black Cat, which starred a female crime fighter who had judo tips in the back of her comics. But Batman, he was my main man.

My mother made me a Batman uniform with ears I was never quite satisfied with. They tended to droop. She solved this to some degree by placing cardboard inside the ears. She made my nephew, who is only a few years younger than me, a Robin outfit. I wish I still had mine.

My nephew and I had plans to solve crimes in Mt. Enterprise, but the place seemed short on the stuff. Nonexistent, in fact. And besides, we had to be in the house at a certain time and go to bed early enough to be up for school. My bedroom may have been the Bat Cave, but it was still in my parents' house.

But Bat Cave it was. With chemistry sets, insect and mineral collections, finger-printing materials, and books on all these subjects.

In my Bat Cave, it was my plan to also include mementos of cases to come, but, alas, the most I ever did was run around with my cape flapping. To remedy this, I began to think of adventures to write and draw about, my own comics. Mom always took time out from whatever she was doing to hear me read my comics and show her the pictures. In time, I preferred the stories to the pictures, possibly because I was better at it.

Mom introduced me to Tarzan movies on television, perhaps to get me out of her hair. Every Saturday morning there was a jungle theater with Tarzan, Jungle Jim, Bomba the Jungle boy, that sort of thing, and every Saturday morning I was glued to the tube. I looked forward to it all week. Later, I discovered Edgar Rice Burroughs, the author of the Tarzan books, and my life was absolutely turned around. I had always wanted to be a writer, but when I started reading Burroughs, I knew I had to be.

Again, I owe it all to Mom.

When I was young, though people find this hard to believe, I was shy. My mother sent me around the corner to a lady who taught what was then called Expression. It was taught at her home, and I learned to memorize poetry and sections from books, and to give recitations. I discovered an unusual knack. I was a pretty good public speaker, a good reader, and could memorize entire poems and pages of books rapidly. I loved it. I didn't know it at the time, and neither did my mother, at least not directly, but she was further grooming me for my future career as writer and public speaker.

When we moved back to Gladewater, we moved there with considerably less money. My father quit Wanda Petroleum and struck out on his own. My cousin made him a wallet card that read: HAVE TOOLS, WILL TRAVEL.

My father loved the independence, and never gave it up again, but it was hard sledding as a freelance mechanic, and it took time for him to get his own garage and build up a clientele. In the meantime, we ate a lot of pinto beans and cornbread. It wasn't until years later I realized we did that because they were cheap. I just thought we liked them.

My mother sold encyclopedias door-to-door, bought things from swap meets and refurbished them, resold them at a higher price and made money for me to join the Boy Scouts, have uniforms and equipment, and to attend Scout camps. One year she raised enough for me to go to Philmont, a prestigious Scout camp in New Mexico. I still remember my scouting days with great fondness.

Later, Mom worked odd jobs so that I was able to go to the Y.M.C.A in Tyler, Texas, and take a variety of martial arts. We had to drive thirty miles every Saturday, and eventually several times a week when I discovered the variety of martial arts offered at night.

I became a fanatic.

Mom even let me try the wrist locks and arm bars on her when my dad wasn't around. She held pillows for me to kick and helped me build punching bags and other simple training devices.

My mother and I were very close until I reached the age of sixteen. That's not unusual. Teenagers strike off on their own for a while, but this was during the turbulent sixties, and though my mother supported much of the change that was going on, civil rights, women's rights, she disliked the long hair, the slovenly clothes, and the antiestablishment mood that the sixties, and now I, represented.

We never became enemies, my mother and I, but we didn't see eye to eye on much. I was troublesome at school, was often expelled, my grades dropped, and I just skimmed through till graduation. I'm sure Mom must have wondered what all the lessons in Expression, Boy Scouts, and martial arts had done for me.

I married when I was eighteen and began attending Tyler Junior College, and then I was off to the University of Texas. My marriage fell apart during that second year of studies, and I came home.

It was really pretty wonderful, and for about a year or so, kind of like a second childhood. At the time I was very much interested in Thoreau. My mother loved him too. She and I read Walden a lot and talked. The closeness returned.

It wasn't until my father's death some years later that things went haywire. From the moment he died, she was lost. She didn't pull in and give up, but she seemed frantic all the time. She had never had the ability to stick to any one thing, even the things she loved, like sales, flower arranging, painting. She dipped into these like a bee at a flower, then moved on. The moment something became a bit difficult, she was out of there. She wanted to keep that high of discovery all the time, and therefore sacrificed the greater high of really becoming good and successful at something.

Finally she remarried. A nice enough fella. Shortly thereafter she was in a wreck that caused her to be thrown through the windshield. She never would wear a seat belt, fearing being trapped, often commenting that she would rather be thrown free. And she was. Right through the windshield that banged her brain and put her in the hospital.

She was operated on, and my brother and I and our families went to see her daily. Her husband, Cecil, received only minor injuries and was soon up and around.

But for mother, it was strange. Even when she was allowed to go home, she didn't know where she was. She couldn't get out of bed. She couldn't care for herself. She didn't know who her family members were. Those same eyes that had looked at me with love, and even frustration, were now more like the eyes of a frightened animal.

Slowly, her memory came back, but though she could remember her past, and me, she had lost the ability to show emotion. It was akin to the novel *The Invasion of the Body Snatchers*, or the movie made from it. She looked like my mother, talked like my mother, but something—a lot—was missing.

Eventually her husband became too ill to take care of her, and my brother tried to keep her in his home, but her injuries resulted in twenty-four-hour-a-day specialized care, and it was a care that working people weren't easily available to do.

We did what we had vowed never to do. We put her in a nursing home near my brother. By this time her memories were not only back, but a lot of her personality. Her emotions returned, but she was never quite the same.

She had periods where she seemed absolutely lost. One time when I visited her she would be fine, lucid, the next confused. She asked for paints, and I bought them for her, and so did my brother, but she never used them. She would give them away, ask for more. The old urges were still there, but not the ability. She would become so frustrated with the fact that she could no longer paint, didn't even know how, that she would rid herself of the kits.

She couldn't do what she loved most. Read. Her mind wouldn't follow the prose; she couldn't visualize the words. She couldn't watch and keep up with a simple television show. She misunderstood the news. During the Gulf War she called to tell me that Iraqis were invading a small Texas community of about two hundred, making terroristic attacks on the gas lines.

She had heard that certain publishing companies were in league with the Mafia, and it became stuck in her mind that I was working for the Mafia by writing for the publishing companies they owned. I often wondered if in her mind she put my martial arts training in league with this and saw me as some sort of freelance hit man for the publishing field.

Having come from the Great Depression, she never could understand how I made as much money as I did. Well, it was a lot by her standards. Not all that special, really, but for someone who every day had to plan their existence down to the penny, she was in awe of the money I made and thought it must come from illegal sources.

Also, the kind of fiction I wrote sometimes led her to believe that I might be crazy, or going crazy. It was all very strange and frustrating, for me as well as her.

On one of her doctor visits, the doctor told me that the X rays revealed she had a cancer on her lung. Here was a woman that had never smoked in her life, who had had nothing but hardship, was badly injured due to a stupid automobile accident, and now she had a cancer on her lung.

Mom refused to have it operated on. She was adamant about that. She had had too many operations due to her injuries, and now in her late seventies, feeling horrible, she felt it was better just to let time take its course. Her belief was she had lived long enough, and that even without the cancer, she didn't have that much time ahead of her anyway, and if she did, who the hell wanted it?

I pursued her about having the operation for a time, but finally dropped it. Her mind was made up. About midMay of 1993 she had a sudden and continued period of lucidness. We began to talk about old times, relive them. My Batman suit. The comics I read by the tons. My room fixed up like the Bat Cave. The martial arts. And my dad. We talked about it all, and it was wonderful.

One night, late May, I got a call from Mom asking if I would come over to see her. Since my family and I lived about a hundred miles away, I told her I would, but I would be there in the morning. She said that was all right.

Early the next morning I got a call from a nurse saying I should come over and see my mother. I told her that was my plan. The nurse didn't indicate that the situation was vital, and Mom and I often went through this. On any morning I was to come see her, she might call two times before I left, two or three times to talk to my wife, Karen, before I arrived, as well as ask the nurses to call while I was en route.

This morning I got ready as usual, and was going out the door when the phone rang.

It was the nurse. My mother was gone.

■ ■ ■

She was buried beside my father. Later I bought them a double tombstone. It was a large funeral. Friends and relatives turned out and told stories of her generosity. I knew she was kind and generous, but I was amazed to learn of the many selfless things she had done, the lives she had changed.

She was an amazing woman who played the hard hand life dealt her. Played it with courage and with a kind of crazy style.

I miss her.

· Mad Dog Summer ·

INTRODUCTION

This one was commissioned for an anthology titled 999, edited by Al Sarrantonio. I actually think the title may have harmed the sales of the book. It's confusing. Had to do with the end of the twentieth century.

"Mad Dog Summer" is a story that had been in my head for years. Not in the plot sense, but in the type of characters I wanted to write about. My parents came of age in the Great Depression, and it influenced them for the rest of their lives. I think it also limited them. Having to work to survive on a day to day basis kept them from having a lot of opportunities. My mother, for example, should have gone to college. She should have been what she most wanted to be all her life. A teacher.

Anyway, stories they told me about the Great Depression, stories I read about, and the fact that, in many ways, the way I grew up was not so far removed from what they knew, led me to write this. It has been compared, mostly favorably, to To Kill a Mockingbird, and that is my favorite novel, and perhaps my favorite film. But, the influence is overrated. I think if you write about the 1930s and the story is told from a young person's view point, and if it has to do with racism, it's then considered influenced by To Kill a Mockingbird.

It was.

But it was more influenced by my parents.

I think it's one of my best works.

■ ■ ■

When I wrote this story, I found that I was constantly editing myself. I had a larger story I wanted to tell, and a few months later, I convinced my editor at that time, Bill Malloy, to let me write a story based on the novella. I had been writing mostly about Hap Collins and Leonard Pine, my series heroes. I love writing about them, but it was never my intent to write one kind of book. I want to return to them soon. But, I felt at the time that, though popular, they weren't getting the push they deserved. I felt, rightly or wrongly, that Warner had determined the series sold a certain number of books, and that was it, and therefore the series was marketed with this in mind. No real growth plan.

I don't accept this.

I believe by treating the books that way it's a self-fulfilling prophecy that the books will sell a certain number, and that's it.

That said, THE BOTTOMS, which is based on this story, "Mad Dog Summer," is unquestionably a broader based book. And it did well.

It also won The Edgar for best Crime novel of 2000.

This is the only award I've ever won that really changed the face of my career.

I believe this is because so many other factors were right.

I had been around a while. I had a body of work. I had a solid following, built up over the years. And I had written, without really thinking about it, a more mainstream style of book.

But it began here. With this story, "Mad Dog Summer." I like the book best, but I still like the story. It is all that I am.

· Mad Dog Summer ·

News, as opposed to rumor, didn't travel the way it does now. Not back then. Not by radio or newspaper it didn't. Not in East Texas. Things were different. What happened in another county was often left to that county.

World news was just that, something that was of importance to us all. We didn't have to know about terrible things that didn't affect us in Bilgewater, Oregon, or even across the state in El Paso, or up northern state way in godforsaken Amarillo.

All it takes now for us to know all the gory details about some murder is for it to be horrible, or it to be a slow news week, and it's everywhere, even if it's some grocery clerk's murder in Maine that hasn't a thing to do with us.

Back in the thirties a killing might occur several counties over and you'd never know about it unless you were related, because as I said, news traveled slower then, and law enforcement tried to take care of their own.

On the other hand, there were times it might have been better had news traveled faster, or traveled at all. If we had known certain things, perhaps some of the terrible experiences my family and I went through could have been avoided.

What's done is done though, and even now in my eighties, as I lie here in the old folks' home, my room full of the smell of my own decaying body, awaiting a meal of whatever, mashed and diced and tasteless, a tube in my shank, the television tuned to some talk show peopled by idiots, I've got the memories of then, nearly eighty years ago, and they are as fresh as the moment.

It all happened in the years of nineteen thirty-one and -two.

■ ■ ■

I suppose there were some back then had money, but we weren't among them. The Depression was on, and if we had been one of those with money, there really wasn't that much to buy, outside of hogs, chickens, vegetables and the staples, and since we raised the first three, with us it was the staples.

Daddy farmed a little, had a barbershop he ran most days except Sunday and Monday, and was a community constable.

We lived back in the deep woods near the Sabine River in a three-room white house he had built before we were born. We had a leak in the roof, no electricity, a smoky wood stove, a rickety barn, and an outhouse prone to snakes.

We used kerosene lamps, hauled water from the well, and did a lot of hunting and fishing to add to the larder. We had about four acres cut out of the woods, and owned another twenty-five acres of hard timber and pine. We farmed the cleared four acres of sandy land with a mule named Sally Redback. We had a car, but Daddy used it primarily for his constable business and Sunday church. The rest of the time we walked, or me and my sister rode Sally Redback.

The woods we owned, and the hundreds of acres of it that surrounded our land, was full of game, chiggers and ticks. Back then in East Texas, all the big woods hadn't been timbered out and they didn't all belong to somebody. There were still mighty trees and lots of them, lost places in the forest and along the riverbanks that no one had touched but animals.

Wild hogs, squirrels, rabbits, coons, possums, some armadillo, and all manner of birds and plenty of snakes were out there. Sometimes you could see those darn water moccasins swimming in a school down the river, their evil heads bobbing up like knobs on logs. And woe unto the fella fell in amongst them, and bless the heart of the fool who believed if he swam down under them he'd be safe because a moccasin couldn't bite underwater. They not only could, but would.

Deer roamed the woods too. Maybe fewer than now, as people grow them like crops these days and harvest them on a three-day drunk during season from a deer stand with a high-powered rifle. Deer they've corn fed and trained to be like pets so they can get a cheap free shot and feel like they've done some serious hunting. It costs them more to shoot the deer, ride its corpse around and mount its head, than it would cost to go to the store and buy an equal amount of beefsteak. Then they like to smear their faces with the blood after the kill and take photos, like this makes them some kind of warrior.

But I've quit talking, and done gone to preaching. I was saying how we lived. And I was saying about all the game. Then too, there was the Goat Man. Half goat, half man, he liked to hang around what was called the swinging bridge. I had never seen him, but sometimes at night, out possum hunting, I thought maybe I heard him, howling and whimpering down there near the cable bridge that hung bold over the river, swinging with the wind in the moonlight, the beams playing on the metal cables like fairies on ropes.

He was supposed to steal livestock and children, and though I didn't know of any children that had been eaten, some farmers claimed the Goat Man had taken their livestock, and there were some kids I knew claimed they had cousins taken off by the Goat Man, never to be seen again.

It was said he didn't go as far as the main road because Baptist preachers traveled regular there on foot and by car, making the preaching rounds, and therefore making the road holy. It was said he didn't get out of the woods that made up the Sabine bottoms. High land was something he couldn't tolerate. He needed the damp, thick leaf mush beneath his feet, which were hooves.

Dad said there wasn't any Goat Man. That it was a wives' tale heard throughout the South. He said what I heard out there was water and animal sounds, but I tell you, those sounds made your skin crawl, and they did remind you of a hurt goat. Mr. Cecil Chambers, who worked with my daddy at the barbershop, said it was probably a panther. They showed up now and then in the deep woods, and they could scream like a woman, he said.

Me and my sister Tom — well, Thomasina, but we all called her Tom 'cause it was easier to remember and because she was a tomboy — roamed those woods from daylight to dark. We had a dog named Toby that was part hound, part terrier, and part what we called feist.

Toby was a hunting sonofagun. But the summer of nineteen thirty-one, while rearing up against a tree so he could bark at a squirrel he'd tracked, the oak he was under lost a rotten limb and it fell on him, striking his back so hard he couldn't move his back legs or tail. I carried him home in my arms. Him whimpering, me and Tom crying.

Daddy was out in the field plowing with Sally, working the plow around a stump that was still in the field. Now and then he chopped at its base with an ax and had set fire to it, but it was stubborn and remained.

Daddy stopped his plowing when he saw us, took the looped lines off his shoulders and dropped them, left Sally Redback standing in the field hitched up to the plow. He walked part of the way across the field to meet us, and we carried Toby out to him and put him on the soft plowed ground and Daddy looked him over. Daddy moved Toby's paws around, tried to straighten Toby's back, but Toby would whine hard when he did that.

After a while, as if considering all possibilities, he told me and Tom to get the gun and take poor Toby out in the woods and put him out of his misery.

"It ain't what I want you to do," Daddy said. "But it's the thing has to be done."

"Yes sir," I said.

These days that might sound rough, but back then we didn't have many vets, and no money to take a dog to one if we wanted to. And all a vet would have done was do what we were gonna do.

Another thing different was you learned about things like dying when you were quite young. It couldn't be helped. You raised and killed chickens and hogs, hunted and fished, so you were constantly up against it. That being the case, I think we respected life more than some do now, and useless suffering was not to be tolerated.

And in the case of something like Toby, you were often expected to do the deed yourself, not pass on the responsibility. It was unspoken, but it was pretty well understood that Toby was our dog, and therefore, our responsibility. Things like that were considered part of the learning process.

We cried a while, then got a wheelbarrow and put Toby in it. I already had my twenty-two for squirrels, but for this I went in the house and swapped it for the single-shot sixteen-gauge shotgun, so there wouldn't be any suffering. The thought of shooting Toby in the back of the head like that, blasting his skull all over creation, was not something I looked forward to.

Our responsibility or not, I was thirteen and Tom was only nine. I told her she could stay at the house, but she wouldn't. She said she'd come on with me. She knew I needed someone to help me be strong.

Tom got the shovel to bury Toby, put it over her shoulder, and we wheeled old Toby along, him whining and such, but after a bit he quit making noise. He just lay there in the wheelbarrow while we pushed him down the trail, his back slightly twisted, his head raised, sniffing the air.

In short time he started sniffing deeper, and we could tell he had a squirrel's scent. Toby always had a way of turning to look at you when he had a squirrel, then he'd point his head in the direction he wanted to go and take off running and yapping in that deep voice of his. Daddy said that was his way of letting us know the direction of the scent before he got out of sight. Well, he had his head turned like that, and I knew what it was I was supposed to do, but I decided to prolong it by giving Toby his head.

We pushed in the direction he wanted to go, and pretty soon we were racing over a narrow trail littered with pine needles, and Toby was barking like crazy. Eventually we run the wheelbarrow up against a hickory tree.

Up there in the high branches two big fat squirrels played around as if taunting us. I shot both of them and tossed them into the wheelbarrow with Toby, and darned if he didn't signal and start barking again.

It was rough pushing that wheelbarrow over all that bumpy wood debris and leaf and needle-littered ground, but we did it, forgetting all about what we were supposed to do for Toby.

By the time Toby quit hitting on squirrel scent, it was near nightfall and we were down deep in the woods with six squirrels — a bumper crop — and we were tuckered out.

There Toby was, a dadburn cripple, and I'd never seen him work the trees better. It was like Toby knew what was coming and was trying to prolong things by treeing squirrels.

We sat down under a big old sweetgum and left Toby in the wheelbarrow with the squirrels. The sun was falling through the trees like a big fat plum coming to pieces. Shadows were rising up like dark men all around us. We didn't have a hunting lamp. There was just the moon and it wasn't up good yet.

"Harry," Tom said. "What about Toby?"

I had been considering on that.

"He don't seem to be in pain none," I said. "And he treed six dadburn squirrels."

"Yeah," Tom said, "but his back's still broke."

"Reckon so," I said.

"Maybe we could hide him down here, come every day, feed and water him."

"I don't think so. He'd be at the mercy of anything came along. Darn chiggers and ticks would eat him alive." I'd thought of that because I could feel bites all over me and knew tonight I'd be spending some time with a lamp, some tweezers and such myself, getting them off all kinds of places, bathing myself later in kerosene, then rinsing. During the summer me and Tom ended up doing that darn near every evening.

"It's gettin' dark," Tom said.

"I know."

"I don't think Toby's in all that much pain now."

"He does seem better," I said. "But that don't mean his back ain't broke."

"Daddy wanted us to shoot him to put him out of his misery. He don't look so miserable to me. It ain't right to shoot him he ain't miserable, is it?"

I looked at Toby. There was mostly just a lump to see, lying there in the wheelbarrow covered by the dark. While I was looking he raised his head and his tail beat on the wooden bottom of the wheelbarrow a couple of times.

"Don't reckon I can do it," I said. "I think we ought to take him back to Daddy, show how he's improved. He may have a broke back, but he ain't in pain like he was. He can move his head and even his tail now, so his whole body ain't dead. He don't need killin'."

"Daddy may not see it that way, though."

"Reckon not, but I can't just shoot him without trying to give him a chance. Heck, he treed six dadburn squirrels. Mama'll be glad to see them squirrels. We'll just take him back."

We got up to go. It was then that it settled on us. We were lost. We had been so busy chasing those squirrels, following Toby's lead, we had gotten down deep in the woods and we didn't recognize anything. We weren't scared, of course, least not right away. We roamed these woods all the time, but it had grown dark, and this immediate place wasn't familiar.

The moon was up some more, and I used that for my bearings. "We need to go that way," I said. "Eventually that'll lead back to the house or the road."

We set out, pushing the wheelbarrow, stumbling over roots and ruts and fallen limbs, banging up against trees with the wheelbarrow and ourselves. Near us we could hear wildlife moving around, and I thought about what Mr. Chambers had said about panthers, and I thought about wild hogs and wondered if we might come up on one rootin' for acorns, and I remembered that Mr. Chambers had also said this was a bad year for the hydrophobia, and lots of animals were coming down with it, and the thought of all that made me nervous enough to feel around in my pocket for shotgun shells. I had three left.

As we went along, there was more movement around us, and after a while I began to think whatever it was was keeping stride with us. When we slowed, it slowed. We sped up, it sped up. And not the way an animal will do, or even the way a coach whip snake will sometimes follow and run you. This was something bigger than a snake. It was stalking us, like a panther. Or a man.

Toby was growling as we went along, his head lifted, the hair on the back of his neck raised.

I looked over at Tom, and the moon was just able to split through the trees and show me her face and how scared she was. I knew she had come to the same conclusion I had.

I wanted to say something, shout out at whatever it was in the bushes, but I was afraid that might be like some kind of bugle call that set it off, causing it to come down on us.

I had broken open the shotgun earlier for safety's sake, laid it in the wheelbarrow and was pushing it, Toby, the shovel, and the squirrels along. Now I stopped, got the shotgun out, made sure a shell was in it, snapped it shut and put my thumb on the hammer.

Toby had really started to make noise, had gone from growling to barking.

I looked at Tom, and she took hold of the wheelbarrow and started pushing. I could tell she was having trouble with it, working it over the soft ground, but I didn't have any choice but to hold on to the gun, and we couldn't leave Toby behind, not after what he'd been through.

Whatever was in those bushes paced us for a while, then went silent. We picked up speed, and didn't hear it anymore. And we didn't feel its presence no more neither. Earlier it was like we was walking along with the devil beside us.

I finally got brave enough to break open the shotgun and lay it in the wheelbarrow and take over the pushing again.

"What was that?" Tom asked.

"I don't know," I said.

"It sounded big."

"Yeah."

"The Goat Man?"

"Daddy says there ain't any Goat Man."

"Yeah, but he's sometimes wrong, ain't he?"

"Hardly ever," I said.

We went along some more, and found a narrow place in the river, and crossed, struggling with the wheelbarrow. We shouldn't have crossed, but there was a spot, and someone or something following us had spooked me, and I had just wanted to put some space between us and it.

We walked along a longer time, and eventually came up against a wad of brambles that twisted in amongst the trees and scrubs and vines and made a wall of thorns. It was a wall of wild rosebushes. Some of the vines on them were thick as well ropes, the thorns like nails, and the flowers smelled strong and sweet in the night wind, almost sweet as sorghum syrup cooking.

The bramble patch ran some distance in either direction, and encased us on all sides. We had wandered into a maze of thorns too wide and thick to go around, and too high and sharp to climb over, and besides they had wound together with low hanging limbs, and it was like a ceiling above. I thought of Brer Rabbit and the briar patch, but unlike Brer Rabbit, I had not been born and raised in a briar patch, and unlike Brer Rabbit, it wasn't what I wanted.

I dug in my pocket and got a match I had left over from when me and Tom tried to smoke some corn silk cigarettes and grapevines, and I struck the match with my thumb and waved it around, saw there was a wide space in the brambles, and it didn't take a lot of know-how to see the path had been cut in them. I bent down and poked the match forward, and I could see the brambles were a kind of tunnel, about six feet high and six feet wide. I couldn't tell how far it went, but it was a goodly distance.

I shook the match out before it burned my hand, said to Tom, "We can go back, or we can take this tunnel."

Tom looked to our left, saw the brambles were thick and solid, and in front of us was a wall of them too. "I don't want to go back because of that thing, whatever it is. And I don't want to go down that tunnel neither. We'd be like rats in a pipe. Maybe whatever it is knew it'd get us boxed in like this, and it's just waitin' at the other end of that bramble trap for us, like that thing Daddy read to us about. The thing that was part man, part cow."

"Part bull, part man," I said. "The Minotaur."

"Yeah. A minutetar. It could be waitin' on us, Harry."

I had, of course, thought about that. "I think we ought to take the tunnel. It can't come from any side on us that way. It has to come from front or rear."

"Can't there be other tunnels in there?"

I hadn't thought of that. There could be openings cut like this anywhere.

"I got the gun," I said. "If you can push the wheelbarrow, Toby can sort of watch for us, let us know something's coming. Anything jumps out at us, I'll cut it in two."

"I don't like any of them choices."

I picked up the gun and made it ready. Tom took hold of the wheelbarrow handles. I went on in and Tom came after me.

■ ■ ■

The smell of roses was thick and overwhelming. It made me sick. The thorns sometimes stuck out on vines you couldn't see in the dark. They snagged my old shirt and cut my arms and face. I could hear Tom back there behind me, cussing softly under her breath as she got scratched. I was glad for the fact that Toby was silent. It gave me some kind of relief.

The bramble tunnel went on for a good ways, then I heard a rushing sound, and the bramble tunnel widened and we came out on the bank of the roaring Sabine. There were splits in the trees above, and the moonlight came through strong and fell over everything and looked yellow and thick like milk that had turned sour. Whatever had been pacing us seemed to be good and gone.

I studied the moon a moment, then thought about the river. I said, "We've gone some out of the way. But I can see how we ought to go. We can follow the river a ways, which ain't the right direction, but I think it's not far from here to the swinging bridge. We cross that, we can hit the main road, walk to the house."

"The swinging bridge?"

"Yeah," I said.

"Think Momma and Daddy are worried?" Tom asked.

"Yeah," I said. "Reckon they are. I hope they'll be glad to see these squirrels as I think they'll be."

"What about Toby?"

"We just got to wait and see."

The bank sloped down, and near the water there was a little trail ran along the edge of the river.

"Reckon we got to carry Toby down, then bring the wheelbarrow. You can push it forward, and I'll get in front and boost it down."

I carefully picked up Toby, who whimpered softly, and Tom, getting ahead of herself, pushed the wheelbarrow. It, the squirrels, shotgun and shovel went over the edge, tipped over near the creek.

"Damn it, Tom," I said.

"I'm sorry," she said. "It got away from me. I'm gonna tell Mama you cussed."

"You do and I'll whup the tar out of you. 'Sides, I heard you cussin' plenty."

I gave Toby to Tom to hold till I could go down a ways, get a footing and have him passed to me.

I slid down the bank, came up against a huge oak growing near the water. The brambles had grown down the bank and were wrapped around the tree. I went around it, put my hand out to steady myself, and jerked it back quick. What I had touched hadn't been tree trunk, or even a thorn, but something soft.

When I looked I saw a gray mess hung up in brambles, and the moonlight was shining across the water and falling on a face, or what had been a face, but was more like a jack-o'-lantern now, swollen and round with dark sockets for eyes. There was a wad of hair on the head like a chunk of dark lamb's wool, and the body was swollen up and twisted and without clothes. A woman.

I had seen a couple of cards with naked women on them that Jake Sterning had shown me. He was always coming up with stuff like that 'cause his daddy was a traveling salesman and sold not only Garrett Snuff but what was called novelties on the side.

But this wasn't like that. Those pictures had stirred me in a way I didn't understand but found somehow sweet and satisfying. This was stirring me in a way I understood immediately. Horror. Fear.

Her breasts were split like rotted melons cracked in the sun. The brambles were tightly wrapped around her swollen flesh and her skin was gray as cigar ash. Her feet weren't touching the ground. She was held against the tree by the brambles. In the moonlight she looked like a fat witch bound to a massive post by barbed wire, ready to be burned.

"Jesus," I said.

"You're cussin' again," Tom said.

I climbed up the bank a bit, took Toby from Tom, laid him on the soft ground by the riverbank, stared some more at the body. Tom slid down, saw what I saw.

"Is it the Goat Man?" she asked.

"No," I said. "It's a dead woman."

"She ain't got no clothes on."

"No, she ain't. Don't look at her, Tom."

"I can't help it."

"We got to get home, tell Daddy."

"Light a match, Harry. Let's get a good look."

I considered on that, finally dug in my pocket. "I just got one left."

"Use it."

I struck the match with my thumb and held it out. The match wavered as my hand shook. I got up as close as I could stand to get. It was even more horrible by match light.

"I think it's a colored woman," I said.

The match went out. I righted the wheelbarrow, shook mud out of the end of the shotgun, put it and the squirrels and Toby back in the wheelbarrow. I couldn't find the shovel, figured it had slid on down into the river and was gone. That was going to cost me.

"We got to get on," I said.

Tom was standing on the bank, staring at the body. She couldn't take her eyes off of it.

"Come on!"

Tom tore herself away. We went along the bank, me pushing that wheelbarrow for all I was worth, it bogging in the soft dirt until I couldn't push it anymore. I bound the squirrels' legs together with some string Tom had, and tied them around my waist.

"You carry the shotgun, Tom, and I'll carry Toby."

Tom took the gun, I picked Toby up, and we started toward the swinging bridge, which was where the Goat Man was supposed to live.

■ ■ ■

Me and my friends normally stayed away from the swinging bridge, all except Jake. Jake wasn't scared of anything. Then again, Jake wasn't smart enough to be scared of much. Story on him and his old man was you cut off their head they wouldn't be any dumber.

Jake said all the stories you heard about the swinging bridge were made up by our parents to keep us off of it 'cause it was dangerous. And maybe that was true.

The bridge was some cables strung across the Sabine from high spots on the banks. Some long board slats were fastened to the cables by rusty metal clamps and rotting ropes. I didn't know who had built it, and maybe it had been a pretty good bridge once, but now a lot of the slats were missing and others were rotten and cracked and the cables were fastened to the high bank on either side by rusty metal bars buried deep in the ground. In places, where the water had washed the bank, you could see part of the bars showing through the dirt. Enough time and water, the whole bridge would fall into the river.

When the wind blew, the bridge swung, and in a high wind it was something. I had crossed it only once before, during the day, the wind dead calm, and that had been scary enough. Every time you stepped, it moved, threatened to dump you. The boards creaked and ached as if in pain. Sometimes little bits of rotten wood came loose and fell into the river below. I might add that below was a deep spot and the water ran fast there, crashed up against some rocks, fell over a little falls, and into wide, deep water.

Now, here we were at night, looking down the length of the bridge, thinking about the Goat Man, the body we'd found, Toby, and it being late, and our parents worried.

"We gotta cross, Harry?" Tom asked.

"Yeah," I said. "Reckon so. I'm gonna lead, and you watch where I step. The boards hold me, they're liable to hold you."

The bridge creaked above the roar of the river, swaying ever so slightly on its cables, like a snake sliding through tall grass.

It had been bad enough trying to cross when I could put both hands on the cables, but carrying Toby, and it being night, and Tom with me, and her trying to carry the shotgun...Well, it didn't look promising.

The other choice was to go back the way we had come, or to try another path on down where the river went shallow, cross over there, walk back to the road and our house. But the river didn't shallow until some miles away, and the woods were rough, and it was dark, and Toby was heavy, and there was something out there that had been tracking us. I didn't see any other way but the bridge.

I took a deep breath, got a good hold on Toby, stepped out on the first slat.

When I did the bridge swung hard to the left, then back even more violently. I had Toby in my arms, so the only thing I could do was bend my legs and try to ride the swing. It took a long time for the bridge to quit swinging, and I took the next step even more gingerly. It didn't swing as much this time. I had gotten a kind of rhythm to my stepping.

I called back to Tom, "You got to step in the middle of them slats. That way it don't swing so much."

"I'm scared, Harry."

"It's all right," I said. "We'll do fine."

I stepped on a slat, and it cracked and I pulled my foot back. Part of the board had broken loose and was falling into the river below. It hit with a splash, was caught up in the water, flickered in the moonlight, and was whipped away. It churned under the brown water, went over the little falls and was gone.

I stood there feeling as if the bottom of my belly had fell out. I hugged Toby tight and took a wide step over the missing slat toward the next one. I made it, but the bridge shook and I heard Tom scream. I turned and looked over my shoulder as she dropped the shotgun and grabbed at the cable. The shotgun fell longways and hung between the two lower cables. The bridge swung violently, threw me against one of the cables, then to the other side, and I thought I was a goner for sure.

When the bridge slowed, I lowered to one knee on the slat, pivoted and looked at Tom. "Easy," I said.

"I'm too scared to let go," Tom said.

"You got to, and you got to get the gun."

It was a long time before Tom finally bent over and picked up the gun. After a bit of heavy breathing, we started on again. That was when we heard the noise down below and saw the thing in the shadows.

It was moving along the bank on the opposite side, down near the water, under the bridge. You couldn't see it good, because it was outside of the moonlight, in the shadows. Its head was huge and there was something like horns on it and the rest of it was dark as a coal bin. It leaned a little forward, as if trying to get a good look at us, and I could see the whites of its eyes and chalky teeth shining in the moonlight.

"Jesus, Harry," Tom said. "It's the Goat Man. What do we do?"

I thought about going back. That way we'd be across the river from it, but then again, we'd have all the woods to travel through, and for miles. And if it crossed over somewhere, we'd have it tracking us again, because now I felt certain that's what had been following us in the brambles.

If we went on across, we'd be above it, on the higher bank, and it wouldn't be that far to the road. It was said the Goat Man didn't ever go as far as the road. That was his quitting' place. He was trapped here in the woods and along the banks of the Sabine, and the route them preachers took kept him away from the road.

"We got to go on," I said. I took one more look at those white eyes and teeth, and started pushing on across. The bridge swung, but I had more motivation now, and I was moving pretty good, and so was Tom.

When we were near to the other side, I looked down, but I couldn't see the Goat Man no more. I didn't know if it was the angle, or if it had gone on. I kept thinking when I got to the other side it would have climbed up and would be waiting.

But when we got to the other side, there was only the trail that split the deep woods standing out in the moonlight. Nothing on it.

We started down the trail. Toby was heavy and I was trying not to jar him too much, but I was so frightened, I wasn't doing that good of a job. He whimpered some.

After we'd gone on a good distance, the trail turned into shadow where the limbs from trees reached out and hid it from the moonlight and seemed to hold the ground in a kind of dark hug.

"I reckon if it's gonna jump us," I said, "that'd be the place."

"Then let's don't go there."

"You want to go back across the bridge?"

"I don't think so."

"Then we got to go on. We don't know he's even followed."

"Did you see those horns on his head?"

"I seen somethin'. I think what we oughta do, least till we get through that bend in the trail there, is swap. You carry Toby and let me carry the shotgun."

"I like the shotgun."

"Yeah, but I can shoot it without it knocking me down. And I got the shells."

Tom considered this. "Okay," she said.

She put the shotgun on the ground and I gave her Toby. I picked up the gun and we started around the dark curve in the trail.

I had been down this trail many times in the daylight. Out to the swinging bridge, but except for that one other time, I had never crossed the bridge until now. I had been in the woods at night before, but not this deep, and usually with Daddy.

When we were deep in the shadow of the trail nothing leaped out on us or bit us, but as we neared the moonlit part of the trail we heard movement in the woods. The same sort of movement we had heard back in the brambles. Calculated. Moving right along with us.

We finally reached the moonlit part of the trail and felt better. But there really wasn't any reason for it. It was just a way of feeling. Moonlight didn't change anything. I looked back over my shoulder, into the darkness we had just left, and in the middle of the trail, covered in shadow, I could see it. Standing there. Watching.

I didn't say anything to Tom about it. Instead I said, "You take the shotgun now, and I'll take Toby. Then I want you to run with everything you got to where the road is."

Tom, not being any dummy, and my eyes probably giving me away, turned and looked back in the shadows. She saw it too. It crossed into the woods. She turned and gave me Toby and took the shotgun and took off like a bolt of lightning. I ran after her, bouncing poor Toby, the squirrels slapping against my legs. Toby whined and whimpered and yelped. The trail widened, the moonlight grew brighter, and the red clay road came up and we hit it, looked back.

Nothing was pursuing us. We didn't hear anything moving in the woods.

"Is it okay now?" Tom asked.

"Reckon so. They say he can't come as far as the road."

"What if he can?"

"Well, he can't...I don't think."

"You think he killed that woman?"

"Figure he did."

"How'd she get to lookin' like that?"

"Somethin' dead swells up like that."

"How'd she get all cut? On his horns?"

"I don't know, Tom."

We went on down the road, and in time, after a number of rest stops, after helping Toby go to the bathroom by holding up his tail and legs, in the deepest part of the night, we reached home.

■ ■ ■

It wasn't entirely a happy homecoming. The sky had grown cloudy and the moon was no longer bright. You could hear the cicadas chirping and frogs bleating off somewhere in the bottoms. When we entered into the yard carrying Toby, Daddy spoke from the shadows, and an owl, startled, flew out of the oak and was temporarily outlined against the faintly brighter sky.

"I ought to whup y'all's butts," Daddy said.

"Yes sir," I said.

Daddy was sitting in a chair under an oak in the yard. It was sort of our gathering tree, where we sat and talked and shelled peas in the summer. He was smoking a pipe, a habit that would kill him later in life. I could see its glow as he puffed flames from a match into the tobacco. The smell from the pipe was woody and sour to me.

We went over and stood beneath the oak, near his chair.

"Your mother's been terrified," he said. "Harry, you know better than to stay out like that, and with your sister. You're supposed to take care of her."

"Yes sir."

"I see you still have Toby."

"Yes sir. I think he's doing better."

"You don't do better with a broken back."

"He treed six squirrels," I said. I took my pocketknife out and cut the string around my waist and presented him with the squirrels. He looked at them in the darkness, laid them beside his chair.

"You have an excuse?" he said.

"Yes sir," I said.

"All right, then," he said. "Tom, you go on up to the house and get the tub and start filling it with water. It's warm enough you won't need to heat it. Not tonight. You bathe, then you get after them bugs on you with the kerosene and such, then hit the bed."

"Yes sir," she said. "But Daddy..."

"Go to the house, Tom," Daddy said.

Tom looked at me, laid the shotgun down on the ground and went on toward the house.

Daddy puffed his pipe. "You said you had an excuse."

"Yes sir. I got to runnin' squirrels, but there's something else. There's a body down by the river."

He leaned forward in his chair. "What?"

I told him everything that had happened. About being followed, the brambles, the body, the Goat Man. When I was finished, he said, "There isn't any Goat Man, Harry. But the person you saw, it's possible he was the killer. You being out like that, it could have been you or Tom."

"Yes sir."

"Suppose I'll have to take a look early morning. You think you can find her again?"

"Yes sir, but I don't want to."

"I know, but I'm gonna need your help. You go up to the house now, and when Tom gets through, you wash up and get the bugs off of you. I know you're covered. Hand me the shotgun and I'll take care of Toby."

I started to say something, but I didn't know what to say. Daddy got up, cradled Toby in his arms and I put the shotgun in his hand.

"Damn rotten thing to happen to a good dog," he said.

Daddy started walking off toward the little barn we had out back of the house by the field.

"Daddy," I said. "I couldn't do it. Not Toby."

"That's all right, son," he said, and went on out to the barn.

When I got up to the house, Tom was on the back porch in the tub and Mama was scrubbing her vigorously by the light of a lantern hanging on a porch beam. When I came up, Mama, who was on her knees, looked over her shoulder at me. Her blonde hair was gathered up in a fat bun and a tendril of it had come loose and was hanging across her forehead and eye. She pushed it aside with a soapy hand. "You ought to know better than to stay out this late. And scaring Tom with stories about seeing a body."

"It ain't a story, Mama," I said.

I told her about it, making it brief.

When I finished, she was quiet for a long moment. "Where's your daddy?"

"He took Toby out to the barn. Toby's back is broken."

"I heard. I'm real sorry."

I listened for the blast of the shotgun, but after fifteen minutes it still hadn't come. Then I heard Daddy coming down from the barn, and pretty soon he stepped out of the shadows and into the lantern light, carrying the shotgun.

"I don't reckon he needs killin'," Daddy said. I felt my heart lighten, and I looked at Tom, who was peeking under Mama's arm as Mama scrubbed her head with lye soap. "He could move his back legs a little, lift his tail. You might be right, Harry. He might be better. Besides, I wasn't any better doin' what ought to be done than you, son. He takes a turn for the worse, stays the same, well…In the meantime, he's yours and Tom's responsibility. Feed and water him, and you'll need to manage him to do his business somehow."

"Yes sir," I said. "Thanks, Daddy."

Daddy sat down on the porch with the shotgun cradled in his lap. "You say the woman was colored?"

"Yes sir."

Daddy sighed. "That's gonna make it some difficult," he said.

■ ■ ■

Next morning I led Daddy out there by means of the road and the trail up to the swinging bridge. I didn't want to cross the bridge again. I pointed out from the bank the spot across and down the river where the body could be found.

"All right," Daddy said. "I'll manage from here. You go home. Better yet, get into town and open up the barbershop. Cecil will be wondering where I am."

I went home, out to the barn to check on Toby. He was crawling around on his belly, wiggling his back legs some. I left Tom with the duty to look after Toby being fed and all, then I got the barbershop key, saddled up Sally Redback, rode her the five miles into town.

Marvel Creek wasn't much of a town really, not that it's anything now, but back then it was pretty much two streets. Main and West. West had a row of houses, Main had the General Store, a courthouse, post office, the doctor's office, the barbershop my daddy owned, a couple other businesses, and sometimes a band of roving hogs that belonged to Old Man Crittendon.

The barbershop was a little one-room white building built under a couple of oaks. It was big enough for one real barber chair and a regular chair with a cushion on the seat and a cushion fastened to the back. Daddy cut hair out of the barber chair, and Cecil used the other.

During the summer the door was open, and there was just a screen door between you and the flies. The flies liked to gather on the screen and cluster like grapes. The wind was often hot.

Cecil was sitting on the steps reading the Tyler newspaper when I arrived. I tied Sally to one of the oaks, went over to unlock the door, and as I did, I gave Cecil a bit of a rundown, letting him know what Daddy was doing.

Cecil listened, shook his head, made a clucking noise with his tongue, then we were inside.

I loved the aroma of the shop. It smelled of alcohol, disinfectants, and hair oils. The bottles were in a row on a shelf behind the barber chair, and the liquid in them was in different colors, red and yellow and a blue liquid that smelled faintly of coconut.

There was a long bench along the wall near the door and a table with a stack of magazines with bright covers. Most of the magazines were detective stories. I read them whenever I got a chance, and sometimes Daddy brought the worn ones home.

When there weren't any customers, Cecil read them too, sitting on the bench with a hand-rolled cigarette in his mouth, looking like one of the characters out of the magazines. Hard-boiled, carefree, efficient.

Cecil was a big man, and from what I heard around town and indirectly from Daddy, ladies found him good-looking. He had a well-tended shock of reddish hair, bright eyes and a nice face with slightly hooded eyes. He had come to Marvel Creek about two months back, a barber looking for work. Daddy, realizing he might have competition, put him in the extra chair and gave him a percentage.

Daddy had since halfway regretted it. It wasn't that Cecil wasn't a good worker, nor was it Daddy didn't like him. It was the fact Cecil was too good. He could really cut hair, and pretty soon, more and more of Daddy's customers were waiting for Cecil to take their turn. More mothers came with their sons and waited while Cecil cut their boys' hair and chatted with them while he pinched their kids' cheeks and made them laugh. Cecil was like that. He could chum up to anyone in a big-city minute.

Though Daddy never admitted it, I could see it got his goat, made him a little jealous. There was also the fact that when Mama came down to the shop she always wilted under Cecil's gaze, turned red. She laughed when he said things that weren't that funny.

Cecil had cut my hair a few times, when Daddy was busy, and the truth was, it was an experience. Cecil loved to talk, and he told great stories about places he'd been. All over the United States, all over the world. He had fought in World War I, seen some of the dirtiest fighting. Beyond admitting that, he didn't say much about it. It seemed to pain him. He did once show me a French coin he wore around his neck on a little chain. It had been struck by a bullet and dented. The coin had been in his shirt pocket, and he credited it with saving his life.

But if he was fairly quiet on the war, on everything else he'd done he was a regular blabbermouth. He kidded me some about girls, and sometimes the kidding was a little too far to one side for Daddy, and he'd flash a look at Cecil, and I could see them in the mirror behind the bench, the one designed for the customer to look in while the barber snipped away. Cecil would take the look, wink at Daddy and change the subject. But Cecil always seemed to come back around to it, taking a real interest in any girlfriend I might have, even if I didn't really have any. Doing that, he made me feel as if I were growing up, taking part in the rituals and thoughts of men.

Tom liked him too, and sometimes she came down to the barbershop just to hang around him and hear him flatter and kid her. He loved to have her sit on his knee and tell her stories about all manner of things, and if Tom was interested in the stories I can't say, but she was certainly interested in Cecil, who was like a wild uncle to both her and me.

But what was most amazing about Cecil was the way he could cut hair. His scissors were like an extension of himself. They flashed and turned and snipped with little more than a flex of his wrist. When I was in his chair pruned hair haloed around me in the sunlight and my head became a piece of sculpture, transformed from a mass of unruly hair to a work of art. Cecil never missed a beat, never poked you with the scissor tips — which Daddy couldn't say — and when he was finished, when he had rubbed spiced oil into your scalp and parted and combed your hair, when he spun you around to look in the closer mirror behind the chairs, you weren't the same guy anymore. I felt I looked older, more manly, when he was finished. Maybe a little like those guys on the magazine covers myself.

When Daddy did the job, parted my hair, put on the oil, and let me out of the chair (he never spun me for a look like he did his adult customers), I was still just a kid. With a haircut.

Since on this day I'm talking about, Daddy was out, and haircuts for me were free, I asked Cecil if he would cut my hair, and he did, finishing with hand-whipped shaving cream and a razor around my ears to get those bits of hair too contrary for scissors. Cecil used his hands to work oil into my scalp, and he massaged the back of my neck with his thumb and fingers. It felt warm and tingly in the heat and made me sleepy.

No sooner had I climbed down from the chair than Old Man Nation drove up in his mule-drawn wagon and he and his two boys came in. Mr. Ethan Nation was a big man in overalls with tufts of hair in his ears and crawling out of his nose. His boys were big, redheaded, jug-eared versions of him. They all chewed tobacco, had brown teeth, and spat when they spoke. Most of their conversation was tied to or worked around cuss words not often spoken in that day and time. They never came in to get a haircut. They cut their own hair with a bowl and scissors. They liked to sit in the chairs and read what words they could out of the magazines and talk about how bad things were.

Cecil, though no friend of theirs, always managed to be polite, and, as Daddy often said, he was a man liked to talk, even if he was talking to the devil.

No sooner had Old Man Nation taken a seat than Cecil said, "Harry says there's been a murder." It was like it was a fact he was proud to spread around, but since I'd been quick to tell him and was about to burst with the news myself, I couldn't blame him none.

Once the word was out, there was nothing for me to do but tell it all. Well, almost all. For some reason I left the Goat Man out of it. I don't know exactly why, but I did.

When I was finished, Mr. Nation said, "Well, one less nigger wench ain't gonna hurt the world none. I was down in the bottoms, came across one of them burr-head women, I don't know, I might be inclined to do her in myself. They're the ones make the little ones. Drop babies like the rest of us drop turds. I might want her to help me out some first, though, you know what I mean. I mean, hell, they're niggers, but for about five minutes the important thing is they're all pink on the inside."

His boys smirked. Cecil said, "Watch your language," and moved his head in my direction.

"Sorry, son," Mr. Nation said. "Your pa's looking in on this, huh?"

"Yes sir," I said.

"Well, he's probably upset about it. He was always one to worry about the niggers. It's just another shine killin', boy, and he ought to leave it alone, let them niggers keep on killin' each other, then the rest of us won't have to worry with it."

At that moment, something changed for me. I had never really thought about my father's personal beliefs, but suddenly it occurred to me his were opposite those of Mr. Nation, and that Mr. Nation, though he liked our barbershop for wasting time, spouting his ideas and reading our magazines, didn't really like my daddy. The fact that he didn't, that Daddy had an opposite point of view to this man, made me proud.

In time, Mr. Johnson, a preacher, came in, and Mr. Nation, feeling the pressure, packed him and his two boys in their wagon and went on down the road to annoy someone else. Late in the day, Daddy came in, and when Cecil asked him about the murder, Daddy looked at me, and I knew then I should have kept my mouth shut.

Daddy told Cecil what I had told him, and little else, other than he thought the woman hadn't gotten caught up there by high water but had been bound there with those briars, like she was being show-cased. Daddy figured the murderer had done it.

That night, back at the house, lying in bed, my ear against the wall, Tom asleep across the way, I listened. The walls were thin, and when it was good and quiet, and Mama and Daddy were talking, I could hear them.

"Doctor in town wouldn't even look at her," Daddy said.

"Because she was colored?"

"Yeah. I had to drive her over to Mission Creek's colored section to see a doctor there."

"She was in our car?"

"It didn't hurt anything. After Harry showed me where she was, I came back, drove over to Billy Gold's house. He and his brother went down there with me, helped me wrap her in a tarp, carry her out and put her in the car."

"What did the doctor say?"

"He reckoned she'd been raped. Her breasts had been split from top to bottom."

"Oh, my goodness."

"Yeah. And worse things were done. Doctor didn't know for sure, but when he got through looking her over, cutting on her, looking at her lungs, he thought maybe she'd been dumped in the river still alive, had drowned, been washed up and maybe a day or so later, someone, most likely the killer, had gone down there and found her, maybe by accident, maybe by design, and had bound her against that tree with the briars."

"Who would do such a thing?"

"I don't know. I haven't even an idea."

"Did the doctor know her?"

"No, but he brought in the colored preacher over there, Mr. Bail. He knew her. Name was Jelda May Sykes. He said she was a local prostitute. Now and then she came to the church to talk to him about getting out of the trade. He said she got salvation about once a month and lost it the rest of the time. She worked some of the black juke joints along the river. Picked up a little white trade now and then."

"So no one has any ideas who could have done it?"

"Nobody over there gives a damn, Marilyn. No one. The coloreds don't have any high feelings for her, and the white law enforcement let me know real quick I was out of my jurisdiction. Or as they put it, 'We take care of our own niggers.' Which, of course, means they don't take care of them at all."

"If it's out of your jurisdiction, you'll have to leave it alone."

"Taking her to Mission Creek was out of my jurisdiction, but where she was found isn't out of my jurisdiction. Law over there figures some hobo ridin' the rails got off over there, had his fun with her, dumped her in a river and caught the next train out. They're probably right. But if that's so, who bound her to the tree?"

"It could have been someone else, couldn't it?"

"I suppose, but it worries me mightily to think that there's that much cruelty out there in the world. And besides, I don't buy it. I think the same man killed her and displayed her. I did a little snoopin' while I was over in Mission Creek. I know a newspaperman over there, Cal Fields."

"He the older man with the younger wife? The hot patootie?"

"Yeah. He's a good guy. The wife ran off with a drummer, by the way. That doesn't bother Cal any. He's got a new girlfriend. But what he was tellin' me was interestin'. He said this is the third murder in the area in eighteen months. He didn't write about any of 'em in the paper, primarily because they're messy, but also because they've all been colored killings, and his audience don't care about colored killings. All the murders have been of prostitutes. One happened there in Mission Creek. Her body was found stuffed in a big ole drainpipe down near the river. Her legs had been broken and pulled up and tied to her head."

"Goodness."

"Cal said he'd just heard the rumor of the other. Cal gave me the name of the editor of the colored paper. I went over and talked to him, a fella named Max Greene. They did do a report on it. He gave me a back issue. The first one was killed January of last year, a little farther up than Mission Creek. They found her in the river too. Her private parts had been cut out and stuffed in her mouth."

"My God. But those murders are some months apart. It wouldn't be the same person, would it?"

"I hope so. Like I said, I don't want to think there's two or three just like this fella runnin' around. Way the bodies are mistreated, sort of displayed, something terribly vulgar done to them. I think it's the same man.

"Greene was of the opinion the murderer likes to finish 'em by drowning 'em. Even the one found in the drainpipe was in water. And the law over there is probably right about it being someone rides the rails. Every spot was near the tracks, close to some little jumping-off point with a juke joint and a working girl. But that don't mean he's a hobo or someone leaves the area much. He could just use the trains to go to the murder sites."

"The body Harry found. What happened to it? Who took it?"

"No one. Honey, I paid to have her buried in the colored cemetery over there. I know we don't have the money, but…"

"Shush. That's all right. You did good."

They grew quiet, and I rolled on my back and looked at the ceiling. When I closed my eyes I saw the woman's body, ruined and swollen, fixed to the tree by vines and thorns. And I saw the bright eyes and white teeth in the dark face of the horned Goat Man. I remembered looking over my shoulder and seeing the Goat Man standing in shadow in the middle of the wooded trail, watching me.

Eventually, in my dream I reached the road, and then I fell asleep.

■ ■ ■

After a while, things drifted back to normal for Tom and me. Time is like that. Especially when you're young. It can fix a lot of things, and what it doesn't fix, you forget, or at least push back and only bring out at certain times, which is what I did, now and then, late at night, just before sleep claimed me. Eventually it was all a distant memory.

Daddy looked around for the Goat Man a while, but except for some tracks along the bank, some signs of somebody scavenging around down there, he didn't find anyone. But I heard him telling Mama how he felt he was being watched, and that he figured there was someone out there knew the woods as well as any animal.

But making a living took the lead over any kind of investigation, and my daddy was no investigator anyway. He was just a small-town constable who mainly delivered legal summonses and picked up dead bodies with the justice of the peace. And if they were colored, he picked them up without the justice of the peace. So, in time the murder and the Goat Man moved into our past.

By that fall, Toby had actually begun to walk again. His back wasn't broken, but the limb had caused some kind of nerve damage. He never quite got back to normal, but he could get around with a bit of stiffness, and from time to time, for no reason we could see, his hips would go dead and he'd end up dragging his rear end. Most of the time, he was all right, and ran with a kind of limp, and not very fast. He was still the best squirrel dog in the county.

Late October, a week short of Halloween, when the air had turned cool and the nights were crisp and clear and the moon was like a pumpkin in the sky, Tom and me played late, chasing lightning bugs and each other. Daddy had gone off on a constable duty, and Mama was in the house sewing, and when we got good and played out, me and Tom sat out under the oak talking about this and that, and suddenly we stopped, and I had a kind of cold feeling. I don't know if a person really has a sixth sense. Maybe it's little things you notice unconsciously. Something seen out of the corner of the eye. Something heard at the back of a conversation. But I had that same feeling Daddy had spoken of, the feeling of being watched.

I stopped listening to Tom, who was chattering on about something or another, and slowly turned my head toward the woods, and there, between two trees, in the shadows, but clearly framed by the light, was a horned figure, watching us.

Tom, noticing I wasn't listening to her, said, "Hey."

"Tom," I said, "be quiet a moment and look where I'm lookin'."

"I don't see any—" Then she went quiet, and after a moment, whispered: "It's him...It's the Goat Man."

The shape abruptly turned, crunched a stick, rustled some leaves, and was gone. We didn't tell Daddy or Mama what we saw. I don't exactly know why, but we didn't. It was between me and Tom, and the next day we hardly mentioned it.

A week later, Janice Jane Willman was dead.

■ ■ ■

We heard about it Halloween night. There was a little party in town for the kids and whoever wanted to come. There were no invitations. Each year it was understood the party would take place and you could show up. The women brought covered dishes and the men brought a little bit of hooch to slip into their drinks.

The party was at Mrs. Canerton's. She was a widow, and kept books at her house as a kind of library. She let us borrow them from her, or we could come and sit in her house and read or even be read to, and she always had some cookies or lemonade, and she wasn't adverse to listening to our stories or problems. She was a sweet-faced lady with large breasts and a lot of men in town liked her and thought she was pretty.

Every year she had a little Halloween party for the kids. Apples. Pumpkin pie and such. Everyone who could afford a spare pillowcase made a ghost costume. A few of the older boys would slip off to West Street to soap some windows, and that was about it for Halloween. But back then, it seemed pretty wonderful.

Daddy had taken us to the party. It was another fine cool night with lots of lightning bugs and crickets chirping, and me and Tom got to playing hide and go seek with the rest of the kids, and while the person who was it was counting, we went to hide. I crawled up under Mrs. Canerton's house, under the front porch. I hadn't no more than got up under there good, than Tom crawled up beside me.

"Hey," I whispered. "Go find your own place."

"I didn't know you was under here. It's too late for me to go anywhere."

"Then be quiet," I said.

While we were sitting there, we saw shoes and pants legs moving toward the porch steps. It was the men who had been standing out in the yard smoking. They were gathering on the porch to talk. I recognized a pair of boots as Daddy's, and after a bit of moving about on the porch above us, we heard the porch swing creak and some of the porch chairs scraping around, and then I heard Cecil speak.

"How long she been dead?"

"About a week I reckon," Daddy said.

"She anyone we know?"

"A prostitute," Daddy said. "Janice Jane Willman. She lives near all them juke joints outside of Mission Creek. She picked up the wrong man. Ended up in the river."

"She drown?" someone else asked.

"Reckon so. But she suffered some before that."

"You know who did it?" Cecil asked. "Any leads?"

"No. Not really."

"Niggers." I knew that voice. Old Man Nation. He showed up wherever there was food and possibly liquor, and he never brought a covered dish or liquor. "Niggers find a white woman down there in the bottoms, they'll get her."

"Yeah," I heard a voice say. "And what would a white woman be doin' wanderin' around down there?"

"Maybe he brought her there," Mr. Nation said. "A nigger'll take a white woman he gets a chance," Mr. Nation said. "Hell, wouldn't you if you was a nigger? Think about what you'd be gettin' at home. Some nigger. A white woman, that's prime business to 'em. Then, if you're a nigger and you've done it to her, you got to kill her so no one knows. Not that any self-respectin' white woman would want to live after somethin' like that."

"That's enough of that," Daddy said.

"You threatenin' me?" Mr. Nation said.

"I'm sayin' we don't need that kind of talk," Daddy said. "The murderer could have been white or black."

"It'll turn out to be a nigger," Mr. Nation said. "Mark my words."

"I heard you had a suspect," Cecil said.

"Not really," Daddy said.

"Some colored fella, I heard," Cecil said.

"I knew it," Nation said. "Some goddamn nigger."

"I picked a man up for questioning, that's all."

"Where is he?" Nation asked.

"You know," Daddy said, "I think I'm gonna have me a piece of that pie."

The porch creaked, the screen door opened, and we heard boot steps entering into the house.

"Nigger lover," Nation said.

"That's enough of that," Cecil said.

"You talkin' to me, fella?" Mr. Nation said.

"I am, and I said that's enough."

There was some scuttling movement on the porch, and suddenly there was a smacking sound and Mr. Nation hit the ground in front of us. We could see him through the steps. His face turned in our direction, but I don't think he saw us. It was dark under the house, and he had his mind on other things. He got up quick like, leaving his hat on the ground, then we heard movement on the porch and Daddy's voice. "Ethan, don't come back on the porch. Go on home."

"Who do you think you are to tell me anything?" Mr. Nation said.

"Right now, I'm the constable, and you come up on this porch, you do one little thing that annoys me, I will arrest you."

"You and who else?"

"Just me."

"What about him? He hit me. You're on his side because he took up for you."

"I'm on his side because you're a loudmouth spoiling everyone else's good time. You been drinkin' too much. Go on home and sleep it off, Ethan. Let's don't let this get out of hand."

Mr. Nation's hand dropped down and picked up his hat. He said, "You're awfully high and mighty, aren't you?"

"There's just no use fighting over something silly," Daddy said.

"You watch yourself, nigger lover," Mr. Nation said.

"Don't come by the barbershop no more," Daddy said.

"Wouldn't think of it, nigger lover."

Then Mr. Nation turned and we saw him walking away.

Daddy said, "Cecil. You talk too much."

"Yeah, I know," Cecil said.

"Now, I was gonna get some pie," Daddy said. "I'm gonna go back inside and try it again. When I come back out, how's about we talk about somethin' altogether different?"

"Suits me," someone said, and I heard the screen door open again. For a moment I thought they were all inside, then I realized Daddy and Cecil were still on the porch, and Daddy was talking to Cecil.

"I shouldn't have spoken to you like that," Daddy said.

"It's all right. You're right. I talk too much."

"Let's forget it."

"Sure...Jacob, this suspect. You think he did it?"

"No. I don't."

"Is he safe?"

"For now. I may just let him go and never let it be known who he is. Bill Smoote is helping me out with him right now."

"Again, I'm sorry, Jacob."

"No problem. Let's get some of that pie."

...

On the way home in the car our bellies were full of apples, pie and lemonade. The windows were rolled down and the October wind was fresh and ripe with the smell of the woods. As we wound through those woods along the dirt road that led to our house, I began to feel sleepy.

Tom had already nodded off. I leaned against the side of the car and began to halfway doze. In time, I realized Mama and Daddy were talking.

"He had her purse?" Mama said.

"Yeah." Daddy said. "He had it, and he'd taken money from it."

"Could it be him?"

"He says he was fishing, saw the purse and her dress floating, snagged the purse with his fishing line. He saw there was money inside, and he took it. He said he figured a purse in the river wasn't something anyone was going to find, and there wasn't any name in it, and it was just five dollars going to waste. He said he didn't even consider that someone had been murdered. It could have happened that way. Personally, I believe him. I've known old Mose all my life. He taught me how to fish. He practically lives on that river in that boat of his. He wouldn't harm a fly. Besides, the man's seventy years old and not in the best of health. He's had a hell of a life. His wife ran off forty years ago and he's never gotten over it. His son disappeared when he was a youngster. Whoever raped this woman had to be pretty strong. She was young enough, and from the way her body looked, she put up a pretty good fight. Man did this had to be strong enough to…Well, she was cut up pretty bad. Same as the other women. Slashes along the breasts. Her hand hacked off at the wrist. We didn't find it."

"Oh dear."

"I'm sorry, honey. I didn't mean to upset you."

"How did you come by the purse?"

"I went by to see Mose. Like I always do when I'm down on the river. It was layin' on the table in his shack. I had to arrest him. I don't know I should have now. Maybe I should have just taken the purse and said I found it. I mean, I believe him. But I don't have evidence one way or the other."

"Hon, didn't Mose have some trouble before?"

"When his wife ran off some thought he'd killed her. She was fairly loose. That was the rumor. Nothing ever came of it."

"But he could have done it?"

"I suppose."

"And wasn't there something about his boy?"

"Telly was the boy's name. He was addleheaded. Mose claimed that's why his wife run off. She was embarrassed by that addleheaded boy. Kid disappeared four or five years later and Mose never talked about it. Some thought he killed him too. But that's just rumor. White folks talkin' about colored folks like they do. I believe his wife ran off. The boy wasn't much of a thinker, and he may have run off too. He liked to roam the woods and river. He might have drowned, fallen in some hole somewhere and never got out."

"But none of that makes it look good for Mose, does it?"

"No, it doesn't."

"What are you gonna do, Jacob?"

"I don't know. I was afraid to lock him up over at the courthouse. It isn't a real jail anyway, and word gets around a colored man was involved, there won't be any real thinking on the matter. I talked Bill Smoote into letting me keep Mose over at his bait house."

"Couldn't Mose just run away?"

"I suppose. But he's not in that good a health, hon. And he trusts me to investigate, clear him. That's what makes me nervous. I don't know how. I thought about talking to the Mission Creek police, as they have more experience, but they have a tendency to be a little emotional themselves. Rumor is, sheriff over there is in the Klan, or used to be. Frankly, I'm not sure what to do."

I began to drift off again. I thought of Mose. He was an old colored man who got around on shore with use of a cane. He had white blood in him. Red in his hair, and eyes as green as spring leaves. Mostly you saw him in his little rowboat fishing. He lived in a shack alongside the river not more than three miles from us. Living off the fish he caught, the squirrels he shot. Sometimes, when we had a good day hunting or fishing, Daddy would go by there and give Mose a squirrel or some fish. Mose was always glad to see us, or seemed to be. Up until a year ago, I used to go fishing with him. It was then Jake told me I ought not. That it wasn't right to be seen with a nigger all the time.

Thinking back on that, I felt sick to my stomach, confused. Mose had taught my daddy to fish, I had gone fishing with him, and suddenly I deserted him because of what Jake had said.

I thought of the Goat Man again. I recalled him standing below the swinging bridge, looking up through the shadows at me. I thought of him near our house, watching. The Goat Man had killed those women, I knew it. And Mose was gonna take the blame for what he had done.

It was there in the car, battered by the cool October wind, that I began to formulate a plan to find the Goat Man and free Mose. I thought on it for several days after, and I think maybe I had begun to come up with something that seemed like a good idea to me: It probably wasn't. Just some thirteen-year-old's idea of a plan. But it didn't really matter. Shortly thereafter, things turned for the worse.

■ ■ ■

It was a Monday, a couple days later, and Daddy was off from the barbershop that day. He had already gotten up and fed the livestock, and as daybreak was making through the trees, he come and got me up to help tote water from the well to the house. Mama was in the kitchen cooking grits, biscuits, and fatback for breakfast.

Me and Daddy had a bucket of water apiece and were carrying them back to the house, when I said, "Daddy. You ever figure out what you're gonna do with Ole Mose?"

He paused a moment. "How'd you know about that?'

"I heard you and Mama talkin'."

He nodded, and we started walking again. "I can't leave him where he is for good. Someone will get onto it. I reckon I'm gonna have to take him to the courthouse or let him go. There's no real evidence against him, just some circumstantial stuff. But a colored man, a white woman, and a hint of suspicion...He'll never get a fair trial. I got to be sure myself he didn't do it."

"Ain't you?"

We were on the back porch now, and Daddy set his bucket down and set mine down too. "You know, I reckon I am. If no one ever knows who it was I arrested, he can go on about his business. I ain't got nothin' on him. Not really. Something else comes up, some real evidence against him, I know where he is."

"Mose couldn't have killed those women. He hardly gets around, Daddy."

I saw his face redden. "Yeah. You're right."

He picked up both buckets and carried them into the house. Mama had the food on the table, and Tom was sitting there with her eyes squinted, looking as if she were going to fall face forward in her grits any moment. Normally, there'd be school, but the schoolteacher had quit and they hadn't hired another yet, so we had nowhere to go that day, me and Tom.

I think that was part of the reason Daddy asked me to go with him after breakfast. That, and I figured he wanted some company. He told me he had decided to go down and let Mose loose.

We drove over to Bill Smoote's. Bill owned an icehouse down by the river. It was a big room really, with sawdust and ice packed in there, and people came and bought it by car or by boat on the river. He sold right smart of it. Up behind the icehouse was the little house where Bill lived with his wife and two daughters that looked as if they had fallen out of an ugly tree, hit every branch on the way down, then smacked the dirt solid. They was always smilin' at me and such, and it made me nervous.

Behind Mr. Smoote's house was his barn, really more of a big ole shed. That's where Daddy said Mose was kept. As we pulled up at Mr. Smoote's place alongside the river, we saw the yard was full of cars, wagons, horses, mules and people. It was early morning still, and the sunlight fell through the trees like Christmas decorations, and the river was red with the morning sun, and the people in the yard were painted with the same red light as the river.

At first I thought Mr. Smoote was just having him a big run of customers, but as we got up there, we saw there was a wad of people coming from the barn. The wad was Mr. Nation, his two boys, and some other man I'd seen around town before but didn't know. They had Mose between them. He wasn't exactly walking with them. He was being half dragged, and I heard Mr. Nation's loud voice say something about "damn nigger," then Daddy was out of the car and pushing through the crowd.

A heavyset woman in a print dress and square-looking shoes, her hair wadded on top of her head and pinned there, yelled, "To hell with you, Jacob, for hidin' this nigger out. After what he done."

It was then I realized we was in the middle of the crowd, and they were closing around us, except for a gap that opened so Mr. Nation and his bunch could drag Mose into the circle.

Mose looked ancient, withered and knotted like old cowhide soaked in brine. His head was bleeding, his eyes were swollen, his lips were split. He had already taken quite a beating.

When Mose saw Daddy, his green eyes lit up. "Mr. Jacob, don't let them do nothin'. I didn't do nothin' to nobody."

"It's all right, Mose," he said. Then he glared at Mr. Nation. "Nation, this ain't your business."

"It's all our business," Mr. Nation said. "When our womenfolk can't walk around without worrying about some nigger draggin' 'em off, then it's our business."

There was a voice of agreement from the crowd.

"I only picked him up 'cause he might know something could lead to the killer," Daddy said. "I was comin' out here to let him go. I realized he don't know a thing."

"Bill here says he had that woman's purse," Nation said.

Daddy turned to look at Mr. Smoote, who didn't acknowledge Daddy's look. He just said softly under his breath, "I didn't tell 'em he was here, Jacob. They knew. I just told 'em why you had him here. I tried to get them to listen, but they wouldn't."

Daddy just stared at Mr. Smoote for a long moment. Then he turned to Nation, said, "Let him go."

"In the old days, we took care of bad niggers prompt like," Mr. Nation said. "And we figured out somethin' real quick. A nigger hurt a white man or woman, you hung him, he didn't hurt anyone again. You got to take care of a nigger problem quick, or ever' nigger around here will be thinkin' he can rape and murder white women at will."

Daddy spoke calmly. "He deserves a fair trial. We're not here to punish anyone."

"Hell we ain't," someone said.

The crowd grew tighter around us. I turned to look for Mr. Smoote, but he was gone from sight.

Mr. Nation said, "You ain't so high and mighty now, are you, Jacob? You and your nigger-lovin' ways aren't gonna cut the mustard around here."

"Hand him over," Daddy said. "I'll take him. See he gets a fair trial."

"You said you were gonna turn him loose," Nation said.

"I thought about it. Yes."

"He ain't gonna be turned loose, except at the end of the rope."

"You're not gonna hang this man," Daddy said.

"That's funny," Nation said. "I thought that's exactly what we were gonna do."

"This ain't the wild west," Daddy said.

"No," Nation said. "This here is a riverbank with trees, and we got us a rope and a bad nigger."

One of Mr. Nation's boys had slipped off while Daddy and Mr. Nation were talking, and when he reappeared, he had a rope tied in a noose. He slipped it over Mose's head.

Daddy stepped forward then, grabbed the rope and jerked it off of Mose. The crowd let out a sound like an animal in pain, then they were all over Daddy, punching and kicking. I tried to fight them, but they hit me too, and the next thing I knew I was on the ground and legs were kicking at us and then I heard Mose scream for my daddy, and when I looked up they had the rope around his neck and were dragging him along the ground.

One man grabbed the end of the rope and threw it over a thick oak limb, and in unison the crowd grabbed the rope and began to pull, hoisting Mose up. Mose grabbed at the rope with his hands and his feet kicked.

Daddy pushed himself up, staggered forward, grabbed Mose's legs and ducked his head under Mose and lifted him. But Mr. Nation blindsided Daddy with a kick to the ribs, and Daddy went down and Mose dropped with a snapping sound, started to kick and spit foam. Daddy tried to get up, but men and women began to kick and beat him. I got up and ran for him. Someone clipped me in the back of the neck, and when I come to everyone was gone except me and Daddy, still unconscious, and Mose hung above us, his tongue long and black and thick as a sock stuffed with paper. His green eyes bulged out of his head like little green persimmons.

On hands and knees I threw up until I didn't think I had any more in me. Hands grabbed my sides, and I was figuring on more of a beating, but then I heard Mr. Smoote say, "Easy, boy. Easy."

He tried to help me up, but I couldn't stand. He left me sitting on the ground and went over and looked at Daddy. He turned him over and pulled an eyelid back.

I said, "Is he...?"

"No. He's all right. He just took some good shots."

Daddy stirred. Mr. Smoote sat him up. Daddy lifted his eyes to Mose. He said, "For Christ's sake, Bill, cut him down from there."

■ ■ ■

Mose was buried on our place, between the barn and the field. Daddy made him a wooden cross and carved MOSE on it, and swore when he got money he'd get him a stone.

After that, Daddy wasn't quite the same. He wanted to quit being a constable, but the little money the job brought in was needed, so he stayed at it, swearing anything like this came up again he was gonna quit.

Fall passed into winter, and there were no more murders. Those who had helped lynch Mose warmed themselves by their self-righteousness. A bad nigger had been laid low. No more women would die—especially white women.

Many of those there that day had been Daddy's customers, and we didn't see them anymore at the shop. As for the rest, Cecil cut most of the hair, and Daddy was doing so little of it, he finally gave Cecil a key and a bigger slice of the money and only came around now and then. He turned his attention to working around the farm, fishing and hunting.

When spring came, Daddy went to planting, just like always, but he didn't talk about the crops much, and I didn't hear him and Mama talking much, but sometimes late at night, through the wall, I could hear him cry. There's no way to explain how bad it hurts to hear your father cry.

They got a new schoolmaster come that spring, but it was decided school wouldn't pick up until the fall, after all the crops had been laid by. Cecil started teaching me how to cut hair, and I even got so I could handle a little trade at the shop, mostly kids my age that liked the idea of me doing it. I brought the money home to Mama, and when I gave it to her, she nearly always cried.

For the first time in my life, the Depression seemed like the Depression to me. Tom and I still hunted and fished together, but there was starting to be more of a gulf between our ages. I was about to turn fourteen and I felt as old as Mose had been.

That next spring came and went and was pleasant enough, but the summer set in with a vengeance, hot as hell's griddle, and the river receded some and the fish didn't seem to want to bite, and the squirrels and rabbits were wormy that time of year, so there wasn't much use in that. Most of the crops burned up, and if that wasn't bad enough, mid July, there was a bad case of the hydrophobia broke out. Forest animals, domesticated dogs and cats were the victims. It was pretty awful. Got so people shot stray dogs on sight. We kept Toby close to the house, and in the cool, as it was believed by many that an animal could catch rabies not only by being bitten by a diseased animal but by air when it was hot.

Anyway, it got so folks were calling it a mad dog summer, and it turned out that in more ways than one they were right.

■ ■ ■

Clem Sumption lived some ten miles down the road from us, right where a little road forked off what served as a main highway then. You wouldn't think of it as a highway now, but it was the main road, and if you turned off of it, trying to cross through our neck of the woods on your way to Tyler, you had to pass his house, which was situated alongside the river.

Clem's outhouse was over near the river, and it was fixed up so what went out of him and his family went into the river. Lot of folks did that, though some like my daddy were appalled at the idea. It was that place and time's idea of plumbing. The waste dropped down a slanted hole onto the bank and when the water rose, the mess was carried away. When it didn't, flies lived there on mounds of dark mess, buried in it, glowing like jewels in rancid chocolate.

Clem ran a little roadside stand where he sold a bit of vegetables now and then, and on this hot day I'm talking about, he suddenly had the urge to take care of a mild stomach disorder, and left his son, Wilson, in charge of the stand.

After doing his business, Clem rolled a cigarette and went out beside the outhouse to look down on the fly-infested pile, maybe hoping the river had carried some of it away. But dry as it was, the pile was bigger and the water was lower, and something pale lay facedown in the pile.

Clem, first spying it, thought it was a huge, bloated, belly-up catfish. One of those enormous bottom crawler types that were reputed by some to be able to swallow small dogs and babies.

But a catfish didn't have legs.

Clem said later, even when he saw the legs, it didn't register with him that it was a human being. It looked too swollen, too strange to be a person.

But as he eased carefully down the side of the hill, mindful not to step in what his family had been dropping along the bank all summer, he saw that it was indeed a woman's bloated body lying face-down in the moist blackness, and the flies were as delighted with the corpse as they were with the waste.

Clem saddled up a horse and arrived in our yard sometime after that. This wasn't like now, when medical examiners show up and cops measure this and measure that, take fingerprints and photos. My father and Clem pulled the body out of the pile and dipped it into the river for a rinse, and it was then that Daddy saw the face of Marla Canerton buried in a mass of swollen flesh, one cold dead eye open, as if she were winking.

The body arrived at our house wrapped in a tarp. Daddy and Clem hauled it out of the car and toted it up to the barn. As they walked by, me and Tom, out under the big tree, playing some game or another, could smell that terrible dead smell through the tarp, and with no wind blowing, it was dry and rude to the nostrils and made me sick.

When Daddy came out of the barn with Clem, he had an ax handle in his hand. He started walking briskly down to the car, and I could hear Clem arguing with him. "Don't do it, Jacob. It ain't worth it."

We ran over to the car as Mama came out of the house. Daddy calmly laid the ax handle in the front seat, and Clem stood shaking his head. Mama climbed into the car and started on Daddy. "Jacob, I know what you're thinkin'. You can't."

Daddy started up the car. Mama yelled out, "Children. Get in. I'm not leavin' you here."

We did just that, and roared off leaving Clem standing in the yard bewildered. Mama fussed and yelled and pleaded all the way over to Mr. Nation's house, but Daddy never said a word. When he pulled up in Nation's yard, Mr. Nation's wife was outside hoeing at a pathetic little garden, and Mr. Nation and his two boys were sitting in rickety chairs under a tree.

Daddy got out of the car with his ax handle and started walking toward Mr. Nation. Mama was hanging on his arm, but he pulled free. He walked right past Mrs. Nation, who paused and looked up in surprise.

Mr. Nation and his boys spotted Daddy coming, and Mr. Nation slowly rose from his chair. "What the hell you doin' with that ax handle?" he asked.

Daddy didn't answer, but the next moment what he was doing with that ax handle became clear. It whistled through the hot morning air like a flaming arrow and caught Mr. Nation alongside the head about where the jaw meets the ear, and the sound it made was, to put it mildly, akin to a rifle shot.

Mr. Nation went down like a windblown scarecrow, and Daddy stood over him swinging the ax handle, and Mr. Nation was yelling and putting up his arms in a pathetic way, and the two boys came at Daddy, and Daddy turned and swatted one of them down, and the other tackled him. Instinctively, I started kicking at that boy, and he came off Daddy and climbed me, but Daddy was up now, and the ax handle whistled, and that ole boy went out like a light and the other one, who was still conscious, started scuttling along the ground on all fours with a motion like a crippled centipede. He finally got upright and ran for the house.

Mr. Nation tried to get up several times, but every time he did that ax handle would cut the air, and down he'd go. Daddy whapped on Mr. Nation's sides and back and legs until he was worn out, had to back off and lean on the somewhat splintered handle.

Nation, battered, ribs surely broken, lip busted, spitting teeth, looked at Daddy, but he didn't try to get up. Daddy, when he got his wind back, said, "They found Marla Canerton down by the river. Dead. Cut the same way. You and your boys and that lynch mob didn't do nothin' but hang an innocent man."

"You're supposed to be the law?" Nation said.

"If'n I was any kind of law, I'd have had you arrested for what you did to Mose, but that wouldn't have done any good. No one around here would convict you, Nation. They're scared of you. But I ain't. I ain't. And if you ever cross my path again, I swear to God, I'll kill you."

Daddy tossed the ax handle aside, said "Come on," and we all started back to the car. As we passed Mrs. Nation, she looked up and leaned on her hoe. She had a black eye and a swollen lip and some old bruises on her cheek. She smiled at us.

■ ■ ■

We all went to Mrs. Canerton's funeral. Me and my family stood in the front row. Cecil was there. Just about everyone in town and around about, except the Nations and some of the people who had been in the lynch mob that killed Mose.

Within a week Daddy's customers at the barbershop returned, among them members of the lynch party, and the majority of them wanted him to cut their hair. He had to go back to work regularly. I don't know how he felt about that, cutting the hair of those who had beaten me and him that day, that had killed Mose, but he cut their hair and took their money. Maybe Daddy saw it as a kind of revenge. And maybe we just needed the money.

Mama took a job in town at the courthouse. With school out, that left me to take care of Tom, and though we were supposed to stay out of the woods that summer, especially knowing there was a murderer on the loose, we were kids and adventurous and bored.

One morning me and Tom and Toby went down to the river and walked along the bank, looking for a place to ford near the swinging bridge. Neither of us wanted to cross the bridge, and we used the excuse that Toby couldn't cross it, but that was just an excuse.

We wanted to look at the briar tunnel we had been lost in that night, but we didn't want to cross the bridge to get there. We walked a long ways and finally came to the shack where Mose had lived, and we just stood there looking at it. It had never been much, just a hovel made of wood and tin and tarpaper. Mose mostly set outside of it in an old chair under a willow tree that overlooked the river.

The door was wide open, and when we looked in there, we could see animals had been prowling about. A tin of flour had been knocked over and was littered with bugs. Other foodstuff was not recognizable. They were just glaze matted into the hard dirt floor. A few pathetic possessions were lying here and there. A wooden child's toy was on a shelf and next to it a very faded photograph of a dark black woman that might have been Mose's wife.

The place depressed me. Toby went inside and sniffed about and prowled in the flour till we called him out. We walked around the house and out near the chair, and it was then, looking back at the house, I noted there was something hanging on a nail on the outside wall. It was a chain, and from the chain hung a number of fish skeletons, and one fresh fish.

We went over and looked at it. The fresh fish was very fresh, and in fact, it was still damp. Someone had hung it there recently, and the other stack of fish bones indicated that someone had been hanging fish there on a regular basis, and for some time, like an offering to Mose. An offering he could no longer take.

On another nail nearby, strings tied together, was a pair of old shoes that had most likely been fished from the river, and hung over them was a water-warped belt. On the ground, leaning against the side of the house below the nail with the shoes, was a tin plate and a bright blue river rock and a mason jar. All of it laid out like gifts.

I don't know why, but I took the dead fish down, all the old bones, and cast them into the river and put the chain back on the nail. I tossed the shoes and belt, the plate, rock and mason jar into the river. Not out of meanness, but so the gifts would seem to be taken.

Mose's old boat was still up by the house, laid up on rocks so it wouldn't rot on the ground. A paddle lay in its bottom. We decided to take it and float it upriver to where the briar tunnels were. We loaded Toby in the boat, pushed it into the water and set out. We floated the long distance back to the swinging bridge and went under it, looking for the Goat Man under there, waiting like Billy Goat Gruff.

In shadow, under the bridge, deep into the bank, was a dark indention, like a cave. I imagined that was where the Goat Man lived, waiting for prey.

We paddled gently to the riverbank where we had found the woman bound to the tree by the river. She was long gone, of course, and the vines that had held her were no longer there.

We pulled the boat onto the dirt and gravel bank and left it there as we went up the taller part of the bank, past the tree where the woman had been, and into the briars. The tunnel was the same, and it was clear in the daytime that the tunnel had, as we suspected, been cut into the briars. It was not as large or as long a tunnel as it had seemed that night, and it emptied out into a wider tunnel, and it too was shorter and smaller than we had thought. There were little bits of colored cloth hung on briars all about and there were pictures from Sears catalogs of women in underwear and there were a few of those playing cards like I had seen hung on briars. We hadn't seen all that at night, but I figured it had been there all along.

In the middle of the tunnel was a place where someone had built a fire, and above us the briars wrapped so thick and were so intertwined with low-hanging branches, you could imagine much of this place would stay almost dry during a rainstorm.

Toby was sniffing and running about as best his poor old damaged back and legs would allow him.

"It's like some kind of nest," Tom said: "The Goat Man's nest."

A chill came over me then, and it occurred to me that if that was true, and if this was his den instead of the cave under the bridge, or one of his dens, he might come home at any time. I told Tom that, and we called up Toby and got out of there, tried to paddle the boat back upriver, but couldn't.

We finally got out and made to carry it along the bank, but it was too heavy. We gave up and left it by the river. We walked past the swinging bridge and for a long ways till we found a sandbar. We used that to cross, and went back home, finished the chores, cleaned ourselves and Toby up before Mama and Daddy came chugging home from work in our car.

Next morning, when Mama and Daddy left for town and work, me and Tom and Toby went at it again. I had a hunch about Mose's old shack, and I wanted to check it out. But my hunch was wrong. There was nothing new hung from the nails or leaned against the wall. But there was something curious. The boat we had left on the bank was back in its place atop the rocks with the paddle inside.

■ ■ ■

It was that night, lying in bed, that I heard Mama and Daddy talking. After Daddy had beaten Mr. Nation and his boys with the ax handle, his spirit had been restored. I heard him tell Mama: "There's this thing I been thinking, honey. What if the murderer wanted people to think it was Mose, so he made a big to-do about it to hide the fact he done it. Maybe he was gonna quit doin' it, but he couldn't. You know, like some of them diseases that come back on you when you think you're over it."

"You mean Mr. Nation, don't you?" Mama said.

"Well, it's a thought. And it come to me it might be one of them boys, Esau or Uriah. Uriah has had a few problems. There's lots of talk about him torturin' little animals and such, stomping the fish he caught on the bank, for no good reason other than he wanted to."

"That doesn't mean he killed those women."

"No. But he likes to hurt things and cut them up. And the other'n, Esau. He starts fires, and not like some kids will do, but regular like. He's been in trouble over it before. Folks like that worry me."

"That still don't mean they're murderers."

"No. But if Nation was capable of such a thing, it would be like him to blame it on a colored. Most people in these parts would be quick to accept that. I've heard a couple of lawmen say when you don't know who did it, go out and get you a nigger. It calms people down, and it's one less nigger."

"That's terrible."

"Of course it is. But there's some like that. If Nation didn't do it, and he knows one or both of them worthless boys did it, he might have been coverin' up for him."

"You really think that's possible, Jacob?"

"I think it's possible. I don't know it's likely, but I'm gonna keep my eye on 'em."

Daddy made sense about Mr. Nation and his boys. I had seen Mr. Nation a couple of times since the day Daddy gave him his beating, and when he saw me, he gave me a look that could have set fire to rocks, then went his way. Esau had even followed me down Main Street one day, scowling, but by the time I reached the barbershop, he had turned and gone between a couple of buildings and out of sight.

But all that aside, I still put my odds on the Goat Man. He had been near the site of the body me and Tom had found, and he had followed us out to the road, as if we were to be his next victims. And I figured only something that wasn't quite human would be capable of the kind of things that had happened in those bottoms with those women.

Poor Mrs. Canerton had always been so nice. All those books. The Halloween parties. The way she smiled.

As I drifted off to sleep I thought of telling Daddy about the Sears catalog pictures and the cloth and such in the briar tunnel, but being young like I was then, I was more worried about getting in trouble for being where I wasn't supposed to be, so I kept quiet. Actually, thinking back now, it wouldn't have mattered.

■ ■ ■

That summer, from time to time, me and Tom slipped off and went down to Mose's old cabin. Now and then there would be a fish on the nail, or some odd thing from the river, so my hunch had been right all along. Someone was bringing Mose gifts, perhaps unaware he was dead. Or maybe they had been left there for some other reason.

We dutifully took down what was there and returned it to the river, wondering if maybe it was the Goat Man leaving the goods. But when we looked around for sign of him, all we could find were prints from someone wearing large-sized shoes. No hoof prints.

As the summer moved on, it got hotter and hotter, and the air was like having a blanket wrapped twice around your head. Got so you hardly wanted to move midday, and for a time we quit slipping off down to the river and stayed close at home.

That Fourth of July, our little town decided to have a celebration. Me and Tom were excited because there was to be firecrackers and some Roman candles and all manner of fireworks, and, of course, plenty of home-cooked food.

Folks were pretty leery, thinking that the killer was probably still out there somewhere, and the general thinking had gone from him being some traveling fellow to being someone among us.

Fact was, no one had ever seen or heard of anything like this, except for Jack the Ripper, and we had thought that kind of murder was only done in some big city far away.

The town gathered late afternoon before dark. Main Street had been blocked off, which was no big deal as traffic was rare anyway, and tables with covered dishes and watermelons on them were set up in the street, and after a preacher said a few words, everyone got a plate and went around and helped themselves. I remember eating a little of everything that was there, zeroing in on mashed potatoes and gravy, mincemeat, apple, and pear pies. Tom ate pie and cake and nothing else except watermelon that Cecil helped her cut.

There was a circle of chairs between the tables and behind the chairs was a kind of makeshift stage, and there were a handful of folks with guitars and fiddles playing and singing now and then, and the men and womenfolk would gather in the middle and dance to the tunes. Mama and Daddy were dancing too, and Tom was sitting on Cecil's knee and he was clapping and keeping time to the music, bouncing her up and down.

I kept thinking Mr. Nation and his boys would show, as they were always ones to be about when there was free food or the possibility of a drink, but they didn't. I figured that was because of Daddy. Mr. Nation might have looked tough and had a big mouth, but that ax handle had tamed him.

As the night wore on, the music was stopped and the fireworks were set. The firecrackers popped and the candles and such exploded

high above Main Street, burst into all kinds of colors, pinned themselves against the night, then went wide and thin and faded. I remember watching as one bright swathe did not fade right away, but
dropped to earth like a falling star, and as my eyes followed it down,
it dipped behind Cecil and Tom, and in the final light from its burst, I
could see Tom's smiling face, and Cecil, his hands on her shoulders,
his face slack and beaded with sweat, his knee still bouncing her gently, even though there was no music to keep time to, the two of them
looking up, awaiting more bright explosions.

Worry about the murders, about there being a killer amongst us,
had withered. In that moment, all seemed right with the world.

■ ■ ■

When we got home that night we were all excited, and we sat
down for a while under the big oak outside and drank some apple
cider. It was great fun, but I kept having that uncomfortable feeling of
being watched. I scanned the woods, but didn't see anything. Tom
didn't seem to have noticed, and neither had my parents. Not long
after a possum presented itself at the edge of the woods, peeked out at
our celebration and disappeared back into the darkness.

Daddy and Mama sang a few tunes as he picked his old guitar,
then they told stories a while, and a couple of them were kind of
spooky ones, then we all took turns going out to the outhouse, and
finally to bed.

Tom and I talked some, then I helped her open the window by her
bed, and the warm air blew in carrying the smell of rain brewing.

As I lay in bed that night, my ear to the wall, I heard Mama say:
"The children will hear, honey. These walls are paper thin."

"Don't you want to?"

"Of course. Sure."

"The walls are always paper thin."

"You're not always like you are tonight. You know how you are
when you're like this."

"How am I?"

Mama laughed. "Loud."

"Listen, honey. I really, you know, need to. And I want to be loud.
What say we take the car down the road a piece. I know a spot."

"Jacob. What if someone came along?"

"I know a spot they won't come along. It'll be real private."

"Well, we don't have to do that. We can do it here. We'll just have to be quiet."

"I don't want to be quiet. And even if I did, it's a great night. I'm not sleepy."

"What about the children?"

"It's just down the road, hon. It'll be fun."

"All right…All right. Why not?"

I lay there wondering what in the world had gotten into my parents, and as I lay there I heard the car start up and glide away down the road.

Where could they be going?

And why?

It was really some years later before I realized what was going on. At the time it was a mystery. But back then I contemplated it for a time, then nodded off, the wind turning from warm to cool by the touch of oncoming rain.

Sometime later I was awakened by Toby barking, but it didn't last and I went back to sleep. After that, I heard a tapping sound. It was as if some bird were pecking corn from a hard surface. I gradually opened my eyes and turned in my bed and saw a figure at the open window. When the curtains blew I could see the shape standing there, looking in. It was a dark shape with horns on its head, and one hand was tapping on the windowsill with long fingernails. The Goat Man was making a kind of grunting sound.

I sat bolt upright in bed, my back to the wall.

"Go away!" I said.

But the shape remained and its gruntings changed to whimpers. The curtains blew in, back out, and the shape was gone. Then I noticed that Tom's bed, which was directly beneath the window, was empty.

I had helped open that window.

I eased over to her bed and peeked outside. Out by the woods I could see the Goat Man. He lifted his hand and summoned me.

I hesitated. I ran to Mama and Daddy's room, but they were gone. I dimly remembered before dropping off to sleep they had driven off in the car, for God knows what. I went back to our little room and assured myself I was not dreaming. Tom was gone, stolen by the Goat Man, most likely, and now the thing was summoning me to follow. A kind of taunt. A kind of game.

I looked out the window again, and the Goat Man was still there. I got the shotgun and some shells and pulled my pants on, tucked in my nightshirt, and slipped on my shoes. I went back to the window and looked out. The Goat Man was still in his spot by the woods. I slid out the window and went after him. As soon as he saw my gun, he ducked into the shadows.

As I ran, I called for Mama and Daddy and Tom. But no one answered. I tripped and went down. When I rose to my knees I saw that I had tripped over Toby. He lay still on the ground. I put the shotgun down and picked him up. His head rolled limp to one side. His neck was broken.

Oh God. Toby was dead. After all he had been through, he had been murdered. He had barked earlier, to warn me about the Goat Man, and now he was dead and Tom was missing, and Mama and Daddy had gone off somewhere in the car, and the Goat Man was no longer in sight.

I put Toby down easy, pushed back the tears, picked up the shotgun and ran blindly into the woods, down the narrow path the Goat Man had taken, fully expecting at any moment to fall over Tom's body, her neck broken like Toby's.

But that didn't happen.

There was just enough moon for me to see where I was going, but not enough to keep every shadow from looking like the Goat Man, coiled and ready to pounce. The wind was sighing through the trees and there were bits of rain with it, and the rain was cool.

I didn't know if I should go on or go back and try and find Mama and Daddy. I felt that no matter what I did, valuable time was being lost. There was no telling what the Goat Man was doing to poor Tom. He had probably tied her up and put her at the edge of the woods before coming back to taunt me at the window. Maybe he had wanted me too. I thought of what had been done to all those poor women, and I thought of Tom, and a kind of sickness came over me, and I ran faster, deciding it was best to continue on course, hoping I'd come up on the monster and would get a clear shot at him and be able to rescue Tom.

It was then that I saw a strange thing in the middle of the trail. A limb had been cut, and it was forced into the ground, and it was bent to the right at the top and whittled on to make it sharp. It was like a kind of arrow pointing the way.

The Goat Man was having his fun with me. I decided I had no choice other than to go where the arrow was pointing, a little trail even more narrow than the one I was on.

I went on down it, and in the middle of it was another limb, this one more hastily prepared, just broken off and stuck in the ground, bent over at the middle and pointing to the right again.

Where it pointed wasn't hardly even a trail, just a break here and there in the trees. I went that way, spiderwebs twisting into my hair, limbs slapping me across the face, and before I knew it my feet had gone out from under me and I was sliding over the edge of an embankment, and when I hit on the seat of my pants and looked out, I was at the road, the one the preachers traveled. The Goat Man had brought me to the road by a shortcut and had gone straight down it, because right in front of me, drawn in the dirt of the road, was an arrow. If he could cross the road or travel down it, that meant he could go anywhere he wanted. There wasn't any safe place from the Goat Man.

I ran down the road, and I wasn't even looking for sign anymore. I knew I was heading for the swinging bridge, and across from that the briar tunnels, where I figured the Goat Man had taken her. That would be his place, I reckoned. Those tunnels, and I knew then that the tunnels were where he had done his meanness to those women before casting them into the river. By placing that dead colored woman there, he had been taunting us all, showing us not only the place of the murder but the probable place of all the murders. A place where he could take his time and do what he wanted for as long as he wanted.

When I got to the swinging bridge, the wind was blowing hard and it was starting to rain harder. The bridge lashed back and forth, and I finally decided I'd be better off to go down to Mose's cabin and use his boat to cross the river.

I ran down the bank as fast as I could go, and when I got to the cabin my sides hurt from running. I threw the shotgun into the boat, pushed the boat off its blocks, let it slide down to the edge of the river. It got caught up in the sand there, and I couldn't move it. It had bogged down good in the soft sand. I pushed and pulled, but no dice. I started to cry. I should have crossed the swinging bridge.

I grabbed the shotgun out of the boat and started to run back toward the bridge, but as I went up the little hill toward the cabin, I saw something hanging from the nail there that gave me a start.

There was a chain over the nail, and hanging from the chain was a hand, and part of a wrist. I felt sick. Tom. Oh God. Tom.

I went up there slowly and bent forward and saw that the hand was too large to be Tom's, and it was mostly rotten with only a bit of flesh on it. In the shadows it had looked whole, but it was anything but. The chain was not tied to the hand, but the hand was in a half fist and the chain was draped through its fingers, and in the partial open palm I could see what it held was a coin. A French coin with a dent in it. Cecil's coin.

I knew I should hurry, but it was as if I had been hit with a stick. The killer had chopped off one of his victim's hands. I remembered that. I decided the woman had grabbed the killer, and the killer had chopped at her with something big and sharp, and her hand had come off.

This gave me as many questions as answers. How did Cecil's coin get in the hand, and how did it end up here? Who was leaving all these things here, and why? Was it the Goat Man?

Then there was a hand on my shoulder.

■ ■ ■

As I jerked my head around I brought up the shotgun, but another hand came out quickly and took the shotgun away from me, and I was looking straight into the face of the Goat Man.

The moon rolled out from behind a rain cloud, and its light fell into the Goat Man's eyes, and they shone, and I realized they were green. Green like Ole Mose's eyes.

The Goat Man made a soft grunting sound and patted my shoulder. I saw then his horns were not horns at all but an old straw hat that had rotted, leaving a gap in the front, like something had taken a bite out of it, and it made him look like he had horns. It was just a straw hat. A dadburn straw hat. No horns. And those eyes. Ole Mose's eyes.

And in that instant I knew. The Goat Man wasn't any goat man at all. He was Mose's son, the one wasn't right in the head and was thought to be dead. He'd been living out here in the woods all this time, and Mose had been taking care of him, and the son in his turn had been trying to take care of Mose by bringing him gifts he had found in the river, and now that Mose was dead and gone, he was still doing it. He was just a big dumb boy in a man's body, wandering the woods wearing worn-out clothes and shoes with soles that flopped.

The Goat Man turned and pointed upriver. I knew then he hadn't killed anyone, hadn't taken Tom. He had come to warn me, to let me know Tom had been taken, and now he was pointing the way. I just knew it. I didn't know how he had come by the hand or Cecil's chain and coin, but I knew the Goat Man hadn't killed anybody. He had been watching our house, and he had seen what had happened, and now he was trying to help me.

I broke loose from him and ran back to the boat, tried to push it free again. The Goat Man followed me down and put the shotgun in the boat and grabbed it and pushed it out of the sand and into the river and helped me into it, waded and pushed me out until the current had me good. I watched as he waded back toward the shore and the cabin. I picked up the paddle and went to work, trying not to think too much about what was being done to Tom.

Dark clouds passed over the moon from time to time, and the raindrops became more frequent and the wind was high and slightly cool with the dampness. I paddled so hard my back and shoulders began to ache, but the current was with me, pulling me fast. I passed a whole school of water moccasins swimming in the dark, and I feared they might try to climb up into the boat, as they liked to do, thinking it was a floating log and wanting a rest.

I paddled quickly through them, spreading the school, and one did indeed try to climb up the side, but I brought the boat paddle down on him hard and he went back in the water, alive or dead I couldn't say.

As I paddled around a bend in the river, I saw where the wild briars grew, and in that moment I had a strange sinking feeling. Not only for fear of what I might find in the briar tunnels, but fear I might find nothing at all. Fear I was all wrong. Or that the Goat Man did indeed have Tom. Perhaps in Mose's cabin, and had been keeping her there, waiting until I was out of sight. But if that was true, why had he given my gun back? Then again, he wasn't bright. He was a creature of the woods, same as a coon or a possum. He didn't think like regular folks.

All of this went through my head and swirled around and confused itself with my own fears and the thought of actually cutting down on a man with a shotgun. I felt like I was in a dream, like the kind I'd had when I'd had the flu the year before and everything had swirled and Mama and Daddy's voices had seemed to echo and there were shadows all around me, trying to grab at me and pull me away into who knows where.

I paddled up to the bank and got out and pulled the boat up on shore best I could. I couldn't quite get it out of the water since I was so tuckered out from paddling. I just hoped it would hang there and hold.

I got the shotgun out and went up the hill quietly and found the mouth of the tunnel just beyond the tree, where me and Tom and Toby had come out that night.

It was dark inside the briars, and the moon had gone away behind a cloud and the wind rattled the briars and clicked them together and bits of rain sliced through the briars and mixed with the sweat in my hair, ran down my face and made me shiver. July the Fourth, and I was cold.

As I sneaked down the tunnel, an orange glow leaped and danced and I could hear a crackling sound. I trembled and eased forward and came to the end of the tunnel, and froze. I couldn't make myself turn into the other tunnel. It was as if my feet were nailed the ground.

I pulled back the hammer on the shotgun, slipped my face around the edge of the briars, and looked.

There was a fire going in the center of the tunnel, in the spot where Tom and I had seen the burn marks that day, and I could see Tom lying on the ground, her clothes off and strewn about, and a man was leaning over her, running his hands over her back and forth, making a sound like an animal eating after a long time without food. His hands flowed over her as if he was playing a piano. A huge machete was stuck up in the dirt near Tom's head, and Tom's face was turned toward me. Her eyes were wide and full of tears, and tied around her mouth was a thick bandanna, and her hands and feet were bound with rope, and as I looked the man rose and I saw that his pants were undone and he had hold of himself, and he was walking back and forth behind the fire, looking down at Tom, yelling, "I don't want to do this. You make me do this. It's your fault, you know? You're getting just right. Just right."

The voice was loud, but not like any voice I'd ever heard. There was all the darkness and wetness of the bottom of the river in that voice, as well as the mud down there, and anything that might collect in it.

I hadn't been able to get a good look at his face, but I could tell from the way he was built, the way the fire caught his hair, it was Mr. Nation's son, Uriah.

Then he turned slightly, and it wasn't Uriah at all. I had merely thought it was Uriah because he was built like Uriah, but it wasn't.

I stepped fully into the tunnel and said, "Cecil?"

The word just came out of my mouth, without me really planning to say it. Cecil turned now, and when he saw me his face was like it had been earlier, when Tom was being bounced on his knee and the fireworks had exploded behind him. He had the same slack-jawed look, his face was beaded in sweat.

He let go of his privates and just let them hang out for me to see, as if he were proud of them and that I should be too.

"Oh, boy," he said, his voice still husky and animal-like. "It's just gone all wrong. I didn't want to have to have Tom. I didn't. But she's been ripenin', boy, right in front of my eyes. Every time I saw her, I said, no, you don't shit where you eat, but she's ripenin', boy, and I thought I'd go to your place, peek in on her if I could, and then I seen her there, easy to take, and I knew tonight I had to have her. There wasn't nothing else for it."

"Why?"

"Oh, son. There is no why. I just have to. I have to do them all. I tell myself I won't, but I do. I do."

He eased toward me.

I lifted the shotgun.

"Now, boy," he said. "You don't want to shoot me."

"Yes, sir. I do."

"It ain't something I can help. Listen here. I'll let her go, and we'll just forget about this business. Time you get home, I'll be out of here. I got a little boat hid out, and I can take it downriver to where I can catch a train. I'm good at that. I can be gone before you know it."

"You're wiltin'," I said.

His pee-dink had gone limp.

Cecil looked down. "So I am."

He pushed himself inside his pants and buttoned up as he talked. "Look here. I wasn't gonna hurt her. Just feel her some. I was just gonna get my finger wet. I'll go on, and everything will be all right."

"You'll just go down the river and do it again," I said. "Way you come down the river to us and did it here. You ain't gonna stop, are you?"

"There's nothing to say about it, Harry. It just gets out of hand sometime."

"Where's your chain and coin, Cecil?"

He touched his throat. "It got lost."

"That woman got her hand chopped off, she grabbed it, didn't she?"

"I reckon she did."

"Move to the left there, Cecil."

He moved to the left, pointed at the machete. "She grabbed me, I chopped her with that, and her hand came off. Damndest thing. I got her down here and she got away from me and I chased her. And she grabbed me, fought back. I chopped her hand off and it went in the river. Can you imagine that…How did you know?"

"The Goat Man finds things in the river. He hangs them on Mose's shack."

"Goat Man?"

"You're the real Goat Man."

"You're not making any sense, boy."

"Move on around to the side there."

I wanted him away from the exit on that other side, the one me and Tom had stumbled into that night we found the body.

Cecil slipped to my left, and I went to the right. We were kind of circling each other. I got over close to Tom and I squatted down by her, still pointing the shotgun at Cecil.

"I could be gone for good," Cecil said. "All you got to do is let me go."

I reached out with one hand and got hold of the knot on the bandanna and pulled it loose. Tom said, "Shoot him! Shoot him! He stuck his fingers in me. Shoot him! He took me out of the window and stuck his fingers in me."

"Hush, Tom," I said. "Take it easy."

"Cut me loose. Give me the gun and I'll shoot him."

"All the time you were bringin' those women here to kill, weren't you?" I said.

"It's a perfect place. Already made by hobos. Once I decided on a woman, well, I can easily handle a woman. I always had my boat ready, and you can get almost anywhere you need to go by river. The tracks aren't far from here. Plenty of trains run. It's easy to get around. Now and then I borrowed a car. You know whose? Mrs. Canerton. One night she loaned it to me, and well, I asked her if she wanted to go for a drive with me while I ran an errand. And she liked me, boy, and I just couldn't contain myself. All I had to do was bring them here, and when I finished, I tossed out the trash."

"Daddy trusted you. You told where Mose was. You told Mr. Nation."

"It was just a nigger, boy. I had to try and hide my trail. You understand. It wasn't like the world lost an upstanding citizen."

"We thought you were our friend," I said.

"I am. I am. Sometimes friends make you mad, though, don't they? They do wrong things. But I don't mean to."

"We ain't talkin' about stealin' a piece of peppermint, here. You're worse than the critters out there with hydrophobia, 'cause you ain't as good as them. They can't help themselves."

"Neither can I."

The fire crackled, bled red colors across his face. Some of the rain leaked in through the thick wad of briars and vines and limbs overhead, hit the fire and it hissed. "You're like your daddy, ain't you? Self-righteous."

"Reckon so."

I had one hand holding the shotgun, resting it against me as I squatted down and worked the knots free on Tom's hands. I wasn't having any luck with that, so I got my pocketknife out of my pants and cut her hands loose, then her feet.

I stood up, raised the gun, and he flinched some, but I couldn't cut down on him. It just wasn't in me, not unless he tried to lay hands on us.

I didn't know what to do with him. I decided I had no choice but to let him go, tell Daddy and have them try and hunt him down.

Tom was pulling on her clothes when I said, "You'll get yours eventually."

"Now you're talkin', boy."

"You stay over yonder, we're goin' out."

He held up his hands. "Now you're using some sense."

Tom said, "You can't shoot him, I can."

"Go on, Tom."

She didn't like it, but she turned down the tunnel and headed out. Cecil said, "Remember, boy. We had some good times."

"We ain't got nothin'. You ain't never done nothing with me but cut my hair, and you didn't know how to cut a boy's hair anyway." I turned and went out by the tunnel. "And I ought to blow one of your legs off for what you done to Toby."

We didn't use the opening in the tunnel that led to the woods because I wanted to go out the way I'd come and get back to the boat. We got on the river it would be hard for him to track us, if that was his notion.

When we got down to the river, the boat, which I hadn't pulled up good on the shore, had washed out in the river, and I could see it floating away with the current.

"Damn," I said.

"Was that Mose's boat?" Tom asked.

"We got to go by the bank, to the swinging bridge."

"It's a long ways," I heard Cecil say.

I spun around, and there he was up on the higher bank next to the tree where me and Tom had found the body. He was just a big shadow next to the tree, and I thought of the Devil come up from the ground, all dark and evil and full of bluff. "You got a long ways to go, children. A long ways."

I pointed the shotgun at him and he slipped behind the tree out of sight, said, "A long ways."

I knew then I should have killed him. Without the boat, he could follow alongside us easy, back up in the woods there, and we couldn't even see him.

Me and Tom started moving brisk like along the bank, and we could hear Cecil moving through the woods on the bank above us, and finally we didn't hear him anymore. It was the same as that night when we heard the sounds near and in the tunnel. I figured it had been him, maybe come down to see his handiwork at the tree there, liking it perhaps, wanting it to be seen by someone. Maybe we had come down right after he finished doing it. He had been stalking us, or Tom, maybe. He had wanted Tom all along.

We walked fast and Tom was cussing most of it, talking about what Cecil had done with his fingers, and the whole thing was making me sick.

"Just shut up, Tom. Shut up."

She started crying. I stopped and got down on one knee, let the shotgun lay against me as I reached out with both hands and took hold of her shoulders.

"I'm sorry, Tom, really. I'm scared too. We got to keep ourselves together, you hear me?"

"I hear you," she said.

"We got to stay the course here. I got a gun. He don't. He may have already given up."

"He ain't give up, and you know it."

"We got to keep moving."

Tom nodded, and we started out again, and pretty soon the long dark shadow of the swinging bridge was visible across the river, and the wind was high, and the bridge thrashed back and forth and creaked and groaned like hinges on rusty doors.

"We could go on down a ways, Tom, I think we got to cross by the bridge here. It's quicker, and we can be home sooner."

"I'm scared, Harry."

"So am I."

"Can you do it?"

Tom sucked in her top lip and nodded. "I can."

We climbed up the bank where the bridge began and looked down on it. It swung back and forth. I looked down at the river. White foam rose with the dark water and it rolled away and crashed over the little falls into the broader, deeper, slower part of the river. The rain came down on us and the wind was chilly, and all around the woods seemed quiet, yet full of something I couldn't put a name to. Now and again, in spite of the rain, the clouds would split and the moon would shine down on us, looking as if it were something greasy.

I decided to cross first, so if a board gave out Tom would know. When I stepped on the bridge, the wind the way it was, and now my weight, made it swing way up and I darn near tipped into the water. When I reached out to grab the cables, I let go of the shotgun. It went into the water without any sound I could hear and was instantly gone.

"You lost it, Harry," Tom yelled from the bank.

"Come on, just hang to the cables."

Tom stepped onto the bridge, and it swung hard and nearly tipped again.

"We got to walk light," I said, "and kind of together. Where I take a step, you take one, but if a board goes, or I go, you'll see in time."

"If you fall, what do I do?"

"You got to go on across, Tom."

We started on across, and we seemed to have gotten the movement right, because we weren't tipping quite so bad, and pretty soon we were halfway done.

I turned and looked down the length of the bridge, past Tom. I didn't see anyone tryin' to follow.

It was slow going, but it wasn't long before we were six feet from the other side. I began to breathe a sigh of relief. Then I realized I still had a ways to go yet till we got to the wide trail, then the road, and now I knew there wasn't any road would stop Cecil or anyone else. It was just a road. If we got that far, we still had some distance yet, and Cecil would know where we were going, and Mama and Daddy might not even be home yet.

I thought if we got to the road I might try and fool him, go the other way, but it was a longer distance like that to someone's house, and if he figured what we were doin', we could be in worse trouble.

I decided there wasn't nothing for it but to head home and stay cautious. But while all this was on my mind, and we were about to reach the opposite bank, a shadow separated from the brush and dirt there and became Cecil.

He held the machete in his hand. He smiled and stuck it on the dirt, stayed on solid ground, but took hold of both sides of the cables that held up the swinging bridge. He said, "I beat you across, boy. Just waited. Now you and little Tom, you're gonna have to take a dip. I didn't want it this way, but that's how it is. You see that, don't you? All I wanted was Tom. You give her to me, to do as I want, then you can go. By the time you get home, me and her, we'll be on our way."

"You ain't got your dough done in the middle," I said.

Cecil clutched the cables hard and shook them. The bridge swung out from under me and I found my feet hanging out in midair. Only my arms wrapped around one of the cables was holding me. I could see Tom. She had fallen and was grabbing at one of the board steps, and I could see bits of rotten wood splintering. The board and Tom were gonna go.

Cecil shook the cables again, but I hung tight, and the board Tom clung to didn't give. I glanced toward Cecil and saw another shape coming out of the shadows. A huge one, with what looked like goat horns on its head.

Mose's boy, Telly.

Telly grabbed Cecil around the neck and jerked him back, and Cecil spun loose and hit him in the stomach, and they grappled around there for a moment, then Cecil got hold of the machete and slashed it across Telly's chest. Telly let out with a noise like a bull bellowing, leaped against Cecil, and the both of them went flying onto the bridge.

When they hit, boards splintered, the bridge swung to the side and up and there was a snapping sound as one of the cables broke in two, whipped out and away from us and into the water. Cecil and Telly fell past us into the Sabine. Me and Tom clung for a moment to the remaining cable, then it snapped, and we fell into the fast rushing water after them.

I went down deep, and when I came up, I bumped into Tom. She screamed and I screamed and I grabbed her. The water churned us under again, and I fought to bring us up, all the while clinging to Tom's collar. When I broke the surface of the water I saw Cecil and Telly in a clench, riding the blast of the Sabine over the little falls, flowing out into deeper, calmer waters.

The next thing I knew, we were there too, through the falls, into the deeper, less rapid flowing water. I got a good grip on Tom and started trying to swim toward shore. It was hard in our wet clothes, tired like we were; and me trying to hang on to and pull Tom, who wasn't helping herself a bit, didn't make it any easier.

I finally swam to where my feet were touching sand and gravel, and I waded us on into shore, pulled Tom up next to me. She rolled over and puked.

I looked out at the water. The rain had ceased and the sky had cleared momentarily, and the moon, though weak, cast a glow on the Sabine like grease starting to shine on a hot skillet. I could see Cecil and Telly gripped together, a hand flying up now and then to strike, and I could see something else all around them, something that rose up in a dozen silvery knobs that gleamed in the moonlight, then extended quickly and struck at the pair, time after time.

Cecil and Telly had washed into that school of water moccasins, or another just like them, had stirred them up, and now it was like bull whips flying from the water, hitting the two of them time after time.

They washed around a bend in the river with the snakes and went out of sight.

I was finally able to stand up, and I realized I had lost a shoe. I got hold of Tom and started pulling her on up the bank. The ground around the bank was rough, and then there were stickers and briars, and my one bare foot took a beating. But we went on out of there, onto the road and finally to the house, where Daddy and Mama were standing in the yard yelling our names.

■ ■ ■

The next morning they found Cecil on a sandbar. He was bloated up and swollen from water and snakebites. His neck was broken, Daddy said. Telly had taken care of him before the snakebite.

Caught up in some roots next to the bank, his arms spread and through them and his feet wound in vines, was Telly. The machete wound had torn open his chest and side. Daddy said that silly hat was still on his head, and he discovered that it was somehow wound into Telly's hair. He said the parts that looked like horns had washed down and were covering his eyes, like huge eyelids.

I wondered what had gotten into Telly, the Goat Man. He had led me out there to save Tom, but he hadn't wanted any part of stopping Cecil. Maybe he was afraid. But when we were on the bridge, and Cecil was getting the best of us, he had come for him.

Had it been because he wanted to help us, or was he just there already and frightened? I'd never know. I thought of poor Telly living out there in the woods all that time, only his daddy knowing he was there, and maybe keeping it secret just so folks would leave him alone, not take advantage of him because he was addleheaded.

In the end, the whole thing was one horrible experience. I remember mostly just lying in bed for two days after, nursing all the wounds in my foot from stickers and such, trying to get my strength back, weak from thinking about what almost happened to Tom.

Mama stayed by our side for the next two days, leaving us only long enough to make soup. Daddy sat up with us at night. When I awoke, frightened, thinking I was still on the swinging bridge, he would be there, and he would smile and put out his hand and touch my head, and I would lie back and sleep again.

Over a period of years, picking up a word here and there, we would learn that there had been more murders like those in our area, all the way down from Arkansas and over into Oklahoma and some of North Texas. Back then no one pinned those on one murderer. The law just didn't think like that then. The true nature of serial killers was unknown. Had communication been better, had knowledge been better, perhaps some, or all, of what happened that time long ago might have been avoided.

And maybe not. It's all done now, those long-ago events of nineteen thirty-one and -two.

Now, I lie here, not much longer for the world, and with no desire to be here or to have my life stretched out for another moment, just lying here with this tube in my shank, waiting on mashed peas and corn and some awful thing that will pass for meat, all to be handfed to me, and I think of then and how I lay in bed in our little house next to the woods, and how when I awoke Daddy or Mama would be there, and how comforting it was.

So now I close my eyes with my memories of those two years, and that great and horrible mad dog summer, and I hope this time when I awake I will no longer be of this world, and Mama and Daddy, and even poor Tom, dead before her time in a car accident, will be waiting, and perhaps even Mose and the Goat Man and good old Toby.